SHADOW CHASERS

PAUL ADAM

LITTLE, BROWN AND COMPANY

A *Little, Brown* Book

First published in Great Britain in 2000
by Little, Brown and Company

Copyright © Paul Adam 2000

The moral right of the author has been asserted.

A CIP catalogue record for this book
is available from the British Library.

C FORMAT ISBN 0 316 85188 4
HARDBACK ISBN 0 316 85187 6

Typeset by Palimpsest Book Production Limited,
Polmont, Stirlingshire
Printed and bound in Great Britain by
Clays Ltd, St Ives plc

UK companies, institutions and other organisations wishing
to make bulk purchases of this or any other book
published by Little, Brown should contact their local
bookshop or the special sales department at the address below.
Tel 0207 911 8000. Fax 0207 911 8100.

Little, Brown and Company (UK)
Brettenham House
Lancaster Place
London WC2E 7EN

ACKNOWLEDGEMENT

I would like to thank the staff of UCLAF for their help in the research for this book.

ONE

Bay of Naples, Italy

The mist hung like drifting smoke over the surface of the water. It was a moonless night, the sky smothered with a dense blanket of low cloud. In the near distance, the lights of Prócida and Ischia burned tiny holes in the darkness and further away, almost due east, a hazy orange glow marked the position of Naples, the aura spreading upwards, dissipating gradually over the shadowy slopes of Mount Vesuvius.

Rob Sullivan stepped out on to the deck of the *Guardia di Finanza* patrol boat. After the warmth of the bridge, the cold sea air momentarily took his breath away. He zipped up his jacket and leant on the port rail next to Stig Enqvist, feeling the hull beneath his feet rocking gently in the swell.

Enqvist shivered and took a drag on his cigarette.

'I didn't think it got this cold down here.'

'Go back inside.'

'It's too stuffy in there. Any sign yet?'

Sullivan shook his head. He peered out into the night, looking for shapes on the water, listening for a sound through the swirling fog though he knew the radar would pick up any movement long before he did.

'You want some *grappa*?'

Enqvist held out a large silver hip flask filled with cheap Italian brandy. Sullivan took a sip and let the liquid slip down slowly, searing his insides. He passed the flask back and Enqvist took a long gulp.

'That volcano gives me the creeps,' Stig said. 'You can feel its presence, can't you? Brooding, menacing. Can you imagine living next to it, wondering when it's going to blow next?'

He swallowed another mouthful of *grappa*.

'Go easy, Stig,' Sullivan said.

'I'm okay,' Enqvist replied, but he slid the flask away into the pocket of his coat.

Sullivan looked at the faint clusters of lights along the curve of the shoreline. The Bay was famous for its beauty, its glorious sunsets, but Enqvist was right, there was something unnerving about it. Not only the threatening bulk of Vesuvius, but the peninsula to the west of the city, the Phlegraean Fields, off which they were anchored, was a throbbing mass of volcanic activity. The whole area was rising and sinking imperceptibly, a fragile crust of rock floating on a subterranean chamber of white hot magma. It was littered with pools of boiling mud and fumaroles belching gas which drifted on the wind to add a hint of sulphur to the salt tang of the ocean.

'You think they're coming?' Enqvist asked.

Sullivan shrugged. 'The tip-off was good.'

'How do you know, unless it pays off?'

'Casagrande's sure. He knows what he's doing.'

Sullivan glanced round at the bridge. The *Guardia* major's profile was visible through the side window, the sharp lines of his nose and jaw softened by the reflected glow from the lights on the control panel below him. He looked relaxed, confident, like the rest of the team of Gico commandos who were waiting patiently in the longroom just aft of the bridge. An elite squad from the *Gruppo investigazione*

2

sulla criminalità organizzata, they were slouched on wooden benches in combat fatigues, smoking or talking quietly in the dialects of Lombardy and Piedmont – northerners to the man, chosen specially to be untouched by the slippery tentacles of the Camorra, Mafia or 'Ndrangheta.

The door to the bridge opened and Casagrande leaned out.

'We have something,' he said quietly in English.

Sullivan and Enqvist pushed themselves away from the rail and went back inside. Tendrils of acrid cigarette smoke curled through from the longroom, adding to the close, oppressive atmosphere on the bridge. The captain and first officer were in shirtsleeves, leaning over the shoulder of a colleague who was seated in front of a luminous green screen dotted with pinpricks of light. They moved aside as Casagrande brought Sullivan and Enqvist forward.

'Just there,' the major said, his fingertip hovering over two pulsing specks.

'How do you know it's them?' Sullivan asked.

'The speed. Most of the traffic out there at this time of night is fishing vessels, the occasional cargo ship. Cruising speed maybe twelve, fifteen knots. These two are going closer to forty.'

'How far away?'

'Inside territorial waters. Fifteen minutes and they'll be here.' Casagrande pulled a wry face. 'The waiting is over, *signori.*'

The Gico commandos were crouched in the bottoms of two inflatable rubber dinghies tied to the starboard rail of the patrol boat. The men were silent now, tense and watchful, their sub-machine-guns braced across their chests as the dinghies dipped and rolled with each lap of the waves.

Sullivan could see them through the window of the bridge. Vague outlines in the blackness. Casagrande was sitting in the stern of the leading dinghy, his left hand cupped around the throttle of the idling outboard motor. It was darker now. The deck and cabin lights had been extinguished, leaving only the ghostly green sheen of the radar screen to illuminate the faces of the men gathered around it. The two glowing dots were moving gradually closer.

'They have radar, don't they?' Enqvist asked.

The captain nodded. 'On those boats they have everything.'

'So they can see us too.'

'Not here, anchored among the rocks. We're completely invisible.'

'Range, half a mile,' the radar operator said softly.

The first officer clicked on the radio and relayed the information to Casagrande. Enqvist threw an anxious glance at the captain.

'Don't they monitor the radio frequencies?' he said.

'You bet they do. That's why we have a scrambler.' The captain smiled reassuringly. 'Relax, Mr Enqvist. This is one time the bastards aren't going to get away.'

'Quarter of a mile,' the radar operator murmured.

They watched the dots on the screen draw nearer. Sullivan lifted his head and looked out of the window, straining to see. Through the gaps in the rocks he thought he caught a glimpse of two indistinct shapes passing by in the mist, but he couldn't be sure.

The pulsating dots disappeared abruptly from the screen.

'They're in the bay, Major,' the first officer said into the radio as the captain threw open the bridge door and rattled off an order at the two ratings waiting on the starboard deck. The mooring lines were quickly untied and the rubber dinghies surged away towards the headland, their undersides slapping the crests of the waves sending glistening showers of spray into the air.

The captain stepped over to the control panel and fired

off more orders, the first officer taking the wheel. The navigation and deck lights snapped back on and there was a muted clanking noise as the anchors were winched in. The patrol boat eased away, manoeuvring carefully through the string of half-submerged rocks, going wide round the jagged tongue of land that protruded into the ocean, its edges concealed beneath a continuous barrage of foaming breakers. The boat had almost reached the shelter of the bay on the other side when there was a distant rattle of tiny explosions that could only be one thing. Gunfire. Sullivan and Enqvist exchanged looks. The first officer opened the throttle and the patrol boat swept round the promontory into the inlet.

Close to the shore, anchored in the shallows, were two sleek, streamlined cabin cruisers. Their decks seemed to be swarming with shadowy figures as the Gico commandos clambered on board from the dinghies. A shot rang out in one of the cabins, answered by a short burst from a machine-gun. Two men threw themselves into the sea and splashed their way towards the shore. One of the dinghies raced after them, scraping to a halt on the shingle beach. Two commandos leapt out and hurled the men brutally to the ground.

Sullivan went out on to the foredeck as the *Guardia* boat moved in closer. The mist was thickening, cloaking the scene with a veil which, coupled with the darkness, was difficult to penetrate. Everything was confused: people yelling, feet thudding on decks, someone screaming in pain, the cacophony all underpinned by the relentless crash of the waves on the beach.

The spotlight on the front of the patrol boat lanced through the fog, illuminating a man struggling out on to the shore. He stumbled on the bank of pebbles and fell headlong. By the time he picked himself up there was a commando standing over him, a sub-machine-gun butt swinging down on to the side of his head. More men went overboard. The sea seemed to be churning with bodies, with flailing limbs. And floating amongst them were several bobbing objects – cardboard boxes which, as the water soaked into them, slowly started to sink.

The commandos dragged the men out of the surf and hauled them up on to the beach, making them lie prone while their hands were cuffed behind their backs. Then the cardboard boxes were salvaged from the sea and others unloaded from the cabin cruisers and stacked above the tide line.

Sullivan and Enqvist were taken ashore in a motorboat. Casagrande was waiting for them beside the pile of boxes. He bent down and ripped open the tops of several. Inside each were dozens of red and white cartons of Marlboro cigarettes. Casagrande lifted out a carton and opened it, removing a couple of packets. He tossed one to Enqvist.

'Keep it,' he said. 'A souvenir from Naples.'

He offered the second packet to Sullivan.

Sullivan shook his head. 'No thanks, I don't smoke.'

Yorkshire, England

'What the hell . . .'

The driver of the prison van rammed his foot down hard on the brake pedal, bracing his arms against the steering wheel as the vehicle skidded to a halt. Slewed across the road in front, almost blocking the narrow country lane, was a maroon Vauxhall Astra, its bonnet crumpled against the stone wall separating the road from the adjoining fields, the glass from its shattered windscreen strewn like diamonds across the asphalt.

A woman with shoulder-length blonde hair was slumped against the side of the car. She turned her head as the van stopped and the driver saw the blood caking her face and neck.

'Jesus!'

He threw open his door. His colleague in the passenger seat climbed out on the other side. The woman staggered towards them, one hand clutching her head. Her eyes were dazed, her mouth contorted in pain and anguish.

'Take it easy, love,' the driver said, catching her in his arms as she fell. 'Better radio for an ambulance, Phil.'

The blonde groaned and pushed herself upright, her hand reaching down into her coat pocket.

'I don't think that will be necessary,' she said coolly, pointing an automatic pistol at the driver's head.

He gaped at her. 'What? Fuck! You bitch!'

The blonde whipped the pistol across his face, cutting open his cheek. A trickle of blood seeped out from the wound.

'No obscenity, please.'

She swung the pistol between the two guards.

'Face down on the road. Both of you. Now!' she ordered.

The guards looked at each other, but didn't move. A man vaulted over the wall behind them.

'Do as the lady says.'

He was wearing a soiled black balaclava, scuffed leather jacket and old Adidas trainers. But there was nothing used about the gleaming silver Beretta pistol he held in his hand. The two prison guards crouched down and lay flat on the road.

'Give me the keys to the back of the van,' the man in the balaclava said in a lazy drawl.

'We don't have them,' the driver replied, twisting his head so he could see the blonde standing over him. Trying to imprint her bloody features in his memory.

The man in the balaclava stepped over and, without warning, shot the driver in the back of the knee.

'I'll ask you again.'

'You fucking bastard,' the second guard spat. The driver was curled up, holding his shattered knee, screaming in agony.

'The keys.'

The second guard rummaged in his jacket pocket and threw a bunch of keys out on to the road. 'Go fuck yourself.'

The man in the balaclava ignored him. He went round to the rear of the prison van and unlocked the heavy steel doors, taking a pace back and levelling his pistol at a third uniformed guard who was sitting on the bench inside next to four handcuffed prisoners.

'Maartens, out,' Balaclava said. Then to the guard: 'Unlock his cuffs.'

Frans Maartens was too stunned to move. Short and plump, his red face rimmed with greying hair and a grizzled beard, he simply stared at Balaclava.

'You hear me? Out!'

The prison guard unfastened the handcuffs. His hands were trembling so much he could barely hold the keys. He seized Maartens and pushed him out through the doors.

'Move down the bench to the back,' Balaclava said, standing aside as the blonde forced the other two guards round from the front. The driver was only half conscious, moaning in pain and shock as his colleague lifted him up into the back of the van.

'At least call an ambulance. He needs to get to hospital,' the guard pleaded.

'Get in, or you're next.'

Balaclava swung the doors closed, locked them and threw the keys over the wall. Then he took hold of Maartens by the collar of his jacket and dragged him along the road. A green VW Golf was parked in a copse down a muddy farm track. Balaclava opened the boot and pushed Maartens inside.

'No sound. You understand?'

He slammed the lid shut and ran round to the driver's door, pulling off his balaclava. He clambered in and turned the ignition. The blonde slipped into the seat next to him. She picked up a towel and wiped the fake blood off her face before removing the blonde wig and shaking loose the dark hair underneath. The Golf was moving fast down the bumpy track and out on to the road when she took out a cosmetic bag and mirror and began to touch up her make-up.

They drove east for more than half an hour, across the flat agricultural land north of Hull, sticking to minor roads and deserted country lanes wherever they could. As they neared the coast, the North Sea crept slowly into view, filling the horizon with a wash of still, grey water that was almost indistinguishable from the overcast sky.

The Golf turned down a narrow metalled lane which, after a quarter of a mile, became a rough dirt track, its surface worn into two deep ruts by the heavy wheels of farm vehicles. At the end of the track was a derelict barn. The Golf drove inside and stopped in front of a pile of dirty straw. The roof of the barn had partially fallen in. Panels of rusty corrugated iron dangled from the wooden rafters, held tenuously in place by a few old nails. The lapboard sides had disintegrated leaving gaping holes through which the clifftop could be seen, only yards away.

Balaclava opened the boot of the car. Frans Maartens stared up at him, seeing his face for the first time. He turned pale, a rat's gnaw of fear in his eyes.

'Get out,' Balaclava said.

'Mr Doyle . . .' Maartens stammered in bewilderment.

9

'What is this?' He spoke English with a marked Dutch accent.

'Get out.'

Maartens clambered awkwardly over the lip of the boot and stood looking at Doyle, licking his fleshy mouth nervously. The woman was over by the door of the barn, gazing out at the patchwork of fields.

Doyle slid a cigarette between his lips and held out the pack. Maartens hesitated, then took one. Doyle lit them both and inhaled deeply, his eyes never leaving Maartens.

'How was your time in prison, Frans?' he said.

'What's going on?' Maartens asked anxiously.

'You had plenty of opportunity for reflection, I hope. To see the error of your ways. You got greedy, Frans. That's not an attractive trait.'

'Greedy?' Maartens attempted a smile, but it came out as more of a grimace. 'Now, I wasn't serious, you know. I didn't mean it. You know how these things are.'

'Of course. You understand our position though, don't you? We didn't want you going through a trial, giving evidence.'

'I wouldn't have said anything. I wouldn't.'

Maartens sucked on his cigarette. His clothes were crumpled, his thinning hair dishevelled. Slightly stooped, cheeks and nose veined with broken blood vessels, he looked much older than his forty-seven years. Doyle smiled icily at him.

'We couldn't afford to take that risk.'

'What am I going to do now?' Maartens said. 'I'm a fugitive, on the run.'

'I expected more gratitude,' Doyle said.

'You should have left me inside. Where am I supposed to go now?'

Doyle threw his cigarette on to the dirt floor and crushed it out with the heel of his shoe.

'You don't need to worry about that, Frans,' he said soothingly. 'We'll take care of you.'

Hendaye, French–Spanish border

The senior customs officer was crowding her, leaning over so close that Claire could smell the residue of the previous night's garlic on his breath.

'How long are you down for?' Bignon said smoothly. 'Perhaps I could show you around. Have you seen the Pyrenees before?'

Claire suppressed a weary sigh and leafed through the documents on the desk in front of her. These Latin men bored her with their predictable chat-up lines, their intrusive hands and tedious insistence on treating her like a little girl in need of a sugar daddy.

Bignon touched her on the shoulder, squeezing her flesh through her jacket and blouse.

'Maybe I could take you out to dinner tonight?' he said.

Claire turned her head to look at him. 'Will your wife be coming too?' she asked.

Bignon took his hand away and smiled thinly. He fingered his pencil-line moustache as if checking it were still there. He wasn't sure quite what to make of this slender young woman whose self-assurance belied her petite, almost fragile, appearance. Claire pulled out a couple of papers from the pile, trying to get back down to business.

'These two interest me. You know the companies?'

The senior customs officer bent over to examine the documents. As he reached out to adjust their position on the desk, his hand brushed against Claire's breast. She gritted her teeth. The first time he'd done that she'd given him the benefit of the doubt, but twice was more than an accident. She pushed back her chair and stood up, digging her heel hard into Bignon's instep. He winced and stifled a cry.

'I'm sorry, was that your foot?' Claire said, picking up the documents and heading for the door.

Outside, the early morning air was thick with diesel fumes from the constant stream of traffic passing over the frontier. To the left, the foothills of the Pyrenees rose in a series of undulating inclines, their grassy slopes dotted with holiday villas; to the right, the sun glinted on the broken waters of the Gulf of Gascony. It was a picturesque setting, but the terrain immediately adjacent to the customs post was depressingly ugly: a vast expanse of grey concrete filled with parked trailers and trucks, a no-man's-land of huge forty-tonne lorries and tired drivers waiting to cross into Spain or France.

Claire absorbed the scene for a moment, watching a group of earnest young men completing an on-the-spot check of a French lorry laden down with crates of wine. They were plainclothes customs officers but they weren't from Hendaye: this was a team from the central anti-fraud division in Paris.

The group leader, Philippe Allard, strolled across to the customs post. A boyish-faced man in his mid-thirties, he had dark hair cut short in a severe *en brosse* style. Claire gave him a quizzical look and he shook his head.

'Everything in order.'

'You sound disappointed.'

'I know. We couldn't even find some trivial technicality to get him on. What's the world coming to when wine exporters, of all people, are honest?'

'Try this one.' Claire held out one of the papers clasped in her hand. 'It's the blue truck over there. Spanish.'

Allard glanced at the paper. 'Okay. We'll do it next.'

'Do what next?'

Christophe Bignon had come out of the customs post behind them.

'Or aren't you going to tell me?' he added acerbically.

His tone and expression left them in no doubt how he felt about a bunch of smug Parisians coming to throw their weight around in the provinces.

'The Spanish lorry,' Claire said. 'Garcia Saez S.L., San Sebastian.'

'You're wasting your time,' Bignon said contemptuously. 'Those trucks go back and forth every few days. We know all the drivers. We've never had any problems with them.'

'There's a first time for everything,' Claire said.

She walked purposefully across to the blue articulated lorry. It was parked at the front of a line of three commercial vehicles which had been selected for random inspection from the dozens which came over from Irun almost every hour of the day. The driver was standing by his cab, smoking and gossiping with two of his compatriots. Allard asked him to open up the back of his trailer and the driver shot a puzzled look at Bignon.

'Just a formality,' Bignon growled, waving an arm dismissively. 'They're from headquarters.' What else can you expect? was the unspoken sneer in his voice.

The driver walked the length of the vehicle and swung open the rear doors, fastening them back against the sides of the trailer. Inside were rows of shiny metal jerry cans stacked five high on wooden pallets. Allard vaulted agilely inside and pulled down one of the cans, unscrewing the cap and peering at the contents. He lowered his nose and sniffed deeply.

'Seems all right.'

'Extra virgin,' the Spanish driver said in French. 'You won't find any better.'

'You see,' Bignon snorted, turning away with a gesture of impatience.

Allard replaced the can on the pile and squeezed through the narrow gap between the pallets, selecting another container from the back of the consignment. That too seemed in order, as did a third jerry can he lifted down from the top of one of the stacks.

'We'll need a sample, for testing,' Claire said. 'Perhaps Monsieur Bignon would oblige?'

The senior customs officer made no attempt to conceal his irritation.

'Is that really necessary?'

Claire's cool blue eyes settled on his sallow face. She was in charge of the operation but she had no direct authority over Bignon. She wasn't part of Allard's team, wasn't even French despite her fluency in the language. But she wasn't going to allow some petty border official to obstruct her.

'Yes, it's necessary,' she said.

She turned away, not willing to discuss the matter further. She heard Bignon draw in his breath, then his heavy footsteps as he stomped back to the customs post.

'You want to check any more?' Allard inquired.

Claire watched the driver. He was standing to one side, still smoking. He seemed a little on edge but she'd have been surprised if he hadn't been. A random customs search was an unsettling experience, even for those with a clear conscience.

'Maybe one more,' she said.

The driver's shoulders slumped. 'Is all good stuff, you know. I see them press the olives myself. The first oil out, it all go in there.'

'One from the top,' Claire said, pointing.

Allard lifted down the heavy jerry can and placed it on the floor of the trailer by the open doors. Claire took off the cap and studied the viscous golden liquid inside. She inhaled. It was certainly olive oil, but whether it was extra

14

virgin as the transit documents specified was something only the laboratory could determine.

Bignon appeared round the side of the lorry, a sample kit dangling from his hand.

'This one?' he said brusquely.

Claire nodded, moving out of the way to let him ladle a small amount of oil into a plastic container. Bignon sealed the container and filled out the label on the side.

'You finish now?' the driver said in his accented French. 'I'm half an hour late.'

'What do you think?' Claire asked Allard.

'I'm satisfied.'

The driver glanced at Bignon and quickly stepped round to unlatch one of the doors. Something about his manner aroused Claire's attention, she wasn't sure exactly what. The look of relief in his face, the haste with which he started to close up the trailer. He was late and in a hurry, but all the same . . .

'Just a moment,' she said.

Allard caught her eye. He was about to jump down from the trailer but stopped. She nodded discreetly at him.

'I'd like to see one from the bottom.'

'What?' the driver said in exasperation. 'Look, you open four already. How many you want to see?'

'We can open every one if we need to,' Claire said sharply.

She ignored the driver's petulant response, the rolling eyes, the arms thrown wide in disbelief, and indicated a jerry can at the bottom of one of the stacks. Allard removed the top four containers and brought the fifth to the rear of the trailer. Claire was conscious of all three men watching her intently as she unscrewed the cap and lowered her eyes to the opening.

She noticed the difference at once. This liquid was paler, cloudier, and had none of the thick amber lustre of olive oil.

She smelt it, then dipped a finger in and tasted it, letting the flavour linger in her mouth.

'So?' Bignon said impatiently. 'Is it good or not?'

'Well,' Claire replied, 'I'm no cook, but I certainly wouldn't put that in my vinaigrette.'

'You know what it is?' Allard said.

'Hazelnut oil.'

He nodded. They both knew what that meant.

'We'll need a lab test to confirm it,' Claire continued, 'but I'm sure.'

She'd encountered it before: it was a common enough fraud. Hazelnut oil was sixty per cent cheaper than olive oil. It had a distinctive flavour on its own, but when mixed with olive oil, to adulterate it, was almost impossible for the human palette to detect provided you kept the proportion below twenty per cent. Which was why the European Union made importers of hazelnut oil pay a substantial security against release for certain authorised uses only.

'Where was it going?' she asked.

Allard referred to the transit documents. 'Just up the road. Fonteneau et Delahaye. A bottling plant in Bayonne.'

'Any previous suspicions?'

'We'll have to do a check.' He studied her shrewdly for a moment. 'You knew, didn't you? That's the one you were waiting for.'

Claire walked over to the window of the customs post and looked out. The Spanish lorry had been moved to a secure compound off the main road where Allard's men, watched by Christophe Bignon, were unloading the jerry cans and checking their contents. The driver was being held in an interview room at the back of the customs post, waiting to be questioned.

'This isn't the first time,' Claire said. 'Those lorries have

16

been doing this run for ages. Months, maybe years. Yet they've never been caught.'

'What are you saying?'

Claire took another look outside, then pulled open the door that led to the rest of the customs post. The corridor beyond was deserted. Closing the door again, she walked across to Allard and kept her voice low.

'How many phones are there here?'

Allard frowned. 'Just this one in here, as far as I know. Maybe a couple of extensions, but they're all the same number.'

'Can you get one of your team in here and keep him here on some pretext until we've finished this job?'

'Why?'

'I don't want this to leak out.'

Allard eyed her narrowly. 'You don't trust the officers here?'

'Let's not take any chances, Philippe.'

'I can arrange that. And the next move?'

Claire smiled. 'I think it's time we took a closer look at this bottling plant, don't you?'

TWO

'It's not exactly riveting television, is it?' Casagrande said laconically, leaning back in his chair and gazing up at the video screen on the wall.

The grainy black and white picture showed the inside of a Gico interview room – a windowless, white-walled box equipped with a scratched metal table, tape recorder, three steel chairs and all the quaint charm of a run-down public lavatory. In one of the chairs, his clothes still damp from his immersion in the sea, sat a squat middle-aged man with a bruised face and thick matted hair like coconut fibre on his forearms. He was gazing stoically at the two uniformed revenue guards sitting opposite him and grunting occasionally in a guttural language that both Sullivan and Enqvist, watching from the quiet seclusion of Casagrande's office, found incomprehensible.

'What's he saying?' Enqvist asked.

Casagrande shrugged. 'Who knows? I need an interpreter too. They speak Italian, these scum, but they pretend not to. It's tiresome, but we're used to it now. What can you do in a foreign country like this?'

His lip curled sardonically. Casagrande was from Milan, a Lombard who regarded all of Italy south of Rome, maybe even south of Florence, as the sub-Sahara. Temperamentally, and culturally, he had more in common with the Swiss than he did with the Neapolitans.

'One thing you can be absolutely sure of,' he continued, 'he won't tell us a single thing of any interest. We can question him from now until Christmas but he won't say anything. He's too scared of his masters.'

Sullivan studied the image on the screen. The prisoner seemed at ease in the bare, intimidating environment of the interview room. Calm, composed, listening to his interrogators politely, he had more the air of a man being interviewed for a job than a smuggler facing a long term in jail. Arrest was just one of the many hazards of his occupation that he accepted with a quiet resignation.

'He's Camorra, I assume,' Sullivan said.

'Of course,' Casagrande replied with a sigh.

He picked up the remote control from his desk and pressed the mute button, killing the sound on the video monitor.

'Which group?' Sullivan asked.

'It hardly matters, they're all the same. I'd guess the Lucianis. Things are pretty unstable at the moment. People's loyalties are wavering. They're waiting to see who ends up on top.'

'Maybe you should pull out for a time and leave them to sort it out among themselves?'

'I'd love that,' Casagrande said. 'Let the bastards knock each other off, one by one, then move in and pick up the survivors. Unfortunately that's not a solution our political masters find acceptable. The shootings last week have made them nervous. You saw that in Brussels?'

Sullivan nodded. It hadn't made the television news but he'd read about it in the paper. In a bar in one of the northern suburbs of Naples, out near Capodichino airport, four men had been killed in a shoot-out between rival Camorra gangs.

'Who's going to win?' Enqvist asked.

20

Casagrande gave the facial equivalent of a shrug.

'Do I care? Luciani's on top at the moment, but Dino Falzone controls a lot of territory and is ruthless enough to capture more. The only thing I can be sure of is that whatever happens, nothing will change.'

There was a knock on the door.

'Yes?' the major called out.

The door opened and an orderly came in carrying a tray of coffee and *cornetti*. He placed the tray softly on the desk and went out. Casagrande poured three cups of steaming black espresso and gestured to the others to help themselves to the pastries.

'What was the haul in the end?' Sullivan said, leaning forward in his chair to take a coffee.

'Four hundred cases. They had them stashed everywhere, even in the toilets and showers.'

'Four hundred?' Sullivan did the arithmetic in his head. Fifty cartons to a case, ten packets of twenty to a carton, that made a total of four million cigarettes. It was a reasonably impressive catch, but a mere fraction of the vast numbers of contraband cigarettes which flooded into Naples every year and even less significant when compared to the figures for the whole of Italy. None of the three men in the room was under any illusions about the true effectiveness of their night's work.

Casagrande reached out for an electronic calculator and punched in the numbers, talking to himself.

'Two hundred thousand packets. Duty per packet, around eleven hundred lire, that makes . . . *Merda*, there aren't enough digits on the calculator.'

'Two hundred and twenty million lire,' Sullivan said.

Casagrande glanced up at him. 'I'll take your word for that. And in Euros?'

'A lot,' Sullivan said.

'Come on, don't be modest.'

'Nineteen hundred lire to the Euro. Roughly a hundred and fifteen thousand Euros,' Sullivan said.

Casagrande did the sum on his calculator and pulled a face.

'Show-off,' he snarled grudgingly, tossing the calculator away across the desk.

Sullivan grinned at him and took a *cornetto* from the plate. Enqvist was already on his second pastry, the buttery crumbs sticking to his lips and the stubble on his plump chin.

'These are good,' he said thickly, chewing on a mouthful. 'Did they come from the canteen?'

'You must be joking,' Casagrande said. 'I sent out to a *pasticceria* for them. One of the perks of rank.'

Sullivan sipped his espresso, looking around the room. There weren't many other perks of rank on show. Casagrande's office was only marginally better furnished than the interview room they could still see flickering on the screen high up on the side wall. He had a piece of tatty carpet on the floor, a functional desk and a few ugly chairs with central stores reject written all over them, but the budget had obviously run out long before the room could be contaminated with anything approaching comfort. Casagrande wasn't the type to even notice, much less care.

The most disconcerting feature was the metal sheeting over the window, but that had been placed there for security rather than aesthetic reasons. Although Gico was a branch of the *Guardia di Finanza*, its regional headquarters in Naples was housed in a separate compound protected by a high steel fence, razor wire and armed guards. Casagrande, like most of his men, lived in the compound twenty-four hours a day, seven days a week, venturing out only when absolutely necessary. To Sullivan, he seemed remarkably serene for a man who was almost certainly on a Camorra hit list.

'What about the mother vessel?' Sullivan asked.

Casagrande's narrow face brightened momentarily. 'Ah yes, I forgot to say. She's under arrest, currently being escorted into port by a *Guardia* cruiser.'

'You got her?' Sullivan found it hard to contain his jubilation. 'What's her name?'

'I know nothing more about her at the moment. As soon as I get any information, I'll let you have it. That's the one thing that cheers me up. Seizing the ship and the cabin cruisers. It should set them back more than confiscating any number of cigarettes. Armando Luciani is going to be shitting himself with fury.'

The major smiled broadly. Then he glanced up at the video monitor and his smile faded. He picked up the remote control and restored the sound to the picture. One of the *Guardia* officers in the interview room was standing up, collecting together his notes, while the other spoke into the tape recorder, terminating the session. The tape was removed, then the two officers walked to the door and knocked on it. It was opened by the guard outside and the two men went out, leaving their interviewee alone in the room.

'It doesn't look as if you got very far,' Sullivan said.

Casagrande pulled a sour face. 'We'll keep at him, make his life difficult at least. He's like all the others. He'll keep his mouth shut, do his time, then come out and start all over again. It's the only way of life they know.'

Up on the video screen, the prisoner turned his head and looked directly at the camera. He appeared tired, but in his eyes was a burning defiance. He shouted something in dialect, then stood up and walked over until he was below the fish-eye lens. He gathered the phlegm in his throat and spat it out and upwards. The image on the video monitor erupted in a shower of frothy saliva.

Casagrande pressed a button and the screen went black.

'Well,' he said dryly. 'He's quite a spitter. All those years of practice, I suppose. They don't learn to read and write, these people, but they could gob for Italy.'

Sullivan and Enqvist laughed. Casagrande spoke English with an accent, but he had an admirable command of the vernacular.

'Sometimes I wonder why we do it,' the major continued, serious now. 'We're just fleas biting on an elephant's backside. I have some sympathy for people like him. He doesn't regard what he does as criminal. After all, cigarettes are a legal product. All he's doing is avoiding excise duty on it. Is that really much different from the wealthy businessmen who pay accountants to fiddle their taxes for them? It's always the same, isn't it? One law for the poor, one for the rich.'

He held out the plate of *cornetti*. 'Come on, finish them off. It was a long, cold night.'

Casagrande poured more espresso into his cup and stirred in some sugar, musing pensively.

'That one in there will go down for a few years. His wife and kids will struggle to survive without him but the *capo* who organised it all, who makes the millions out of it, will carry on as before. Sitting in his villa up in the hills, drinking his expensive wine and planning the next shipment. *He's* the one we'll never catch.'

He was talking more to himself than anyone else. And more in sorrow than anger.

'That doesn't mean we shouldn't try,' Sullivan said.

Casagrande eyed him, the beginnings of a frown wrinkling his forehead.

'Ah, an idealist,' he said. 'But then in Brussels it is possible to have ideals. Here at the sharp end it is not so easy. We were lucky last night. But we shouldn't kid ourselves that we're ever going to do more than scratch the surface, cause some minor inconvenience to these Camorra barons.'

Casagrande lifted his coffee cup and said mockingly: '*Signori*, I give you a toast. To futility.'

He tilted the cup to his lips and downed it in one.

There had always been something fundamentally untrustworthy about Rupert Bird. Looking at him now across the starched linen tablecloth, Hal Montague had a clear, and none too affectionate, recollection of the various indiscretions and betrayals which had marked their joint progression through school and university and which had, in adulthood, made Bird an ideal recruit for the Secret Intelligence Service.

At Harrow, Bird – Bird Minor as he was called, to distinguish him from his older brother, a joke which both masters and boys had persisted in finding funny for about five years longer than its natural lifespan – had been a sneak of the worst kind. Conniving and deceitful, he had been imbued with an instinct for lying and treachery which his fellow pupils had found loathsome but which Her Majesty's Government had regarded as a perfect qualification for a job at the Foreign Office.

Montague had never liked him. They'd never been friends and, after Oxford, where Montague had been at pains to avoid Bird's company, he had broken with him entirely. They'd lost touch for many years, Bird making steady progress through the stuffy ranks of the civil service, Montague making rather more of a mark on the world of business and finance where his talent for taking calculated risks had paid impressive dividends. But a chance encounter at an old boys' fundraising function had renewed their acquaintanceship and led to occasional social contact which had proved mutually beneficial. Montague had a knack of identifying people who could be of use to him and Bird, in the corridors of Whitehall at least, was extremely well-connected.

'Have you chosen yet, Rupert?' Montague asked, aware of the waiter hovering near their table.

'I'm not sure.'

Bird inspected the menu again. Montague contained his impatience, knowing his companion would have the fillet steak as usual. He didn't have the imagination to try anything new.

Montague beckoned the waiter over. 'The rack of lamb for me. And—' He waited.

'The fillet steak, why not?' Bird said.

'New potatoes and vegetables?' the waiter asked.

Montague nodded and ordered a bottle of the house red. He was rich enough to be a wine snob but he didn't see the point. A 'plain bottle of plonk' – as he was fond of saying, generally in a cod Yorkshire accent – was all he required with his food. That was one of the reasons he liked the Parkside, it had no pretensions. The food was simple and English, well-cooked and plentiful enough to fill his beefy frame. No ridiculous garnishes, no trickles of raspberry sauce with the meat, no main courses balanced in a pile in the middle of the plate so it might as well have been served in a drainpipe.

There were other advantages too, notably the fact that there was an absolute ban on mobile telephones in the dining room. Montague hated mobile phones, regarding them as the status symbol of the office boy, a sign of enslavement rather than liberation. He had one himself, outside in the Bentley, but that was different. He never allowed it to intrude on his life; the whole point of power was to dictate whom you spoke to and when.

But the main advantage of the Parkside was its location: a quiet Kensington backwater, if Kensington really had any backwaters, far enough away from the watering holes of the City and Whitehall for neither of them to be recognised by colleagues or rivals. For what they had to discuss, on the infrequent occasions they met, was always confidential and very often politically and commercially sensitive.

They made idle small-talk while the wine was brought and poured, then Bird leaned forward over the table and said: 'So when exactly are you going?'

'Next week.'

'And your itinerary?'

'Unchanged. Kiev, Odessa, Zhdanov.'

Bird nodded. He knew all this already but he liked to check his facts, if only to cover his back with his superiors.

'And you're meeting the Ukrainian trade minister when?'

'Thursday.'

Bird sipped some of his wine. 'How do you rate your prospects?'

'Good. Zuganin is a man of growing influence. He wants to see this project go ahead as much as I do. His political future depends on it.'

Montague didn't add that the minister's bank balance in Zürich also depended on it. Bird didn't need to know the details of the deal.

'Most of the former Soviet republics are teetering on the verge of bankruptcy,' Montague continued. 'They're as desperate for hard currency now as they were in the communist era. The only way they're going to get any kind of political stability is to bring some economic prosperity to their countries. And they're only going to achieve that through Western investment. You know what the average annual earnings in the Ukraine are?'

'No.'

'Forty pounds. That's all they make.'

'No wonder you're so keen to get in there.'

Montague smiled, but his eyes remained cold.

'We'll be using skilled labour,' he said. 'They'll get more than that. But not much more,' he added with a grim chuckle.

Montague liked doing business in Eastern Europe and the old USSR. He had investments in manufacturing in Poland, Russia and the Ukraine, in agriculture in Hungary, and was now spearheading a consortium seeking to explore for petroleum and natural gas near the Sea of Azov. The possibilities for an entrepreneur with guts and guile were limitless. All the people with power in the former communist states were infatuated with capitalism. They wanted to get rich quick and they weren't too scrupulous about how they did it. They'd rejected a system of state control with all its corruption and inefficiencies and replaced it with a culture of uncontrolled laissez-faire gangsterism that, although it didn't work either, had one major advantage over communism: it made the people in charge wealthy enough not to care whether it worked or not. It was little different from the heyday of the robber barons in the United States. Rockefeller and Vanderbilt and Jay Gould would have found a home from home in modern Ukraine, or Russia or Belarus, it didn't matter which. And Montague, who had much in common with those old rogues, was equally comfortable there.

Bird fingered the stem of his wine glass, casting an eye around the restaurant. There were no other diners near enough to overhear what they were saying.

'I've had a word with Our Man in Kiev,' he said pompously.

Montague was amused that people in the FO still talked like that, as if there were some in-house style book dating back to the Thirties that they were all obliged to use.

'And what did Your Man say?'

'They'd be interested in anything you can pick up. General background information. Economic data, political stuff, you know what I mean. It's all useful.'

'Tittle-tattle, gossip, which minister has a boyfriend, that kind of stuff?' Montague said sarcastically.

Bird forced a weak smile. 'Anything. You can leave it to us to sort the wheat from the chaff.'

'I'm sure I can,' Montague said, though he had his doubts. He regarded the words British Intelligence as something of an oxymoron. Its employees, if Rupert Bird was anything to go by, would probably be hard-pressed to tell the difference between a classified document and a shopping list. But Montague indulged them because it suited his purposes to do so. He'd supplied snippets of information in the past, nothing that would compromise his own self-interest, and was happy to go on doing it. It appealed to the small boy inside him, a childish love of intrigue which he'd never lost. And it created an obligation between him and his old schoolmate, a debt that could be called in whenever he needed it.

A liveried figure appeared at the door of the restaurant: Montague's chauffeur. He walked across the room, manoeuvring his way between the tables.

'I'm sorry to interrupt, sir, but you said I was to let you know immediately. Mr Doyle called.'

'And?' Montague said.

'He said the job had been completed to his satisfaction. He's on his way back to London now.'

'Thank you.'

Bird waited for the chauffeur to leave, then said, as if the interruption hadn't occurred: 'We'd be particularly interested in anything you hear about the hardline Nationalists. They're picking up a lot of support out in the provinces, we gather.'

Montague nodded. 'Hedging your bets?'

'We want to make sure we support the right side.'

'And which is the right side?'

'Whoever wins, of course,' Bird said.

'Rupert, you're beginning to sound like a politician.'

'You'll keep me posted, as usual?'

Montague saw the waiter coming out of the kitchen with their food. He flicked open his napkin and spread it across his lap.

'You know you can rely on me to do my bit for my country,' he said. 'Provided it does its bit for me.'

Simon Doyle switched off his mobile phone and slipped it away into the pocket of his jacket. The balaclava, the leather jacket and trainers had gone – dumped in three separate dustbins in different suburbs of Kingston upon Hull – and he was now dressed in a smart charcoal suit and sober tie, the picture of a junior executive or travelling sales rep. The stolen Golf was a burnt-out skeleton in a wood near Beverley and he was once again sitting behind the wheel of the Ford Mondeo he'd hired the previous day in London. He felt good. His body was pulsing with the kind of fresh vitality he usually associated with a hard work-out in the gym.

He turned his head to look at Serena Montague in the seat next to him. She was flushed, her eyes shining.

'You get a high out of this, don't you?' he said.

She smiled and stretched her long limbs. She reminded Doyle of a resting puma. Sleek, watchful and very dangerous.

'God, if only Hal could see me now,' she said.

'You'd enjoy it if he found out, wouldn't you?'

'I think I might. I do love getting under his skin.'

It was raining outside, the view of wet fields and hedgerows partially obscured by the streaming water on the windscreen. They were parked in a deserted picnic area a few minutes' drive from the westbound M180.

Serena reached across and ran her hand under Doyle's jacket, feeling the muscles of his chest and washboard stomach.

'I think we deserve a little bit of relaxation now,' she said.

Her fingers dropped to his fly. He pushed them away.

'What if someone comes?'

'Who's going to come here on a day like this?'

She started to kiss his neck, watching to see what he did. She liked taking risks. A part of her wanted to get caught.

'We could find a hotel for an hour or two,' he said.

'I don't want to wait.'

'It's either that, or the back seat.'

'What's wrong with that?' Serena said.

Claire looked out of the window of the car as they sped north up the coast road from Hendaye. The waves were rolling in, their crests spewing angry froth, along a huge stretch of beach between the fishing port of St Jean-de-Luz and the more sophisticated haunts of Biarritz. The surf here was renowned as some of the best in Europe. Claire had swum in it, when was it? Eighteen years ago. The realisation numbed her for a second. Where had all the intervening years gone?

She'd been eighteen years old. A group of surfers and their girlfriends had come down from the University of Amsterdam for the long vacation, sleeping rough, living out of camper vans parked near the beach. The girls had lain around on the sand all day while the men surfed. Claire couldn't believe she'd been a surfer's girl, hanging about all summer watching a bunch of brainless boys riding boards. As a joke, the girls had made cardboard stencils of their boyfriends' names and taped them across their stomachs so that the skin didn't tan. For two years after, until it finally faded, she'd had Wim blazoned across her navel. She'd never done anything so silly in her life. Actually, she had. She'd married the guy.

They were on the outskirts of Biarritz now, heading slightly inland away from the sea. Claire remembered

Biarritz as a chic, elegant town, full of fashionable shops and cafes that were too expensive, and too snooty, for penniless students. But none of that was visible from the road which descended to the River Adour and across a bridge into the old port of Bayonne.

Bayonne felt like a real town to Claire, a place where people lived and worked rather than simply idled away their holidays. It had none of the faded charm of its neighbour but it was attractive nonetheless in a plain, stolid sort of way.

The olive oil bottling plant, Fonteneau et Delahaye, was on the northern fringes of the town, in one of the character-less *zones industrielles* with which the French cluttered their sprawling suburbs. A local customs officer was waiting in a car at the entrance to the industrial park with the search warrant he'd obtained on Allard's instructions. There was a brief conference on the verge beside the road, then they drove in convoy to the factory, a large, modern building constructed – like all the others on the site – with great quantities of concrete and steel and very little style.

It was a slick, orderly raid – Allard and his men had carried them out many times before and each member knew exactly what had to be done. Claire kept out of their way, assuming the role of an observer. They went in at the front, asking the receptionist to summon the manager to the foyer, then while Allard and Claire waited for him to emerge from his office, the other customs officers – six in total – went through to the production and storage areas.

The manager, Alain Delahaye, was pushing sixty, a tubby little man with thick black spectacles and wobbly pink jowls like a sow. Allard showed him the warrant and explained what was happening. Delahaye blinked at him, too surprised to speak at first, then he assumed a manner of servile politeness.

'Of course, monsieur. You will have my full cooperation, but I assure you there is nothing here to warrant the attentions of the *Douane*. It's just a simple olive oil bottling plant.'

'You have dealings with a firm in San Sebastian, Garcia Saez?' Allard said.

'Yes. They supply us with much of our oil.'

'Olive oil?'

'Of course.'

'Do you also bottle hazelnut oil?'

Delahaye started, his jowls flapping as his head jolted backwards. Then he recovered himself.

'Hazelnut oil? I'm not sure I understand.'

'Do you bottle it here?'

'Why no.'

'We stopped a lorry at Hendaye earlier this morning,' Allard said. 'It contained a cargo destined for your factory. Concealed among the cans of olive oil were a number filled with what we believe to be hazelnut oil.'

'It wasn't coming here,' Delahaye protested indignantly. 'See for yourself.'

'My men are already doing that,' Allard said. 'Perhaps we should join them.'

The factory floor was a clean, airy space about the size of a football pitch. Rows of fluorescent lights hung on chains from the high vault of the ceiling, illuminating a complex circuit of conveyor belts which looped round and round the floor like a child's train set. Glass bottles rattled along the conveyor, the empty ones passing through a series of machines which filled them with olive oil, then capped and sealed them with a plastic sheath. Labels were stuck on and the bottles removed from the belt to be packed into cardboard boxes. Most of the process was mechanised but there were workers in blue overalls supervising the various stages who turned and stared curiously as Delahaye came out on to the floor.

'Where are the storerooms?' Allard asked.

Delahaye lifted a hand to point but the gesture was unnecessary, for one of Allard's men was already beckoning to them from a doorway on the other side of the production line.

The storeroom had been sealed off and customs officers were sorting through the rows of metal drums and jerry cans inside.

'I think you should see this,' the officer said to Allard.

Stacked at the back of the room were dozens of metal containers identical to the ones on the lorry at Hendaye. The caps of several had been removed. Allard peered into them, then dipped in a finger and tasted the liquid. He turned to Delahaye.

'Do you have a lawyer?' he said.

'Yes.'

'I think you'd better call him.'

The production line had been shut down. Customs officers were inspecting the machinery, taking samples from the tanks of olive oil and from the filled bottles to send away for analysis. The workforce, except those helping on the factory floor, had been asked to wait in the canteen until their turn came to be interviewed.

Allard and Claire were upstairs in Delahaye's office, which had windows on two sides, one set overlooking the production line, the other the yard at the rear of the factory. Claire was leaning on the windowsill while Delahaye's secretary brought in the company's books and other records for Allard to inspect. Delahaye himself was sitting stiffly in a chair, refusing to say anything until his lawyer arrived.

Claire looked down into the yard where an empty lorry was waiting forlornly by the shuttered entrance to the loading bay. She needed a cup of coffee badly but it didn't seem an appropriate moment to ask if there was a machine anywhere. She could always go for a walk, see if she could find one. She pushed herself off the windowsill and stopped dead as she noticed the door next to the loading bay open and a man come out. He was wearing blue overalls like the rest of the workers. Claire frowned. No one was supposed to leave the factory until Allard gave the okay. She watched the man cross the yard and go into a smaller one-storey building on the other side.

Curious, she walked away from the window and, with a nod at Allard, out of the office. There was a corridor outside leading to a flight of stairs which descended to the front foyer. Claire ran down them and paused to take her bearings. She had only a vague idea of the layout of the plant but she knew the loading bay must have access to the storage area where the packaged bottles of olive oil were kept prior to distribution.

She went through the doors on to the factory floor and walked hurriedly around the conveyor belts. Two of Allard's men were still checking through the production storeroom. She could see them as she walked past. Further on was a wide opening which led through into a bay filled with cardboard boxes stacked on pallets. A couple of yellow fork-lift trucks were standing idle against the wall. She pulled open the door beside the high metal loading bay shutters and stepped out into the yard.

Walking across to the other building, she cautiously opened the door. Inside was what looked like another storeroom or perhaps, from the stench of petrol fumes, a garage, with additional access from outside through a pair of double doors. The man in the overalls was loading cardboard boxes into the back of a Renault transit van.

'You need any help?' Claire said.

The man spun round and stared at her.

'Piss off, little girl, this is none of your business,' he snarled angrily.

35

'You want to show me what you've got in there?'

In reply, the man reached into the van and pulled out a steel tyre wrench. He brandished it in her direction.

'Get out of here. If you've any sense.'

Claire sized him up. He was much bigger than she was but running to fat. He looked strong, certainly, but also out of condition. She could have walked out to get assistance but he might have gone by the time she got back. Besides, she loathed seeming the helpless woman. In many ways it made her more reckless than a man. She took a couple of paces towards him.

'I don't want to hurt you,' he warned. 'But I will if I have to. Now fuck off out of here.'

'Put it down,' Claire said calmly. 'Don't make things worse for yourself.'

He snorted incredulously. 'Worse for me? Don't make me laugh.'

Claire sighed. Basic self-defence techniques had been part of her training, but it seemed a shame to waste her judo skills on a big oaf like this. She took another step towards him, unfastening the buttons on her blouse to expose the flimsy lace cups of her bra.

'Do you want me here, or in the back of the van?' she said.

The man gaped at her. The tyre wrench dropped to his side and his eyes to her cleavage.

'Uh?'

Men, sometimes they were so stupid, Claire thought as she swung back her leg and kicked him hard in the balls. He made a harsh, choking sound and doubled up clutching his groin. Claire gave him a push and he toppled over to the floor. She walked round to the back of the van and ripped open the top of one of the cardboard boxes.

She didn't know what she expected to find, but the contents took her by surprise. She stepped backwards, regaining her composure, then went round all the other boxes, tearing open each one in turn. The man was still moaning in a ball on the floor when Claire walked past him to the door, fastening up the buttons on her blouse.

THREE

It was raining heavily when Sullivan left his apartment for the twenty-minute drive to work across the Forêt de Soignes – or Zoniënwoud, if you preferred the Flemish version. He'd lived in Brussels long enough to get used to the bilingual nature of the city, the double names on all the streets and public buildings. Sometimes it still confused him – he'd hear the Flemish name for something he knew only in French and be perplexed for a time until he realised it was the same thing. It was usually that way round. French was a more familiar language to him and, though he lived in a Flemish-speaking suburb, his command of that language was poor. Like most Englishmen, he was lazy about languages, but the Flemings spoke such good English it seemed unnecessary, perverse even, to converse badly with them in their own tongue. He might have managed it in French but one of the things he'd learnt very quickly about Belgium – a country demarcated along complex linguistic and geographical lines – was that the Flemings spoke French only when it was absolutely unavoidable and the Walloons, well, the Walloons would rather cut out their tongues than utter a single word of Flemish.

The rain had eased a little by the time he emerged from the forest into the built-up area on the south-eastern edge of the city. It was no longer a cold, depressing downpour, merely a cold, depressing drizzle which, he'd come to realise, was an almost permanent meteorological feature of Brussels. It was just his luck that his first, and probably only, job overseas had to be in a country – and there weren't many – where it rained more than it did in England.

The headquarters of UCLAF, the *Unité de Coordination de la Lutte Anti-Fraude* – the European Commission's fraud investigation unit – was in a small part of a vast complex of offices on the Avenue de Beaulieu which also accommodated the directorates for the Environment, Transport, Telecommunications, Personnel and Research and Technology. Constructed on a skeleton of steel girders overlaid with a skin made of huge sheets of glass, the building bore a curious resemblance to an opulent greenhouse, except that the species inside it were anything but tender seedlings in need of protection from the elements. They were hardy perennial bureaucrats and administrators, germinated on the rich manure of tax-free salaries, fed on subsidised food, mulched by first-class travel and special allowances, watered with golden showers of Euros and never ever subject to the painful snip of the pruning shears.

The marble-floored atrium inside was filled with real trees and shrubs bathed in sunlight from the glass roof. Six floors of offices, their windows overlooking the atrium, rose upwards on either side, serviced by banks of glass-walled lifts and open spiral staircases. Sullivan had been told that the complex had originally been designed as a shopping centre but at times, particularly on dank winter days, with its security guards, locked doors, steel gantries and bridges, it had more the feel of a high-tech prison. But it was clean, modern and, above all, light. Sullivan wouldn't have minded the window-cleaning contract for the building, if he weren't almost certain that some *fonctionnaire* had already awarded it to themselves.

The UCLAF offices were on the top three floors at one end of the complex, accessed through doors which could only be opened with a special pass card. Sullivan walked down the corridor to the room he shared with Stig Enqvist and threw himself immediately into the most important business of the day – filling the filter machine with water and coffee and monitoring the liquid carefully for strength and purity as it dripped through. Stig wasn't in yet, but then he rarely was this early in the morning. His timekeeping, never good, had got worse recently, his attendance undermined by a jaded disillusionment which Sullivan found disturbing.

There was a pile of messages waiting for him on the desk, and a further stack of papers which Antonio Casagrande – a man determined to contradict all the common preconceptions about Italian efficiency – had faxed through overnight. Sullivan dealt with the most pressing messages first then turned his attention to the faxes, calling Casagrande on the phone to get an update on the information they contained. He was on his second cup of coffee by the time Enqvist slouched into the office and slumped down in his chair, his overcoat dripping wet from the rain.

'This fucking weather,' the Swede grumbled in his fluent, idiomatic English that Sullivan sometimes thought he'd picked up from some passing unit of linguistically-challenged troopers. 'Every bloody day it's the same. I swear my skin's shrunk since I came here.'

'I've noticed you doing many things,' Sullivan said dryly, 'but shrinking is not one of them.'

Enqvist sniffed and pulled off his coat, draping it over the back of a spare chair to dry. He straightened the jacket of his grey suit and looked down, holding in his stomach. He wasn't fat – not yet anyway – but he was showing noticeable signs of middle-aged spread. Too many waffles and burgers, not enough exercise. He gripped the roll of flesh around his waist and wobbled it up and down.

'Not bad for my age,' he said. 'It just needs a bit of toning.'

'Liposuction more like,' Sullivan said.

'Look, I'll show you.' Enqvist untucked his shirt.

'No thanks,' Sullivan interjected quickly. 'Not this early in the morning. Besides, Carlsen wants to see us in his office.

'About Naples?'

'Casagrande's faxed through the interview transcripts and a few other things. You want to look at them before we go?'

'Nah, I'll let you do all the talking.'

'Well, that'll make a change.'

They walked down the corridor then took the stairs to the sixth floor and the office of their section head, Ole Carlsen – a soft-spoken Dane in his early fifties with short hair and an iron-grey moustache which gave him a misleading military air, for he was actually a career *fonctionnaire* within the Commission with a distinguished career in the Danish civil service behind him. He waved them to a couple of chairs and pushed the file he'd been reading to one side of his immaculate desk.

'I hear it went well,' he said.

Sullivan glanced at Enqvist. Carlsen had an unnerving habit of being particularly well-informed about every operation his section undertook, even when the investigators involved hadn't told him a thing.

'RAI 1,' Carlsen said by way of explanation, seeing the puzzled looks on their faces. 'Not the details, but I got the gist. One dead, that was unfortunate.'

Italian television, of course. Like the BBC, Dutch, French and German stations, RAI 1 was a standard part of the cable package provided to virtually every home in the city. It was one of the reasons the residents were such phenomenal linguists.

'It sounded an exciting night.'

Sullivan briefed him on the details of the operation.

'Four hundred cases, two speedboats impounded, eight smugglers in custody, that's a good result,' Carlsen said. 'How much excise duty evaded?'

'About a hundred and fifteen thousand Euros.'

'Not bad.'

'A drop in the ocean compared to the total,' Sullivan said.

'But a setback for the Camorra nevertheless.'

'True,' Sullivan conceded. 'But the trail ends there. Eight small fry in jail, no big fish. Gico questioned them all but got nothing.'

'So we don't know where the contraband came from?'

'Oh yes,' Sullivan said casually, saving the best bit till the end. 'A bonded warehouse in Rotterdam. They were supposed to be going to West Africa. At least, that's what the papers on the mother vessel said.'

Carlsen raised an eyebrow. 'They got the mother vessel?'

'Picked her up seventy-five miles off the coast. The master denied any involvement, of course. The usual story. As soon as the *Guardia* cruiser came alongside he contacted Lloyd's for a satellite fix, then started screaming about acts of piracy. They arrested her anyway and brought her into Naples.'

'What nationality is she?'

'Liberian.'

'Now that's a surprise,' Enqvist said ironically.

'The *Maria Vasquez*,' Sullivan said. 'A general cargo freighter, about four thousand tonnes.'

'Can they establish a link?' Carlsen asked.

Although as a general rule it was unlawful to arrest a ship on the high seas, the Geneva and Montego Bay conventions permitted it if you could establish a link between the vessel and the smuggling of contraband.

'Enough,' Sullivan said.

'Aerial surveillance?'

'Only radar. They didn't want to use a plane in case it was spotted and they aborted the drop.'

'But no one actually witnessed the transfer of the cigarettes?'

'No. The circumstantial evidence is pretty damning though. There were thirty thousand master cases on board. Mostly American – Winston, Marlboro, Lucky Strikes.'

'Thirty thousand,' Carlsen said. That was three hundred million cigarettes. 'Going elsewhere?'

'No one knows at the moment. The boys we picked up might have been going back for a few more runs. According to the freight manifest they were all going to Senegal. But it's a funny way to go to Senegal.'

Carlsen nodded in agreement. 'Excellent. I'm very pleased. You did well. That was a damn fine show.'

Carlsen said things like that. He spoke five languages fluently, six if you included the language of bureaucracy which, this being the European Commission, was *de rigueur* in the senior position he occupied. But while Enqvist, for example, spoke the English of the football terraces, Carlsen sometimes appeared to have learnt his during a sojourn at a Home Counties golf club.

'The ship owners are going to court, I assume?' Carlsen continued.

Sullivan nodded. 'I spoke to Casagrande this morning. They've hired a team of heavyweight lawyers, five of them, to fight the seizure.'

'How does Casagrande rate their chances?'

'It's difficult to say. You can never tell with an Italian court. We know it was the *Maria Vasquez*, but there's no absolute conclusive proof that it was her. Not in legal terms.'

'Have Gico sent you any material from the ship?' Carlsen asked.

'I haven't been through it all yet,' Sullivan replied

evasively. He knew exactly what was in the faxes, but he guessed what was coming next and didn't want to show his hand.

'Should the courts force the release of the ship,' Carlsen said carefully, 'I want anything you have sent back to Naples immediately. We can't hold material that has resulted from an illegal search.'

Sullivan nodded. Carlsen was a Dane, but he had an almost Germanic obsession with procedure – an essential characteristic given the legal, transnational nature of UCLAF's work, but one that wasn't always shared or appreciated by his staff.

'Okay.'

'Thank you for your time. Keep me informed.'

Carlsen reached over for the file on his desk and opened it again.

'By the way,' he added, 'speak to Claire Colmar. She has something that might interest you.'

Sullivan and Enqvist went out. They were ten metres down the corridor when Sullivan said: 'I'll take Colmar.' Then: 'The pile of faxes on my desk from Casagrande. Why don't you photocopy them and put the copies somewhere safe?'

Enqvist grinned at him. 'Shit, it's uncanny how you can read my mind.'

Claire Colmar was seated at her desk, tapping away at the keyboard of her computer, when Sullivan walked into her office. She finished her sentence and swung round in her chair.

'Hi.'

'Ole says you've got something for us.'

Sullivan pulled up a chair and sat down. Claire crossed her legs and smoothed her skirt over her knees. Sullivan took in her appearance without any conscious scrutiny.

She was simply dressed – powder-blue blouse and grey suit – but there was a sort of effortless elegance about her which he'd come to associate with continental professional women. She obviously took care about what she wore, and wasn't averse to spending a lot on her clothes, but there was nothing ornamental about her. Her shoes were flat-heeled and practical, her nails trimmed short and unvarnished, her hair a dark bob that was easy to keep groomed. There was something lithe, athletic about her. Sullivan could see her in a gym or a swimming pool.

'I was down in the Basque country yesterday,' she said. 'With the *Douane*. We raided a factory in Bayonne. In one of the storerooms we found some cases of cigarettes. I think they're contraband. In fact, I'm sure of it.'

'What makes you so certain?'

'Well, it was an olive oil bottling plant for a start. And I caught one of the employees in the act of moving them. They didn't want us to find them.'

'How many cases?'

'Sixteen.'

'Any indication where they came from?'

'We questioned the factory owner. He said they were for personal consumption.'

'Oh yeah? He's a heavy smoker?'

'So he claimed. But assuming he was on, say, fifty a day, that would give him enough supply for . . .' She paused, hunting around on her desk for her notes.

'About eight and three quarter years,' Sullivan said.

Claire pulled out the sheet of paper on which she'd earlier worked out the numbers with a calculator, just for the hell of it. Eight point seven six seven, she'd scribbled at the bottom. She lifted her head and stared at Sullivan.

'You just figured that out? In your head?' she said.

Sullivan waved a hand as if to dismiss the subject.

46

'Maybe he likes to buy in bulk. Some people do,' he said. 'You can save a lot of money.'

Claire slid her notes back on to her desk.

'There were no records of purchase,' she said. 'No receipts, no invoices. You'd expect something for that many cigarettes. The owner says he's lost them but I don't believe it.'

'Did he say where he got them?'

'He can't remember.'

'All that smoking, it must have affected his memory,' Sullivan said.

Claire laughed. 'The *Douane* are still questioning him. I doubt he'll say much, but I have a hunch those sixteen cases were all that's left of a much bigger consignment. Has Bayonne featured in any of your investigations?'

'Not until now. What's the name of the plant?'

'Fonteneau et Delahaye.'

Sullivan shook his head. 'It's new to me. What sort of cigarettes were they?'

'Marlboro.' Claire handed him a piece of paper. 'The serial numbers on the cases. You want me to follow it up?'

'That's okay. We'll look into it. Who's in charge at the French end?'

'Philippe Allard.'

Sullivan folded the sheet of paper and slipped it into his pocket. Then he stood up.

'How's Nicoletti?' Claire asked.

Maurizio Nicoletti was the third member of the Cigarette Task Group, temporarily absent after breaking his right leg in a skiing accident at Cortina d'Ampezzo.

'He's out of hospital,' Sullivan said, 'but still a long way from being fit enough to come back.'

'I'm sorry.'

'He's okay. Thanks for your help.'

'Any time.'

She watched him walk away. He was attractive. A little reserved in that curious way the English had, so that you couldn't be sure whether they were cold or merely shy. But she didn't mind that; it gave you more to discover. She hardly ever spoke to him. He wasn't one of the men in the department – and there were several – who made a point of stopping by her office on the flimsiest pretext and flirting with her. She wondered why not.

She turned back to her computer and finished her mission report on the random customs checks in Hendaye. For once, a tip-off on one of the UCLAF freephone fraud lines had paid off. There was a number in each member state but they all came through to an answering machine at Beaulieu. Claire thought of it as the loony line because most of the calls were from either weirdos or people with gripes: disgruntled employees shopping their boss, businessmen stirring up trouble for their rivals, jealous neighbours taking revenge by telling malicious lies. Most, particularly the anonymous complaints, could safely be ignored, but just once in a while one turned out to be true, in this case information from an accountant in San Sebastian who had his suspicions about Garcia Saez.

Claire filed the report, then rang Allard. He was still at the bottling plant in Bayonne, overseeing his team as they questioned the employees and combed through every piece of paper they could lay their hands on.

'We've had the report on the lab samples,' he said.

'And?'

'Seventeen per cent hazelnut oil. In the tanks and the bottles. I doubt this place has ever produced a bottle of pure olive oil.'

'You're having them withdrawn, I take it?'

'We're contacting every wholesaler and retailer on the

company books, instructing them to remove any oil from their shelves and return it.'

'And the consumer?'

'There's a press conference this afternoon; newspapers, TV. Same message: return any bottle of oil to the shop where they bought it.'

'You're going to be on television?'

'I'm having my hair done specially,' Allard said. 'You get French TV, don't you? Watch the evening news.'

'I can hardly wait,' Claire said.

It was quite a coup for Allard's team. The publicity would increase their prestige and public awareness of what they did. UCLAF's role in uncovering the fraud would get barely a mention, but Claire didn't resent that. She didn't expect recognition for what she did. That was their job: to remain in the background, an unknown EU support group, while the national agencies took the credit for any successes.

'Philippe, I know you're very busy down there, but I've been thinking. You remember in Hendaye I said this had been going on for years and I wondered why no one had been caught until now?'

Allard saw where she was heading. 'You think the whole customs post is on the take?'

'I don't know. Maybe some of them.'

'You have anyone in mind?'

'Bignon.'

Claire heard him suck in air through his teeth. Then he said: 'He's a senior, well-respected officer. He's got a good record.'

'Can you check the factory files for when deliveries were made, then crosscheck them against the customs roster? See exactly who was on duty when the Garcia Saez lorries went over.'

There was a silence on the line.

'We're snowed under already, Claire.'

'I know. It's just an idea. It might be important, but it's your decision entirely.'

Allard grunted. 'Jesus, you don't give a guy much chance, do you?'

'That's what they all say,' Claire replied and hung up.

'So you made it back in one piece,' Enqvist jeered as Sullivan came into their office. 'Balls still intact, dick still dangling?'

'I never have any problems with Claire,' Sullivan replied.

'That's because you're the only man in the unit who's never tried it on with her.'

'Have you?' Sullivan was surprised. 'You never said.'

'Before your time. You think I could spend four years here and not have a shot, a woman like that?'

'And she turned you down?'

Enqvist pulled a face but didn't reply.

'I knew she had good taste,' Sullivan continued.

'Piss off.'

'Ah, the wit of the Swedes.'

'So what did she have for us?'

Sullivan told him. Enqvist leaned back in his chair and picked idly at one of his teeth with a fingernail.

'Sixteen cases, that all?' he said. 'It's hardly worth bothering with. American, of course?'

'Marlboros.'

American cigarettes sold well on the European black market. A malicious observer might have added that they were easy for a smuggler to get hold of too, but that would have been to single out the US companies and tar them with a brush that could equally well have been applied to any multi-national cigarette manufacturer. It was true that back in the early Nineties the Italians had accused Philip Morris of dealing with smugglers and temporarily banned the sale of their products in state tobacconists. But there was no absolute proof that they, or any of the other companies, traded with traffickers. Certainly there were vast amounts of contraband cigarettes swilling around the black and grey markets and, equally certain, it was of no concern to the manufacturers whether excise duty was paid on them, but it would have been a gross libel to even suggest that the tobacco barons knew anything about it.

Sullivan sat down at his desk and noticed the wad of papers Enqvist was holding in his hand.

'What's that you've got there?'

'I was looking through the faxes from Casagrande. These are copies of the log from the *Maria Vasquez*. You seen them?'

'I didn't study every page in detail.'

'I noticed something interesting. Two weeks ago the ship was detained by Customs and Excise in Hull. Held for two days. And at the end of those two days the master was replaced.'

'Why?'

'It doesn't say. Suddenly there's a new captain in charge, a Vladimir Strakhov.'

'Russian?' Sullivan said.

'Possibly. These Liberian ships have every nationality in their crews. The previous master was Dutch by the sound of him. Maartens. Frans Maartens.'

Enqvist held out the papers. 'I'll let you take care of it.'

'Why me?'

'Hull, that's in Yorkshire, isn't it? I won't understand a bloody word they say.'

'It's clean,' Doyle said, coming out of the conference room holding a small black box about the size of a brick and an electronic probe which bore a resemblance to a miniature metal detector, only its job was to locate the presence of unauthorised listening devices.

He stowed the equipment in his attaché case and followed Montague back into the room he'd just swept. There was a long polished table in the centre with seating for sixteen around it, although only four of the places were set with the standard appurtenances of a business meeting: notepad and pen, glass for mineral water, a bone china cup and saucer for coffee. It was the middle of the morning, but the blinds over the windows were shut and the fluorescent strips on the ceiling turned on, casting a garish sheen over the mahogany surface below. It seemed a pity because the view from the window, looking out across the Singel canal to the floating flower market, was one of the prettiest in Amsterdam.

Montague went to the chair at the head of the table and tossed down the copy of the *Daily Telegraph* he'd been flicking through outside. A headline near the bottom of the page read: 'Remand prisoner freed in ambush.' Inserted in the text of the story was a police photofit of an unremarkable-looking blonde woman.

'Did you have to shoot the fucking guard?' Montague said acidly, removing his jacket and sitting down.

'We were in a hurry,' Doyle replied. 'He was pissing us around.'

'You know he's likely to lose his left leg below the knee?'

Doyle shrugged. 'So?'

'So was it necessary?'

'You gave me a job to do, Hal. I did it the way I thought best. If you don't like it, do it yourself next time.'

'Let's hope there won't be a next time,' Montague said smoothly, ignoring his assistant's belligerent tone. 'Who was the woman? Some tart of yours?'

'You don't want to know.'

'No, I don't.' Montague glanced at the photofit drawing. 'Can they identify her from that?'

'Not a chance. Doesn't look remotely like her. She was wearing a wig, her face smeared with a bucketload of fake blood. The guards wouldn't recognise her again if they sat next to her on a bus.'

'Is she reliable?'

Doyle's mouth twisted into a sour grin. 'Oh yes, she's reliable.'

He took his place next to Montague as an attractive middle-aged woman entered the room pushing a trolley bearing a large jug of coffee, more cups and two plates of the sweet cinnamon biscuits the Dutch call *spekulaas*.

'Is everything to your satisfaction?' she asked.

'Perfect, as always, Ilse,' Montague said with exaggerated gallantry.

'Your colleagues have just arrived.'

She wheeled the trolley to the side of the room and waited while a group of four other men entered. Only when they were settled into their seats with coffee and biscuits in front of them did she discreetly leave.

Montague looked around the table. The chair next to Doyle was occupied by Gilles Lafon, a stocky French businessman in his early sixties with leathery skin and tufts of coarse grey hair on the backs of his hands. Strip away his expensive suit and diamond tiepin and he would have looked like an ageing manual labourer, or a trucker, both of which he had been in the early years of his career.

Opposite him was a thick-set tanned man with jet-black hair and a battered face that Montague always likened to a knobbly potato, a simile that would have annoyed Armando Luciani intensely for he prided himself on his rugged good looks. Behind him, seated against the wall, were the two younger men who always accompanied Luciani on his travels. Montague regarded them as a

53

superfluous, and far too conspicuous, entourage but it was none of his business; the Camorra boss probably didn't go to the toilet without a bodyguard to watch his backside.

'Shall we begin?' Montague said, easing effortlessly into the role of chairman of the board. It was such second nature to him that he sometimes had to remind himself that this was no ordinary business meeting despite its formal setting. There was no agenda, no minutes, no voting. The notepads on the table were purely for show: not a single word would ever be written down.

He turned to Luciani and said: 'What happened?'

Luciani grimaced, the expression emphasising the coarseness of his face.

'What happened? I tell you what happened,' he said in English, the language they always used in their meetings. Montague spoke fluent French and passable Italian, acquired from long and regular holidays at his villa in Umbria, but neither Lafon nor Luciani spoke the other's tongue.

'I lost two high-speed motorboats, worth two hundred and fifty thousand dollars each. I lost eight men to the fucking *Guardia* and a whole shipment of cigarettes. That's what happened.'

The anger was still seething beneath the surface, controlled but potentially explosive. Montague chose his next words carefully.

'Are we compromised in any way?'

'What?' Luciani frowned at him.

Montague rephrased the question. 'Are we in danger?'

'You? I'm the one in the fucking shit. What have you lost, eh?'

'I've lost my ship. That's worth a lot more than your speedboats.'

Luciani made a placatory gesture, conceding the point.

'Okay, I'm angry, that's all. When I find the *cazzo* who tipped them off, well, he won't have a fucking *cazzo* for long, that's for sure.'

'You have any indication who it was?'

'No.'

'You'd better find him,' Lafon muttered darkly.

'How do you know it was in Italy?' Luciani demanded. 'It could have been someone in England, someone on the ship.'

'We're all at risk here, Armando,' Montague said diplomatically. 'We're not apportioning blame. We don't want it happening again.'

'You think *I* do? I've just lost a shipload of fucking cigarettes.'

'So have I,' Lafon said. 'So shut up about what *you've* lost.'

'What?' Luciani glared at the Frenchman. 'What shipload?'

'Not a ship. But I've lost a consignment, part of it.'

Montague turned to Lafon, suddenly disturbed.

'What are you talking about, Gilles?'

The Frenchman dipped a biscuit in his coffee and chewed it. Montague noticed the oil and dirt around his fingertips. Lafon never looked spotlessly clean, but he made such a show of being a horny-handed son of toil that Montague sometimes wondered if the oil weren't applied from a bottle the way a woman put on nail varnish. Surely a man worth five hundred million francs could afford a tub of Swarfega.

'The *Douane*,' Lafon said. 'They raided Fonteneau et Delahaye.'

'They knew the cigarettes were there?' Montague was alarmed now.

'It was pure chance. Fortunately, most of them had already been shipped out.' Lafon picked up another biscuit.

'Maybe we should stop for a time. Things aren't going very well.'

'Stop?' Luciani exploded. 'Listen, if I don't get some more, and soon, Dino Falzone will be all over my territory. I can't afford to be off the streets for even a few days. I have some reserves but I'm going to need a big shipment soon.'

'You'll get it, Armando,' Montague said.

'How? They have your ship.'

'You think I only have one? You'll get your supplies, you can depend on that.'

The girls came in shortly after the meeting was over, opening bottles of champagne and circulating around the room. A tall, slim blonde in a halterneck dress slit to the crotch handed a glass to Montague, then took a Cuban cigar from the humidor on the table, cut off the end and slipped it between his lips. She lit it with a silver lighter adorned with a small sculpture of a couple fornicating and perched herself on the arm of Montague's chair, one hand stroking his hair lightly.

'Christine, my dear, how nice to see you again,' Montague said.

He inhaled on his cigar and let the smoke out slowly, noticing Doyle already leaving the room with a statuesque brunette. Young men, they were always in such a hurry.

'I know those fine gentlemen at the Harvard Business School wouldn't agree with me,' Montague pontificated. 'But there's a hell of a lot to be said for mixing business and pleasure.'

The apartment was in darkness, splashed with icy puddles of light from the streetlamps outside. Sullivan pulled the curtains and switched on a couple of table lamps. It felt

warmer then, but no amount of soft lighting could overcome the basic coldness of the flat. Not its temperature –
that was kept uncomfortably high by the heating system
which served the whole block – but its atmosphere. The
floors were bare wood, covered in places by bald rugs,
the ceilings high and the walls a plain cream colour that
exuded a chilly dampness, as if they'd been painted with
melted ice cream.

There was very little furniture. What there was came with
the apartment and Sullivan had not chosen to supplement
it with any of his own. He didn't see the point. He was
only on secondment for three years, four at the most,
and buying furniture seemed a waste of money. What
did he need it for anyway, except to fill up the sterile
emptiness of the flat? It was far too big for one person:
three bedrooms, a big gloomy sitting room, a long walled
garden outside the French windows. He'd rented it shortly
after arriving in Brussels when it had been their intention
that his wife and sons would join him, the boys going to
the European School in the city. But in the end they'd
decided it was better not to interrupt their schooling in
England, nor to separate them from their friends. His
wife, too, had been reluctant to give up her teaching
job and relocate so they'd compromised and he'd kept
on the flat so they could all come over and stay in the
school holidays.

Sullivan wished it were more welcoming. He was temporary, and felt it, yet three years was still a long time
to live out of a suitcase. He liked the comforts of home,
missed them, especially on these dark winter nights when
he came back to face a long evening alone, but he couldn't
be bothered to recreate them for himself. That was something he'd always relied on his wife to do. The decor, the
furnishings, the personality, that transformed a four-walled
box into a home had always been Kate's. Without her, he

didn't feel inclined, or able, to build a second home for himself in Brussels. His home was in England, with her and the boys, and it seemed somehow wrong to create an alternative life without them. So he endured the dismal ambience of the apartment, working long hours to reduce the time spent in it, and consoled himself with the thought of his two weekends a month back in Colchester where he belonged.

Going into the kitchen, he boiled the kettle and made himself a cup of tea. He was too tired to even think about cooking so he worked his way through half a packet of chocolate biscuits then, feeling guilty and not remotely full, wished he'd had something healthier and more substantial. He was losing his discipline. There'd been a time when he would have gone out jogging and then made himself a proper meal, but the willpower was deserting him. The cautionary spectre of Stig Enqvist loomed up before him, a classic example of a man living alone and away from home who was slowly letting his body deteriorate through laziness and indifference. Sullivan didn't want that to happen to him, yet he could see all too clearly how easy it was to let things go and never regain them.

He took his tea through into the sitting room and switched on the television with the sound turned off. He didn't want to watch it; he simply found its colourful glow comforting. Then he picked up the phone and rang home. It was Kate who answered, though he could hear Patrick and James squabbling noisily in the background. Their incessant fighting drove him mad when he was there but now he found himself almost – but not quite – missing the sibling warfare.

'Hi,' he said.

'Hello.'

She sounded tense, under strain. She broke off for a second to tell the boys to shut up, then came back on.

'Sorry.'

'How's things?' Sullivan said.

'Okay.'

'What's the matter?' He could always sense when something wasn't right.

'Nothing.'

'Kate.'

'I'm tired, that's all. It's been a trying couple of days.'

'Why?'

'Oh, nothing in particular. It's all fine now.'

'What's all fine?'

She was being a martyr again. The wife coping on her own, struggling through adversity, not wanting to bother him with what she saw as trivia. But it was the trivia he missed; the boring details of their lives which he wasn't there to share but which, when taken together, gradually built up and solidified to form the bedrock of a happy family.

'It's James,' she said eventually. 'He had an accident last night. He was knocked off his bike.'

'What! Was he hurt?'

'Fortunately not. The car wasn't going very fast. He was lucky, he landed on a grass verge.'

'Was he wearing his helmet?'

'Yes.'

'So there were no injuries at all?'

'A few bruises. He was taken to hospital. We were in Casualty from eight o'clock to gone midnight. The usual waiting around for doctors, X-rays.'

'You should have called me.'

'It was too late by the time we got home.'

'Too late?' Sullivan said in exasperation. 'It's never too late to tell me my son's had an accident. I don't mind what time you call.'

'Yes, okay. Don't get cross about it.'

59

'I'm *not* cross.'

Silence. Sullivan sighed. It was difficult sustaining a marriage on the end of a phone. They'd had too many of these conversations. They both loathed the instrument. It had the advantage of immediacy, but despite that it didn't seem to bring you closer, only make you more distant.

'Kate?' Sullivan said gently. 'I'm not cross, okay? It's just a shock to find out. I'm worried and I'm too far away to be of any help.'

'I know,' she said. 'But he's fine.'

'And you?'

'I'm fine too.'

'I'm coming home tomorrow,' he said.

'Oh.'

She didn't sound overly excited at the prospect.

'I have to go to Hull. I'll be with you early evening, I hope, depending on the trains.'

'You know we're all tied up on Saturday. I've the school trip and the boys are going up to Norwich with the Mackinnons. I told you weeks ago.'

'Did you?' He didn't remember, but then he wasn't there to be reminded. 'Anyway, it'll be nice to have an extra weekend together.'

'Yes.'

Another silence.

'Do the boys want to say hello?'

'I'll ask them.'

He caught the muffled sounds as she passed on the question to his sons, then heard their blunt, indifferent replies.

'They're a bit tied up at the moment,' Kate said down the phone, softening the blow.

He kept the disappointment out of his voice. 'Okay, I'll see you tomorrow then.'

He replaced the receiver, feeling the silent emptiness of the apartment all around him. Then he picked up his cup of tea and sipped it, his eyes fixed unseeingly on the flickering television.

FOUR

If Sullivan had drawn up a list of places he'd like to be on a wet February day, Kingston upon Hull would have come somewhere below Ulan Bator and Vladivostok. It wasn't that he felt any particular antipathy towards the city – it was actually quite an attractive place, certainly more attractive than its reputation suggested – but when the rain beat down in a continuous barrage and the wind swept across from the North Sea, cutting deep into the bones like a blunt saw, he could imagine few locations on earth more miserable.

He'd taken an early morning flight from Zaventem to Leeds – Bradford, then a slow train east across Yorkshire, stopping at Selby, Brough and a half dozen godforsaken outposts in between. He could have carried out his business on the phone, or by fax, but he preferred to visit people in person whenever possible. On the phone he was a faceless Brussels bureaucrat, a distant apparatchik working for an organisation most people in Europe had never heard of. In the flesh, whatever their nationality, they could see him for what he was: an ordinary working man with the same worries and aspirations, the same common decency and basic outlook as they had. And most importantly – particularly in England, given the paranoid suspicions about 'Europe' – they could see he was one of us, not one of them.

From the centre of Hull, he took a taxi out along the Humber to the customs post which served the King

George and Queen Elizabeth docks. It was an uninspiring drive: three miles of tatty houses and boarded-up shops interspersed with warehouses and small metal-bashing workshops. He'd been to ports all over the world. Like airports, they were all different yet all essentially the same. The storage sheds, the grain silos and oil tanks, the vast yards full of containers and lorry trailers were identical wherever you went. They were small towns with their own private roads and security guards, strange coastal enclaves where the stench of oil and ship's diesel was always more powerful than the smell of the sea.

Climbing out of the taxi, Sullivan saw the dockside cranes and the superstructure of a roll-on roll-off ferry poking up above the roof of the warehouse across the road. There was a cowl of grey cloud over the estuary and, on the horizon beyond the dipping flocks of gulls, the flat shoreline of Lincolnshire emerged hazily from the mist.

Jeff Goodman, the customs officer he had spoken to on the phone from Brussels, met him at reception and took him through to his office. They had coffee and made small-talk for a while, chatting mostly about the job, the universal gripes of government employees. Sullivan, though he was working for the European Commission, was still a UK customs officer and would return to the service at the end of his secondment. It was a moot point whether he still had the powers of a customs officer or whether they were temporarily held in abeyance, but as far as Goodman was concerned he was an insider and would be given all the assistance he needed.

'You wanted to know about the *Maria Vasquez*,' Goodman said. 'I've got the file here. How can I help you?'

'We've seen a copy of the logbook which indicates the ship was detained here a few weeks ago.'

'That's right,' Goodman said. He was a little younger than Sullivan with curly blond hair and freckles spattering his cheeks and nose. 'January twenty-fourth, that's when she docked.'

'Coming from?' Sullivan asked.

'Rotterdam. Bringing in a mixed cargo of goods: palm oil, nuts, dried fruit, odds and sods. She's one of those freighters that will carry anything, you know the kind. Look at her and you'd think she'd sink before she got a couple of miles down the Humber estuary, but she was built to last. The owners probably picked her up for a song, tarted her up a bit – and I mean a bit – then chartered her out to some bargain basement outfit interested only in doing things on the cheap.'

'She's Liberian, isn't she?'

'Yeah. But the crew were mostly Filipinos. You should have seen the quarters. Jesus, I'd keep pigs in better conditions.'

'You went on board?'

'Searched it from bow to stern.'

'Why?'

'Drugs.'

'You find any?'

Goodman shook his head. 'It was clean.'

'But you thought there were some on board?'

'We knew there were. The master, bloke named Maartens, was bringing the stuff in. Not big quantities, mostly cannabis as far as we can tell. He's Dutch, you can buy it dead easy over there. It's quite a temptation. Pick up a few kilos in Rotterdam, put it in your cabin then sell it once you get to the UK.'

'You caught him at it?'

'Not us. Humberside police. Drugs Squad. They were watching a known dealer in the city. They caught Maartens in the act of handing over four kilos in the toilets of a nightclub. They contacted us and we went on board and took the ship apart. Nothing.'

'You think he'd been bringing it in regularly?'

Goodman shrugged. 'Hard to tell. I met Maartens last year, he was over here every few weeks. He didn't strike me as the criminal mastermind type. He was more your foolhardy chancer. Saw an opportunity to make a bit on the side and couldn't resist it.'

'The police charged him, I assume?'

'Of course. The CPS in Hull have the file. We gave them our report too.'

'I'd be interested in talking to him. About the movements of the *Maria Vasquez* while he was the master. Who's the CPS lawyer handling the case?'

Goodman checked the file. 'Cosgrove. Kenneth Cosgrove. You may have a long wait.'

Sullivan frowned. 'What?'

'You obviously don't know. Maartens has disappeared. Sprung from the van on his way from the Wolds prison to the remand hearing in court.'

'That was *him*?' Sullivan said. He only occasionally read the English papers, but he vaguely recalled a mention on the BBC news bulletins he received in Belgium.

'Two days ago,' Goodman said. 'He hasn't been seen since. Not as far as I know anyway. You want to call the CPS?'

'Could I?'

Goodman flicked through the pages of the file, then reached out for the phone on his desk and dialled a number.

'I'm afraid we can't help you,' the CPS lawyer said when Sullivan came on the line. 'The case against Maartens is closed.'

'Don't you think he'll turn up somewhere?' Sullivan said.

'Oh he has. He turned up this morning in a derelict barn near the coast. Unfortunately he was dead.'

'Dead?' Sullivan paused, absorbing the information. 'In suspicious circumstances?'

'A bullet through the head. Is that suspicious enough for you?' Cosgrove said.

'Who found him?' Sullivan asked.

Kenneth Cosgrove shifted in his high-backed leather chair and put his hands behind his head, flexing his fingers together. He was a big man with a dark five o'clock shadow across his jawline though it was only just gone noon. It felt insufferably hot in the stuffy warren of offices which the Crown Prosecution Service occupied in the centre of Hull. Already there were damp patches of sweat under the arms of Cosgrove's shirt.

'A farmer. He has a place out near Hornsea. There are some old long abandoned farm buildings on his land. On the clifftop. The farmer uses the barn for storing hay, a few bits of machinery. He doesn't go there all that often, but he did this morning. Maartens was slumped in a corner, a bullet hole in his left temple.'

Sullivan stroked his cheek pensively. 'The same people who ambushed the prison van?'

'Without a doubt. Shows how wrong you can be. When it happened we thought it was friends of his wanting to free him, smuggle him out of the country. It all makes sense now.'

'How do you mean?'

'Maartens was a nobody, a stupid small-time criminal. Okay, he brought in drugs, but it was only cannabis, not the hard stuff. He'd have gone down for a time, a year, maybe two. He had no record, at least not for drugs. Twelve months inside and he'd have been out. So why go to the trouble, and the risk, of springing him from an armoured prison van? We know now.'

'Yet why kill him, if he was such a small fish?'

Cosgrove gave a shrug. 'Your guess is as good as mine. The police are still out there, obviously, picking over the scene. We won't know what they find for a couple of days.'

Sullivan stood up and removed the jacket of his suit, hanging it over the back of his chair.

'You hot?' Cosgrove said. 'Open a window if you like.'

'Do you mind?'

'We get used to the temperature. These new buildings, no proper ventilation. Go ahead.'

Sullivan unlatched one of the windows and swung it open. Down below in Lowgate the rain was spitting on the gleaming pavements, peppering the pedestrians as they hurried about huddled beneath their umbrellas. There was a dazzling gilt statue of William III on an island in the middle of the road, its plinth – in a jarring and some-how disrespectful juxtaposition – immediately above the entrance to an underground public convenience. Sullivan took a breath of the damp sea air. It seemed cold and heavy on his lungs. Then he went back to his chair and sat down.

'Can I ask what the circumstances of his arrest were? Jeff Goodman said it was in a nightclub.'

'That's right. Although I'd use the word nightclub advisedly. It was an old warehouse down by the river. Some wideboy converted it, put in a few bright lights, a bar, a sound system. It's still an old warehouse but the kids who go there are too pissed to notice. I think it's supposed to have atmosphere although what's atmospheric about mouldy walls and the stink of mud at low tide I don't know.'

Sullivan smiled at him. 'You're showing your age.'

'Yeah, I know. Mind, even when I was a teenager you wouldn't have caught me dead in a place like that.' He paused. 'I suppose that's why I became a solicitor.'

'And Maartens?' Sullivan prompted.

'Stuck out like a prick in a convent. He must have been the oldest person there by a long way. Even the undercover cops were only in their twenties. They were watching a guy named Vasili Kravchenko, a known dealer.'

'Kravchenko?'

'You know the name?'

'What nationality is he?'

'Ukrainian originally. Naturalised British. We have quite a problem here with Eastern Europeans: Poles, Ukrainians, Serbs. They're muscling in on every racket you can think of. Drugs, prostitution, contraband cigarettes. But then you probably know all about that already.'

'It occasionally comes to our notice,' Sullivan said dryly.

'Maartens had a holdall with him containing four and a half kilos of weed,' Cosgrove continued. 'The police burst in on them when he was handing it over to Kravchenko.'

'Was he a regular courier?'

'We'll never know now. Maartens was a seedy character. No master with a clean sheet would have touched a tub like the *Maria Vasquez*.'

'He had previous convictions?'

'Not in this country. But the Dutch police knew him. He was linked to a handling case a few years back but there wasn't enough evidence to convict him. There was an attempted extortion too. He demanded money from a married secretary at a shipping agent's in Rotterdam in return for keeping quiet about an affair she was having with her boss. She went to the police but Maartens denied it. It was his word against hers so he was never charged.'

'A pretty unsavoury character,' Sullivan said.

'He was. I reckon he got what was coming to him.'

'Do you mind if I look at the file?'

'Help yourself. You over here for the day?'

'Yes.'

'You want some lunch first? There's a pub down the road serves a nice pint.' Cosgrove smirked. 'On you, of course. This is a deprived area, we need all the help we can get from Brussels.'

Sullivan put on his jacket and raincoat and waited for Cosgrove to get ready. They were downstairs in the foyer, bracing themselves for the penetrating cold outside, when Sullivan said: 'Do the police have any idea who might have killed him?'

Cosgrove pulled open the glass door to the street, letting in a gust of biting wind.

'Some dealer with a grudge, maybe someone scared of what he'd say in court.'

'You think it was a drugs-related murder?'

'What else could it be?' Cosgrove said.

It was nearly eleven o'clock that night when Sullivan arrived home in Colchester. He'd left Hull at four o'clock, relaxed and looking forward to the weekend. By the time the taxi pulled up outside his house he was seething with a frustrated anger that could only be described as 'train rage'.

It was a hundred and twenty miles as the crow flies from Hull to Colchester. It had taken him seven hours, an average speed – as he'd worked out during one of the many longueurs on the journey – of a fraction over seventeen miles an hour, which was probably about the speed at which a crow actually flew.

First of all he'd had to go to York – completely the opposite direction to the one in which he wanted to go – in a clapped-out collection of carriages with a heating system which circulated only marginally more warmth than a pair of bellows and a lighted match. Then in York he'd had to wait close on two hours for the East Coast express which was running late due to some unexplained 'technical problems', a delay which meant he missed his connection at Liverpool Street and had to wait almost another hour for the next train to Colchester.

Kate could tell he was in a foul mood the moment he walked in through the door. She'd got ready for bed earlier and was waiting up in the sitting room in her dressing gown.

'We got anything to eat, I'm starving?' was the first thing he said, coming in and tossing down his overnight bag and briefcase. 'Those bloody trains. No wonder this shitty country is going down the tubes. Seven hours it's taken me, seven bloody hours. It's just up the road, Hull. Stephenson's fucking Rocket could have done it quicker. D'you leave me any dinner?'

'It's nice to see you too, Rob,' Kate said.

But he wasn't listening. He turned and went out. Kate heard him go into the kitchen and open the fridge. She followed and stood in the doorway, leaning on the frame with her arms folded.

'What did you have?' he said, rummaging around the shelves.

'Some pasta. The sauce is in a bowl.'

'You leave me any pasta?'

'I threw it away.'

'Why?'

'You know it's horrible cold. You never eat it.'

'You could've put it in the oven.'

'It's eleven o'clock. I expected you at eight.'

'It's not my fault. I was stuck on a bloody train.'

'God, you're in a mood.'

'What d'you expect? I thought you'd leave me some food. I've been on the go all day.'

'You think I haven't?'

'What did you throw it away for?'

'Don't shout at me.' Kate sighed, trying to cool things down. 'Why don't you have some bread and cheese?'

'Bread and cheese? I want more than bread and sodding cheese. What else have we got?'

He closed the fridge door and circled the kitchen, pulling open the cupboards and slamming them shut.

'There's never anything to eat in this house.'

'I'm going to bed,' Kate said, wanting only to get out of his way.

'What, already?'

'I'm tired. I have to be up early.'

'Why?'

'The school trip. I told you on the phone.'

'Oh.'

She went out before the atmosphere deteriorated any further. It was always the same when he came home. Friday night they always had a row, some trivial but acrimonious exchange which left them both feeling resentful. She knew it was the process of adjusting to the other's presence after a time apart, but knowing the cause of the arguments didn't seem to stop them happening. After nearly two years of seeing Rob only every other weekend, and during the school holidays when she and the boys went and stayed with him in Brussels, she thought she would have got used to it by now. But it seemed to be harder than ever.

At the beginning it had been difficult, but they'd both expected that and made an extra effort to overcome the problems. Now living apart was the norm, the problems were still essentially the same, but neither of them was inclined to try so hard to smooth them out. Kate had got used to the arrangement: organised her life to cope with her husband not being there most of the time. So when he burst back in twice a month, expecting everything to be dropped for him, expecting their family life to be the same as it had been before he left, it annoyed her. She knew it was tough for him being away from home, but he didn't seem to appreciate how hard it was for her. She was virtually a single mother, holding down a full-time job and bringing up her sons on her own. She would have preferred him to be there to help but she was coping just fine by herself. The last thing she needed were these pointless Friday-night squabbles.

She was drifting off to sleep when Rob finally came upstairs and got into bed. She waited for him to say something, to touch her, put his arms around her and hold her. It had always been an unspoken rule in their marriage, before he went to Brussels, that after a row they would kiss and make up before they went to sleep. But he just lay there and did nothing. She could sense the tension, the contained anger in him, but she was damned if she was going to be the one to make the first move. So they rolled over and ignored each other, two silent, resentful shapes sharing a bed.

By morning they were still a little tentative, unsure what mood the other was in. But Rob came over to her side and slipped his arms around her warm body, gently exploring her contours as if reminding himself what she felt like. Kate rolled over and kissed him.

'Are we friends now?'

'Yes. I'm sorry about last night,' he said sheepishly. 'I just wanted to be here with you, not hanging around some freezing station platform.'

He stroked her softly.

'Don't get any ideas,' Kate said. 'I have to get up.'

'Can't you miss the trip?'

She removed his hands and climbed out of bed, slipping on her dressing gown.

'Why don't you come with us?' she suggested. 'There'll be room on the coach and we could do with another adult.'

Rob pulled a face. Spending the day with a bunch of over-excited nine-year-olds was not his idea of fun.

'You're leaving me on my own,' he said. 'What am I going to do?'

'You could always put up the curtain rail in the kitchen. It's been sitting there for two months.'

'Why is it that whenever I come home, you always have some DIY for me to do?'

Kate smiled. 'Well, you've got to be useful for something.'

She went out of the bedroom. Rob heard her going next door to wake the boys. It was ironic really, he reflected ruefully, that in the early days, when the boys were little and he and Kate desperately needed a lie-in, they never managed one because Patrick and James always came in at the crack of dawn to disturb them. Now things were different and they practically had to drag the boys from their beds, a late rising was a real possibility, yet there was always some pressing reason not to take advantage of it.

Reluctantly, he dragged himself out from the duvet and threw on his clothes. He was in the kitchen, making tea and toast, when his sons came downstairs, a pair of yawning, tousle-haired slobs.

'Morning,' he said.

The boys grunted indistinctly and helped themselves to Weetabix and milk.

'You sleep well?'

They nodded, not looking up from their bowls. He wondered if he should be flattered by their indifference, the way they regarded him as such a fixture in their lives that there was no need to acknowledge his presence. They were beyond the stage of showing how they felt about him, no longer the little boys who got excited when he came home from work, who wanted to be picked up and cuddled. He missed that.

Kate came in and grabbed a slice of toast and a gulp of

tea. She'd put on her make-up and her field trip clothes: jeans, woolly jumper, thick socks.

'Come on,' she urged the boys. 'I'll drop you at the Mackinnons on my way.'

'Where exactly are you going?' Rob asked his sons.

'I told you,' Kate said. 'They're going to Norwich. Eric Mackinnon's taking them with David.'

'To do what?'

'It's an Inlines competition.'

'Inlines?' Rob couldn't get used to the new terminology. He still thought of it as Rollerblading. He was perturbed how out of touch he was. He knew the boys had taken up the sport but he didn't realise they were good enough to enter a competition.

'Is James up to it?' he said. 'After his accident.'

'I'm okay,' James protested. 'There's nothing the matter with me.'

'Are you sure?' Rob said, looking at Kate.

She nodded. 'He'll be fine. He wasn't hurt on Wednesday. Go and clean your teeth, boys, we have to leave.'

Rob waited for his sons to go upstairs before saying: 'Is this a good idea?'

'They're resilient things, kids.'

'They're also fragile.'

'Stop worrying. They've been looking forward to this for weeks.'

'Maybe I should go with them.'

'I thought of that, but it's too late. You need a spectator's ticket and I know it was sold out ages ago.'

She kissed him lightly on the lips. 'See you tonight. Enjoy your DIY.'

The house was very quiet after they'd gone. Rob made himself another pot of tea and tried to read the newspaper, but his heart wasn't in it. Did all fathers feel they were losing contact with their children? All parents, maybe. Or just the ones who worked away?

He remembered clearly the day, twelve years ago, when he'd gone to register Patrick's birth. The Registrar, a smiling, chatty woman in her fifties, had said to him, and he could recall her words exactly: 'Make the most of him. It won't be long before you have to give him back.' He knew now what she'd meant, how being a parent was a slow, inexorable process of letting your children go.

It started very early. At playgroup, at school, where your offspring soon created a world of their own from which you were excluded. And later, when they formed friendships and ventured further from the home, asserting their need for independence which, in time, would take them away from you altogether. He knew it was inevitable, wanted, for their sakes, for it to happen because that was what growing up was all about. But he couldn't help feeling a pang of nostalgia for the early days, for the two babies whose entire universe had revolved around their mother and father.

He roused himself and went upstairs to wash and change into his tatty, paint-stained trousers and shirt. Then he returned to the kitchen, took out his toolkit and began the task of putting up the new curtain rail.

There was always the same pattern to his attempts at DIY. He would start off confidently, enthusiastically even, convinced that the job would be a complete doddle. But after half an hour discovering that the walls weren't flat, or vertical, or that the plaster came away like brittle toffee when he touched it and that nothing was ever, ever as simple as the *Reader's Digest* sodding manual said it was, he suddenly remembered how much he loathed the whole business and wished he'd never begun. But he had to carry on; drilling holes that were too big for the wallplugs, making new ones nearby that were just as bad, trying to patch things up as best he could and getting more and more frustrated until he was in such a state of fury he thought his head would explode. And what was more, there was no one there to share, or alleviate, his rabid frenzy. One of the things he'd noticed over the years was that whenever he undertook any tasks around the house, the rest of the family somehow contrived to be elsewhere while he botched them up.

Two hours later the curtain rail was finished; not quite straight and slightly wobbly, but he was too fed up to care. He retired to the local pub for a pint of bitter and a roast pork sandwich, enduring an hour of motorcycling – a sport well up there on the watching-paint-dry scale of fascination – on the satellite screen before going home to wait for Kate and the boys to return.

Patrick and James arrived first, tired but elated, both having done quite well in their respective age groups. Rob gave them tea and sat with them, listening as they told him about their day. Kate came in a while later and paused to admire the new curtain rail – 'I love the way it dips in the middle' – before going upstairs for a soak in the bath.

They put the boys to bed early and had an Indian takeaway delivered. Rob had spent a large part of the day anticipating making love to Kate that night, but in the end they were both too stuffed with lager, nan bread, chicken dupiaza and prawn biryani to even contemplate sex. They sogged on the sofa in front of the TV then dragged themselves upstairs and curled up together in bed, comfortable, familiar with each other.

The Sunday passed in the quiet family routine of the papers, lunch and a walk in the woods then, just as they were all getting used to each other again, Rob had to pack and prepare himself for the journey back to Brussels. Kate drove him to Colchester station and they sat in the car park, suddenly subdued. They both hated these depressing Sunday nights.

'We'll see you in Brussels next weekend,' Kate said.

Rob nodded. 'It seems a long way off.'

'We'll have a whole week together.'

She reached across and hugged him. They kissed. Gently at first, then more passionately. He slipped his hands under her jumper. She pulled him closer then broke away.

'The timing's never right, is it?' she said disconsolately. 'You'd better go, you'll miss your train.'

He went into London and across to Waterloo on the Underground. The Eurostar departure lounge was full of men just like him, peripatetic fathers returning to exile in Belgium. He wondered if they felt the same way as he did, but from the outside it was impossible to tell.

He got on to the train and stared out of the window as it purred slowly through the suburbs and on into the Kent countryside. Then he pulled some papers from his briefcase, shut down the part of his brain marked 'personal' and immersed himself in the anodyne therapy of work.

FIVE

Stig Enqvist poured himself another cup of coffee, loosened his tie and undid the top button of his shirt, then sat down in his chair and stretched out his arms and legs as if he were sunbathing.

'So what's your theory?' he said.

Sullivan shrugged. 'I don't have one. But I don't think it had anything to do with drugs.'

'Why not? Maybe the CPS guy is right. Someone was scared Maartens would do a deal to get his sentence reduced. Say too much.'

'About what?'

'Where he got the cannabis, who he delivered it to.'

'The police know who he delivered it to. The Ukrainian's in custody. Guy named Vasili Kravchenko. That mean anything to you?'

'No, should it?'

'It sounded familiar so I looked it up on the data base before you came in. You remember last summer, UK Customs raided a clothing warehouse in Nottingham on a tip-off it was being used for storing cigarettes?'

'The abortive one, you mean?'

'Yeah. Place was empty. I called Tony Fitzpatrick who organised the raid. To check on the facts. The manager of the warehouse was called Ivan Kravchenko.'

'Related?'

'Vasili's younger brother.'

'Well, well. So they're into drugs as well as cigarettes. That doesn't surprise me. Maartens brings in cigarettes and does a bit of dope-smuggling on the side. He gets caught so they knock him off. These guys don't take chances. What's one more killing to them?'

Sullivan lifted his leg and placed the sole of his shoe on the edge of his desk, rocking back in his chair.

'I'm not sure it's quite so simple. You find out who owns the *Maria Vasquez* yet?'

'I contacted New York Friday afternoon,' Enqvist said.

For some mysterious reason, probably because no one knew where the hell Monrovia was, the Liberian register of shipping was kept in New York City.

'The answer was waiting for me this morning.' Enqvist picked up a fax from the desk. 'It's owned by a Liberian corporation, of course. Buchanan Investments. But naturally that's just a front. The beneficial owners could be anyone.'

'Dun and Bradstreet?'

'It lists a firm of lawyers in Monrovia as the registered office and a business address in Vaduz.'

'Liechtenstein? Shit, well that's a dead end for a start. We got anything else?'

'There's the stuff from Casagrande, the logbook and so on.'

'We're going to have to go through the log day by day, plot the movements of the *Maria Vasquez*, see exactly where she went and when.'

'Well, as you're volunteering.'

Enqvist pushed the pile of documentation across the desk. Sullivan picked up the logbook and riffled through the photocopied pages without much enthusiasm.

Enqvist sipped his coffee. 'How was your weekend?'

'Okay. Yours?'

'You know, pretty much as usual.'

'You go anywhere?'

'No. Where would I go?'

Enqvist's marriage had broken down three years earlier, before Sullivan was seconded to UCLAF. His wife and daughter were still in Stockholm but Stig rarely visited them. He seemed to spend his weekends either working or talking to strangers in bars. He held his drink well, but Sullivan sometimes worried about him. His eyes were getting increasingly bloodshot and there were moments during the working day when he disappeared to the toilet for ten minutes and came back smelling of mint toothpaste which didn't always disguise the underlying odour of brandy.

Sullivan put down the logbook and glanced at one of the other bits of paper Casagrande had sent from Naples. It was a list of the names of the crew on the *Maria Vasquez*. Something about it struck Sullivan as odd. He rummaged in his briefcase and took out a photocopy he'd brought back from Hull.

'What's the matter?' Enqvist asked.

Sullivan compared the two pieces of paper, then searched through the logbook for something that wasn't there.

'This is the crew list from Naples,' he said. 'And this is one I got from the CPS file in Hull. The master is different on each one, we know why. But so is the first officer. When the ship was detained in Hull, and when Customs finally let her sail, he was someone called Joop Broekhuizen. When the *Guardia* arrested the ship the first officer was one Nikolai Tonkov. There's no entry in the log to explain when or why he was replaced.'

'So? Maybe the first guy was tainted by Maartens so the owners got rid of him. Maybe the new master wanted to bring his own first officer with him. There could be any number of reasons why it happened.'

'Yes, perhaps,' Sullivan conceded.

He returned the papers to the collection on the desk and noticed Enqvist holding up another document.

'What's that?'

'Take a look. It's from Dutch Customs. I asked them for it when you were in Hull. It's a copy of the clearance for the cigarettes on the *Maria Vasquez*. They came from a bonded warehouse owned by a Willem Van Vliet.'

Sullivan's brow furrowed as he ran the name through his memory banks.

'I don't recognise it. Any form?'

'Not in our files.'

'Dutch Customs?'

'They're checking, but unlikely. By all accounts it's a reputable, long-established business.'

Sullivan studied the information in the fax.

'You notice the figures?' Enqvist said.

Sullivan didn't reply. He was hunting through the drawers of his desk, taking out wads of paper and flicking through them quickly.

'What are you looking for?' Enqvist asked.

'Got it.'

Sullivan held up a scrap of paper with a few numbers scribbled on it.

'Got what?'

But Sullivan was already on his feet, collecting together the assortment of documents scattered over the surface in front of him.

'We're going to see Carlsen.'

Sullivan spread the papers over the section chief's desk and talked him through them, Stig Enqvist looking on from a chair to one side.

'The *Maria Vasquez* left Rotterdam on February seventh, carrying a cargo of American cigarettes which had been stored in a bonded warehouse belonging to Van Vliet Entrepôt NV. No duty was paid because the cigarettes were being re-exported to Senegal. So far, everything above board.

'Eight days later, on the morning of the fifteenth, the ship is arrested in the Tyrrhenian Sea off the coast of Italy. On board her the *Guardia* find nearly thirty thousand master cases of cigarettes, plus the four hundred cases we recovered from the speedboats. But look at the Rotterdam customs clearances. When she left Holland, the *Maria Vasquez* was loaded with forty-five thousand master cases. Somewhere between Rotterdam and Naples she offloaded a hundred and fifty million cigarettes and you can bet your life it wasn't done legitimately.'

'They made another drop?' Carlsen said, looking up from the documents.

'Offshore,' Sullivan said. 'According to the log, she didn't put in anywhere after she left Rotterdam.'

'That's a lot of coastline. France, Spain, Portugal. Several thousand kilometres.'

'Now look at this,' Sullivan said. 'Claire Colmar gave me the serial numbers of the cases of cigarettes she found in Bayonne. Check them against the Rotterdam customs clearances and the *Guardia di Finanza* seizure list. It was the same consignment.'

Carlsen leaned back, looking directly at Sullivan.

'What do you want me to do?'

'Authorise a raid on the bonded warehouse in Rotterdam. I want to know who ordered the cigarettes, who shipped them and who paid for them.'

'Just us?'

'With Dutch Customs. I think they should be in on it.'

Carlsen gave a nod. That was one of his strengths, the ability to make quick decisions, to trust the professionalism of his investigators.

83

'I'll talk to Hellendoorn immediately,' he said. 'Have you spoken to Colmar about this?'

'Not yet.'

The section chief mused on something for a time, tugging at the lobe of his left ear with his forefinger and thumb.

'What's the latest on Nicoletti?' he said.

'I spoke to him last week,' Enqvist said. 'Another three weeks, at least. And then he'll probably be on crutches for a time.'

'I'm going to have a word with Pierre Serot,' Carlsen said. 'See if he can spare Colmar for a while. You could use another person on the team. Especially in Rotterdam. She's Dutch, she knows the people there, speaks the language.'

'She might not want to join us,' Sullivan said.

Carlsen smiled knowingly. 'Oh, I think she will.'

Claire Colmar had been with UCLAF for nearly three years, her first twelve months on general agricultural import and export investigations and latterly on the Olive Oil Task Group which, along with the task groups on cigarettes and alcohol, dealt with the high-risk, high-return frauds which were dominated by organised crime gangs. She enjoyed the work, but agriculture had none of the glamour of cigarettes or alcohol. Checking bottles of olive oil was hardly the stuff of dreams and she'd been angling for some time for a transfer to one of the other two task groups. But there'd been no opening until Maurizio Nicoletti slid into a pine tree and snapped his tibia venturing off-piste in the Dolomites. After that she'd approached Carlsen again and made another pitch for a transfer. He'd been cool at first, but Claire had a feeling she'd get her own way eventually. She usually did.

Sullivan and Enqvist were relatively unknown quantities to her. There were almost eighty investigators in the unit and most were so engrossed in their particular special-isations that they had no time to cross over and mix with their colleagues in other sections. Enqvist was probably one of the few who was familiar to everyone in some way. He was coming to the end of his term of secondment so he'd been around for nearly four years, longer than most, and he was a sociable, gregarious individual. Loud would be another, less complimentary way of putting it. He was friendly, talkative – too talkative for some – and always willing to go for a drink after work or to help out a colleague in need. He'd made a pass at Claire once and she'd given him the brush-off, but he didn't seem to resent it and she certainly didn't hold it against him. She was used to working in predominantly male environments and was accustomed to the unwanted attentions that always brought.

Sullivan was harder to categorise. Seemingly distant, contained, he had none of Enqvist's boisterous energy, but he had a quiet, unassuming determination about him, a tough grittiness that was reassuring. Claire sensed almost immediately that, of the two, Sullivan was the one she'd rather have beside her in a tight corner.

But right now they were in a car on the motorway north of Brussels, heading towards Antwerp and then Rotterdam. Enqvist was driving, Sullivan next to him. Claire was in the back listening to the two men talking.

'I like Antwerp,' Enqvist was saying. 'You know why? Because it's a Flemish town. There's something about the Flemings I like. They're friendlier than the Walloons.'

'You mean they drink more,' Sullivan said.

'They're less stand-offish, more parochial in some ways, but that gives the city more character than Brussels, which is too full of foreigners for me.'

'Especially Swedes.'

'You know what I mean. Brussels bores me, particularly stuck there at weekends. You can only wander around the Grand-Place so many times.'

'There's more to see than the Grand-Place, if you want to play tourists.'

'Like what?' Enqvist said. 'The Manneken Pis?'

'There's the Atomium, the Château Royal, the parks, the museums.'

'The museums? I can't think of anything more boring. The only interesting one was the Underpants Museum but that shut a few years ago.'

'There was an Underpants Museum?' Sullivan said incredulously.

'Yeah.'

'You're kidding.'

'No, there was.'

'Containing what?'

'What do you think? Celebrities' underwear.'

'Like whose? Sharon Stone's?'

'Funnily enough, no. That's what made it interesting. It was the only underpants museum in the world not to contain a pair of Sharon Stone's knickers. People flocked there from all over to see why not.'

'Bollocks.'

'It's true,' Enqvist protested.

'Okay, whose underpants were in it?'

'I can't remember exactly. Famous Belgians'.'

'So it was a very small museum?'

'Ho, a cheap jibe.'

'In England, the Belgians are famous for not being famous. I bet you can't name me ten famous Belgians.'

'Easy.' Enqvist paused.

'See,' Sullivan said.

'Wait on, I'm just collecting my thoughts. Okay, Simenon, the writer; César Franck, the composer; Hercule Poirot, the detective.'

'He's not real.'

'He is to me.'

'You might just as well include Tintin, Captain Haddock and Snowy.'

'Hergé, he's another. How many's that?'

'Three.'

'Shit, there must be more than that.'

Claire looked out of the window, marvelling at this stream of drivel, only half listening to these grown men playing the sort of silly game you indulge in when you're drunk, or on surveillance duty to pass the time. They were both former customs officers, maybe that's where they'd acquired the habit.

Claire had once thought that women were better at talking to one another, just chatting easily about whatever happened to occur to them, but men needed a specific subject. Men had to talk *about* a particular topic: about football, or about cars or about women. But over the years, working with men, she'd realised how wrong that was; that men had an innate ability to talk to each other for hours on end about absolutely nothing at all.

'Jean-Claude Van Damme, so-called actor,' Enqvist said. 'The Muscles from Brussels.'

'Is he famous?' Sullivan inquired.

'He thinks he is.'

'That's four.'

They were silent for a long time, Enqvist concentrating on negotiating the ringroad around Antwerp, Sullivan gazing through the windscreen with the kind of fixed focus that implied he wasn't actually looking at the view. Claire put them out of their misery.

'Hieronymus Bosch, Brueghel, Pierre Cuilliford,' she said.

'Who?' Sullivan said.

'The artist. He created the *Schtroumpfs*. Smurfs, you call them in English.'

'Those little blue gits are Belgian? That explains a lot.'

'Rubens, Van Dyck, Magritte.' Claire finished the list. 'I think that's ten.'

That shut them up.

There was a pause, then Enqvist glanced across at Sullivan and said: 'Okay, ten famous Norwegians.'

The grey Renault saloon was two hundred metres from the customs post, anonymous and completely unnoticed amongst the dozens of other vehicles in the car park beside the River Bidassoa. Queyras and Pigout, the two plainclothes customs officers inside the car, had long since run out of things to say to each other. The former was flicking idly through a motoring magazine, looking at the same pictures, the same articles he'd already read at least twice; the latter was listening to Johnny Halliday on his personal stereo and chewing on a slightly stale *pain aux raisins*, his third of the day.

They were old hands at the surveillance game, practised at filling the long hours of tedium it entailed. They had an ability to draw out the simplest activities to an inordinate length: to extend a brief exchange that might normally take five minutes into a half-hour conversation, to stretch a newspaper feature from a two-minute browse to a twenty-minute detailed study, and to break up the numbing boredom of a day's shift with the undercover operative's great solace: food. The inside of the Renault was littered with the debris of their indulgence; crumbs and torn fragments of *baguette*, orange peel, apple cores, discarded pastry bags and innumerable chocolate bar wrappers.

The vacuum flask on the floor had held two litres of coffee but that had now all been drunk, the evidence clearly visible in the gleaming pools of liquid outside on the asphalt beside the doors. Like professional cyclists who could urinate whilst in the saddle, the two men –

not daring, or often finding it impossible, to leave their posts – had perfected the technique of pissing out of the side of a stationary car without drawing attention to themselves.

Queyras checked his watch. 'It's time,' he said, tossing down his magazine.

Pigout switched off his stereo and removed the head-phones from his ears. In the distance, three figures came out of the door of the customs post and split up, heading for their cars parked in the lot next to the building. Christophe Bignon climbed into a shiny green Citroën and drove out on to the main road.

'They don't hang around, do they?' Queyras said, starting the engine and spinning the wheel to bring the Renault out on to the highway a hundred metres behind the Citroën. 'The minute the shift finishes, they're off.'

'Can you blame them?' Pigout said.

'It's all right for some.'

'You want to swap with them? Sit around all day in a shitty little backwater like this, counting lorries as they go past?'

Queyras didn't reply. They'd both served their time in the provinces before finally making it to *Douane* headquarters in Paris. Their job had its drawbacks but neither of them wanted to return to the monotonous routine of a frontier posting.

Bignon's car headed north-east up the N10 towards St Jean-de-Luz, but turned off in Urrugne to take a narrow country road which ascended the foothills leading to La Rhune, the 900-metre peak which dominated this part of the Basque Coast. A couple of kilometres up the hill he turned into the driveway of a large stone farmhouse commanding a panoramic view of Hendaye, Fuenterrabia and Irun.

Queyras and Pigout drove past the house and found a

junction higher up where they turned round and went back down the hill, stopping on the verge next to a stone wall which hid their car from sight of the house. The only problem was that the wall also prevented them seeing the entrance to the driveway. Queyras took out the surveillance log and made a note of the time and Bignon's route home. Then he produced a five franc coin.

'I'll toss you for the first stint.'

Pigout lost. Muttering darkly, he hauled himself out of the car and walked down the hill to a point from which he could see the house without himself being observed. Night had already fallen and there was a cool wind blowing off the black sheet of the ocean far down below him, beyond the scintillating lights of Hendaye Plage. Pigout shivered and buttoned up his coat.

After half an hour, Queyras relieved him and they alternated throughout the evening, freezing their balls off on the roadside before returning to the car to thaw out. Approaching nine o'clock, Bignon came out of the drive in the Citroën and went back down the hill towards the coast. A little more than thirty minutes later he was in the casino at Biarritz.

Queyras and Pigout went in after him and took turns loitering near the roulette table as Bignon played with an intense fervour that marked him out as more than just a casual gambler. He remained there until eleven thirty, then drove home.

Following him in the Renault, Pigout remarked: 'How much do you reckon he just blew?'

'I made it nearly sixty thousand francs.'

'And what does he earn? Thirty thousand a month maximum, even with overtime.'

'So he just lost two months' wages in one evening.'

Pigout nodded. 'And his house, that must be worth, what, two million?'

They held back a little, letting the Citroën get well ahead of them as they went up the hill.

Then Pigout said: 'I think I'd like to have a look at his bank account, wouldn't you?'

'What is the point of these places?' Enqvist demanded rhetorically. 'There are dozens of them all over the world. Not just Andorra. Monaco, San Marino, Liechtenstein, the Channel Islands, every fucking banana republic in the Caribbean. What are they for? We having another bottle of wine, by the way?'

'I'm okay,' Sullivan said.

Claire shook her head, but Enqvist had already made the decision for them. He flagged down a passing waiter and ordered another bottle of Alsace Riesling.

'I'll tell you what they're for,' he said, continuing his train of thought. 'They exist because the rich need them to avoid taxes and if there's one golden rule that applies to every fucking thing in this world, it's that whatever the rich need, they get. The western governments, if they really wanted to, could shut down these ridiculous havens overnight: close their borders, cut off their supplies, invade. You think the French couldn't walk into Monaco and say, 'Okay, guys, the party's over, you're part of France now and we want all the billions you've stashed away.' What are the Monegasques going to do? Send out a bunch of pop stars and playboys in their luxury yachts to stop the French Navy? Wheel out Rainier, Albert, Caroline and all those other royal parasites to lie down in front of the tanks?'

Sullivan caught Claire's eye across the table and smiled.

'Stig is something of a Republican, as you'll notice now you're working with us,' he said.

'I'm just explaining the problems we have to face,' Enqvist said. 'Cigarettes and olive oil are different. Every investigation we undertake sooner or later – and it's usually sooner – we find it somehow involves one of these pisspot little states. Like Andorra, as I said.'

He paused as the waiter brought the second bottle of wine to the table, pulled the cork and let him taste it. Enqvist nodded his approval and waved the waiter away, filling his glass himself.

'Anyone else?'

Sullivan was still on his first glass of the previous bottle and Claire had barely started her second. They both shook their heads.

Enqvist took a gulp of the new wine and said to Claire: 'You ever been to Andorra?'

'No.'

'You should go. Everyone should. I recommend it as a salutary example of what a base, materialistic species we are. It's the most revolting, obscene place I've ever been. Think of all the worst souvenir shops you've seen and put them in the same street and you've got Andorra la Vella, that's the capital. Although capital is a grand word for what is basically the world's largest duty-free shop. That's all there is there. Two long rows of stores selling the same stuff: booze, cigarettes, cameras, perfume. Plus a few bars and some hotels – but not many. No one actually stays in the shitty little hole, they just go there for the day to shop.

'And you know who the Head of State of Andorra is? Well, there are two, it's joint rule. The President of France and, wait for it, the Bishop of Urgel. Isn't that hilarious? A Catholic bishop presiding over the tackiest, most commercialised place on earth.'

Enqvist paused, concentrating on his food. They were in the top floor restaurant of their hotel in Rotterdam, sitting by a window which afforded a view of the modern, high-rise centre of the city and in the distance, beyond the glowing lights of the tower blocks, the Nieuwe Maas waterway which led to the massive Europoort complex, and, ultimately, the North Sea.

Enqvist was filling Claire in on some of the background to the Cigarette Task Group's work, describing how they'd stopped the trafficking from Andorra which had once been a major centre for smugglers.

'We looked at the figures, it was as simple as that,' he said. 'Andorra has a resident population of about sixty-three thousand, plus a few hundred thousand tourists spread out over the year. Yet they import – or at least they did then – several billion cigarettes annually. Not to mention the ones they manufacture under licence within the country. On the figures – and I can't remember them exactly – every man, woman and child in the country must have been smoking something like four hundred cigarettes a day. Now that's what I call a habit.'

Enqvist helped himself to more sauté potatoes from the dish in the middle of the table and used them to mop up the creamy sauce that had come with his veal cutlets.

'What's more,' he continued, 'a large part of the cigarettes imported into Andorra came from the UK, brands that the Andorrans – or for that matter, the Spanish and French – have never traditionally smoked. What was going on?

'Quite simple: the cigarettes were manufactured in Britain, then exported on a T1 to Andorra. Goods in transit across the EU to a non-EU country so no duty payable. The Andorrans then smuggled them over their borders into France and Spain, either across the mountain passes by donkey, or by road declaring them as something else. The cigarettes were then back in the EU and could be moved freely between member states without customs checks. So the smugglers put them on a lorry and took them all the way back to the UK where they sold them on the black market. How much duty evaded? In 1997 alone, about four hundred million ECUs. And that's just one trafficking route. I tell you, the more I do this, the more I realise I'm in the wrong job.'

Claire finished the last morsel of her chicken and sipped her wine, looking across at the two men. Enqvist was shovelling potatoes into his mouth and chewing on them, his cheeks bulging; Sullivan was going slower, eking out his food as if he didn't want to finish first. He hadn't said much during the meal, he'd left all that to Enqvist, but there was nothing intimidating or hostile about his reticence. His manner was warm, welcoming. He seemed glad to have her on the team.

'The Spanish Civil Guard sealed off the entire border,' Enqvist went on. 'Tightened up their frontier controls, stopped and searched as many lorries as they could. The smugglers soon got the message.'

'They stopped doing it, you mean?'

Sullivan shook his head. 'They just moved elsewhere. That's how they work. They go where the smuggling is easiest. If one country gets too hot, they simply find another base. We sorted out Andorra but the truth is we just moved the trafficking into someone else's back yard.'

'Anywhere in particular?'

Sullivan grinned. 'Now if we knew that . . .'

'The bastards are everywhere,' Enqvist said. 'Every mafia-type outfit in the world wants a share of the cake. The Cosa Nostra, Camorra, the Triads, the Turkish Grey Wolves, the Chechens, the Ukrainians, the Colombians, the Serb warlords.'

'The Serbs are into trafficking?' Claire said.

'It's one of the key ways they fund their war machine.'

'But how do all these people get hold of the cigarettes?'

'The manufacturers sell to them. Not directly, of course.'

Enqvist's voice took on a tone of heavy sarcasm. 'Cigarette manufacturers are all men of honour, fine law-abiding citizens who would never dream of trading with traffickers. Unfortunately, there are plenty of middle men who have no such scruples. It's hardly the fault of the manufacturers if those middle men sell on what they buy to a bunch of gangsters, now is it?'

'They must know what's going on, surely?' Claire said.

'I'll give you some more statistics, let you draw your own conclusions,' Enqvist said. 'In October 1997 alone, before the clampdown on smugglers by the Civil Guard and the French, the British cigarette firm Gallaher exported a hundred million cigarettes to Andorra. One month later, in November 1997, after the clampdown, they exported precisely zero to Andorra. In October, the other big British manufacturer, Imperial, exported nearly eighty million cigarettes to Andorra. By January 1998, that too was down to zero. The companies say they had no idea where the cigarettes were ultimately going, but who did they think was buying them, the Bishop of fucking Urgel?'

Claire laughed. She had a feeling she was going to enjoy working with these two.

'The middle men are the problem,' Sullivan explained. 'Some of them are traders who deal with legitimate outlets and siphon off a part for sale to traffickers. Others flog on everything they buy to smugglers.'

'You know who they are?'

'Some. A lot of them are Swiss: clever, unscrupulous lawyers and accountants. Rich men in suits who mix with politicians and bankers, sophisticated businessmen who go to black-tie dinners at international finance conferences, who can borrow millions on the shake of a hand. They're crooks, but catching them at it is nigh on impossible. They're always protected by a trail of companies, many of them bogus and all eventually ending up in places like Liechtenstein and the Bahamas and Jersey where their secrets are safe from people like us.'

'Which I think is where we came in,' said Enqvist.

He cleared his plate and poured himself another glass of wine, looking around for a waiter.

'We having dessert?'

He signalled to one of the waiters and asked for the dessert menu. Then Sullivan's mobile phone rang. He answered and had a brief conversation.

'Hellendoorn,' he said, putting the phone back in his jacket pocket.

'Everything fixed?' Stig asked.

'Warrants arranged, his men all ready to go. He'll pick us up from the foyer at seven thirty.'

Enqvist winced. 'So early?'

'He wanted earlier, but I told him you were here so he made a concession. It somehow spoils the impact if one of the team is still wearing his pyjamas.'

'I don't wear pyjamas.'

'Even worse.'

'Are we having dessert or not? Do something useful with your mouth,' Enqvist said, turning his attention to the menu.

Claire could feel the easy rapport between them. They made a good partnership. She'd seen ones like it before in Dutch Customs: men who worked well together, who respected each other but indulged in a smokescreen of casual joshing to disguise the genuine affection they felt for one another.

They went straight to their rooms after they'd finished dinner. They had three next to each other down a long corridor. Enqvist went into his first with a murmured, 'See you in the morning'. Claire unlocked her door as Sullivan walked past her to his room. He paused on the threshold and smiled briefly at her.

'Good night.'

'Good night,' she said.

She watched him disappear through the doorway, then pushed open her own door, went inside and locked it behind her.

SIX

Claire had grown up in Haarlem in the province of Noord-Holland, a small parochial town she'd found stiflingly dull as a teenager, and from which she'd taken every possible opportunity to escape. Fortunately, the beach resort of Zandvoort was only a few kilometres away to the west, a refuge during the summer months where she and her friends had spent many a long weekend sunbathing or wandering along the seafront chatting up boys. In winter, and in the evenings, there was Amsterdam, a fifteen-minute train journey away to the east. She'd loved the city back then. It seemed to offer everything Haarlem lacked: bright lights, teeming bars and nightclubs, exotic haunts and the wicked, tantalising flavour of sex, which she was just beginning to try out for herself. Now she was older, Amsterdam was no longer so appealing. The red-light district had lost its fascination and the city was a curious mixture of the tawdry and the picturesque. A centre for tourists that she regarded as Heritage Holland, like windmills and tulip fields and women in clogs and lace shawls.

Rotterdam, in contrast, had almost nothing to offer the tourist. It had none of the charm of the capital, and the prostitution and drug-dealing were not for sightseers, they were for real. Claire had never really liked the city, but it had an energy and a culture of enterprise that made it an exciting place to live. Virtually destroyed during the war, it had been rebuilt with a fervour and an optimism that had transformed it from the busiest port in Holland into the busiest in the world. Whilst Amsterdam seemed to wallow in its past, Rotterdam, its past bombed to rubble by the *Luftwaffe*, looked only to the future.

No one would have called the vast complex of port facilities that lined the waterway to the North Sea beautiful, but it was impossible not to be impressed, even overawed, by their scale. For thirty kilometres, from Waalhaven docks to the Maasvlakte container terminal opposite the Hook of Holland, the banks of the man-made Nieuwe Waterweg were cluttered with moorings, harbours, refineries, petro-chemical plants, oil and dry bulk storage containers and hundreds of warehouses and 'distriparks' from which goods were distributed across continental Europe.

There was a vibrancy about it that Claire found stimulating. The huge supertankers discharging their crude oil; the container ships – their decks stacked high with multicoloured boxes which, from a distance, looked like Lego bricks – unloading next to ranks of towering cranes; the incessant activity day and night; the lorries moving in convoy along the perimeter roads and all of it tainted with the windblown taste of the ocean. It was a testament to what man, motivated by the desire to rebuild and reshape his environment, could achieve. And it was a testament to the greed and the ruthlessness which underpinned that desire.

The warehouses of Van Vliet Entrepôt NV were in a distripark adjacent to the Europoort. There were three of them in total, each the size of several supermarkets put together, but only one used for storing bonded goods – cigarettes and alcohol imported duty free and only removed for distribution under the supervision of Customs.

The two navy-blue BMWs drove on to the quayside beside the warehouses and parked near the entrance to the company offices. Claire, Sullivan and Enqvist climbed out of one of the vehicles. With them was Piet Hellendoorn, the anti-fraud liaison officer for the Dutch customs service. Tall and craggy, he had flowing blond hair, ice-blue eyes and – quite apposite considering the task in hand – a nicotine addiction which meant a cigarette was never very far away from his lips. Claire found him passably attractive but he smelt like a four-day-old ash tray.

They went through a pair of glass doors into the foyer and asked to see the owner. Willem Van Vliet was small and wiry with a skein of straw-coloured hair plastered across the top of his head and a blotchy, broken-veined complexion which implied he was no stranger to the bottle, a first impression which was confirmed when he invited them all up to his office and offered them coffee or a shot of *jenever* from the drinks cabinet he kept by his desk. They accepted the coffee but declined the spirit; it was too early, even for Enqvist, to be drinking gin.

The office was spacious but hardly luxurious. To reach it involved a climb up a flight of metal steps and a short walk along an open steel gantry that overlooked the cavernous interior of the bonded warehouse where cases of cigarettes and alcohol were stacked to the roof as far as the eye could see. The desk and chairs were bottom-of-the-range catalogue furniture and the flooring a thin industrial carpeting singed in places by what appeared to be cigarette burns. Van Vliet waved them to the seats and slumped down behind his desk. He was so short that only the upper part of his chest and head were visible.

'This is an unexpected pleasure,' he said in Dutch, smiling to reveal a set of yellowing teeth.

'Perhaps we could speak English,' Hellendoorn said, introducing the others. 'It would be easier for my colleagues from UCLAF.'

'UCLAF?' A flicker of his eyes betrayed Van Vliet's unease. 'So this isn't a routine visit?' he said in English.

'No, I'm afraid not. We'd like to take a look at your records.'

'Which ones?'

'All of them. Is there someone who can show my officers where they are kept, and explain your system to them?'

'Of course. Has there been some irregularity?'

'The records first, Mr Van Vliet.'

Van Vliet shrugged and pushed himself up out of his chair. If it weren't for his aging features, it would have looked as though a schoolboy had sneaked in to take charge of the office. He went through into the adjoining room and barked instructions at the middle-aged woman sitting behind a computer terminal.

'My secretary will take care of everything you need,' he said, returning to his desk.

'Thank you,' Hellendoorn said.

He dispatched his team of investigators. Enqvist went with them, leaving Sullivan and Claire in Van Vliet's office. Hellendoorn deferred to them.

'Miss Colmar and Mr Sullivan are with the Cigarette Task Group. This visit is being carried out at their instigation.'

'For what reason?' Van Vliet enquired politely.

'Are you familiar with a ship named the *Maria Vasquez*?' Sullivan said.

'Yes.'

'She was arrested off the Italian coast last week on suspicion of supplying cigarettes to smugglers. Did you know that?'

'I'd heard something,' Van Vliet replied. 'But I know nothing about any smuggling.'

'We understand the cigarettes she was carrying came from your warehouse.'

'Yes, they did. You want to see the papers?'

'Please.'

'Erik!' Van Vliet called. 'Erik! Excuse me.'

Van Vliet went back out into the adjoining office just as a shirtsleeved young man came in from the gantry outside. They exchanged a few inaudible words and the young man went to a shelf and took down a box file. Van Vliet tucked it under his arm and returned to his own office. Claire, seated at an oblique angle to the desk, had a clear view of the young man outside reaching for the telephone before Van Vliet closed the door and resumed his seat. Claire stole a furtive glance at her watch. It was 8.25 am.

Van Vliet opened the file and perused its contents.

'She was loaded on the seventh. Forty-five thousand cases. The list of brands is here if you want to see it. Every case was checked out by Customs. They always are. Not a single cigarette leaves this warehouse without customs clearance.'

'She was going to Senegal, according to documents found on board.'

'That's right. Dakar.'

Van Vliet took out a pouch of tobacco and some papers and rolled himself a cigarette, licking the gum and pinching off a few protruding strands of leaf.

'I've run this warehouse for twenty years and I have never had any problems with Customs,' he said, lighting the cigarette and puffing on it. 'What happens to the ships after they leave Rotterdam is not my business. All I do is arrange for the goods to be loaded.'

'You've done business with the *Maria Vasquez* before?' Sullivan said.

'Many times. She's a regular carrier of all sorts of goods.'

'Cigarettes?'

'Yes, but other things too.'

'Do you know who owns the ship?'

'A Liberian corporation, I believe. All Liberian-registered

ships have to be owned by a Liberian citizen or corporation. Who owns it is immaterial to me.'

'Who gave you the order for the cigarettes?'

Van Vliet consulted the file. 'A company in London. Cannadine Export Limited. The address is there, if you want it.'

'You've dealt with them in the past?'

'For about six months only. They're a relatively new customer.'

'Who did you deal with there?'

Some ash fell off the tip of Van Vliet's cigarette. He flicked it from his shirtfront with his fingers.

'No one at the company,' he explained. 'My instructions came from their agent, a Herr Walter Busch. He's a lawyer in Vaduz.'

'And payment for the cigarettes?'

'A cheque drawn on a bank in Vaduz.'

Liechtenstein again. Sullivan had never been there but he knew in his gut he wouldn't like it. There were too many lawyers.

'You know Mr Busch?' he said.

'I've never met him. I rarely meet the people I do business with. We communicate by telephone and fax. All I know about him is that he is efficient and pays his bills promptly. Those are great virtues in commerce.'

Van Vliet brushed more ash off his shirt. It was less effort than using an ash tray.

'This company, Cannadine Export Limited,' Sullivan continued. 'Did they only deal in cigarettes?'

'With me, yes.'

'How many shipments in the six months you've been associated with them?'

'Six. One a month.'

'All on the *Maria Vasquez*?'

Van Vliet nodded.

'All bound for Senegal?'

'No. The destinations have all been different. They're here in the file too.'

'Did this company ever use other ships to move cigarettes?'

'I wouldn't know. They never did with me, but there are other bonded warehouses in Rotterdam. You'd have to ask them.'

Sullivan reached out for the file. 'I can take this?'

'It's what you came for, isn't it?' Van Vliet said.

'You never had any suspicions that the *Maria Vasquez* was involved in trafficking?'

'Why would I? I don't check what happens to the cargoes I sell. My only concern is ensuring the legal formalities are observed and that my bills are paid. Believe me, you won't find a single irregularity in that file, or any of the others here. But you're welcome to try.'

They found Stig Enqvist downstairs with the other customs officers in a large, airy room which was obviously used for meetings. The long table in the centre was already covered with stacks of files and printouts which the men were sifting through with laborious thoroughness. In theory, the entire operation of the warehouses was done by computer, but in practice, for Van Vliet and every other business Sullivan had ever encountered, the paperless office was a myth. There was always paper. Piles of it. Invoices, receipts, order forms, letters, cargo manifests, customs clearances. Computers had revolutionised the working of commerce, sped up its cogs and wheels so that transactions could be completed in fractions of a second and with an accuracy previous generations could only have dreamt of. But for all their magical efficiency, the machines had been unable to overcome a basic human need to hold something tangible in the hand. People still wanted to see it written on paper

105

and for that small weakness Sullivan would be eternally grateful, because it was in those pieces of paper that a company's secrets were always hidden.

'You finished yet?' Sullivan asked facetiously.

'We were waiting for you,' Enqvist replied. 'What happened to that coffee we were promised?'

Sullivan dropped the file from Van Vliet's office on to the table and sat down.

'The company that owns the *Maria Vasquez*,' he said. 'What was its name? Buchanan Investments?'

'That's right.'

'You said they had a business address in Vaduz.'

'Yeah, a lawyer's office.'

'You remember his name?'

'Busch. Something like that.'

'Walter Busch?'

'Yeah, that's him. Why?'

Sullivan sighed and flipped open the box file. 'It's a very small world,' he said, taking out a thick wad of papers.

He glanced up. On the other side of the room Claire was deep in conversation with Hellendoorn. He caught just a few words of Dutch, picking out a couple he understood but making no sense of them. He turned his attention back to the papers and started to read.

They were there for the rest of the day, going over the company records, examining invoices, payments, every detail of Van Vliet's business. Sullivan found this aspect of his job tedious. He wasn't an accountant and, though he'd done a customs audit many times before, he was only too aware that a clever and careful operator could hide a multitude of sins in the morass of facts and figures. But one of the key guidelines for a fraud investigator was 'follow the paper trail', and this monotonous routine of checking and crosschecking was an essential, and unavoidable, part of the process.

In the middle of the afternoon he left Van Vliet's offices and went across to the nearby customs control post to use the fax machine. When he'd finished he was handed a piece of paper to take back to Hellendoorn. It was a fax that had arrived earlier, listing a series of telephone numbers and times.

'What's all this, Piet?' he asked when he returned to the bonded warehouse.

'Claire asked for it,' Hellendoorn replied, waving the paper in her direction.

Claire got up from the table and came over. She scanned the list of numbers.

'That one,' she said, underlining it with her pen. 'The Amsterdam number. Can you do the same thing for me again? Get a printout of the calls made from there today?'

Hellendoorn looked at his watch. 'You probably won't get the answer until tomorrow.'

'That's okay.'

'What's going on?' Sullivan asked.

'I'm not sure,' Claire replied. 'But I think it's worth checking.'

By six o'clock Sullivan had had enough. His eyes and neck and shoulders ached and his concentration was so diminished he knew it was silly to continue. It was when you were tired that you made mistakes, started to overlook even the obvious. He approached Claire and perched himself on the edge of the table next to her.

'Are you up to a short trip?' he said.

She pushed back her chair and rubbed her eyes.

'A trip where?'

'Gouda.'

'You want to buy some cheese?'

'To talk to someone. I may need an interpreter.'

'Why not?' she said with a shrug. 'I've had more than I can take of this.'

Enqvist sniffed and made a pretence at appearing wounded when they told him they were going.

'And leaving me here with all this shit?' he said, gesturing at the mounds of files.

Sullivan patted him on the shoulder. 'It's where you're most at home,' he said.

One of Hellendoorn's officers gave them a lift back to their hotel where they picked up their own car and drove the twenty-five kilometres north-east to the small town of Gouda. It was Sullivan's first time there but he knew it was famous for its cheese and its handmade candles, an appropriate combination considering that, in his opinion, they both tasted of wax.

The address he was looking for, lifted from the CPS file he'd studied in Hull, was near the centre of the town, a first-floor apartment accessed through a door next to a shop whose window was jammed with blue Delft pottery. Claire pressed the bell and had a short exchange in Dutch with a woman on the entryphone. The lock clicked open and they went through and up a steep flight of stairs. A plump woman with a soft face and a cast-iron perm was waiting for them on the landing at the top.

Claire showed her ID card. 'Mrs Maartens?'

'My name is Faassen. Gerda Faassen.'

The woman said something else in Dutch and Claire turned to Sullivan.

'She's Maartens' sister, not his wife. He wasn't married.'

'May we come in?' Claire said.

Mrs Faassen looked puzzled rather than hostile. 'What are you, police?'

'Something like that,' Claire said, which wasn't strictly true. UCLAF had no police powers, but it was sometimes helpful if people believed they did.

108

Mrs Faassen showed them through into her sitting room. It was small and dim and so crammed with furniture you had to pick your way through an obstacle course to reach a seat. There were ornaments and vases and all manner of bric-a-brac on every surface. A glass-fronted cabinet contained shelves of polished silver and glassware and on the mantelpiece and hanging from brackets on the walls were dozens of china plates, many of them very old. It was like living in an antiques shop where nothing was ever sold.

Claire explained why they were there and – having ascertained that Mrs Faassen spoke little English – translated the conversation for Sullivan's benefit.

Mrs Faassen was quite happy to talk. She'd lived with her brother in the apartment for the previous ten years.

'Since my husband left me,' she explained. 'That's when Frans moved in. To help pay the rent, keep me company. Not that he was here very often. It worked quite well as an arrangement. This place is too small for two people but Frans only came back for a few days every month.'

'How long had he been master of the *Maria Vasquez*?' Claire asked.

'About two years. It wasn't a very good post, he was worthy of better but . . . well, you take what you can when jobs are scarce. He had a bit of trouble with the police – all nonsense of course – but it puts people off.'

That would have been the attempted blackmail charge, Sullivan reflected as Claire told him what Mrs Faassen had said.

'He loved the sea. We grew up in Rotterdam and as a boy he'd always be down in the harbour watching the ships. He couldn't do anything else. The *Maria Vasquez* was a bit of a comedown for him – he worked on tankers in the Eighties. The pay was dreadful, the hours terrible.'

Mrs Faassen glanced apologetically at Sullivan. 'No offence, but the English work their crews like slaves.'

Sullivan frowned as Claire translated the remark.

'It's a Liberian ship,' he said.

Mrs Faassen waved away the objection. 'Yes, yes, but no one really believes that. It was Liberian-registered but owned and run by the English.'

'Are you sure?' Claire said.

'Oh yes. Frans mentioned his boss a few times in passing. He only met him once, I think, but he said he was a typical arrogant Englishman.'

'Did he mention a name?'

'Not that I can remember. To tell you the truth, I wasn't very interested.' She paused. 'Frans and I weren't close. He was my brother but he was always away. He had been since he was eighteen.'

'His death must have shocked you,' Sullivan said.

'Yes, it did.' For a moment she looked away, her expression hidden in shadow. 'Why would anyone do that? I don't understand it.'

'He was involved in smuggling drugs. That's a murky, violent world.'

'Drugs!' Mrs Faassen exclaimed bitterly. 'It was only a bit of marijuana. The English are so ridiculous about these things. It's much less harmful than cigarettes or alcohol.'

'Did your brother ever talk about the cargoes the *Maria Vasquez* carried, where she went?' Sullivan asked casually.

'No. He went all over. The travelling bored him – it does if you're a sailor, doesn't it? He sent me regular postcards but he never said much in them.'

'From where?'

'Oh.' She stopped to think. 'West Africa, Egypt, Istanbul. I've quite a collection. He'd been almost everywhere over the years. I liked getting his cards. It brought a bit of glamour into the house. I'll miss them.'

She tried a smile which didn't really come off. 'They won't even let me have his body back for burial,' she continued sadly. 'Not until they've finished their investigations.'

She looked at them both, her eyes watering a little. 'Why are you interested in Frans?'

Claire translated the question. 'You want to answer that?' she said in English.

'Ask her if she knows the former first officer, Joop Broekhuizen?'

Claire put the question. Mrs Faassen nodded.

'Joop? Yes, he came here a few times with Frans. A nice enough young man, but a bit wild,' she added unenthusiastically. 'Drank a little too much for my liking. I was very sad to hear about him.'

'Hear what about him?'

'His death. Didn't you know he'd died?'

Claire translated again and Sullivan started with surprise.

'He's dead? When? How?'

Claire conversed with Mrs Faassen for a while. Then she said in English: 'Two weeks ago. He was killed in a hit-and-run accident in northern Holland.'

SEVEN

It was dark outside, but Sullivan was still aware of the monotonous flatness of the terrain as they drove north through Holland. From Gouda to Utrecht and on across the rural plains of Overijssel and Drenthe, the uniform nature of the countryside broken up only by gleaming canals and dykes and isolated patches of forest. This was as far off the beaten track as it was possible to go in Holland, a land of fields and scattered settlements that the urban Dutch, never mind the foreign tourist, rarely had much cause to visit.

Approaching nine o'clock, they stopped at a service station on the A28 and had hamburgers and *vlaamse*, Flemish chips with mayonnaise, for dinner. Rotterdam was a hundred and twenty kilometres behind them, Groningen, their ultimate destination, a further eighty kilometres to the north. They chatted idly for a time, Sullivan telling Claire about his trip to Hull.

'Do you ever talk about anything other than work?' Claire said eventually.

'Sure.' He gave her a clear-eyed look, a smile grazing the corners of his mouth. 'You have a subject in mind?'

'Not particularly. I'm just tired of all this. It's been a long day.'

'You want to go on tonight, or find somewhere to stay?'

'Let's get there.'

Sullivan dipped a chip into a puddle of creamy mayonnaise. 'I'll drive the next bit. Let you enjoy the view.'

Claire smiled. 'That should keep me awake for all of five minutes.'

'You know this area?'

'Not well.'

'Where's your home?'

'Noord-Holland. The province, that is, not the region. Friesland and Groningen are both further north.'

'Colmar, that's not a very Dutch-sounding name.'

'My father was French.'

'Was?'

'He died a few years ago. And your home?'

'Yorkshire originally. Colchester now. It's a bit like this round there. Flat, agricultural, dull.'

'Do you get home to your wife very often?' Claire said, steering the conversation into an area of greater interest to her.

'How did you know I was married?' Sullivan said.

Men were so naive, or pretended to be. Claire could never be sure which. Did he not realise that the first thing the women in the office did when a new man arrived was ascertain his marital status? Not because they were after husbands, but because it was sensible to know what complications might arise. Nothing made a man hornier than living away from home on a tax-free salary.

'I can tell,' she said.

'I'm not sure that's a compliment. What are the signs?'

She shook her head, not wanting to get too specific. He was warming up. For the first time there was a hint of flirtation in their exchanges. He was looking at her differently too: more like the single guys in the unit.

'What do you do in Brussels when you're not working?' she asked.

'More work. Watch TV. Sometimes I go out with Stig.'

'That must be exhausting.'

'What do you mean?'

'He's hard to keep pace with, isn't he? He's quite a drinker. And a talker.'

'You noticed? I've told him he should form a support group for compulsive talkers. He could call it On and On Anon.'

Claire laughed and he was struck by how easy it was to talk to her. Her understanding of English, even silly jokes, was so effortless that he had to remind himself she was Dutch.

'How about you?' he said. 'Are you attached?'

'Not at the moment.'

'Never married?'

'Once. A long time ago.'

'It didn't work out?'

'Something like that,' Claire said.

She didn't want to tell him too much. In business, knowledge was power. In romance, it was boredom. She was attracted to him. He had a wife but she was used to that. When a woman reached her age all the decent men were married. She'd had affairs with several married men. Too many times. She wondered if that was a coincidence. The relationships were always fundamentally unsatisfactory even though their casual nature appealed to her. There was too much deception involved, too much waiting, having to fit in with his domestic arrangements, and Claire didn't like to wait.

Single men were even worse. She didn't want to get married again, not after her experiences with Wim, and sooner or later a single man's demands always became too much for her. They wanted more of her time, more of her, than she was willing to give and she found herself, sometimes deliberately, sometimes only half consciously, destroying the foundations of the relationship so it couldn't last. She liked

115

the sex, the companionship, when it suited her, but she also liked the freedom to be alone. She'd never subscribed to the extremist view that marriage was a form of legalised prostitution, but it was certainly legalised drudgery. She had no intention of ever cooking another meal or washing another pair of sweaty socks for a man again.

Sullivan was watching her, sipping his cup of coffee slowly. She knew he was curious but he didn't press her. She liked that in a man; the ability to leave things unspoken, undiscovered. She'd dumped her last guy because he dug under her skin too much. That was three months ago. Since then there'd been only a one-night stand with a pilot for Sabena she'd met at a party, and that had been a disaster. She knew the English joked about the initials of the Belgian national airline standing for Such A Bad Experience Never Again. The same could be said of the pilot's performance in bed.

'Shall we go?' Claire said.

They went back out to the car. The wind was blowing from the west, across the reclaimed land on the shores of the Ijsselmeer. With no hills, not even a slight undulation in the ground to block its progress, the gusting air swept over the fields like the backdraft from a jet engine, buffeting the body so it was hard to stay upright. They shut it out with the car doors, listening for a moment to the mournful threnody as the currents wailed and whistled around the contours of the vehicle. Then they started up and continued their journey across the empty darkness of the plain.

Enqvist stayed on late at the warehouse, then left with Hellendoorn and the rest of his team, the files they'd been examining safely locked away under the watchful eyes of a security guard from the customs post in the Europoort. Van Vliet and his staff had made every effort to be as helpful as possible, but no one was going to take the chance that they might stay on into the night with a shredder to hand.

Back at the hotel, Enqvist took a call from Sullivan saying that he and Claire were going north and wouldn't return to Rotterdam until the following day. Enqvist was annoyed. If they'd told him earlier, he could have seen what Hellendoorn was doing for the evening and tagged along. Now he was stuck on his own and he hated that.

He took a shower and changed, then went up to the hotel restaurant and ate dinner alone, looking around for any other single diners – male or female – he could strike up a conversation with. Eating by himself in a strange hotel, surrounded by couples and groups of businessmen, was one of the most depressing activities Stig could think of. He didn't enjoy his own company and was constantly aware of the voices and laughter around him that seemed to increase his feeling of isolation. He ate quickly and left the restaurant as soon as he could.

On the way out he glanced into the bar, but it was deserted except for the barman and a middle-aged couple silently nursing a pair of cocktails at one of the tables. They didn't look much fun and, besides, Enqvist disliked hotel bars. They had no character, no atmosphere. He picked up his coat from his room and got a taxi to the Oudehaven, the old harbour area of the city which had been redeveloped and turned into a lively enclave of restaurants and clubs.

He wandered along the quays for a time then selected what seemed to be the busiest bar and went inside, forcing his way through the crowds of young people and perching himself on a high stool by the counter. He ordered a shot of *jenever* and peered around in the dim lighting, enjoying the sounds of voices and the underlying throb of the taped music. This was the kind of bar he liked. Where you could forget your own loneliness by sharing vicariously in the friendly conviviality of the groups around you, and where you could get slowly, and anonymously, drunk.

At the other end of the bar, hidden in the shadows and shielded from view by the ranks of boisterous drinkers, a pinch-faced young man was watching Enqvist. He'd spoken to him several times during the day, but he had no interest in socialising with him outside the office. Erik Wissing wasn't there for pleasure, nor was he there by chance. He'd followed Enqvist from his hotel and would stay close to him, unnoticed, until he returned. This was business. Wissing was acting under instructions but he didn't resent the loss of his evening. There were worse ways of earning a bit of overtime.

It was eleven o'clock by the time Sullivan and Claire found a hotel in Groningen and checked in. They went up to their rooms and said good night, two colleagues being polite, friendly, but nothing more. Sullivan washed and cleaned his teeth and was getting undressed when the phone on the bedside table rang. He picked it up.

'Why don't you come next door for a drink?' Claire said.

'I'm not sure that's such a good idea.'

'Come on. I've opened a bottle of wine from the mini-bar. The door's unlocked.'

The line went dead. Sullivan didn't move. He could have rung back and declined, but he didn't. He thought for a time, then put his shoes and shirt back on and went out. He was a grown man, alert and stone-cold sober. He knew exactly what he was doing.

Claire was leaning back on the headboard of the double bed, her legs stretched out on the covers. She still had on her make-up but she'd removed her tights and the jacket of her suit. Sullivan noticed that her toenails were painted with pearl varnish. She was poised, confident and very beautiful.

There were two glasses of wine on the table next to the bed. She handed one to him then took a drag on the cigarette she was holding between her fingers. For the first time, Sullivan noticed the smell in the room: the sweet, distinctive odour of marijuana. She passed him the joint and he sucked in the smoke.

'Have you smoked pot before?' she said.

'Of course.'

'I thought it was illegal in Britain.'

'It is.'

Claire looked at him, this straight Englishman in his button-down shirt and suit trousers.

'Where do you get hold of it?'

'I'm a customs officer,' Sullivan said. 'I confiscate it.'

Claire's eyes widened. 'And use it yourself?'

'You should come to a customs party. The booze, the cigarettes, you think we buy any of it?'

Claire leaned forward and took back the joint.

'I thought you were supposed to burn contraband marijuana?'

'Oh, we do,' Sullivan said. 'We just inhale at the same time.'

He drank some of his wine, wondering if he should leave now. But he'd already made the decision. Claire gave him the joint again. He felt the drug relaxing him as he drew it into his lungs. He closed his eyes.

'Good?' Claire said.

'It makes me want to go to sleep.'

'I'm sure we can think of something to keep you awake,' she said, reaching for him.

Afterwards, lying back on the pillows, naked, smiling at him, Claire said: 'Well, one thing's for sure. You'll never make it as a pilot for Sabena.'

Sullivan said: '*What?*'

*   *   *

119

There were two empty bottles of vodka on the table and Yevgeny Drozhkin was opening a third and refilling the glasses. Montague didn't touch his, he'd had enough already. He wondered why the Russians seemed able to do business only in a state of semi-intoxication. Actually, Drozhkin was Ukrainian and would have been offended to be mistaken for one of his northern neighbours, but the difference was immaterial to Montague. He thought of all the former Soviets as essentially the same. They were all unpredictable, all coarse and greedy and all endowed with a tolerance to alcohol that was truly terrifying.

Drozhkin was more sophisticated than most. He'd lived in the West and had acquired a patina of cosmopolitan culture to go with his expensive Italian suits, but there was still something of the peasant in his heavy features and pudgy hands. And in his fondness for thirty-per-cent-proof vodka that quite literally took the surface off your throat as you swallowed it.

'Chin-chin,' Drozhkin said in his thick-accented English and raised his glass, draining it in one swift movement.

'You've made the payment?' Montague asked.

'Half has already been transferred to your account in Zürich. The remainder will be paid, as usual, when I've checked the consignment is complete.'

'It's all there,' Montague said. 'You can be sure of that.'

'I'll need more next month.'

'How much?'

'Thirty thousand cases.'

'Business must be booming.'

Drozhkin shrugged non-committally. 'Can you deliver?'

'Oh yes.' Montague paused. 'And the other matters? In Holland?'

'One has been dealt with,' Drozhkin replied.

'And the second?'

'My son is taking care of it.'

Drozhkin nodded at the young man sitting beside him. Mikhail Drozhkin had none of his father's educated veneer. Surly, unshaven, his hair cropped so short you could see every contour of his skull, he looked like a hardened thug or a career soldier, which in the Ukraine were virtually the same thing.

'I want it finished quickly,' Montague said. 'If there's one thing I hate it's blackmailers.'

'We know what we're doing,' Mikhail Drozhkin replied with a dismissive sneer.

'I hope so.'

Yevgeny Drozhkin smiled. It was his teeth that betrayed his nationality. He could buy Western clothes and cars, Rolex watches and French perfumes, but his teeth would always bear the unmistakable stamp of Soviet dentistry.

'Mikhail and his colleagues are good,' he said reassuringly. 'You have nothing to worry about.'

Doyle stood up. 'I'm going to check the containers.'

He went outside on to the quayside. Mikhail Drozhkin came out after him and together they walked across the broad expanse of floodlit concrete towards a shabby freighter that was tied up to the dock. A crane was unloading cardboard boxes, lowering them to the quay where they were transferred by forklift trucks to containers mounted on the backs of articulated lorries.

Doyle pulled up the collar of his coat, hunching his shoulders against the breeze gusting in from the Black Sea. This was his sixth or seventh visit to Odessa, but it didn't get any more attractive. The docks were an ugly sprawl of concrete jetties and decrepit warehouses infested with rats the size of small cats. In winter it was bitingly cold, raked by winds that seemed to come all the way from Central Asia. In summer it stank of fetid water and rotten fish. It amazed him that this was one of the

Ukraine's premier holiday resorts. During July and August the beaches outside the city were crammed with fat sweaty tourists, lined up in rows along the sand like sausages on a barbecue. Drozhkin had taken him there one afternoon, but the sight had turned his stomach. Doyle preferred the Ukrainians, even the women – particularly the women – fully clothed.

They watched the ship being unloaded for a time in silence. Then Doyle said: 'Is everything arranged?'

Mikhail Drozhkin nodded. 'They'll be on their way before midnight.'

'And the frontiers?'

'All taken care of.'

Doyle took a wad of dollar bills from his jacket and passed them across to Drozhkin, who counted them carefully.

'It's all there,' Doyle said.

'I like to be sure.'

'Who else knows?'

'Just you, me and my father.'

'Let's keep it that way,' Doyle said.

EIGHT

Sullivan was very quiet at breakfast, but maybe that was the way he always was. The hotel had laid on a full Dutch *ontbijt*: cheese, ham, hard-boiled eggs. Sullivan only had a cup of coffee and a roll. Claire wondered if he was feeling guilty.

In the car later, driving out of the city, he was still subdued, wrapped up in himself. Claire left him alone. They both needed time to reflect on what had happened. The sun was low in the sky. The pale rays glistened on the fields which were dusted with a coating of frost like icing sugar. It was very still. The reeds in the marshes, frozen and brittle, barely moved, and in the distance, by one of the canals, stood a tall windmill, its sails motionless against the blue-grey backdrop of the horizon.

This was how Sullivan had pictured rural Holland. How he'd imagined it from illustrations in children's books, from paintings of ice-skaters and dykes and plump, rosy-cheeked infants wrapped up against the cold. He'd thought they were glamorised, chocolate-box images of the countryside and was captivated to find that they really existed.

A few kilometres south of Groningen, they turned off into a small hamlet and found the address Frans Maartens' sister had given them. It was on the edge of the village, a tiny cottage with two bedroom windows peeping out from the slope of the thatched roof. Behind it, across an expanse of meadowland, was a lake, its surface a mottled sheet of ice.

Sullivan and Claire walked through the garden to the front door, the grass cracking like porcelain beneath their feet. Their breath steamed in billowing clouds that rose and melted away into the thin air.

Joop Broekhuizen's widow was in her early thirties, her face pale and hollow-eyed. Claire explained why they'd come and the woman just turned on her heel and walked back into the house leaving the door open. Two blonde little girls, not yet at school, peeked out curiously from the kitchen and were hastily pulled back as an older woman, presumably Broekhuizen's mother-in-law, came to the front of the house to speak to Claire.

'She doesn't want to talk about it,' the older woman said brusquely. 'It's too upsetting. You can get all the information you need from the police.'

'In Groningen?'

'Across the way.' She gestured with a hand. 'There's a substation in the village. Ask them.'

She retreated into the house and closed the door behind her.

The police station wasn't difficult to find. In the centre of the village, next to a bakery from which the aroma of fresh bread wafted on the breeze, it had a patrol car parked outside and a uniformed constable sitting at a desk just inside the door. Save for his presence and the trappings of a law and order establishment – the sign above the entrance, the official posters on the walls – it could have been any kind of small-town office.

The constable himself was in his forties, a solid but unambitious officer who would no doubt remain at the same lowly rank until he retired and be content with it. He had fat red cheeks, a bushy blond moustache and a beer gut so pronounced he probably had to take his annual fitness test in his patrol car.

'You're investigating Broekhuizen?' he said. 'Well, it's not the first time he's been in trouble.'

'He had a criminal record?' Claire said.

'Nothing serious. Stupid kid's things. He was quite a tearaway when he was a teenager. Going to sea sorted him out, gave him some discipline.'

'You knew him well?'

'Everyone knew Joop round here. He was a bit of a lad, you know. Came home on leave and drank too much, got in a few fights. But he wasn't a bad sort really. He wasn't malicious like some of the kids. Getting married calmed him down a bit. Women do that, don't they?'

The constable guffawed and swivelled round in his chair to open a filing cabinet behind him. He seemed to have organised his office so that once he was settled in his chair he never had to get up for anything. He pulled out a file and swung back to open it on his desk.

'You'll want the details of how he was killed, I suppose.'

Claire nodded. 'We understand it was a hit-and-run.'

'That's right. One of those senseless accidents. I've seen a few in my time. All stupid, all avoidable. Driver was probably drunk. Here we are. It was the third of this month. Joop was walking home along the road down by the lake. He'd been to a bar with a friend. It was dark, the road was icy. The road's quite narrow there, a ditch on either side, so you have to walk along the carriageway. The car hit him from behind on a bend, killed him outright.'

'Was the friend with him?'

The constable nodded. 'That's how we know what happened. He was lucky. He turned and saw the car coming. Threw himself into the ditch just in time.'

'Do you have his name?'

'Kuypers. Jan Kuypers. His address is there if you want it.'

'What about the driver?' Claire asked.

'Never traced. Kuypers gave us a description of the car but no licence plates.'

'You're still looking for him?'

'Groningen took over the case, but they haven't made any progress. Won't either now. Cases like that, the more time goes by the harder it is to solve them.' The constable shook his head. 'It's a sad business. He had two little daughters, lovely girls. His wife's all torn up about it. You're not going to bother her with this, are you?'

Claire glanced at Sullivan and translated what the constable had said. Sullivan shook his head.

'That won't be necessary,' Claire said. 'We don't know for certain he was involved in anything. Can I take his friend's address?'

The constable turned the file round so she could write down the details.

Then she said: 'He was replaced as first officer on his ship a few weeks ago. You wouldn't have any idea why, would you?'

'Sorry,' the constable said. 'It's not the kind of thing I'd know. But he chopped and changed quite a bit. He wasn't the type to hold down a job for too long.'

'First officer is a responsible post.'

'It was only some cheap freighter, wasn't it? I don't know who gave him the job, but I can't see any reputable shipping line making Joop Broekhuizen a first officer. I wouldn't have put him in charge of a rowing boat.'

'The *Maria Vasquez* sounds a fun ship to have been on,' Sullivan said as they drove away from the police station. 'A drug-smuggling master with a handling and extortion record. A first officer with a drink problem.'

'And both of them dead now,' Claire said.

They headed back north, crossing over the motorway

and taking a country road which ran along the edge of Groningen airport.

'Do you believe the hit-and-run was an accident?' Claire asked.

'Let's see what Kuypers says.'

The house was almost within spitting distance of the airport, a dilapidated wooden bungalow with flaking white paint on the exterior walls and rusty metal window frames; a prefabricated building which looked as if it had been erected after the war as a temporary home and been kept habitable – although only just – ever since. It was in a row of similar houses in varying states of repair, an isolated little estate with fields at the back and the perimeter fence and runway of the airport across the road at the front. In the distance could be seen a couple of hangars, the small terminal building and an assortment of aeroplanes, mostly weekend fliers, but also a large commercial cargo plane.

There was no answer when they rang the bell at the front. Sullivan went round to the back and peered in through the windows. The curtains were open but there was no sign of anyone. The house had a closed-up look to it, like a rented holiday cottage out of season.

He returned to the front and saw Claire talking to an old woman on the step of the house next door. They disappeared inside and Claire emerged a few moments later, the old lady right behind her. Sullivan walked across in time to catch Claire handing one of her business cards to the old lady and saying: 'When he comes back, could you ask him to call me on this number?'

'He's a pilot,' Claire explained to Sullivan, walking back to the car. 'Goes away a lot.'

'Pilot for whom?'

'Some freight company. Flies from the airport. Mostly internal stuff.'

'You get a name?'

Claire held up a scrap of paper. 'And the number. From her phone directory. Paterswolde Air Transport.'

They sat in the car, Sullivan watching a small single-engined aircraft take off while Claire phoned the freight company on his mobile. He was only half listening, and the Dutch was too fast and fluent for him to follow, but he heard in her voice that something was wrong. He turned to look at her, trying to guess what she was saying from her intonation.

She ended the call and handed him back his telephone.

'Kuypers has gone missing,' she said. 'He hasn't shown up for work for two weeks. No one has any idea where he is.'

The cafe was in the centre of Bayonne, in one of the narrow crowded shopping streets near the cathedral. Bignon went in and sat down at a table towards the back from where he had a clear view of the door. It was raining outside. Through the window he could see the pavements wet and glistening like a fishmonger's slab.

Pigout strolled in a few minutes later and found a table up against the side wall. He ordered a coffee and a *pain au chocolat* and began reading a copy of *L'Équipe* he'd picked up at the newsagent's across the street. Five minutes or more had elapsed when a hefty, unshaven man in a black leather jacket came in and walked across to Bignon's table. The two men nodded at each other. Leather Jacket sat down opposite Bignon and lit up a cigarette, his eyes wandering casually around the interior of the cafe. Pigout took a bite of his *pain au chocolat* and concentrated on his newspaper. He'd done this so many times before that it was almost second nature to him: watching out of the corner of his eye, then sensing instinctively the exact moment to glance across without being observed.

Leather Jacket was an amateur, Pigout could tell immediately. His caution was tainted with complacency and, though his movements were slick enough, they weren't sufficiently discreet to prevent Pigout seeing the thick brown envelope that he passed under the table to Bignon.

Almost immediately, Leather Jacket stood up and left the cafe. Pigout stayed where he was and gave a slight nod through the window. On the other side of the street, browsing through a rack of magazines, Queyras acknowledged the signal with a subtle inclination of his head, then set off in pursuit.

Pigout finished his coffee and remained in his seat reading the paper even when Bignon got up and left. The Hendaye customs officer was a secondary concern now. It was Leather Jacket who mattered.

Paying for his drink and buying another *pain au chocolat* to take out, Pigout drifted back through the streets to their car. He'd eaten the pastry and was listening to the cassette player, his lap sprinkled with greasy crumbs, when his partner climbed in next to him.

'He had a car. Var licence plates,' Queyras said.

'He's a long way from home.'

'How much d'you want to bet he's got a record?' Queyras said, leaning forward to pick up the radio handset.

'I hope you enjoyed yourselves,' Stig Enqvist said sourly as Claire and Sullivan walked into the conference room at Van Vliet's bonded warehouse.

'Very much,' Claire said, smiling enigmatically.

'And you?' Sullivan said.

'Me?' Enqvist waved a hand around the table. 'I've been wading through this crap all day.'

'You find anything of interest?'

Enqvist picked up a thin sheaf of papers. 'Those faxes you sent yesterday. We've had the replies.' He thumbed out the sheets one at a time. 'Dakar, Freetown, Abidjan, Accra, Lagos. All saying the same thing.' He paused for effect.

'You know, Stig,' Sullivan said. 'When you joined the *Tullverk*, the Swedish theatre lost a great ham. What do they say?'

'Guess.'

Sullivan picked up the faxes and skimmed through their contents. When he looked up, Enqvist was smirking at him.

'Better than sex, isn't it, this job?'

'What are you talking about?' Claire said.

'The *Maria Vasquez*,' Sullivan replied. 'She carried five cargoes of cigarettes from here before the last one we intercepted. All for this British company, Cannadine Export Limited. They were all declared as going to five different West African countries, yet according to Customs in those countries, she never went to any of them.'

'A hundred and fifty thousand master cases,' Enqvist said. 'That's one and a half billion cigarettes. All smuggled back into the EU. Duty evaded?' He glanced at Sullivan.

'Depends on which country they ended up in,' Sullivan said. 'But a conservative estimate, about a hundred and thirty million Euros.'

'Jesus!' Claire breathed.

'And that's just one ship, just five cargoes. You see the scale of the problem,' Enqvist said.

'You're checking other vessels?' Sullivan asked.

Enqvist gestured unenthusiastically at the files. 'Going through every export Van Vliet has made for the last two years. You know how many records that entails? I'll be here for fucking days.'

Piet Hellendoorn came into the room, bringing with him the smell of the Dunhills he'd gone outside to smoke. He gave Claire a phone company printout.

'Is that what you wanted?'

'Thanks, Piet.'

'I made a few enquiries for you. The Amsterdam number is a brothel on the Singel Canal.'

'A brothel?'

'It calls itself a hotel – the Golden Valley Inn. Very exclusive, very expensive. You can't just walk in off the street and ask for a room. It's very selective about its clients, caters for wealthy businessmen and celebrities.'

'People with things to hide.'

'Exactly.'

Sullivan looked over Claire's shoulder as she examined the printout.

'Why are you so interested in an Amsterdam brothel?'

'Yeah,' Enqvist said. 'And can we have the number too?'

'Just before we interviewed Van Vliet,' Claire said, 'he said something to his assistant. What's his name?'

'Erik Wissing,' Hellendoorn said.

'I saw Wissing pick up the outer office phone as Van Vliet shut his door. He phoned this brothel, hotel, whatever you want to call it. That was at twenty-five past eight. Immediately after that three consecutive calls were made from the brothel; at eight thirty, eight thirty-four and eight thirty-seven. All international calls. You recognise the codes?'

She held out the paper. 'The first one is a French prefix. Paris. The second?'

'London,' Hellendoorn said.

'And the third. Three nine zero. That's Italy. I don't know the other numbers. Eighty-one. What city is that?'

'It's the code for Naples,' Sullivan said.

Willem Van Vliet rocked back and forth in his high office chair, his mouth puckered into a pout as he looked pensively across the desk at his assistant.

'You think he's vulnerable?'

Wissing nodded. 'I watched him carefully. He's the right type. Away from home, lonely, drinks too much. You know the symptoms.'

'He didn't see you?'

'It was very crowded. He never even glanced my way.'

'What kind of bar was it? Gay?'

'No, he's straight. He tried to chat up a couple of women but they weren't interested.'

Van Vliet let his chair spring upright, then rested his forearms on the top of the desk.

'Thank you, Erik. That was a job well done.'

'You have something in mind for him?'

'Oh yes,' Van Vliet replied. 'I have something in mind for him.'

NINE

'We've been ordered to release the *Maria Vasquez*,' Casagrande said.

The telephone line was clear enough but, nevertheless, Sullivan thought he must have misheard.

'Did you say release?' he asked incredulously.

'The court hearing was yesterday,' Casagrande continued. 'I tried to reach you in the evening but you weren't there.'

'I was in Rotterdam. I got back very late.'

'The *Tribunale* magistrate ruled the seizure was unlawful.'

'What the hell is he talking about? Unlawful?'

'No direct link between the ship and the traffickers.'

Sullivan swore out loud. 'No direct link? Where else did the fucking cigarettes come from?'

'It's politics, Rob,' Casagrande said in a tone of weary resignation. 'In Italy, everything is politics.'

'Are you saying the judge was nobbled by Rome?'

'Nobbled?' Casagrande said, puzzled.

'Influenced.'

'Who knows? The Liberian government has been making a big noise ever since we arrested her. For all I know the magistrate is in the pocket of the Camorra. He wouldn't be the first Neapolitan judge.'

'You're appealing, I hope?'

'You bet we are. The hearing's next week.'

'The *Maria Vasquez* stays impounded until then?'

'Yes. But if we lose the appeal we'll have to release her immediately.'

'Shit! They don't have a case, do they?'

'They have five very good, very well-connected lawyers acting for them. There were twenty ships out in the Tyrrhenian Sea that night. They're saying the cigarettes could have been offloaded from any one of them.'

'And how do they explain what the *Maria Vasquez* was doing off Italy when she was supposedly going to Senegal?'

'She diverted to pick up an additional cargo from Naples. They have all the paperwork. Forged, of course, but we'll have a hard time proving it. These people are good, Rob. We had no aerial surveillance, no photographs or eye-witness evidence to show the cigarettes being offloaded on to the cabin cruisers. The appeal could go either way without something stronger to link the *Maria Vasquez* with trafficking.'

'How about a pattern of fraudulent shipments? Five cargoes that disappeared en route to West Africa.'

'You have proof?' Casagrande said, his voice rising a couple of tones.

'The paperwork's in Rotterdam. Stig's still up there. I'll get him to send you everything he has.'

'That would be a big help.'

'And can you do something for me, Antonio?'

'Name it.'

'Check a phone number in Naples.'

'Easy.'

Sullivan gave him the number, then hung up and called Enqvist, who had remained behind to complete the inspection of Van Vliet's records.

'No problem,' Stig said. 'I'll fax him this morning. You looked into Cannadine Export yet?'

'Just about to,' Sullivan replied.

He replaced the receiver and called a contact in the Metropolitan Police Fraud Squad. He gave him the address of Cannadine Export Limited in Streatham and asked if he could have someone check it out. Finally, he rang the London number Piet Hellendoorn had given Claire, rehearsing in his head the lines he was going to deliver. He needed some information but he didn't want to arouse their suspicions.

'Corvex Limited,' a woman's voice said.

'I'm sorry, what did you say?' Sullivan asked.

'Corvex Limited,' the woman repeated.

'I think I've got the wrong number. Are you a car spares company?'

'We're shipping agents.'

'I have got the wrong number. I'm sorry to have troubled you.'

He hung up and pulled out the keyboard of his computer. He typed in some commands and waited as the computer accessed the Companies House Direct database which listed records of every company registered in the United Kingdom. He tapped in the name Corvex Limited and the company information appeared on his screen: the names and addresses of its directors and secretary, a list of documents filed, the dates of accounts and annual returns made, and details of disqualified directors. The company secretary was named as Michael Bruton and only one director was listed, a Simon Doyle. Sullivan came out of the database and punched into UCLAF's own records. He ran the names of both men through the system but there was no mention of either. He went back into Companies House Direct and searched under the men's names, looking for any other appointments they had. Bruton was secretary and director of two more companies, Doyle of four more. Sullivan called up each of these additional six companies in turn and made a note of all their directors. In total, excluding Bruton and Doyle, there were twenty-six names. Sullivan checked each one through the UCLAF database.

It was a time-consuming, laborious task but he knew it was essential. Organised criminals were adept at covering their tracks through numerous bogus companies and false names, but most of them, at some point, needed a legal front to assist their activities, if only to launder the proceeds of their fraudulent operations. Finding that one legitimate company, that one director who turned out to be genuine, not some man of straw, was often the key that could unlock the doors leading to the real brains behind a fraud.

All twenty-six names were clean. Sullivan went back to Companies House Direct and searched for any other directorships the men had. He came up with the names of another thirty-two British companies. 'Shit,' he breathed. This was going to take him hours.

He ran all thirty-two names through the UCLAF database. Thirty-one of them turned out to be negative, but one came up positive, a company called Horningtoft Limited with a registered address of Horningtoft Priory, Norfolk. There was no UCLAF file on the company itself but it was listed in a cross-reference to a TF7 report on fraud in the European wheat industry. Sullivan made a note of the serial number of the file and logged off. TF7 was the UCLAF department covering the agricultural sector of the European Union – Claire Colmar's old department. Sullivan got up from his desk. It was about time he saw her again.

Claire's phone rang as she was refilling her coffee cup from the filter machine on the windowsill of her office. It was Philippe Allard.

'I was just about to call you,' she said in French, sitting down behind her desk and crossing her legs.

'That sounds ominous,' Allard replied with a dry chuckle.

'Write this down.'

She read out the Paris number which had been called from the brothel in Amsterdam and asked Allard if he could get her the name and address of the subscriber.

'I'll put someone on to it,' he said. 'Is it urgent?'

'Any time in the next ten minutes will be fine,' Claire said. 'Now what can I do for you?'

'Christophe Bignon. You guessed right. Every time a Garcia Saez lorry came over through Hendaye, Bignon was in charge of the customs shift. He's living well beyond his official income. Expensive lifestyle, a gambling problem.'

'Did you check his bank account?'

'Nothing suspicious about it. No unexplained or regular deposits apart from his salary. We kept an eye on him and got lucky yesterday. Watched him meet a go-between who slipped him an envelope almost certainly full of cash.'

'Go-between for whom?' Claire asked.

'We can't be certain, but the go-between was an old lag named Thierry Lannay. Done time for assault and theft. Lannay is an associate of a businessman called Gilles Lafon who operates a haulage business out of Paris and Toulon. A big operation, several hundred trucks.'

'You think Lafon is the paymaster?'

'That would be my guess. He's a rich man, but not what you'd call respectable. No convictions but a lot of underworld connections, particularly in Marseille.'

'Is he linked to Fonteneau et Delahaye or Garcia Saez?'

'We're looking into it. I'll let you know what we find.'

'Thanks, Philippe.'

Claire hung up and sipped her coffee. A haulage business, shady friends in Marseille, the organised crime capital of France. She rather liked the sound of Gilles Lafon.

Sullivan had been married for fifteen years, but that night in Groningen was the first time he'd been unfaithful to his wife. Put starkly like that it didn't seem such a terrible transgression – one night in several thousand – but he knew the quantity didn't really count. Once was all it took to break that bond of trust he had with Kate. Yet it disturbed him how easy it had been, how little guilt he felt afterwards. He wasn't sure why he'd succumbed. He'd never felt the inclination before, at least not strongly enough to do anything about it. He was happily married, still passionate about his wife. If Claire hadn't taken the initiative, he certainly wouldn't have attempted to seduce her. That wasn't to put all the responsibility on Claire – he'd been a more than willing partner in the encounter – but it had tipped the balance, making his own complicity easier to reconcile with his conscience.

That wasn't an excuse for his behaviour, it was a rationalisation. Adultery, as some ancient sage had once remarked, was like burglary: ten per cent motivation, ninety per cent opportunity. Sullivan was lazy about sex. Unless they were inveterate womanisers, in which case the chase was as important as the conquest, most men were. Which was why marriage was such a splendid institution – it saved you no end of time and effort and included all sorts of fringe benefits which would have cost a fortune to get someone other than a wife to provide.

Claire had made it easy for him. She'd missed out all the awkward, tentative foreplay and cut straight to the sweaty climax, simultaneously removing the need for much work on his part whilst giving his common sense no chance to override the immediate imperatives of his groin. Strangely, Sullivan hadn't enjoyed it as much as he'd expected. Nothing to do with Claire, more the fact that he wasn't as relaxed as he was with his wife. He'd felt a pressure to perform, sensed she was trying him out in some way. It was better with Kate. They were so easy with each other, so uninhibited together that over the years making love had become more erotic, more satisfying than ever. But Kate – and this was the real, fundamental reason – was in England and he saw her only twice a month. Claire was on the doorstep, available and willing. Those were powerful temptations for a lonely man, living by himself in a foreign city.

Sullivan went upstairs and along the corridor to Claire's office. He had no intention of having an affair with her. He'd had one moment of weakness but there'd be no more. He regarded middle-aged men who cheated on their wives as pathetic. That night in Groningen would be quietly forgotten. Claire was a colleague – she probably regretted it herself – and working together was only going to be possible if they re-established a formal, professional relationship.

She looked up and smiled as he came in. He felt an instinctive warmth towards her that he made himself suppress.

'Hi,' he said.

'You want some coffee?'

'Sure.'

She filled a cup for him and sat back down, cool, not overly familiar. He sensed that, like him, she was taking a step backwards, reassessing what had happened and resolving not to let it happen again. He was relieved but also, perversely, if he was honest, a little disappointed.

They discussed what they'd been doing for a time, exchanging information. Claire told him about Allard's call and Sullivan briefed her on the *Maria Vasquez*. Then he gave her the reference number of the file he was looking for.

'Fraud in the wheat industry?' Claire said. 'That's a bit remote from cigarette-trafficking.'

'You know how it is. Every possible lead, no matter how tenuous, is worth examining.'

'It's outside my area, but I can check it out. What was the name again?'

'Horningtoft Limited.'

Claire scribbled it down. 'If I find anything, I'll bring it to your office.'

'Thanks for the coffee.'

He went back downstairs and almost immediately the telephone rang. It was Mick Linstead, his contact in the Met Fraud Squad.

'Cannadine Exports,' Linstead said. 'I had one of my boys go round. It was just an empty office above a hairdresser's shop. A desk and a phone line. The hairdresser says she sub-let it to the company six months ago.'

'Any names?' Sullivan said.

'She only ever dealt with one man, bloke named Wilson. He paid the rent, monthly in cash, and came round to collect the mail every few days. Then last week he gave notice, paid what he owed her and cleared the place out. No forwarding address. You want me to take it any further?'

'No. Thanks for your help, Mick. I owe you one.'

Sullivan had absolutely no doubt what it was. It bore all the classic hallmarks: an office in some cheap, run-down part of London, no staff, no files, rent paid in cash and no one there when the police came knocking on the door. He'd have to check the names and addresses of the directors but he knew they'd be false, they always were. Setting up a limited company was ridiculously easy. A couple of forms, some Table A Memorandum and Articles of Association you could pick up in a legal stationer's for a fiver, a twenty-pound registration fee and you were in business. No one ever checked whether the directors existed until something went wrong, and by then it was too late.

He pulled out his contacts book and rang the UK Customs and Excise payments centre in Southend-on-Sea. This was where every VAT-registered business in the country sent their quarterly returns. He was put through to one of the records clerks and asked him if they had a listing for Cannadine Exports. The clerk tapped into the computer system.

'Registered August of last year. Import–export business,' he said.

'How many returns filed?' Sullivan asked.

'Two.'

'Let me guess, each one with a higher input than output tax.'

'Yes, how did you know?'

'How much has been reimbursed to them?'

'In total, nearly eighty thousand pounds.'

Sullivan sighed, thanked the clerk and rang off. These guys had every trick covered. Still, if you were going to be hung, why bother with lambs when there was a whole flock of sheep out there for the taking? It was a simple scam, but relatively risk-free. You set up a company and registered it for VAT. You then charged tax on goods you sold but pocketed it instead of passing it on to the Excise; or you claimed reimbursement of VAT supposedly paid on fictitious goods you'd never actually bought in the first place. Either way the VAT man was cheated and, as your chances of undergoing a random inspection were almost negligible, you got away with it if you didn't push your luck and do it for too long. Then you just disappeared and set up a new company at a new address and started all over again. You could make a tidy living and the only work involved was filling in a form every three months and pushing a wheelbarrow down to the bank to withdraw the proceeds.

Claire walked into his office shortly afterwards, carrying a file under her arm.

'The report you asked for,' she said, dropping the cardboard folder on to his desk with a thud.

Sullivan eyed it apprehensively.

'It looks very thick.'

'It does, doesn't it? I'm glad I'm not the one having to read it.'

'Maybe you should. You know more about agriculture than I do.'

'Nice try, Rob, but do I look like an idiot?'

'It's your area.'

'Wheat? I was in olive oil.'

'It's almost the same thing.'

'Enjoy yourself,' she said, turning to leave. 'Oh, by the way, Philippe Allard just rang back. That Paris number he was checking for me. It was a freight depot near Orly. And you know who it belongs to?'

Sullivan grinned at her. 'Gilles Lafon gets more interesting by the minute.'

'I'll see what else I can dig up.'

She looked directly at him. 'You want to go for a drink later?'

Sullivan met her eyes, remembering his resolution, his loyalty to his wife, his determination not to be another libidinous fool.

'I'll give you a call when I'm finished,' he said.

There was a word for it in Swedish: *höst depression*, autumn depression, a phenomenon so common it had earned not only its own terminology but recognised medical symptoms to go with it. Other Europeans, even North Europeans like the Germans and the British whose climates were far from perfect, had no idea what a Scandinavian winter was like. They couldn't comprehend just what the prospect of those long bitter nights and all too brief days did to the human spirit; what misery it was to say goodbye to the three short months of summer and contemplate a horizon of unremitting gloom and rain and bone-numbing cold.

Stig Enqvist, like most of his compatriots, had suffered from *höst depression* to varying degrees so he knew what it felt like. And he knew that what he was feeling now was very similar, although he was depressed not at the impending arrival of winter, but the impending end to his attachment to UCLAF.

His four years were nearly up. In six weeks' time he would be gone, his place taken by some other investigator, and he would never come back. One secondment was all you were allowed. It wasn't the thought of returning to Stockholm, or his job at the *Tullverk* that made him despondent. It was more the thought of picking up the pieces of his old life, facing up to the problems which he'd managed to put on hold during his time in Brussels. Living abroad had enabled him to, if not forget, then certainly relegate to an isolated corner of his brain his ex-wife and daughter. He'd helped them financially since the divorce but done little else to form any kind of relationship with the little girl who was now – he had to think about it – nearly five years old. The thought of seeing her again, of coping with the guilt he felt at abandoning her, frightened him. He would have to face up to all that emotional turmoil now. And face up to his remaining years back in his homeland, middle-aged, unattached and lonely.

He helped himself to a miniature whisky from the mini-bar in his hotel room and flicked through the channels on the television set. He'd had enough of Rotterdam, enough of Van Vliet Entrepôt. He wanted to get back to Brussels and . . . and what? What did he have in Brussels that was so special? He downed the whisky angrily and threw on his coat. He was damned if he was going to sit on his bed watching television all evening. He went downstairs and ordered a taxi at reception, then went outside on to the steps to wait.

The taxi arrived a few minutes later. Enqvist watched

it pull in and started down the steps, aware of a figure emerging from the hotel and hurrying down next to him. He glanced sideways. It was a woman with long blonde hair cascading over the collar of her black overcoat. She got to the taxi first and pulled open the door.

'I think this is for me,' Enqvist said in English.

The woman turned to look at him. She was strikingly beautiful. She answered in the same language.

'I'm sorry. I ordered one too, I thought this was mine.'

She stepped away from the door. 'Please.'

'No, you take it,' Enqvist said. 'I can wait.'

'Where are you going?'

'I'm not sure. The Oudehaven maybe. I don't care, I'm just going out.'

'You can share it with me,' she said.

'Are you sure?' Enqvist said.

She shrugged. 'I'm going that way.'

He held the door open for her and climbed in after her. She gave the driver instructions in Dutch and settled back in the far corner of the seat. The streetlights touched her hair with a halo of silver, throwing shadows over the curve of her cheeks and the pale outline of her neck.

'Are you staying in the hotel?' Enqvist said.

'Yes. You're English?'

'Swedish,' Enqvist replied.

'From where? Stockholm?'

'You know it?'

'I've been there. I love the old town, what's it called? Gamla . . .'

'Gamla Stan,' Enqvist said.

They chatted intermittently throughout the short journey to the Oudehaven. The taxi pulled in outside a restaurant and the woman got out. Enqvist followed her.

'This will do me too,' he said, paying the driver.

'Here.' She offered him half the fare. 'No, I insist,' she said when he tried to refuse.

She looked at the gold watch on her wrist.

'I'm meeting some friends for dinner. I'm a little early.'

She bit her lip and glanced awkwardly at him. 'I hate sitting on my own in restaurants. You wouldn't have a drink with me, would you? Just until they get here.'

Enqvist pretended to give it some thought, resisting the urge to race into the restaurant and order a couple of aperitifs.

'Sure,' he said as coolly as he could. 'I've nothing planned.'

They sat on a sofa in the bar area, surrounded by diners perusing menus, waiting to be seated. She was easy company: warm, relaxed, with a girlish, slightly giggly personality which took the edge off her intimidating good looks. After ten minutes the head waiter approached her and asked hesitantly: 'Miss Rietveld?'

'Yes.'

'A Miss Noorlander telephoned. She sent her apologies but she and her partner are unable to come. Their baby-sitter hasn't shown up.'

'Ah, thank you.'

Enqvist saw the look on her face though he hadn't been able to follow the Dutch.

'Is something the matter?'

'My friends have cancelled.'

'Do you want a table for two instead?' the head waiter said, speaking in English now.

She was embarrassed. 'Well . . .'

'It would be my pleasure,' Stig said. 'Will you have dinner with me?'

Her name was Juliana Rietveld. She was from Amsterdam, but down in Rotterdam on a two-day modelling assignment.

'Nothing very exciting,' she said. 'Just a clothing catalogue for a mail-order company.'

Enqvist nodded. He'd never been much of a fan of
mail-order catalogues, but if the models in them all
looked like this girl he'd take out a life subscription
immediately.

'It's mostly very boring studio work,' she continued. 'A
bit of outdoor shooting but that's even worse. It's summer
clothes we're modelling. You've no idea how cold it gets.
Your skin goes blue all over.'

Enqvist drank some of his wine and tried not to think
about it. He couldn't quite believe he was sitting there
having dinner with this young woman who must have
been – he guessed – in her late twenties. Old enough for
the age gap between them to be not altogether ridiculous.
He didn't want to be mistaken for either her father or a
cradle snatcher.

He'd never been out with a model before, never actually met one, in fact – Swedish customs officers were
not renowned for moving in fashion circles. Juliana was
dauntingly pretty, but seemed to be completely unaware
of it and the effect it had on men. Enqvist knew it had to
be partly a pose, an artifice to prevent accusations of vanity
or narcissism, but she carried it off well. After the first few
moments at their table, when they were both on edge, the
evening progressed with a disarming ease. Enqvist was an
entertaining companion when he chose to be and Juliana
was a good listener, which certainly helped. By the time
they went back to the hotel there was a comfortable rapport
between them, almost an intimacy.

They went up in the lift and stopped on the fourth
floor – Enqvist's floor. He pressed the button to hold the
doors open.

'I enjoyed tonight,' he said.

'So did I.'

Enqvist hesitated. Juliana gave him his cue.

'I go to Brussels quite often on assignments.'

'Really? Look me up, if you like.'

He took out his wallet and gave her one of his business cards.

'Maybe I will,' she said.

'Do you want another drink? In my room?'

She shook her head. 'No thanks. Good night.'

He stepped out of the lift.

'Stig.'

He turned.

'Perhaps I will have that drink.'

They walked down the corridor to his room, not saying anything. He opened the door and as he fumbled for the light switch, he brushed against her, inhaling the smell of her perfume. He didn't know which of them made the move first, whether she came to him or he pulled her, but her body was suddenly pressed hard against him and they were kissing with a ferocious abandon.

They edged their way to the bed, still kissing, discarding clothes as they went. Juliana tugged off his shirt and tie and pushed him down on to the covers. Then her fingers unfastened the zip at the back of her dress and she stepped out of it. Enqvist lay back on the pillow and gazed at her. Rotterdam was the last place on earth he would have thought of as Heaven, but he knew he'd died and gone somewhere.

There was a jaundiced view of male sexuality – often attributed to embittered feminists – that held that a man would shag a revolving door if it had big enough tits. Sullivan didn't subscribe to the theory, regarding it as an offensive slur, but nevertheless he couldn't help wondering what he was doing in Claire Colmar's apartment at eleven o'clock at night.

They'd been for a drink after work, driving into the centre of the city because the residential suburbs around Beaulieu were noticeably devoid of bars. It had seemed natural then to move on to a restaurant and have dinner together. They were in Ixelles, not far from Claire's flat, and when she'd suggested he came back with her for coffee he'd said yes without stopping to think what that signalled. Or rather, he *had* stopped to think, but deluded himself that coffee didn't necessarily entail anything more.

He was a fool, and knew it. There'd been no pressure, Claire had been careful about that. He could have made a clean break and walked away with no feelings hurt, but he'd chosen not to. He knew what he was doing, although he wasn't prepared to admit it to himself: he was allowing himself to be carried along, hoping that he would get to the point where it was too late to pull out and that would justify his actions. It would make him feel that, if he slept with Claire again, it hadn't been a conscious decision on his part, it had just happened. Events had taken over and simply swept them both away.

It was a feeble rationale, but who really concerned themselves with reason when the loins were hot with lust? Claire was attractive, desirable. Being with her gave him a sense of exhilaration, of heightened arousal. He was forty-two years old and a part of him – an immature part, it was true, but that didn't lessen its influence – wondered if he was missing out on some marvellous sexual experience that would never come his way again. Mid-life crisis, the urge to regain lost youth were trite concepts that he didn't really believe in. But he wished he'd slept with more women over the years. That was what it was: he wanted the novelty and the excitement of an affair.

The apartment was on the second floor of a converted house near the Avenue Louise. It had two bedrooms and a big living room with a dining table at one end and French windows leading out on to a small balcony at the other.

They sat on the sofa, beneath a framed Magritte print of a giant apple filling a room, and drank their coffee, lost for words for the first time that evening. Neither of them wanted the drink, it was just a pretext, a formality which had to be observed. Claire waited for him. She appeared composed but Sullivan could sense she was nervous. Tonight it was his turn.

He put his arm along the back of the sofa. She half turned towards him. He stroked her hair gently, feeling the thick dark strands. Then he leaned across and kissed her. Her arms came up around his neck, pulling him to her.

When they broke apart, breathless, Claire said: 'Was it a mistake the other night?'

'Probably.'

'You regret it?'

'No, I don't think I do. You?'

'No,' she said. 'The bedroom's through there.'

He took her hand and pulled her to her feet. It was another mistake. But right now he didn't care.

TEN

Sullivan spent most of the following morning going through the TF7 file on fraud in the European wheat industry, not reading it in detail but scanning the pages for any mention of Horningtoft Limited. He couldn't find a single reference so he rang Claire on the internal line.

'Why would it be mentioned on the database but not in the report?' he asked her.

'I don't know. Maybe it wasn't important enough to include. Have you checked the appendices?'

'Yes, there's nothing.'

'I'll look through the supporting materials on which the report was based. They often log things on the database which don't then find their way into the finished report. You could always try the Intervention Board. They might have something.'

'Anyone in particular?'

'Ask for Chris Carmichael. He's helped me in the past.'

Sullivan rang the Reading headquarters of the Intervention Board, the government agency which distributed EU subsidies to United Kingdom farmers. Chris Carmichael had a chirpy Cockney voice which made him sound like a dodgy East End barrow boy, but he was helpful enough. He made a note of the name and called back ten minutes later.

'Yeah, we've got a listing for Horningtoft Limited. Can't

fink why you've got it though, there's no mention of any irregularity.'

'Do you know anything about it?' Sullivan said.

'Only what I've got here on the screen. It's a big client.'

'What does it do?'

'Manages farms. A few dozen, all over East Anglia mostly.'

'Manages them? For the farmers?'

'Absentee landlords. It's a growing business. The land-owner pisses off to the Bahamas, Sarf of France, wherever, leaves the management company to run his farm in return for an agreed share of the profits. A right old bleedin' doss if you ask me.'

'How much EU support does it get?'

'A lot. It's a big operation, manages a ton of land, all prime arable. Cereals – mainly wheat – sugar beet, oilseed rape, milk and dairy as well.'

'Why would we have a reference to it when you have no record of any irregularity?' Sullivan said.

'Can't fink,' Carmichael said. 'Either the reference never came from us or, if there was an allegation, we investigated it and found it to be baseless.'

'Wouldn't that be in your records?'

'Depends how long ago it was. What year we talking abaht?'

'Four years ago.'

'It would be here if we had anything. Can't help you, mate, sorry. As far as we're concerned it's clean. Not a stain on its character.'

'Okay, thanks anyway.'

'Any time.'

Sullivan rang off and stared out of the window. He was overlooking something obvious here. If Horningtoft Limited, a British company receiving EU support payments in the UK, had been suspected of any irregularity, the case would have been dealt with solely by the Intervention Board which had its own investigation department. UCLAF would only have been notified if a second member state were involved, if the irregularity had somehow become a transnational case. Sullivan called Claire.

'The Intervention Board have no record of any suspected fraud,' he said. 'There must have been another country in the frame. Who compiled the report?'

'Mercier and Feenstra, both long gone. There's no one left in TF7 who would remember the details of any investigation. The file is all we've got.'

'There must be a document somewhere. Someone had a reason for putting the company on the database.'

'I'll see what I can do.'

Sullivan was on the phone, talking to Casagrande in Naples, when Claire walked into his office. She sat down in Enqvist's chair and waited for him to finish. Sullivan eyed her slim legs, the dark skirt slipping up above the knee. Then he looked up to see her watching him with detached amusement. He smiled at her and came off the line.

'That Naples number,' he said. 'It was just a bar down near the docks.'

'Camorra?'

'Probably. We'll never know what the message was and for whom. What's that you've got there?'

'It was in the supporting materials for France, not the UK.'

She passed the piece of paper across the desk. It was a letter addressed to UCLAF from the Crown Prosecution Service office in Norwich. Sullivan read through it. The CPS lawyer who'd sent it, a Jim Bristow, was outlining the general nature of an Intervention Board investigation into financial irregularities at Horningtoft Limited, a file which had been passed on to the CPS for legal proceedings to begin. Bristow was asking if UCLAF had any information on the activities of the company in France where they also managed farms and where they were also claiming, and receiving, EU agricultural subsidies.

Sullivan read the letter again, frowning.

'This doesn't make sense. Have you read this? There was clearly an Intervention Board inquiry into Horningtoft, so why isn't it mentioned in the Intervention Board records? And it wasn't just some insignificant irregularity if it had already been passed on to the Crown Prosecution Service. The CPS was ready to prosecute Horningtoft. Can you do something for me, Claire? Check with the French, see what they've got on this.'

'Sure.' She stood up. 'You going for lunch later?'

Sullivan nodded. 'With Stig. He's on his way back this morning. Why don't you join us?'

'A *ménage à trois*? How could I refuse?' Claire said, walking out.

Sullivan watched her go, listening to the sound of her heels receding down the corridor, thinking about the previous night. Wondering what it had meant to him. And to her. Then he focused back on his work and telephoned the CPS in Norwich. He asked to speak to Jim Bristow.

'Who?' the girl on the switchboard said.

'Jim Bristow,' Sullivan repeated.

'We don't have anyone of that name here.'

'He's a lawyer.'

'I'm sorry. Are you sure you've got the right office?'

'I have a letter from him here, dated May 1996.'

'That was before my time. He's not here now.'

'I have a query about one of his cases. Is there anyone else who can help me?'

'I'll put you through to Mr Newman, he's the Area Chief Crown Prosecutor.'

Newman was terse, in a hurry. 'Who's this?' he said curtly.

Sullivan told him who he was and why he was calling.

'1996?' Newman said. 'That's four years ago. My God, you people are even slower than we are. But then you're Brussels,' he added with a sarcastic sneer. 'You have a reputation to keep up.'

Sullivan didn't bother explaining the circumstances. Newman was clearly one of those people – and Sullivan came across a lot – who regarded anyone employed by the European Union as a high-living, contemptible parasite.

'Perhaps you could look up the case for me?' Sullivan said politely.

'I could,' Newman said. 'If I had nothing better to do.'

'It would be very helpful. I gather Jim Bristow is no longer there.'

'He retired a few years ago.'

'Is he still in Norwich?'

'How the hell would I know that? I never knew the fellow.'

'I'd appreciate any information you have on the case,' Sullivan said diplomatically.

He had no power to make the CPS cooperate. He had to depend entirely on their good will, which in Newman's case appeared to be in singularly short supply.

Newman made an impatient clicking noise with his tongue. Sullivan pictured some ferret-faced provincial solicitor, sitting in a high leather chair acting the autocrat in his dismal little empire.

'What was the name of the company again?'

'Horningtoft Limited,' Sullivan said.

'I'll put someone on to it.'

Sullivan gave him his telephone number. 'Will I hear today?'

'You'll hear when we're ready,' Newman said rudely. 'You've waited four years. What's the big hurry now?'

'Thank you for your help,' Sullivan said.

He released the phone from his clenched fist and replaced it carefully, taking a couple of deep breaths to control his temper.

'And screw you too,' he said with a quiet ferocity.

'What kind of a welcome is that?' Stig Enqvist said from the door.

He came in, pulling off his wet overcoat.

'I leave in a rainstorm, return in one. It's good to know nothing changes,' he said acidly.

He brushed the droplets off his hair, wiping his fingers on the back of his trousers.

'You ready to eat? I'm dying for a drink.'

'So where do we stand?' Sullivan said.

Enqvist took a long pull on his Rodenbach beer and helped himself to a chunk of bread from the basket in the middle of the table.

'Van Vliet is a crook,' he said. 'I'm certain of that. He knows full well that he's dealing with traffickers. Not just Cannadine Export but I found a number of other recent shipments, some by rail, some by sea, that looked suspicious. Several were ordered and paid for by Steinhammer Weiss in Zürich.'

'You're kidding?' Sullivan said. 'I thought Wolf had retired.'

'Apparently not.'

'Who's Wolf?' Claire said.

'Julius Wolf, Swiss lawyer and businessman,' Sullivan said. 'We have a file on him about this thick. He's getting on a bit now but in his day he was one of the largest cigarette traders in Europe. One of those middle men we told you about who buy from the manufacturers and sell on to traffickers. Steinhammer Weiss is one of his front companies.'

'It would seem he's back in the game,' Enqvist said. 'Unless someone else has taken over his business.'

'Any indication from Van Vliet's records?'

Enqvist shook his head. 'Van Vliet is a very careful man. He makes damn sure every legal nicety is observed, every regulation followed to the letter. His books are clean. He trades in cigarettes quite legitimately. Everything he sells is cleared with Customs. If it's distributed within the EU the duty is paid on the nail. If it's in transit the T1s are perfect. You can't flaw his business methods.'

'But?' Sullivan said.

'But what?'

'Are you saying he's untouchable? You've gone through his records and found no irregularities at all?'

Enqvist shrugged. 'Nothing worth pursuing.'

'Come on, Stig, there must be something. What was the point of raiding the place if we come away with nothing?'

'There's no evidence to implicate Van Vliet in trafficking.'

'But he might just be our conduit to the smugglers.'

Enqvist chewed on his crust of bread, sitting back to allow the waitress to place a pot of steaming beef carbonnade on the table. The vegetables came next; sliced potatoes garnished with chopped parsley, pickled red cabbage and asparagus tips dripping with melted butter.

He waited until they each had their plates full before he said wearily: 'We all know the obstacles we're up against. Clever, well-organised smugglers with access to virtually unlimited supplies of cigarettes; a huge black market it's impossible to even identify much less stamp out; a shortage of law enforcement resources to adequately police the frontiers of the EU. We're on a hiding to nothing. We confiscate millions of contraband cigarettes each year

157

but billions more slip through the net. We spend our time locking the stable door after the horse has bolted.'

'So isn't it time we caught the nag before she gets out?' Sullivan said.

'We've tried that before. Unless we get a tip-off, like we did in Naples, we have no idea when or where the smugglers are going to strike next.'

'That's still true,' Sullivan said. 'But we have the advantage of more information now. We know that a large number of contraband cigarettes originate from Van Vliet's warehouse.'

'But the smugglers know we have that information,' Claire interjected. 'They'll simply find their supply elsewhere, won't they?'

Sullivan shook his head. 'Finding a new supplier isn't that straightforward. The cigarette companies only deal with a limited number of bonded warehouses. And besides, these guys are arrogant. They think – no, they *know* – they can outsmart us because they've been doing it successfully for years. They're going to rely on the fact that although we may suspect Van Vliet of supplying them, we still don't know which shipments are legitimate and which aren't. And we certainly don't know how they're going to smuggle the cigarettes back into the EU. The odds are huge and in their favour. The EU has – what? – something like forty thousand kilometres of external frontier. All the smugglers need is a strip fifty metres wide and they can walk in with impunity.'

Sullivan ate some of his stew. He speared a chunk of beef with his fork and loaded it into his mouth, savouring the beer-flavoured sauce.

Le Chasseur Georges – a reference to the proprietor who was a renowned local hunter and celebrated cook of the game he shot for the pot – was one of their favourite restaurants. Just outside Brussels, a short drive across the

Forêt de Soignes in Jezus-Eik, it was an unpretentious, noisy place with good plain food and a rustic ambience which – unlike many country restaurants outside the city – owed more to its local clientèle and ancient decor than an interior designer's concept.

'What are you suggesting?' Claire said.

She was sitting next to Sullivan on a narrow bench. She could feel the warmth of his leg pressing against hers.

'You made notes of all those recent shipments from Van Vliet's warehouse, I assume,' Sullivan asked Enqvist.

'Of course. But they're long gone.'

'And we can find out from Dutch Customs when any new consignments leave. Some of them are going to be legitimate cargoes, some are going to be smuggled back into the EU. The trick is identifying which is which.'

'And how do we do that?' Claire said.

'Well, these guys are big-time. This is organised trafficking on a vast scale. However they smuggle the cigarettes, they'll probably have done a similar, if not identical run before. The infrastructure will be in place, the black marketeers will be expecting a regular supply along certain routes. You don't smuggle a hundred and fifty million cigarettes at a time with a suitcase and a couple of couriers.

'Now, some of the cigarettes are going out by road and rail and will be offloaded illegally in transit across the EU. But the big cargoes will go by sea, we know that from past experience. It's the best way of moving large quantities and the hardest for us to keep tabs on. The *Maria Vasquez* wasn't their only ship, there'll be others. I think we can identify which they are.'

Enqvist drank some of his beer to wash down a mouthful of potatoes.

'That's not going to be easy,' he said gloomily.

'But it's possible. We go through the previous shipments

159

and check every component: the ships, the quantity ordered, the declared destination, the company paying for them. We've got the log of the *Maria Vasquez*. We know where she went and when. We compare her movements with those of the other ships and see if anything is similar, see if there's a pattern of cargoes and destinations. We check with Customs and see if the ships actually went where they were supposed to.'

Sullivan looked at Claire and Enqvist in turn, a raw determination in his eyes and the set of his jaw.

'You've got six weeks left, Stig,' he said. 'Wouldn't you like to go out in a blaze of glory?'

In the middle of the afternoon, Sullivan received a call from the Crown Prosecution Service in Norwich.

'My name's Russell,' the voice on the line said, a hint of a Norfolk burr in his words. 'John Newman asked me to give you a bell.'

'I appreciate it,' Sullivan replied. 'Mr Newman didn't seem exactly keen on helping me.'

Russell gave an abrupt snort of laughter, like a sneeze.

'Take no notice of him. It's just his manner. You wanted to know about Horningtoft Limited.'

'Yes. One of your former colleagues, Jim Bristow, was handling a case against them.'

'Jim? Was he, when?'

'Four years ago.'

'He retired about four years ago. Are you sure?'

'We have a letter from him on file.'

'That's more than we have,' Russell said. 'We have nothing at all. No file, no computer record.'

'That can't be possible. According to Bristow's letter he was about to initiate proceedings against the company. You must have something.'

'I'm afraid not. I've looked everywhere. We have no

record of a case against Horningtoft Limited. Are you sure that was the name?' He spelt it out.

'That's the one,' Sullivan said. 'Are you absolutely certain? Could it have been misplaced?'

'It's possible. It was a while ago. All I know is I can't find any trace of it.'

Sullivan screwed up his forehead, staring intensely at the stark walls of his office.

'Are you still there?' Russell said.

'What? Oh, yes, I'm sorry. Tell me, have you seen Jim Bristow since he retired?'

'No, I haven't. I'm not sure anyone in the office has. He moved away from Norwich.'

'Do you know where?'

'I don't have an address, but I believe it was somewhere up near the coast. Wells, Burnham Market, around there.'

Sullivan thanked him for his help and hung up. Stig Enqvist looked at him across the cluttered surfaces of their desks.

'Something the matter?'

'I don't know. Yes, I think something is the matter.'

Sullivan picked up the phone and rang UK Directory Enquiries. Bristow wasn't a particularly common name and there were only three listed for the Wells area of north Norfolk. Sullivan tried each one. The first didn't answer, the second was a Bed and Breakfast in Little Walsingham and the third a mother with two young children – he could hear them screaming in the background – in Brancaster Staithe.

'I'm trying to get in touch with a Jim Bristow who used to work for the Crown Prosecution Service in Norwich,' Sullivan explained.

'That's my father-in-law.'

'It is? You couldn't give me his number, could you?'

It was the first number he'd tried.

'He'll be out in the marshes,' the woman said. 'He's there most afternoons. Try him again around tea-time.'

Sullivan rang at intervals over the next few hours. It was six thirty Brussels time, five thirty in the UK, when he finally got an answer. Bristow's voice was deep, peremptory, a little intimidating.

'How did you get this number?' he asked before he would even confirm his identity.

Sullivan told him.

'And you're from UCLAF?' Bristow said, checking his facts like a good lawyer.

'That's right. I've been reading a letter you wrote to us about a company called Horningtoft Limited.'

'Horningtoft?' Bristow exclaimed, his tone harsh, cynical. 'Ah well, better late than never.'

'What do you mean?'

'What do you want, Mr . . .'

'Sullivan. Rob Sullivan. To talk to you about it.'

'I'm retired. I'm not sure I can help you.'

'No one else seems to be able to either. I'd like to know why neither the CPS nor the Intervention Board have any record of an investigation into the company.'

'It's no longer my business, Mr Sullivan,' Bristow said firmly.

'You're the only lead I have. This is important.'

'Not to me.'

'Don't shut me out, please. You pursued this case once. I don't know what happened to it, but I think you do. I need your help, Mr Bristow.'

There was a long silence. Sullivan controlled the urge to say more. Bristow's conscience, his sense of duty would have to do the rest.

'Not on the phone,' Bristow said finally. 'You'll have to come and see me.'

'That's not a problem. What's your address?'

Bristow gave him the name of a house and a street in Burnham Overy Staithe.

'You know this area?' he added.

'I've been there on holiday,' Sullivan said. 'I'll come tomorrow.'

'Mr Sullivan,' Bristow said. Then he paused. 'This sounds rather silly, but don't tell anyone you're coming. I mean that, no one at all.'

ELEVEN

Claire was nervous. She wasn't sure exactly why, but she could feel it in the tightness of her stomach, the insistent thud of her heartbeat. It was a sensation she'd experienced only once before in the course of her work. She and a colleague had been in Italy, in the depths of the rural south, checking stocks of olive oil which the EU had bought into intervention to maintain the price level in the market. There was a suspicion that the olive oil in many of the huge tanks was either Tunisian, smuggled in to fraudulently claim European support payments, or adulterated with hazelnut oil and therefore not eligible for any subsidy. They'd toured the area taking samples for analysis, accompanied by an official from AIMA, the Italian intervention board who, it rapidly became apparent, was in the pocket of the local mafia. In one warehouse Claire had caught the AIMA man in the process of substituting the UCLAF sample bottles for identical ones he'd filled earlier. Then unidentified men in dark glasses had started following them around, tailing their car through the remote villages of Campania.

One night, Claire and her colleague had checked into a hotel and left the olive oil samples locked in their car in the hotel's car park. Within minutes of their leaving the vehicle, its alarm had gone off as someone tried to force the boot. Two men were caught running away by the hotel staff and Claire recognised one of them as the chairman of the agricultural cooperative they'd visited earlier in the day. Fearing a second attempt to tamper with the samples, Claire and her colleague had moved them into their hotel rooms – about 2,000 small plastic bottles in total. Claire had vivid memories of that night, trying to sleep in a room which reeked of olive oil.

The next day the unidentified men in dark glasses had been behind them again, keeping twenty metres away, going everywhere Claire and her colleague went. Claire had been terrified, genuinely scared for her life. They'd abandoned the mission, driven straight to Naples airport and left the country. When they went back, several months later, they had to be escorted by a team of armed officers from the *Guardia di Finanza*. And this wasn't alcohol or cigarettes they were investigating, it was olive oil.

Claire was frightened now. Or rather, on edge. No one was following her, there was no logical reason for her to be worried, but she was. She was driving along a narrow country lane to the west of Bruges, heading towards the Belgian coast which was only a few kilometres away. It was pitch dark outside. Her headlights cut a bright tunnel through the surrounding blackness, glancing off the surface of the road and the patchy hedgerows along the edges of the adjoining fields. It was very quiet. Claire felt as if she were sealed inside the car, moving in a capsule through the flat countryside whose empty spaces and lowering sky seemed to threaten her.

She braked for a junction, peering out to decipher the names on the road sign, then turned right, following the instructions she'd been given. She had no clear idea where she was going, this whole area was unfamiliar to her. Not for the first time she wondered what she was doing, driving alone at night for a rendezvous with a man she'd never met.

He'd called as she was about to leave the office to go home.

'You left your card with a neighbour of mine,' he'd said in Dutch and she'd realised it was Jan Kuypers, the missing pilot from Groningen.

He'd refused to say any more on the telephone, simply told her she'd have to come to him if she wanted to talk. He was at a friend's house near De Haan on the North Sea coast. For one night only, he was leaving in the morning. Claire didn't feel she had a choice.

Outside, the fields were giving way to sparse woodland, stunted poplars and low shrubs which had been planted as windbreaks and to stabilise the sandy dunes that ran in a broad strip along this whole stretch of coast. Claire wound down her window a little. She could smell the sea on the breeze gusting in through the gap, catching at her hair.

Beside the road a weathered wooden sign appeared in the beam of her headlights. Claire slowed. The wording on the sign was too faded to read but she knew this must be the place. She turned off left down an unmetalled track, feeling the bumps and jolts of the water-filled potholes under the wheels of the car. The thin woodland on either side became gradually denser, the broadleaf deciduous trees being assimilated into a thicker swathe of dark pines. They closed in around the car, coming right down to the edge of the track, shutting out the sky with a canopy of spiky fronds. Claire twisted her hand around to depress the button below the window, centrally locking all the doors. She didn't know why she did it, it just came instinctively. As instinctively as the knot of nervous tension that was tightening around her stomach.

After two hundred metres the track came to an end in a cramped turning circle. Claire swung her car round to face back the way she'd come and switched off the engine. The silence was smothering. Claire resisted an impulse to twist the key in the ignition, to restore the reassuring noise and vibration of the motor. The headlights were still on. It took real willpower to make herself extinguish them. She sat in the darkness listening to the sound of her heart, tempted to drive away immediately. But what was the point of coming all this way if she was going to lose her nerve at the last minute?

She let her eyes adjust to the night, then climbed out, scanning the ranks of pine trees all around. She wished she'd brought a torch. She hadn't expected the house to be quite so isolated. Nothing moved. There was no sound except the faint rustle of the wind in the branches and a distant, almost inaudible murmur that she realised was the sea breaking along the beach.

Kuypers had said there was a path through the forest from the end of the track, but she couldn't see it. She scoured the perimeter of the turning circle and noticed a break in the undergrowth and a patch of earth beyond it where the soil had been trodden down hard. She took a deep breath, trying to relax, and plunged into the trees.

It was too dark to follow a path, too dark to even see if there was one. She just had to feel her way blind, sensing where a path might have been, and hope for the best. The ground started to go uphill. She could feel the pine needles crunching beneath her shoes, the loose soil crumbling as she dug in her toes. On the brow of the hill she saw ahead of her the lights of a house glowing orange and flickering like candle flames as the branches of the trees danced in front of the windows. She increased her pace, knowing where she was going now, anxious to escape the claustrophobic clutches of the forest.

The house was on the edge of the dunes, separated from the trees by a grassy clearing. It was a small, two-storey wooden cottage with smoke trickling from its chimney and its ground-floor windows ablaze with light, their curtains pulled open to reveal the interiors of the rooms.

Claire walked across the clearing. On the other side of the cottage the hillocks of sand rolled in swollen waves down to the beach. The sea was grey and choppy, the breakers crashing and fizzing along the shoreline.

Claire knocked on the door of the cottage. There was no answer. She tried the handle. The door swung open. She hesitated.

'Kuypers?' she called.

The atmosphere inside the house seemed to seep out and envelop her in a chilling embrace. She realised her legs were trembling.

'Kuypers?' she called again, not because she expected a response but because she wanted to delay going inside.

She looked down across the dunes. Maybe he'd gone for a walk. But there was no sign of any movement on the sand. She couldn't put it off any longer. She stepped over the threshold into the tiny hall of the cottage. Coats and waterproofs were hanging on pegs on the wall and the door leading to the living room beyond was ajar. Claire pushed it with her foot. The sudden creak of the hinges made her start. She got a grip on herself, controlling her breathing, making herself relax. The living room was deserted. The furniture was old and shabby: a couple of armchairs, a sofa draped with a moth-eaten throw. The floor was varnished wood, thick with dust. In the hearth a wood fire burned, the logs charred on the outside but still solid underneath. It had been stoked not all that long ago.

Claire moved cautiously across the room. She felt frighteningly exposed in the glare of the overhead light. She couldn't see out through the windows though she knew she would be clearly visible to anyone outside. She wanted to close the curtains but didn't. She couldn't bring herself to step in front of the glass. There was another door on the far side of the room. She took a couple of quick paces and pressed herself against the wall beside the door. She was aware of the throbbing pulse inside her head, the chemicals flooding her bloodstream with the overwhelming urge to flee. But she had to go on.

She took hold of the door handle and jerked it down, pulling the door open in one swift movement. There was a small vestibule on the other side from which a darkened flight of stairs ascended to the floor above. Another open door gave access to the brightly lit kitchen. Claire glanced up the stairs and moved quickly across into the kitchen. There was no one there. Her eyes flickered around the room, taking in the chipped stone sink, the bottled gas stove, the back door with clear glass panes through which she could see the brick walls of an outhouse. She pulled open the drawers below the worktops, looking for something. In the fourth drawer, by the sink, she found it, a plastic tray full of cutlery. She rummaged through it and pulled out a wooden-handled chopping knife. She grasped it tight, wondering if she was overreacting. But she felt better with it in her hand.

She went back out into the vestibule. The stairwell was a dark cavity above her. She was reluctant to go up, but she had to make sure. She felt around on the wall and clicked on the light. Slowly, she went up the stairs. The first room at the top was a bathroom. She pushed open the door and turned on the light. Again, it was empty. There was one other door off the landing, presumably leading to the bedroom. Claire pushed it open with her left hand, her right holding the chopping knife at the ready. The room beyond was in darkness, but there was enough light on the landing for her to see a double bed and wardrobe. She reached in, her fingers fumbling then finding the switch. The bedroom light snapped on. There was a blue and white striped duvet on the bed, a couple of thin rugs on the floor. The wardrobe, a big heavy piece with brass handles, and a low chest of drawers were the only other items of furniture. Claire leaned back on the wall and took a deep breath, her relief at concluding her search tempered by a nagging worry that kept her on edge. What the hell had happened to Kuypers?

Leaving the lights on, she went back downstairs and checked the kitchen and living room, looking to see if he'd left her a note or a message of any kind. There was nothing.

She thought about waiting, but there didn't seem much point. She had the impression he'd left in a hurry and not too long before she'd arrived. The signs were there: the fire still burning strongly in the grate, the lights on, the house unlocked. But where had he gone? She wondered if he'd had a car. The cottage was in the middle of nowhere; getting to and from it without transport wouldn't have been easy. Maybe he'd driven off somewhere, to buy food, drink, cigarettes. The options were too complicated to consider. But she didn't feel like hanging around for him, not in the house at least. Something about it unnerved her.

She went back outside and gazed down over the dunes again. It was too dark, and there were too many dips and valleys in the sand, for her to be absolutely sure there was no one lurking out there. She gave him one last chance.

'Kuypers!' she called.

Nothing. She waited a few moments, then turned and went back across the clearing to the forest. It was only as she entered the trees that she realised she was still holding the chopping knife. She shrugged. No one would miss it.

The path was just as hard to see this time, but she moved quicker, knowing where she was going. She dropped over the brow of the hill, slithering down the muddy slope on the other side. It was darker here, out of the reach of the light from the cottage. She lost her footing momentarily and overbalanced, tumbling to the ground and rolling a few metres to the bottom of the incline. Winded but unhurt, she knelt up and paused to recover her breath. Then she clambered to her feet and pressed on, no longer on the path but trusting to her sense of direction to bring her out by her car.

She stumbled against something on the ground and almost fell over again, steadying herself with a hand on a nearby tree trunk. She peered down, trying to make out what was blocking her path. It was about six feet long, with dark limbs outstretched on the earth. A body. Claire reached down and touched it tentatively. Jesus, what was the matter with her? She felt damp bark and moss and a couple of snapped-off branches. It was just a fallen log. Straightening up, she took a few deep breaths, forcing the tension out of her muscles. She wasn't normally this jumpy. In the distance she could see a smear of sky where there was a break in the forest. She headed towards it and broke out through the undergrowth into the turning circle where she'd parked. She froze.

There was someone in her car.

Someone sitting in the driver's seat.

Claire was behind and a little to the side of the vehicle so she couldn't make out the features, but she could see the outline of the shoulders and head and knew it was a man. She approached the car in a wide loop, circling round to the driver's door but stopping dead before she reached it. The man was slumped in the seat, his head lolling back against the headrest. There was enough light for her to see his eyes and mouth gaping like wounds, but the real, sickening injury was lower down – a livid, blood-seeping laceration across the full width of his neck.

Claire stared at him, oblivious for a second to anything except that terrible frozen face, those empty lifeless eyes gazing back at her while the dark, sticky gore below glistened and coagulated on his shirt. Then she became

172

aware of her surroundings again and spun round, suddenly terrified. The parking space was deserted. She strained to see into the forest, to see if she was being watched, but the files of trees were as blank and solid as a wall.

Her instincts were to get out immediately. To jump in her car and drive down the track to the road and keep going, it didn't matter where. But two things stopped her. To use her car would entail moving Kuypers' body – she knew for certain it was him – from the driver's seat and she couldn't bring herself to touch that bloody corpse. And the police would want her to leave everything exactly the way she'd found it. There would be forensic evidence that might be important in identifying the killer. Claire was a law enforcement officer herself, she knew what was required, and her sense of responsibility forbade her to disturb the scene.

She went round to the rear of the car and opened the boot, reaching inside and lifting out the tyre iron from the toolkit. There was no avoiding it: she had to go back to the cottage – there'd been a telephone on the dresser in the living room – and call the police.

She never knew how she made it back through the forest. Her nerves were strung so tight, her guts so twisted with nausea that only a fierce willpower stopped her from throwing up. She ran. Chopping knife in one hand, tyre iron in the other. Ran almost blind, thrusting branches out of the way, tearing at the undergrowth, not caring how much noise she made until she burst out into the clearing on the other side and the reassuring glare of the cottage's lights. She went inside the house and across to the dresser. She picked up the phone. There was no dialling tone. She depressed the button a few times. The line was dead.

'Shit!' she breathed.

She looked around, considering what to do next.

Then the lights went out.

Claire was too shocked to move. She stood there in the darkness, watching the wood embers glowing in the fireplace, then she crouched down automatically, making herself less obtrusive. She was too stunned to be frightened. But she knew that fear preyed on the mind, feeding off insecurity and helplessness. Doing nothing was the surest way of surrendering to it.

She dropped to her belly and snaked across the room. When she reached the corner she twisted round and squatted with her back to the walls. She was thinking quite clearly. Outside in the forest she'd been scared of the unknown, of hidden eyes watching her. Now she was almost relieved. She knew there really was someone there and could work out what to do about it. Imaginary fears were suddenly tangible but that made them easier to deal with. They'd emerged from the dark corners of her mind and taken on human form.

She slowed her breathing, feeling the comforting bulk of the walls behind her, thinking through the alternatives. She could go back outside and hope to run for it, but that would make her an easy target. There was the forest on one side of the cottage, the exposed dunes and beach on the other. Where would she run? Or she could hide somewhere in the house. That seemed equally hazardous, even assuming she could find a suitable place. Claire didn't like the idea of sitting waiting, it wasn't in her nature to be passive, and besides, she had an idea that whoever was out there liked playing games with their victims. Kuypers' body dumped in her car, the electricity supply being cut. Those were the actions of a man showing his power, toying with her before he finished her off. The thought chilled her, but she shut it out, concentrating on her next move.

She had to take the fight to him. He'd expect her to be terrified. She was a woman, vulnerable. He would be sure of himself, perhaps over-confident. He wouldn't expect her to make the first move. She guessed he was somewhere out at the back. He must have cut off the electricity at the fuse box, but where was that? She hadn't seen it in the kitchen. It was probably in the outhouse by the back door. She listened hard. She could hear nothing except her own pulse drumming in her ears.

The embers in the hearth made a faint crackling noise. A glowing sliver of wood burst suddenly into flame for a moment. Claire stared at it, then stood up quickly. She hadn't heard anything, but the fire was more sensitive than her ears. Something had created a draught. Something like the back door opening. Claire crept quietly along the side of the room and stopped by the door to the stairwell. She had the knife in her left hand, the tyre iron raised in her right, ready to strike. She held her breath, listening.

Whoever it was, he was light on his feet. She heard nothing until the door next to her slowly started to open. Claire waited, the tyre iron weighing heavily on her arm. The door swung wider. She expected a figure to appear and prepared herself to strike. But no one came in.

She looked across the room, noticing for the first time in the firelight a faint silvery sheen on the far wall. A sheen dulled in places by distinct shadows. She recognised the shape of one of the shadows and realised too late what it was: her own reflection in a mirror. She started to move, but the man outside was quicker. The door slammed back hard into her body. It would have knocked her off her feet if the wall behind hadn't been there to hold her up. She felt a shudder of pain as her spine crashed against the brickwork. Then a hand grabbed hold of her wrist and tossed her across the room. She landed on her side and slithered along the wood floor. The tyre iron and knife went flying. Claire heard them clatter against the wall, but it was too dark to see where. The impact had knocked the breath out of her. Her right shoulder and hip were throbbing. She rolled over and saw the man towering above her, his face burnished with light from the fire. His hair was cropped short in military fashion, accentuating the hard leanness of his features, his mouth twisted into a curve that might have been either a grin or a snarl. He crouched down, reaching out for her. Claire kicked him. Her foot smashed into his torso but he barely flinched. The vibrations shuddered up her leg, jolting her backwards. She twisted her head, looking around for a weapon, her fingers groping across the floor, trying to find something – anything – to use against him.

One of his hands tore at her jacket, ripping it open. He fumbled for the waistband of her jeans. Claire felt a surge of hope. He was a powerful man. He could have killed her instantly, snapped her neck like balsa wood, but he wanted to draw it out. He wanted to see her frightened, to hurt her first. That was a mistake she could turn to her advantage.

His fingers were hooked under the top of her jeans, tugging them down. Claire stopped struggling suddenly, letting her body go limp. The man paused, glancing up at her face. He had cruel, icy eyes. A sadist's eyes. Claire waited for him to drop his guard. She saw his lips move in a smile of triumph, his gaze drop to her crotch. Then, simultaneously, she clawed at his face with her fingers and brought her right knee up hard into his groin. The man grunted and clutched himself. Claire's fingernails dug into his eye sockets, gouging at the delicate membranes. The man flailed out, trying to grasp her arms, but Claire was already rolling over, twisting sideways and squirming out from under him.

He spat out an exclamation in a language she didn't understand and went for her angrily. Claire kicked out desperately, sliding backwards across the floor. She knew she had to get to her feet to give herself any chance of survival. To run for it, escape the house and seek refuge in the forest. His fingers closed around her right ankle. Claire kicked him in the face with her other foot and wriggled free. She got to her knees and was almost upright when he threw himself at her, his weight crushing her to the floor. He slapped her face, shouting something in his own language. Claire's head snapped round, her eyes watering with pain. She blinked, feeling his hands on her breasts, between her legs.

Then she saw it.

A length of steel glinting at the base of the wall. The tyre iron. Her hand stretched out. Just a bit further. Just a few more centimetres. She could almost touch it. She summoned all her strength, twisting round to give herself that extra bit of reach. Her fingers closed around the metal. She brought the tyre iron up in an arc and smashed it hard into the side of the man's head. He slumped over, moaning in agony, his hands trying to stanch the blood. Claire hit him again. His eyes went suddenly blank. He rolled on to the floor and was still.

Claire slithered away and stood up. She gazed down at him, panting for breath. It was a while before she could bring herself to touch him. Her fingers felt for the pulse on the side of his neck. It was there, faint but detectable. He was still alive. She left him lying on the floor and went out of the cottage, running hard through the forest, down the muddy track on to the main road and back towards a farmhouse whose lights glimmered dimly on the horizon.

Claire let the police go in before her. One of the officers found the fuse box in the outhouse and restored the electricity supply. The cottage lights blazed back on, blinding them all for an instant. Claire let her eyes adjust, then stared around the living room. There was a puddle of blood on the wooden floor and more red smears by the door. But the wounded man had gone.

TWELVE

Hal Montague liked a full house for the weekend. He was a gregarious man who was fond of company and took genuine pleasure in seeing others enjoying themselves, but what he liked most – and he was honest enough to admit it – was showing off. And he had plenty to show off. His country house in Norfolk was a handsome red-brick mansion, parts of which dated back to the sixteenth century, with six hundred acres of parkland and woods and some of the finest shooting in East Anglia. Though small by stately-home standards, it was grand enough to impress almost anyone except the landed aristocracy and royalty – two categories of people with whom he never had the slightest inclination to mix. They were too inbred, too stupid and too terminally dull for his tastes. Yet even they would have been hard-pressed not to admire the opulence of the house, the rich furnishings and antiques that filled it, the stable of twenty horses and the extravagant quantities of food and drink lavished on the guests. Montague might not have had much of a pedigree, but what he lacked in lineage he more than made up for in hard cash.

It was his custom, whenever he was in the UK for a weekend, to invite a group of friends and acquaintances to stay. Or rather, to get his wife to invite them for him. Serena was good at organising house parties. She had a knack of selecting exactly the right combination of guests, choosing people who would gel well together but who were sufficiently different to ensure that the weekend stayed lively without becoming acrimonious. She was also skilled at inviting individuals who might be of assistance to her husband – he was often astonished at just how astute some of her choices turned out to be.

Montague watched her now, sitting at the opposite end of the table orchestrating the lunchtime conversation to make sure everyone was included. She was a very beautiful woman. A cynic – and plenty of people were cynical about Hal Montague – would have called her a trophy wife. There was some truth in the accusation, even Montague acknowledged that. She was twenty years younger than he was, a second wife acquired after a bitter divorce, and she fitted many of the other stereotypes of the breed: she was attractive, well-dressed, nubile. But she was no one's trophy. Serena Montague would never be dressing for any man's table or bed, nor a bimbo to hang off his arm or an exhibit to bolster his ego – and anyone foolhardy enough to suggest it to her face would have rapidly found themselves in need of the nearest Casualty Department.

Montague caught her eye and smiled. She'd selected an interesting collection of guests this weekend. Simon Doyle and another business colleague; a pony-tailed artist whose work Serena liked buying though Montague would have baulked at even hanging his canvases in the stable block for fear of frightening the horses; a showbiz couple who thought they were rather more fascinating than anyone else did; and a pompous but insecure junior minister at the Department of Trade and Industry and his wife who seemed overawed by the whole occasion.

Montague disliked politicians as a species. He regarded them as vain, avaricious, essentially talentless individuals, elevated to a station well above their abilities and fit only for the House of Commons, which he saw as an anachronistic club for sycophants and ambitious no-hopers. He despised them, but recognised they were influential people worth cultivating. He had several backbenchers on his books as paid consultants – tame poodles who could be relied on to put the interests of their wallets before the interests of the country – and there were many more who'd enjoyed, and been subtly corrupted by, his hospitality. Politicians couldn't resist the high life. They were starstruck by successful businessmen, in thrall to them. They thought businessmen could do anything, run anything, even though the only thing businessmen really knew how to do was make money. Montague was adept at exploiting that delusion. A weekend in the country, a few days on his yacht in the Med, and it was amazing how receptive politicians became not just to his particular brand of free-market ideology – of which he had practical experience – but to his opinions on a dozen or more other subjects about which he knew absolutely nothing.

The dining-room door opened and the housekeeper came in. She went straight to Simon Doyle and whispered in his ear. Doyle got up from his chair and headed for the door, glancing across at Montague who raised an enquiring eyebrow at him. Doyle shook his head and left the room.

Montague topped up his wine glass with Puligny-Montrachet and passed the bottle to the elderly man sitting on his right hand. Dr Julius Wolf was a regular visitor to the house but he was hardly the life and soul of the party. He spent most of his time in his room, watching a catholic selection of pornographic movies which Montague always provided for his amusement. Montague didn't know why he watched them – nostalgia perhaps – for the old duffer was almost certainly impotent, age and the three bottles of wine he consumed daily would have seen to that. Montague invited him out of pity and a sense of obligation for it was Wolf who had introduced him to the lucrative possibilities of cigarette-trafficking and who, though now a sleeping partner in the enterprise – sometimes literally – was still a valuable source of advice.

Montague liked doing business with Swiss traders like Wolf. You knew where you stood with them. Unlike the Latin races, or even the north Europeans, the Swiss never did anything for sentimental or altruistic reasons. The bottom line was the only thing that concerned them. They were crooks, of course, but Montague understood that. He was one himself. But the key thing about Switzerland – that perfectly placed Fifth Column, at the very heart of Europe, yet outside the EU and so ideal for trafficking and money-laundering – was that because of its commercial secrecy laws no one could ever find out exactly how crooked you were.

Doyle came back into the room and crossed immediately to Montague, bending down and saying quietly: 'I think you'd better come. Frank Barron's on the phone.'

'What does he want?' Montague said after they'd left the dining room and were walking down the hall towards the study. Frank Barron was a senior civil servant in the Ministry of Agriculture, Fisheries and Food.

'Someone has been asking questions about the Intervention Board investigation into Horningtoft.'

Montague jolted to a halt. 'What? Who?'

'UCLAF.'

'Shit!'

Montague went into the study and picked up the phone as Doyle shut the door behind them.

'What the fuck's going on, Frank? I thought you'd buried that investigation.'

Barron let out a feeble sigh. 'So did I, Hal, believe me.'

'So how did UCLAF get on to it?'

'I don't know. As far as MAFF is concerned it's dead in the water. The file has been destroyed, all mention of it deleted from the computer records. I have no control over UCLAF but there's nothing for them to find.'

'There'd better not be,' Montague said menacingly. 'Not if you think you're retiring from Whitehall and slipping into some nice cushy non-executive directorships with my companies.'

'Relax, Hal, there's nothing to worry about. Everything remotely incriminating has been destroyed. I'm just letting you know, that's all.'

'I expect to be protected on this one, Frank, you understand me? It's your neck on the block as well as mine. If I go down I'll make sure a lot of others go with me.'

Barron swallowed. 'There's no need to get so angry about it.'

'There's every fucking need. You were supposed to have taken care of all this. Why do you think I paid you all that money?'

'Hal, I assure you . . .'

'Yes, yes,' Montague interrupted. 'I want no excuses. What's the name of the UCLAF investigator?'

'Sullivan. Rob Sullivan.'

'British?'

'Yes.'

'Good. You keep your eye on this one, Frank. I want this investigation blocked.'

'I'll do my best, but it may not be easy. Brussels is outside my jurisdiction.'

'Don't give me that shit,' Montague spat down the phone. 'You're a civil servant. Stalling, delaying, sitting on your hands, it's what you're fucking trained to do. And I expect you to do it for me.'

Montague slammed the receiver down hard and stood up, pacing agitatedly around the study.

'Those UCLAF bastards are sticking their noses into my affairs,' he said furiously, clenching his teeth and fists.

'Why would they be interested in some four-year-old investigation that went nowhere?' Doyle said calmly.

'They're not, you know that as well as I do. They're on our fucking tails. Or they think they are.'

Doyle rested his backside on the edge of the desk, watching his employer roaming restlessly across the room. It wasn't often that he saw Montague this rattled.

'Maybe we should be careful, lie low for a while.'

'No way,' Montague said irascibly. 'Those Brussels wankers don't scare me. Bunch of narrow-minded bureaucrats who couldn't investigate their way out of a paper bag.'

'Van Vliet's worried about them.'

'No wonder, they've been taking his warehouse apart. But nothing can be traced directly back to us. The important thing is not to panic, to carry on exactly as normal. But just as a precaution I want you to make sure everyone involved knows to keep their mouths shut. If anyone comes asking questions, they say nothing and let me know immediately.'

Doyle nodded. 'You trust Barron?'

'He'll do his best, but that's not really good enough. As with everything else, if you want something doing properly, do it yourself. Get me Rupert Bird.'

Doyle pushed himself off the desk, looked up a number in his contacts book and dialled it. He handed the receiver to Montague.

'Go and see to the guests. I'll be in shortly,' Montague said.

A voice came on the line.

'Hello?'

'Rupert? Hal Montague.'

Serena was upstairs in her bedroom, changing into her riding clothes, when Doyle walked in. He closed the door and leaned back on it, watching her doing up the buttons on her white, high-necked blouse. She looked good in jodhpurs and boots. They showed off her legs, her tight buttocks. She turned away from the mirror and smiled at him.

'Lock the door, Simon.'

'What?'

'Do you want Hal to walk in on us?'

She took hold of her dark hair and twisted it up on to the back of her head, fastening it in place with a metal clip. Doyle locked the door and came across the room to her.

'How are the guests?' she said.

'Whitton is fixing the ladies up with hard hats and boots. Hal's showing the men the billiards room and then they're going out shooting. Well, all except Wolf. He's gone to his room with a bottle of port.'

'He give me the creeps, that man. I wish Hal wouldn't invite him.'

'Be nice to him, Serena. We may need him. He's an old drunk but he still has a lot of influence.'

Serena adjusted her cravat and slipped on her riding jacket.

'He's a pervert. Every time he looks at me I get the feeling he wants to strip me naked and do God knows what to me.'

Doyle's mouth curled. 'I thought you liked that.'

She glanced at him over her shoulder. 'It depends who's doing the stripping.'

She buttoned up her jacket and turned to face him.

'Well?'

Doyle studied her dispassionately, trying to suppress the stirrings she always aroused in him. They were playing a dangerous game. He knew that was part of the appeal for Serena. In everything she did, riding, skiing, sex, it was the element of risk she liked. The greater the danger, the greater her enjoyment. But he was more careful. Risk for him was something you calculated and eliminated. It was a means, not an end.

'Very nice,' he said coolly.

'Is that all?' she said, feigning disappointment.

'You look good in riding clothes.'

'But better without them, eh?'

She picked up her riding crop from the bed and ran the tip of it up the inside of his leg. He took hold of the crop and pulled her to him, kissing her roughly.

Serena pushed him away, her objective fulfilled.

'That's better,' she said. 'I hate your self-control.'

She turned to look at herself in the floor-length mirror again.

'What was the phone call?' she asked. 'Hal looked absolutely livid when he came back in.'

'His lapdog at MAFF.'

'Trouble?'

Doyle shook his head. 'Nothing we can't handle.'

'Are you sure?'

'Trust me, Serena.'

She glanced at her watch and pouted.

'I suppose I ought to join the ladies. What are you going to do, go shooting?'

Doyle sneered. 'What, potting a few bloody rabbits with the green-wellie brigade? You must be joking.'

'Poor Simon,' Serena said, stroking his face sympathetically. 'We'll have to find something to amuse you later.'

The tide had gone out, leaving the boats stranded on the mud flats, some tilted over sideways on their hulls, others with their keels half buried in the sticky brown ooze. Mooring ropes hung loose from the harbour wall, straddling the channel which the sea and river had cut deep into the salt marshes. Only a narrow ribbon of dirty water meandered its way out to the ocean, navigable in a rowing boat or canoe but nothing bigger. It was a bright, clear day. A stiff breeze was blowing in over the land, tugging at the metal halyards on the yachts so they tinkled against the masts like tin cans on a string.

'There you are,' Jim Bristow said, pointing across the flats at a bird with black and white plumage and a deep orange-red bill. 'Oystercatcher. You see it?'

He handed Sullivan his binoculars and Sullivan felt obliged to look though he had no interest whatsoever in birds.

'Beautiful, isn't she?'

'Mmm,' Sullivan murmured.

'They're here all winter. Oystercatchers, grey plovers, curlews, dunlins, all manner of shore waders. People say it's a dull time of year, February, before the spring migrants arrive, but I find plenty to look at.'

Sullivan gave him back his binoculars and buried his hands in his pockets. He wasn't dressed for a walk along the Norfolk coast in mid-winter, but Bristow had insisted they went out, whether because he wanted the fresh air or because he felt more comfortable talking in the open Sullivan wasn't sure. There was something cautious about him: the way he'd refused to say much on the telephone, his reluctance to discuss anything inside his house. Paranoid was too strong a word, but Bristow was certainly taking no chances that anyone might eavesdrop on their conversation.

'Horningtoft,' Sullivan prompted him.

Bristow took a last look at the oystercatcher and walked on along the path which followed the top of a raised dyke between the mud flats and the Overy marshes.

'I took early retirement,' he said. 'I'd had enough of all the crap you get in the CPS. The bureaucracy, the constant reorganisation, patronising magistrates who know damn-all about the law, whingeing coppers who moan on and on about guilty criminals who're never brought to trial but who don't give you the evidence to make a case in the first place.

'I couldn't wait to get out. My son and his family had settled up here so I moved from Norwich to be near them. I do a bit of painting, watercolours mostly – this coast is beautiful for painting, you should see the light on an autumn evening. And I've always liked birds. I've been here nearly four years now. I'm reasonably contented. Why should I dig up old memories of some trivial legal case I'd rather forget all about?'

'Would you?' Sullivan said. 'Then why did you invite me here?'

'You won't manage to revive it, you know.'

'That's not what I want.'

Bristow turned his head to look at him. He had a walker's build, tall and rangy with long legs and a measured gait that gave the impression he could keep going all day without feeling fatigue.

'What *do* you want, Mr Sullivan?' he said.

'I'm not sure at the moment. If you tell me about Horningtoft, I might have a clearer idea.'

Bristow was silent for a time, collecting his thoughts.

Then he said: 'Have you heard of a man called Henry Montague?'

'No.'

'He's a businessman. Calls himself Hal, like Henry the Fifth – an absurd affectation, but he's rich enough to afford a little vanity. He has a big estate not far from here, Horningtoft Priory, hence the name of his company. *One* of his companies, I should say. He has dozens, maybe hundreds. He's that kind of businessman. Everything concealed behind a web of impenetrable corporations.'

'What's his principal business, agriculture?' Sullivan said.

'Hardly. Montague is a hobby farmer. That's not to say he doesn't take it seriously – he takes everything he does very seriously – but he doesn't devote much time to it.

188

He comes into the country at weekends, talks to his estate manager, strolls around in wellies and pokes the occasional pig. But he doesn't know the first thing about farming. His main interests are in the City.'

'Doing what?'

Bristow smiled sardonically. 'What does anyone in the City do? He's what you might call a 'player'. Buys and sells companies, invests in speculative ventures, moves bits of paper around – well, it's all done electronically now, you don't even need to lift any paper, just press a few buttons and the computer does the rest for you. Nice work if you can get it. If you're part of the coterie of old school and university chums who pass jobs around between themselves, charging vast commissions, scratching each other's back with large wads of cash.'

'You've met him?'

Bristow shook his head. 'But I made a few enquiries after the Intervention Board report landed on my desk. Got him worried enough to reveal his true nature. He made it his business to threaten me.'

'He *threatened* you?' Sullivan said.

'Why do you think I wasn't anxious to talk about him on the phone? He's a dangerous man with powerful connections.'

'What did he do?'

'Oh, nothing overt, nothing you could ever prove against him, but it was a threat nonetheless. He didn't do it himself, of course. He got his assistant to do it for him. A nasty piece of work named Simon Doyle.'

'Doyle?'

'You know him?'

'Just the name. He's a director of another company I've been looking into.'

'Oh yes, he's on the board of quite a few of Montague's companies. Men like Hal Montague always need a Simon

Doyle, a reliable sidekick who doesn't mind getting his hands dirty, a lackey – well-paid, but still a lackey – who's always there to wipe his arse for him.'

'I see you're a fan of Montague's.'

'He has the arrogance of a certain class of Englishman who thinks he can do anything, get away with anything. He was outraged that anyone – particularly a provincial prosecutor like me – could be so presumptuous as to question his probity.'

'He's a criminal?' Sullivan said.

'I doubt he'd use the word. He'd be affronted. To Montague, criminals are working-class people who mug old ladies in the street or break into houses and steal your video recorder. Montague is a businessman, an entrepreneur who plays the system. A system which glorifies people like him.'

Bristow sighed. 'Maybe it's my age, maybe I'm old-fashioned, but I don't understand this modern cult of the businessman. We're supposed to admire them for their energy, their daring, but what are they except well-dressed wideboys flogging dodgy goods off the back of a lorry? The only difference between Hal Montague and some East End gangland thug is that Montague knows the words to the Eton Boating Song.'

'He went to Eton?'

'Harrow, actually, but you get my point. Harrow's on a hill, isn't it? Maybe they have a Mountaineering Song.'

Sullivan smiled. At his Leeds comprehensive they hadn't concerned themselves much with vocal tradition.

'So what did the Horningtoft report say?' he asked.

Bristow lifted his binoculars and trained them on a bird far out on the rippled surface of the mud flats.

'Curlew,' he said. 'You want a look?'

'No thanks,' Sullivan said.

'You know, what I like most about birds is that you can

see them. They don't hide in burrows or only come out at night. They're there every day, all around you. On the ground, in the air, I never tire of watching them.'

They were nearing the sea now, the salt marshes petering out against the base of the dunes that formed a long ridge behind the beach. The sky, veined with torn strands of cloud, filled the horizon. Sullivan could almost feel its weight pressing down on the thin sliver of earth around him. He looked across to the mouth of the estuary where a strip of sand was bathed in sunshine. It was so quiet he could hear the rushes swaying in the breeze. Then the shrill cry of birds broke the silence. A distant flock of gulls rose into the air like flecks of dirt, curling around and swooping away towards the sea.

'You work for the European Commission,' Bristow said. 'You must know better than anyone what a target the EU is for criminals. There's a lot of money swilling around over there in Brussels. It's a gravy train that everyone wants to jump on to, but not everyone wants to pay for their ticket. The farmers around here have benefited enormously from the CAP. Sometimes I wonder how anything got grown before we joined the Common Market. There's a culture of subsidy in the agricultural industry. Farmers can't even fart without being given a methane support grant from Brussels. But they've become so dependent on handouts they've become greedy. And a lot take advantage of the system.'

'Did Montague?'

'Of course. Horningtoft is a farm management company. You knew that, I assume. There are economies of scale in running several farms together, even the ones round here which are some of the largest in Europe. The EU support payments can be huge – up to half a million pounds for a single farm. Horningtoft were suspected of breaking their milk quota, producing more than their allocation and selling it on the black market. It's quite a temptation to a farmer. If he produces too much milk, he has to pour it down the drain. He's not allowed to sell it. And yet we import milk from other EU countries to meet our needs. It's crazy.'

Sullivan nodded. It was one of the many absurdities of the Common Agricultural Policy. The UK could have been self-sufficient in milk production, but because of its quota allocation was forced to buy in part of its requirements from overseas. Many dairies and cheese manufacturers, starved of home-produced milk and so obliged to pay more for imports, were not averse to buying a little extra non-quota milk from their local farmers at a knockdown price.

'There were also irregularities in applications for crop subsidy and set-aside,' Bristow continued. 'Discrepancies in the tonnage of wheat eligible for price support, and doubts over the growing of wheat for industrial use on set-aside land. A very grey area, as you know.'

Sullivan shook his head. 'I'm not an agricultural specialist. What do you mean?'

'A farmer can claim payment for setting aside land, but that doesn't mean he has to leave it fallow. He's allowed to grow crops on it provided they're not for human consumption. So he can grow wheat for industrial purposes – fuel for example – and sell it without losing his set-aside allowance. You can see the problem. Do you know anyone who can tell the difference between wheat grown for human consumption and wheat grown for some other purpose? The whole thing's a farce.'

'Irregularities, you said?'

'Administrative errors was what Montague called them.'

'How much was involved?'

'Over a period of several years, about five and a half million ECUs.'

Sullivan paused for a second, astonished, then he walked on.

'That's some administrative error.'

'Montague claimed one of his managers was responsible and sacked him. Paid him off to keep his mouth shut was the rumour I heard. It was clearly fraud.'

'Yet he wasn't prosecuted.'

'No, he wasn't.'

'Why not?'

'That's a good question. I wish I knew the answer.'

They walked up a slight incline on to the top of the dunes. The whole sweep of Holkham Bay, a vast expanse of gleaming wet sand, was before them. Apart from a woman walking her dog, the shoreline was deserted.

'The case was taken out of my hands by my superior,' Bristow continued.

'Newman?'

'His predecessor, a man named Charmbury. But it's no use asking him. He retired shortly after I did and was dead two years later – liver cancer. No further action was taken. Charmbury said there wasn't enough evidence to prosecute.'

'Was there?'

'In my opinion, yes.'

'You couldn't persuade Charmbury to proceed?'

'I tried.' Bristow hesitated. 'I was told in no uncertain terms to leave it well alone. I think it was one of the reasons they offered me early retirement. I've no real proof of this, but I got the feeling that someone further up the line had made the decision not to prosecute.'

'What do you mean, "further up the line"?'

'In London.'

Sullivan stared at him. 'You mean the DPP's office?'

Bristow nodded.

'Why?' Sullivan said.

193

'Montague is an influential man. He has a lot of friends.'

'Enough to influence the DPP?'

Bristow laughed cynically. 'Who can tell? I know one thing though, I worked for the CPS long enough to realise that decisions whether to prosecute are not always taken for legal reasons.'

'You're saying someone's protecting him?'

'What do you think? Who destroyed the CPS and Intervention Board records of the case?'

They walked on along the dunes. The sand was soft and fine as dust, held in place by clumps of tall marram grass whose stalks were bent almost to the ground by the wind. Down on the beach the dog was splashing in and out of the water, retrieving a ball thrown by its owner. An occasional bark ripped through the cold afternoon air.

Then Bristow said: 'If you're not an agricultural specialist, Mr Sullivan, why are you interested in Horningtoft?'

Sullivan took a moment to reply. 'I'm fishing, I suppose. Looking for possible links with another case I'm working on.'

'Some other kind of fraud?'

'Something like that,' Sullivan replied evasively.

'Don't insult me. You came here asking for confidential information. Do me the courtesy of telling me why.'

'I'm sorry,' Sullivan said. 'Yes, you're entitled to know. Cigarette-trafficking.'

Bristow turned his head. He had a thin, bony face and bushy salt-and-pepper eyebrows. Wisps of untidy light hair protruded from beneath the sides of his pork-pie hat.

'You suspect Montague of cigarette-trafficking?' he said, disbelief in his voice.

'You think it unlikely?'

'No, I don't. It just took me by surprise. I wouldn't put anything past a man like Montague. But I'd be careful, Mr Sullivan. He may be too big to get caught.'

'His friends, you mean?'

'There's an old adage in business,' Bristow said. 'If you borrow ten thousand pounds from the bank, you're at their mercy. If you borrow ten million, they're at *your* mercy. It's the same everywhere. Fiddle a hundred pounds on your tax bill and the Inland Revenue will spend thousands chasing you to get it back. Fiddle millions and you get a knighthood for services to industry. It never pays to be a small fish in the sea. You get eaten too easily.'

'I don't follow you.'

'Prosecuting someone like Montague would be an embarrassment to the government. The amounts involved are too great. They'd prefer to sweep it all under the carpet and pretend it never happened. Besides, do you really want to be the Eliot Ness of Eurofraud?'

'Pardon?'

'Don't waste your bullets. You'll only get one shot at a man like Hal Montague. Remember Al Capone. A bootlegger, murderer, one of the worst gangsters in history and yet all Ness managed to pin on him was a charge of tax evasion. If Montague's trafficking in cigarettes, cheating the EU of millions, you don't want to prosecute him for fiddling his milk quotas, do you?'

Bristow turned away, raising his binoculars and focusing them on a tiny bird of prey hovering over the marshes.

'Merlin,' he murmured softly.

Sullivan lifted his head and watched as the merlin plummeted into a steep dive, sleek and streamlined, its wings swept back. It raced towards the ground then pulled up suddenly into a perfect glide, swooping low over the salt grass to take its unseen, unsuspecting prey.

THIRTEEN

When Sullivan first joined UCLAF, he'd been taken for lunch in the Beaulieu canteen by a colleague, a garrulous Welshman named Barry Morgan who worked in TF4, the unit responsible for fighting fraud against the structural funds of the EU.

Morgan had told him a story about a poor village in southern Spain which was twinned with an equally poor village in Greece. One summer, the mayor of the Greek village visited his counterpart in the Spanish village and was taken aback by his host's opulent house – a large, porticoed villa with lush gardens and its own swimming pool.

'How on earth can you afford a place like this?' the Greek asked in astonishment. 'You're only a struggling farmer like me.'

The Spanish mayor took his visitor out into his garden and pointed down into the valley.

'You see that bridge across the ravine? We got funds from Brussels to build a four-lane highway across it, but we made it one lane instead and put traffic lights at each end. *That's* what paid for this house.'

A few years later the Greek mayor returned the favour and invited the Spaniard to his village in southern Greece. The Spanish mayor walked into the Greek's house, his jaw dropping at the marble floors, the paintings on the walls, the patio and large swimming pool he could see outside in the garden.

'What the hell were you going on about *my* house for?' he said. 'Look at this place. How does a poor farmer like you afford a home like this?'

'Ah,' said the Greek, leading his visitor outside into the landscaped gardens. 'You see that bridge down there in the valley?'

The Spaniard squinted into the distance. 'No, I don't see any bridge.'

'That's what paid for this house,' said the Greek.

It was a joke, but only just, as Sullivan discovered when Morgan took him back to his office and pulled out a pile of files which detailed the misappropriation of EU structural funds.

'It's all in there,' Morgan said. 'The projects which never happened: bridges which were never built, roads which go nowhere, community sports centres which turned out to be a pool and tennis court in the mayor's back garden. We have the names, the towns, the amounts involved. Millions and millions embezzled. All of it true.'

'Jesus,' Sullivan said, flicking through the documents. 'Have you recovered any of it?'

'Almost none. We prepare reports and send them to the public prosecutors in the responsible member states, but most of them do sod-all about it. No legal proceedings, no money repaid, not a single penny. It happens all the time. That's the depressing thing. We have no powers to prosecute ourselves, we depend on the member states to do it. If they choose not to, we can do nothing to make them.'

Morgan grinned. 'Welcome to UCLAF, boyo. I'm telling you, by the time you finish your attachment you'll have a big bruise right here in the middle of your forehead from banging your head against a brick wall.'

So far, Sullivan had escaped the bruise, but he'd had quite

a few headaches. The system was a mess, a fraudster's dream. A budget of eighty billion Euros distributed around fifteen different countries by twenty-plus directorates within the Commission, none of whom had the slightest idea what the others were doing, and all of it monitored, in theory, by a tiny unit of eighty investigators with no police or prosecuting powers.

There was a lot of truth in what Bristow had said about Montague being too big and influential to prosecute. It was common knowledge that EU governments didn't report a large proportion of the frauds they detected in their own countries. It made them look bad if their citizens were seen to be dishonest and there was a real possibility that money lost to fraud would have to be repaid to the Commission, something no government was keen to do. Sullivan had no illusions about his fellow countrymen, but it had still surprised him that no action had been taken against Hal Montague and Horningtoft.

It was late afternoon when he left Burnham Overy Staithe, still frozen from the walk along the coast despite the tea and toast Bristow had given him afterwards at his house. The village of Horningtoft was only a couple of miles off his route to Colchester and, on impulse, he made a detour to take a look at it.

It was a tiny place, more a hamlet than a village. The Priory, being the only building of any size, was easy to find. Sullivan stopped outside the open gates and looked down the drive at the imposing brick mansion silhouetted against the dusk sky. It was partially hidden behind the skeletal outlines of a copse of leafless trees so Sullivan got out of his car and walked down the drive to get a better look. The house had four storeys, a separate stable block at one end and at the other, incorporated into the fabric of the building, a chapel with ornate Gothic windows which Sullivan guessed had been part of the original priory.

199

The ground-floor windows were illuminated, throwing pools of misty light out on to the gravel forecourt. One of the first-floor windows was also lit up. A figure appeared behind the glass. An elderly man, a little bowed at the shoulders with black-framed spectacles and a shock of silver-grey hair. It was a striking face. Not a face you could easily mistake for any other. Sullivan stared up at it, absorbing the features, trying to recall where he'd seen it before. When it came to him, it was with a sudden jar that momentarily nonplussed him. Surely not. He studied the face again. There was no doubt about it.

'You know you're trespassing, don't you?' a harsh voice said behind him.

Sullivan turned and saw a large hefty man in a Barbour jacket, wellies and flat cap. Tucked under his right arm was a Purdey shotgun.

'Pardon?'

'This is private property,' Montague said. 'I suggest you leave before I call the police.'

Sullivan studied him intently, guessing who he was. He was bigger, fleshier than he'd imagined, his face getting puffy around the cheeks and jowls, his double chin sagging above the neck.

'I was just going. I only wanted to look at the house,' Sullivan said.

'When we want tourists and day-trippers rubbernecking around the place, we'll put a sign up by the gates,' Montague replied with a sneer. 'Robinson, see this man off the estate.'

Five other men had come across the lawns behind Montague, all carrying shotguns. One of them, a game-keeper by the look of him, stepped forward out of the group and waited for Sullivan to walk away up the drive. He followed him to the gates and watched as Sullivan climbed into his car and drove away. Then he took a pen out of his inside coat pocket and scribbled the number of the car on the palm of his hand.

The road took a loop around the side of the Priory, heading away from the village. Looking across through the gloom, Sullivan could vaguely make out the shapes of figures going up the steps into the house. He turned off right, negotiating his way back to the main road through the twilit countryside. The horizon was a vista of dark clouds slashed with pale streaks of light which glanced off the bare fields, tinting the furrows of frozen earth with a sheen of platinum. Sullivan barely noticed. He had other things on his mind.

The first thing that struck him when he got home was the noise level. Living on his own for most of the time he got used to silence, and the return to family life was always a rude awakening.

Patrick and James were playing some indefinable game which, like most of their games, seemed to involve charging around the house at high speed, shouting and yelling and hitting each other with whatever came to hand. Sullivan and Kate retreated to the kitchen and sat at the table drinking tea, talking about what had happened since they last spoke on the telephone. It was an unsatisfactory way of keeping in touch, these catch-up conversations which could never hope to recapture the immediacy and spontaneity of actually living the experiences together. But it was a method they'd evolved over the previous two years to keep each other informed about the separate strands of their lives.

Sometimes Sullivan got the impression that it was becoming an effort for Kate to recount to him what had occurred during his absence. Every time he came home she seemed more tired, more rundown than before. It was particularly bad this time, but then she'd just come to the end of the first half of the spring term – the most depressing of the school year with its dark, cold days – and was in need of a break.

'Would you mind if we didn't come back with you tomorrow?' she said, broaching something which had obviously been troubling her.

'Why? What's happened?' Sullivan said sharply.

Kate and the boys always came over to Brussels for the half-term holiday. His wife had given no hint on the telephone that she wanted to change the arrangement.

'I thought we might make our own way over later. Maybe Tuesday. I'm tired, so are the boys. And I've got a lot of stuff to prepare for school. I need a couple of days here.'

Kate listened to the appeasing tone in her voice and wondered why she had to justify herself. She knew he didn't understand what hard work it was uprooting every holiday to stay with him. He just carried on as normal, taking the occasional day off to do something with them, but for her and the boys it was disruptive and exhausting. They had to pack, arrange their travel, endure the journey, adapt to the apartment in Tervuren where none of them felt at home. The whole thing was a chore and the boys were starting to resent it. They had friends in England they wanted to see in the holidays and Brussels bored them. Kate put up with all the hassle – and most of it fell on her – because she believed it was important to keep the family together. But even she was beginning to wonder if it was worth it.

'Oh,' was all Sullivan said.

'We'll still have most of the week with you,' Kate continued, trying to sound upbeat.

'Fine, that's okay.'

'You don't mind?'

'No, why should I?'

Kate was a little taken aback. She'd thought he would

be more difficult. School holidays in Brussels had hitherto been a sacrosanct part of their family life, something that was fixed and untouchable. She knew that Rob, for all his veneer of modern enlightenment – his approval of women having careers, of equal rights and the rest of it – still deep down believed a wife's place was with her husband. She'd expected much more hostility to a change in their routine.

'Are you sure?' she said.

'Yes. Come over whenever you're ready.'

He smiled at her. He was thinking of Claire Colmar, remembering the night in her apartment and anticipating, with a mixture of exhilaration and guilt, another clandestine encounter.

The Eurostar terminal at Waterloo had been deliberately – and expensively – designed to look nothing like a traditional British railway station. There were carpets on the floor of the departure lounge, soft lighting and overpriced souvenir and gift shops. The toilets had fake marble washbasins and individual hand-dryers next to each one, and the coffee shop served espresso and cappuccino and six different types of tea. It was all very comfortable and pleasant yet somehow bland and characterless, just like the airport terminals it had been built to resemble – as if airport architecture were something worth emulating.

Sullivan arrived early for his train back to Brussels. He slid his ticket into the automatic check-in machine and passed through the barrier into the terminal. In a glass-walled booth to one side, a Eurostar employee and a tall, cadaverous man in a dark mackintosh were scrutinising the passengers as they went through passport control. Sullivan glanced at them casually and made his way out into the crowded departure lounge.

Queuing up at the coffee shop, he bought a cup of Earl Grey and a Danish pastry which, from the price, must have been flown in specially from Copenhagen. Then he found an empty table and sat down, feeling almost nostalgic for the days of British Rail: the draughty platforms; the waiting rooms which were stuffy in summer, freezing in winter; the stewed tea strong enough to remove the enamel from your teeth and the appalling standard of service which – like the Blitz – gave the British a feeling of solidarity, of common purpose and, above all, a universal, enduring subject to moan about.

The Eurostar terminal was too artificial, too regulated an environment to create any kind of rapport between the diverse passengers scattered around the departure lounge. Sullivan had waited there on countless occasions but not once had any other traveller attempted to converse with him. Which was why he was so surprised when the cadaverous man he'd seen in passport control came up to him and said curtly: 'Mr Sullivan?'

'Yes.'

'I wonder if I might have a word with you?'

'What about?' Sullivan said, thinking it was probably some customer service or marketing survey. He'd been cornered before and persuaded to answer a few harmless questions, killing time while he waited for his train. But the questioners had always been attractive young women in Eurostar uniforms, not middle-aged men with red noses, and none of them had ever known his name.

The man glanced around and gestured towards the side of the lounge.

'Perhaps we could talk somewhere a little more private?' he said nasally, exuding a faint aroma of menthol cough sweets.

Sullivan was intrigued enough to pick up his bags and follow the man over to the seating area by the windows which was almost empty.

'How did you know my name?' he asked.

Rupert Bird ignored the question. It was hardly worth an answer. The registration number of the car at Horningtoft – easily traceable to a hire company at Waterloo – a description from Montague plus the Eurostar passenger reservations list made the identification elementary even for a desk man like him.

'I work for the government,' he began. 'The British government,' he added in case there was any doubt.

'Oh yes. Which bit?'

'The Foreign Office,' Bird said reluctantly, gauging how much he should reveal. 'We understand you've been asking questions about Henry Montague.'

Sullivan kept his face expressionless, wondering who had told them. Not Bristow, surely. He was a cynic, an outsider, whilst this man with his chalk-striped suit and his plummy public-school drawl had Establishment stamped all over him.

'How do you know that?'

Bird gave a dismissive shrug. 'That doesn't need to concern you.'

He took a soggy handkerchief out of his coat pocket and blew his nose, wiping his nostrils carefully.

'And what if I say it does concern me?' Sullivan asked.

Bird put his handkerchief away and said thickly: 'Would you mind telling me why you're interested in him?'

'Yes, I would mind,' Sullivan replied. The man's manner, patronising, arrogant, annoyed him.

'Ah,' Bird said. 'I was hoping you would be a little more cooperative.'

'I'll cooperate if you tell me who you are and why you want to know. Show me some ID.'

'This is an unofficial approach, Mr Sullivan. All off the record.'

'What's your name?'

'You don't need to know that.'

'Tell me,' Sullivan said acidly. 'Can you give me any good reason why I should talk about my work to a complete stranger who approaches me at a railway station and won't tell me who he is? If not, I suggest you piss off before I call the police.'

'That wouldn't be a good idea.'

'You could be anyone. How do I know you work for the government?'

'You'll have to take my word for that.'

Sullivan gave a snort of disbelief. 'You're going to have to do better than that.'

Rupert Bird cleared his throat. Damn Hal Montague for making him come back into London on a wet Sunday night when he should have been home in bed with a couple of aspirin and a bucket of hot toddy.

'I'm sure you're a loyal British citizen, Mr Sullivan,' he said. 'Even though you do work in Brussels.'

'The two aren't mutually exclusive, you know,' Sullivan replied.

'Aren't they? What if there's a conflict of interest? Which side would you take then?'

'Conflict of interest?'

'Yes. Which would you put first, your duty to Europe or your duty to your country?'

'I'm not aware of any conflict of interest,' Sullivan said. 'What do you mean?'

'You can't serve two masters, can you? There's your country of birth, where you grew up, where your family lives, where you acquired your cultural and historical ident-ity. Then there's the European Commission, an unelected quango of bureaucrats serving fifteen different countries. When push comes to shove, who do you put first?'

Sullivan was amused by the phrasing, the blatant mani-festation of the Europhobia which infected the corridors of power in London.

206

'Do I have to choose between the two?' he said.

'Don't be naive,' Bird said, turning his head away to sneeze. He blew his nose again on his sopping hanky. The skin around his nostrils was raw and tender. Sullivan drew back as far as his seat allowed, trying to keep away from the germs. 'Do you really think the interests of the UK and Europe are the same?'

'Politicians are always telling us they are,' Sullivan said provocatively.

Bird grunted contemptuously. 'What politicians say and what politicians mean are not always the same thing.'

'But you're a Foreign Office civil servant, aren't you?' Sullivan said. 'Don't you write their speeches for them? Or is that a different bit of the FO?'

Bird didn't reply. Sullivan probed him some more, to see the reaction rather than because he expected an answer.

'Which bit of the Foreign Office are you in, Mr . . . ? And what has Henry Montague, or my work, got to do with you?'

'I believe I asked first,' Bird said, as if they were two kids arguing in the playground. 'What is your interest in Montague?'

Sullivan weighed up his answer. He was inclined to believe the man really did work for the FO. He had all the marks of a particular kind of civil servant: the voice, the clothes, the class traits of condescension and impatience which an impostor could never have mastered this well. But Sullivan's investigation was still none of his business.

'I'm not prepared to tell you that,' he said.

Bird's mouth tightened angrily. He rubbed the edge of his forefinger across the base of his nose, trying to suppress a sneeze which came anyway. The shower of mucus sprayed out on to his coat and he rummaged desperately for his handkerchief to wipe it away. Sullivan watched him, reflecting how the common cold could reduce all men to the same level of spluttering indignity.

'I'm appealing to you as a British citizen,' Bird said eventually. 'Henry Montague does valuable work for this country. We don't want him to be compromised by some misguided investigation into his business affairs.'

'What are you talking about, "valuable work"?'

'You would hardly expect me to tell you that.'

Sullivan realised suddenly, belatedly, which bit of the FO the man worked for.

'You think I'm compromising him?' he said. 'Have you ever thought he might be compromising you?'

Bird brushed aside the question. 'There is nothing for you to find. It might be better if you called off your investigation.'

'Let me get this straight,' Sullivan said. 'You're telling me, an employee of the European Commission, to stop an investigation because it might embarrass the British government?'

'I'm not telling you. I'm merely making a suggestion.'

'And if I say no?'

'That would be unfortunate,' Bird said. 'Let's not be hasty. I hope you give it your full and ample consideration.'

'And if I still refuse?'

'That is your decision entirely.'

'I sense a proviso here,' Sullivan said.

Bird attempted a smile but it twisted mid-way into a sneer. He leaned closer and said menacingly: 'You're not really an employee of the European Commission, are you? You still work for UK Customs and Excise, and when you've finished your junket in Brussels, you'll have to come back to this country. When you do, don't think we won't remember which side you chose.'

Sullivan stared at him. 'You're threatening me?'

'I'm sure you're fully aware of the situation. You're an intelligent man. You can work it out for yourself. Give it some thought, eh?'

'I don't need to think about it,' Sullivan replied, controlling his anger. 'I know exactly where my duty lies. You can take your "suggestion", wrap it up in that snotty handkerchief of yours and shove it so far up your arse you can wipe your nose from the inside.'

He stood up. 'Excuse me, I have a train to catch.'

Montague sometimes wondered what defect in his character had made him deviate from the path of lawful commerce, what fundamental flaw in his make-up had led him to become a trafficker in cigarettes. A fortuitous encounter with Julius Wolf, when the Swiss lawyer was brokering a legitimate business deal for him, had opened up the doors of the smuggling world, but nothing had forced Montague to walk through them, or to seize the opportunity with quite such determined relish. It was easy money, it was true, but money had never been the most important thing in his business life, and besides, he'd made more than he could spend through his legitimate enterprises. He had absolutely no need to turn to crime for the money alone.

So what was it? He knew psychologists recognised that certain types of people required an abnormal level of danger and risk in their lives to keep them happy. Bungee jumpers, powerboat racers, mountaineers, obsessives who parachuted off skyscrapers or slid down Everest on kitchen trays. They were people who were constantly finding some new challenge to stimulate themselves and stave off boredom, even though they knew it might kill them. Montague shared something in common with these individuals – most of whom he regarded as certifiably insane. He'd never felt an overwhelming need for physical danger in his life but he needed risk as surely as he needed air and water. He'd succeeded in business because he lacked the sense of caution most people possessed and, once he'd achieved a certain level of wealth and satisfaction, had turned to trafficking to provide the new challenge his personality and intellect demanded.

He had an immense belief in himself. He'd failed at very few things in his life and though, like any businessman, he'd experienced setbacks, he had always recovered and returned to the fray with renewed vigour. But he was too intelligent not to be aware that self-confidence could easily slip over into hubris. For that reason he'd spent most of Sunday reconsidering his strategy in the light of what Frank Barron had told him the previous day. If he was now under scrutiny by the fraud investigators of the European Commission, it made sense to draw up contingency plans to protect his interests.

He was still in his study, drinking Chablis and talking to Doyle, when Rupert Bird rang him.

'Where are you, Rupert?' he asked.

'On my mobile outside Waterloo Station,' Bird replied, breaking off momentarily to sneeze.

'You located him?'

'Yes.'

'And?'

'No deal, I'm afraid.'

Montague gritted his teeth and rolled his eyes at Doyle.

'What do you mean? You turned the screws, I hope?'

'I appealed to his sense of patriotism,' Bird said.

'You did *what*?' Montague said incredulously. 'What did you do, stand up and sing Land of Hope and Fucking Glory?'

'There's no call for that, Hal. I've come all the way into town for you, and with a streaming cold. You might be a little more grateful.'

'You poor thing,' Montague said sarcastically. 'What did you tell him?'

'I did everything I could. He wouldn't be persuaded.'

'Everyone's persuadable. You just need to know their weaknesses.'

'There are limits to how far I can go,' Bird said stiffly. 'I had to keep it unofficial, you understand that.'

'That should have made it easier. You can say what you like, make threats without any comeback.'

'He refused to cooperate. I spelt out the consequences to him, but it made no difference. What did you expect me to do, knock him over the head and bundle him into a waiting car? This is the real world, not some trashy film.'

'You know, Rupert,' Montague said with a sigh, 'you always were a useless prick.'

He put down the phone and turned to Doyle.

'I've taken a dislike to those UCLAF bastards. I think it's time we clipped their wings.'

It was a dark rainy night, a pungent fog hanging low over the city, swirling in eddies across the surface of the sea. The navy-blue Fiat van slowed and pulled in by the kerb at the edge of the harbour road. The driver waited for a couple of cars to go past, then reversed out along a small concrete jetty which protruded into the bay. He climbed out and opened the rear doors of the van. A second man jumped down and together they lifted out a long, streamlined object which resembled a small bobsleigh but without the runners. It had two handles at the back and a propeller protected by a mesh guard. The men peered around through the fog to ensure no one was watching and lowered the object – an underwater sledge – into the sea.

A third man emerged from the rear of the van. He was dressed in diving gear: wet suit, flippers, mask, a compressed air tank strapped to his back. He moved swiftly to the edge of the jetty, shielded by the bulk of the van, and dropped over the side with barely a splash. The two other men passed down to him four heavy metal discs which he stowed in a well in the centre of the sledge. The diver switched on the electric motor, then adjusted the buoyancy of the sledge, flooding the tanks along its sides to make it sink. As the sledge slowly disappeared under the water, the diver grasped the handles at the back and twisted the throttle. The sledge surged away into the inky depths, towing the diver behind. The whole operation had taken less than five minutes.

Twenty minutes later, he was in the main harbour, coming up beneath the rusty hull of a freighter. He clamped the four magnetic discs to the bow plates of the ship and set the timers. Then he grabbed hold of the sledge and turned back the way he'd come.

The navy-blue van with its three occupants was on the A3 south of Vesuvius, near Torre Annunziata, when the charges detonated, blowing four large holes in the hull of the ship. The holds flooded with water and very slowly the *Maria Vasquez* keeled over and sank.

FOURTEEN

'Take a seat. Help yourselves to coffee.'

Ole Carlsen was standing up behind his desk, drifting about aimlessly, fidgeting with the buttons on his jacket as if he didn't know what to do with his hands. Claire had never seen him so tense.

Carlsen waited for the three of them to settle in their chairs, cups and saucers on their laps, before he sat down.

'I think it's time we reviewed this operation,' he said. 'Claire, tell them what happened on Friday night.'

Slowly, calmly, Claire described her ordeal at the cottage on the coast. She'd had the weekend to recover but was still surprised that she could recount the details without feeling unduly distressed. It had happened, it was over now, that was all she felt.

No one spoke for a time after she'd finished. Then Sullivan said: 'Jesus! Are you okay?'

Claire nodded. 'A few bruises, that's all.'

'And mentally?'

'I'm fine.'

Sullivan glanced at Carlsen, the concern apparent in his expression.

'I've suggested Claire takes a few days off,' Carlsen said, answering Sullivan's unspoken question. 'But she'd rather continue working. That is her decision.'

'Are you sure?' Sullivan said.

'Yes,' Claire replied brusquely.

Men always reacted in the same way to any kind of threat to a woman. Shock, then anxiety giving way to an over-protectiveness she found patronising. They would never have condescended in the same way to a male colleague.

'Do we know who your attacker was?' Sullivan asked.

'No. I've given a description to the police. He was young, fit, tough, with cropped hair like a soldier.'

'A soldier? What nationality?'

'I don't know. He said a few words in a language I didn't understand. It sounded Eastern European, Slavic.'

'Can you remember any of the words?'

'Just one. *Sooka*, something like that.'

'*Sooka*?' Stig Enqvist said.

'You know it?' Sullivan asked.

'*Cyka*, it's Russian for bitch.'

'I didn't know you spoke Russian.'

Enqvist smirked, easing the tense atmosphere. 'Only the rude words.'

'Why the hell would a Russian want to kill you?' Sullivan said to Claire.

'I don't think he knew who I was. I just happened to be there at the wrong time. It was Kuypers they wanted.'

'Why?'

'If I'd got there earlier, he might have told me.'

'And your attacker's body?'

'He had an accomplice, it's the only possible explanation. There was no way he was going to walk out of that house in the state I left him. The police found fresh tyre marks on a track through the forest to the east of the cottage. They had a car waiting.'

'Is there any trace of them?'

Claire shook her head. 'The police alerted all the hospitals in the area, set up roadblocks, but there's been no sign of them. He was badly injured, in need of urgent medical treatment. He must have gone somewhere.'

'From now on,' Carlsen said gravely, looking at each of them in turn, 'you must exercise the greatest caution in everything you do. I don't like the way this investigation is going. You do nothing without telling me first, and you go nowhere without the appropriate police or customs support. These are clearly violent people we are dealing with and I'm concerned about some of the military elements that seem to be creeping into the situation.'

'What military elements?' Sullivan said. 'The fact that Claire's attacker looked like a soldier?'

'Not just that,' Carlsen said. 'Did you see the breakfast news at all?'

'No.'

'It was on RAI. The *Maria Vasquez* was blown up in Naples harbour last night.'

'It was *what*? Shit!' Sullivan said. 'How? Who by?'

'I suggest you call Casagrande for the details. But it was done from under the water. The ship was moored in the Italian navy docks, with guards on the quayside. No one went on board her.'

'A diver?' Claire said.

'And underwater charges, probably mines of some sort. Who would have the expertise, the trained personnel and access to explosives like that except the military? You see why I'm concerned.'

'Which military?'

'I don't think we'll gain anything by speculating. We must leave it to the Italians,' Carlsen said. 'Now where are we going next? Rob?'

'I have a lead which is interesting. A British businessman named Henry Montague who's linked in a complicated chain of companies and directorships to Corvex Limited, a British firm we believe has some kind of connection with Van Vliet in Rotterdam.'

'How firm a lead?' Carlsen said.

'Well, out of curiosity, I went to look at his country house in Norfolk over the weekend and saw someone in the window I recognised. Dr Julius Wolf.'

Carlsen sat back abruptly in his chair. He stared at Sullivan.

'Are you certain?'

'No doubt about it. And Wolf's been trading again. Or at least, Steinhammer Weiss has.'

'You think he has a new partner?'

'Maybe not so new,' Sullivan said.

'What do you know about this man Montague?' Carlsen said.

'Not much at the moment. I have to find out more, but that may not be easy.'

'You have the usual sources, don't you? Police, SFO, Customs?'

'In theory, yes,' Sullivan said. 'The problem is, he has influential friends in the British government.'

'Meaning?'

'Well, it would seem he has links with the intelligence services.'

Carlsen blinked at him in disbelief. 'How can you possibly know that?'

Sullivan told them about his encounter at Waterloo Station.

'This man didn't actually say Montague worked for them?' Carlsen said.

'It was the impression I was intended to get. Either way, Montague has powerful friends protecting him. I can check him out, but the confidential stuff may be difficult to obtain.'

'And the way this Foreign Office man threatened you? Do

you want to make a formal complaint? I'm prepared to go to the Commissioner.'

Sullivan shook his head. He'd cooled down since the previous evening. 'They'd only deny it and we'd end up looking foolish.'

Carlsen stroked his moustache pensively. 'It has to go on the record. They're attempting to influence our investigation. That's a serious matter. And they're putting pressure on one of my investigators, jeopardising your career. I can't allow that. We have to make this official, and at the highest level of the Commission. I want a written report of exactly what happened, what was said. Now, while it's fresh in your mind.'

'Okay,' Sullivan said wearily. 'I'll do it this morning.'

'Good man.'

Carlsen turned to Enqvist. 'What about you, Stig?'

Enqvist was gazing distractedly at the wall, as if he hadn't been listening.

'Did you say Kuypers?' he asked Claire suddenly, going off at a tangent. His forehead was ridged with a frown of puzzlement.

'Yes, Jan Kuypers,' Claire replied. 'Why?'

'Wait here a minute.'

Enqvist went out of the office and walked away down the corridor. The others sat in silence, drinking their coffee, until he returned carrying a thick file under his arm. He slumped down and opened the file on his knees.

'I thought it was familiar,' he said. 'Vitoria. The Ilyushin-76 the Spanish seized. It came from Ostend originally, remember?'

'So?' Sullivan said.

'But the cigarettes started off in Holland. The pilot who flew them to Ostend was called Jan Kuypers.'

'I don't remember that.'

Enqvist twisted the file round and showed it to him.

217

'He was a minor player. He was questioned by the delinquents, but never charged with anything.'

The 'delinquents' was the Cigarette Task Group's affectionate nickname for the OCRDEFO, the *Office Central pour la Répression de la Délinquance Économique et Financière Organisée*, the Belgian organised crime investigation unit.

'Would someone mind telling me what you're talking about?' Claire said.

'A smuggling operation we broke last year,' Sullivan said. 'A Ukrainian Ilyushin-76 cargo plane took a consignment of cigarettes from Ostend airport to Belgrade. It stopped to refuel in Greece and the cargo manifests were changed. The plane then flew to Vitoria in northern Spain and declared the freight as electrical spare parts. We were there on the runway waiting for them with the *Guardia Civil*. We found seventeen hundred cases of contraband cigarettes on board.'

'They'd been doing it for months,' Enqvist added. 'Nearly eighteen thousand cases had already been flown in. That's about fifteen million Euros in lost customs duties.'

'And Kuypers was involved in it?'

'Not directly. He was part of the supply chain but he did nothing illegal. All he did was fly the cigarettes from a bonded warehouse in Rotterdam to Ostend.'

'Not Van Vliet's warehouse?' Claire said.

Enqvist shook his head. 'Snoeck and Verheggen, another warehouse company. But this is the best bit: the Spanish impounded the Ilyushin but had to give it back because it turned out it belonged to the Ukrainian government, and the crew were all former Soviet airforce personnel. And what's more, the Ukrainian government, despite the protocols on mutual assistance with the EU, refused to give us any help at all in our investigation.'

Enqvist leaned forward, his eyes gleaming.

'You know what,' he said. 'I'm willing to bet a large

chunk of my salary that the Russian and Ukrainian words for bitch are the same.'

It was early afternoon when Casagrande called back.

'I'm sorry about the delay,' he said apologetically. 'I've been busy.'

That was something of an understatement. Sullivan knew from the Gico duty officer in Naples that Casagrande had been up most of the previous night.

'I appreciate your time, Antonio. What happened?'

'Someone swam into the harbour under cover of darkness and stuck magnetic mines to the bottom of the ship. We've had divers down there but it's hard to tell exactly how many charges. Three, maybe four. Enough to take away half the bow plates.'

'Is she salvageable?'

'That depends what you mean. We're certainly going to get her out of the water. She's blocking off a large part of the Navy docks. But she'll never sail again. It wouldn't be worth patching her up, not a rusty old boat like that.'

'One less ship for our smuggling friends.'

'That's true. We're not crying about it here.'

'Antonio,' Sullivan said. 'It wasn't you, was it?'

Casagrande chuckled. 'If it were, I would hardly tell you, would I? I wish it had been actually. It would save me a hell of a lot of time tracking down the culprits.'

'You have anything?'

'Someone saw a blue Fiat van parked on a fishing jetty down towards Pórtici, but we haven't managed to trace it.'

'Who would have done it? Rival *camorristi*?'

'It's possible. Falzone's boys wouldn't have the skill to do a job like that themselves, but they've got the money to hire someone to do it for them. There are plenty of mercenaries around if you know where to look. Listen, I have to go, Rob. The pricks in Rome are shitting themselves over this.

The ship was in a military zone. It could have been a Navy cruiser that went up. The Minister of Defence is flying down later to look at the wreck for himself and shout at the easiest person to blame.'

'You?'

'Probably.'

'Can I leave something with you? Not for now. Maybe for one of your men when this is all out of the way. Two names. Henry Montague and Simon Doyle.'

'Who are they?'

'I have a hunch, and that's all it is at the moment, that behind all the Liberian bullshit Montague is the real owner of the *Maria Vasquez*.'

'I'll see if we've got anything,' Casagrande said.

'Give my regards to the Minister of Defence.'

Casagrande laughed cynically and hung up.

Sullivan pushed back his chair and got to his feet, walking to the window to look down into the shrub-filled atrium of the building. He thought about Claire, wondering whether he should go and see her. In Carlsen's office he'd felt a powerful urge to touch her, a palpable ache of sexual desire that was with him still.

'Something on your mind?' Enqvist asked.

Sullivan turned and shrugged, focusing his mind on less personal matters.

'The bodies are piling up, aren't they?'

'Smuggling's a dangerous game.'

'It's never been like this before. Maartens, Broekhuizen, now Kuypers. Why?'

'To punish them, to silence them,' Enqvist said. 'Maybe both.'

'The Ukrainians?'

'Kuypers, certainly. The others, who knows?'

'The hit-and-run near Groningen. What if they were after Kuypers, not Broekhuizen?'

'What difference does it make? They're both dead now.'

Sullivan looked back out of the window, reverting to his earlier thoughts.

'Have you ever committed adultery?' he asked casually.

'What?'

'Were you ever unfaithful to Anna?'

'Not when I was sober,' Enqvist said.

'I'm serious. Were you?'

Stig put down his pen and pushed himself away from the desk.

'You having problems with Kate?'

'No, I'm just interested. You can tell me it's none of my business.'

'Once,' Stig said. 'With a girl at the *Tullverk*. After a party.'

'Why did you do it?'

'Because she was there, I suppose.'

'Did you feel guilty?'

'I can't remember. Probably. Everyone does, don't they?'

'Did you tell Anna?'

'God, no. Never tell them. Not if you want to keep them.'

Enqvist broke off to answer the telephone on his desk.

'UCLAF, Enqvist.'

'This is Juliana. You remember me?'

Stig's mouth went dry. He licked his lips and said coolly:

'Sure. How are you?'

'I'm in Brussels. How are you fixed for dinner tonight?'

'I think I'm free. I'll just check my diary . . .'

Sullivan turned away, shutting out Stig's voice on the telephone. Was that why he'd slept with Claire? Was that why he'd cheated on his wife? Because she was there? It seemed a tawdry reason, but then affairs *were* tawdry, weren't they?

Enqvist put down the phone and gave Sullivan a shrewd look.

'You been playing around, or are you just thinking about it?'

'I was simply wondering,' Sullivan said. 'In an abstract sort of way.'

'Adultery is never abstract,' Enqvist said.

Claire was sitting at her desk, writing on a large pad of lined paper. Sullivan stood in the doorway and watched her for a moment. Her face was hidden. All he could see was the dark bob of shiny hair, the glint of a silver ring in one of her ears. Sensing his presence, she looked up. She smiled uncertainly.

'I came to see how you were,' Sullivan said.

'I'm fine.'

'You sure? Can I do anything?'

'I'm not a little girl,' Claire said with a note of irritation.

'I noticed.'

They looked at each other. Sullivan wanted to go to her and hold her, but he couldn't tell how she'd react. How she felt. It was strange how you could sleep with someone and yet not be close to them.

'Okay, I just thought I'd check.'

He turned to go.

'Rob.'

Claire came out from behind her desk and walked over to him. She pushed the door to.

'Stay for a bit, if you like.'

She was only a couple of feet away. Small, slender, desirable. Sullivan reached out and took her hand. She didn't stop him. He pulled her closer, slipping his arms around her waist. Claire stretched upwards and kissed him. He felt her lips soft and yielding, her hands on his neck, his hair. She broke away and pressed herself against him. Sullivan held her, stroking her back. His fingers slid down over the curve of her buttocks. Claire pulled them away.

'Not here.'

She walked back to her desk and took out a small mirror and make-up holder from her shoulderbag. She studied her face in the mirror and wiped away the smeared lipstick with a tissue before applying a fresh layer. Sullivan wondered how many times she'd done this with other men, other colleagues. It didn't make him want her less.

'Can I see you tonight?' he said.

She put the mirror and cosmetics away in her bag.

'I'd like to, but I'm busy. A long-standing appointment with an old friend. A woman,' she added, knowing how men's minds worked.

'Oh.'

'Maybe later in the week.'

Sullivan shrugged non-committally. Kate and the boys would be with him then, but he banished the thought from his head. It weighed too heavily on his conscience.

After he'd gone, Claire couldn't concentrate on her work. Why did relationships never get any easier? She'd been cooler with Sullivan than she'd intended. It was a form of protection that was second nature to her. He was married and she'd learnt that married men, whatever they said, had ties with their wives that were hard to sever. Ties of shared experience, of familiarity, of children that were bonded together and reinforced with a steel core of responsibility and loyalty. She knew never to underestimate the power of male guilt.

She wondered what she was doing, getting involved with yet another attached man. Hadn't she had enough of all that? She was thirty-six years old and was getting tired of the emotional stress an affair put her through. Yet she seemed addicted to it. She seemed unable to make things easy for herself; there always had to be complications.

She'd always been attracted to unsuitable men, it was one of her failings. Since her divorce from Wim, there'd been a series of partners, some more serious than others but none she regarded as long-term prospects. And now there was Rob Sullivan. If he'd been single . . . She didn't concern herself with hypothetical questions. If he'd been single, she probably wouldn't have been attracted to him.

She abandoned what she was doing and went to the window to look out at the darkening sky.

'Shit!' she said to herself, wondering why she'd told him she was busy that evening. It was true, she did have an appointment with an old friend, but she would much rather have cancelled and spent the time with him. So why hadn't she? She wanted him, yet instinctively she shied away from getting too emotionally involved with him.

She went to the telephone and dialled an internal number.

'Rob.' She paused. 'Why don't you come round later? I'll be home after eleven.'

She was even more beautiful than he remembered. Enqvist found himself looking away deliberately during dinner because to gaze at that perfect face for too long was more than he could take. She was utterly breathtaking – so flawless she left him struggling for air, his heart beating as if he'd just run up four flights of stairs. It had never happened to him before, even when he first met Anna, who was a very attractive woman. But Anna had been real, with the defects and imperfections of a real woman. Juliana Rietveld seemed unreal, her beauty like a hallucinatory vision or a mirage that would disappear if you dared to reach out and touch it. Yet Stig *had* touched it that night in Rotterdam, and the possibility, the hope, that he might do so again afflicted him with a nervous tension that was akin to a fever. His hands were clammy, his mouth like sandpaper, his stomach a tight ball of writhing eels. For probably the first time in his life he was tongue-tied until a couple of dry martinis began to relax him.

They were in a restaurant in the centre of Brussels, a quiet, exclusive cordon bleu cathedral where the *maître d'* was the archbishop, the waiters priests ministering to their congregation, the chef God and the bill large enough to re-roof the nave and still leave enough change for a trip to Lourdes. Enqvist didn't take much notice of the food, or the prices, he was too preoccupied with entertaining his guest and wondering what on earth she was doing there with him. He was forty-five years old, an obscure customs officer from Stockholm with a spare tyre and thinning hair, a modest amount of charisma and a salary which, though comfortable enough, was hardly much to get excited about. What did she see in him? he thought periodically during the meal, dismissing such negative reflections immediately with the reassuring riposte, who cares? She was there opposite him, chatting easily, laughing at his jokes and the focus of so much drooling attention the waiters' tongues were practically scraping the carpet. Stig intended to make the most of it.

Dinner over, they went for a walk around the Grand-Place. Stig sucked in a few deep breaths of the damp night air. His head felt thick, his legs a little unsteady. How much had he drunk? Two martinis, a bottle and a half of wine, a liqueur. No more than he was used to, but he could feel the effects nevertheless.

Juliana held his arm, pressing close to him as they strolled the short distance to her hotel. They went up to her room and she opened a couple of miniature brandies from the mini-bar. Stig sipped his slowly, wishing he'd said no. His head was starting to swim, the dizziness turning to nausea.

They sat in armchairs talking in the desultory fashion of two people who know that conversation is not the main reason for their being together. Stig waited for her to make the first move. She'd invited him back to her room, but he was taking nothing for granted.

Finally, she stood up and came across to him. She'd kicked off her shoes and removed her silk jacket. Underneath she was wearing a tight black dress which clung to her figure like a second skin, revealing only her slim arms and a curve of tanned flesh between her neck and breasts. She knelt down beside his chair and kissed him with a lingering sensuousness. Stig ran his hands through her soft blonde hair and then down over her shoulders and back.

They moved to the bed, pulling off each other's clothes, slipping naked beneath the sheet. They kissed again. Juliana touched him. Stig was aware immediately that something was wrong. The desire was there, emerging even through the haze of drunkenness, but it made no difference. He tried to focus his thoughts, to concentrate. Juliana stroked him, kissing him hard. Stig broke away, overcome with embarrassment.

'I'm sorry,' he said.

'That's okay.'

'I really am.'

'It happens, don't worry about it.'

'I've drunk too much.'

'It doesn't matter, Stig.'

He sat up. The dizziness was getting worse. The room was starting to spin. He swung his legs off the bed and staggered into the bathroom, closing the door behind him. A hot and cold wave of nausea overwhelmed him. He threw himself to his knees and was sick in the toilet.

He crouched there on the floor, holding the sides of the bowl until the retching stopped. Even then he waited a while, too faint to stand up.

'Are you all right, Stig?' Juliana called.

'Yes,' he mumbled.

He flushed the toilet and pulled himself to his feet, leaning on the washbasin. He was ashamed to go back out into the bedroom.

'Stig?'

He rinsed his face with cold water and rubbed it dry on a towel. Then he steadied himself and pulled open the door. Juliana was outside. He expected to see disgust in her expression but she seemed more concerned than repulsed.

'I'm sorry,' he said. 'I'm so sorry.'

He stumbled over to the bed, searching for his clothes.

'I'd better go.'

'Don't be silly. You're in no state to go anywhere.'

'I'm sure you want me to leave. I'm sorry.'

'Stop saying sorry. Lie down.'

'Juliana . . .'

She pushed him gently down on to the pillow.

'Lie down.'

She slid in beside him.

'Don't you want me to go?' he said.

'I want you to stay.'

She curled up against him, her head on his shoulder. She was warm, comforting. Stig stared at the ceiling, trying to blot out his thoughts, until his eyes grew heavy and he drifted off into a leaden sleep.

Dr Julius Wolf poured himself another three fingers of cognac and took a long gulp, washing away the feelings of self-revulsion in a torrent of alcohol. A decade ago he would have paid the night porter to find him a companion; there were always call girls on hand for appetites which the official hotel room service was unable to satisfy. But he'd long passed the point where they could do anything for him. He was seventy-five years old, a frail man living on memories, taking his bitter vicarious pleasure by watching others enjoying what he had lost and blotting out the present and the future with the numbing anaesthetic of booze.

The bottle of Courvoisier on the table beside him was three quarters empty, the smoked salmon and avocado sandwich next to the bottle barely touched. On the television screen at the foot of the bed a repetitive, obscene hard-core porn movie was flickering. His watery eyes blinking behind his thick spectacles, Wolf watched the images of young bodies writhing and coupling. He'd seen it all before, loathed himself for his addiction, but had nothing else to give him solace in his declining years. He was a childless widower, his wife taken by cancer twelve years earlier, and what few friends he had were far away in Zürich. He had money enough to afford a luxury suite in the best hotel in Antwerp but not enough – or too much – to buy someone to share it with him.

He refilled his glass with cognac and drank it, feeling his vision blurring. The pictures on the television screen started to shake and Wolf closed his eyes momentarily, trying to clear the fug in his head. Slowly, he became aware of a knocking noise which he thought at first was on the movie. But when he opened his eyes he realised it was coming from the door to his room. He ignored it but it continued, low and insistent.

Wolf swung his legs off the bed and pushed himself unsteadily to his feet. He staggered awkwardly across the room, supporting himself on the edge of the bed and then the wall.

'Who is it?'

'Me,' a voice said softly through the panel.

Wolf snapped back the lock and opened the door. Simon Doyle stepped inside and pushed the door to. Wolf was already stumbling back towards the bed. As he neared the footboard, his legs gave way and he tumbled over sideways, hitting the floor with a shuddering thud. Doyle walked across to him and knelt down, checking Wolf's pulse. Then he glanced around, taking in the almost empty bottle of brandy and the naked bodies on the television. He watched the movie for a few moments before switching it off.

Leaving Wolf where he'd fallen, Doyle went into the bathroom and ran a bath. He still had on his winter coat and black leather gloves. He added some of the hotel's complimentary foambath to the water and let it rise hot and steaming to a good depth. Then he went back out and stripped Wolf of his clothes, tossing the garments on to the bottom of the bed. He lifted the old man up by his arms and dragged him through into the bathroom.

Wolf's body was pale and emaciated, the skin loose and blotchy. Doyle picked him up easily and lowered him into the bath. The feel of the water, the sudden change in temperature, something, brought the old man round. His eyes fluttered open and he stared up at Doyle.

'What . . .' he murmured feebly, barely emerging from his alcoholic stupor.

'Relax, Julius,' Doyle said emolliently. 'Go back to sleep.'

Wolf reached out for the edges of the bath, fumbling for a handhold to stop himself slipping lower into the water.

'Why are you here?' he mumbled, slurring his words so they were almost indistinct.

Doyle gripped Wolf's hair in one hand, his shoulder in the other and pushed him under the surface. The old man struggled, flailing out with his bony arms, the air bubbling up from his mouth and mingling with the perfumed froth of the foambath. Even when sober he would have been no match for Doyle. His body saturated with brandy, he had no hope of escape.

Doyle held him under implacably, showing no emotion. Wolf, finding some final, desperate reserves of strength, fought to free himself. The water splashed out over the sides, soaking the floor and bathmat. But Doyle held on, pushing the old man's head to the bottom, pressing down until the convulsions stopped and Wolf lay still.

Doyle straightened up and rubbed the moisture off his clothes with a towel, then wiped the tiles on the floor, soaking up the overspill from the bath. He hung the towel on a radiator to dry and took a last look at Wolf's lifeless face staring up grotesquely from beneath the water.

'I'm sorry, Julius,' he said. 'We all have to make sacrifices.'

They started kissing the moment he walked through the door. No attempt at conversation, no drinks, no pretence. Just a basic animal desire that overwhelmed them both.

They went through into the bedroom and tore off their clothes. Claire's body was warm and soft. Sullivan touched her, stroked her. She kissed him hard, her hands roving over his skin. He thought fleetingly of his wife before a wave of intense physical pleasure swept over him, drowning out all feelings of guilt and doubt.

Enqvist awoke as Juliana extricated herself from his arms and climbed out of the bed. He blinked. His head ached as if someone had buried a tomahawk in his skull and was joggling it to and fro. He watched her walk naked into the bathroom, the shafts of sunlight breaking through the curtains touching her buttocks and legs with a warm glow. The memories of the previous evening flooded back and he winced with renewed shame and embarrassment. Juliana had been very understanding about the whole sorry episode. Perhaps too understanding.

Stig sat up, wondering about that, asking himself again what she saw in him. He was as vain as most men, but he tried not to let his vanity interfere with his intellect. And he tried not to let it make a fool of him.

Throwing aside the sheet, he slipped out of bed and stood up, pausing to let his head settle. Juliana's handbag was on the top of the desk. Enqvist padded across and looked down at it. She'd have her Dutch identity card inside, perhaps a passport. All he had to do was open the bag. He hesitated. He couldn't bring himself to do it. It seemed underhand, treacherous. Maybe he didn't want to know. He heard the bathroom door click open and went quickly back to the bed.

'How're you feeling?' Juliana asked, walking over and sitting down next to him.

'Not too bad. Look . . .'

She stopped him. 'It's all forgotten. Okay?'

Stig nodded. Juliana smiled and reached out, running her fingers over his bare chest.

'How are you fixed for time?' she said.

'I'm in no hurry. Why?'

'We've some unfinished business from last night.'

FIFTEEN

The two desks were almost hidden beneath a stack of thick reference books and a large spread-out map of Europe, North Africa and the Middle East. Stig Enqvist was sitting in his chair, leafing carelessly through the photocopied logbook of the *Maria Vasquez* while Sullivan and Claire pored over the map.

'What if they were unloaded somewhere along the Basque Coast?' Sullivan said.

'Spain or France?' Claire asked.

'Spain. Maybe somewhere here between San Sebastian and Bilbao.' He followed the indented coastline with his finger.

'I'm not sure,' Claire said doubtfully. 'That's a well-populated stretch, a major port at either end. Too much customs, coastguard activity.'

'Where would you go?'

Claire pointed to the west coast of France. 'Here. The Landes. It's perfect. From Arcachon to Biarritz there's no coastal town of any size. Just a hundred kilometres of deserted beach backed by pine forest. I've been there. There are dozens of places you could bring cigarettes in by speedboat. You have lorries waiting and an hour later you're unloading in the warehouse at Bayonne. That's what I would do if I were a smuggler.'

'It's persuasive,' Sullivan admitted. 'You could use all

233

these minor roads. Who would notice you?'

He reached out to indicate the possible routes the lorries could take and accidentally touched Claire's hand. The contact sent a shiver up his arm and he had to stop himself from taking hold of her fingers and squeezing. He glanced across at Enqvist but his colleague hadn't noticed, he was too engrossed in the logbook. Sullivan looked at Claire, acutely conscious of how close she was. Her perfume was in his nostrils, her hair near enough to touch. She smiled, as if she knew what he was thinking, and leaned sideways, brushing his body with her shoulder for an instant before bending over the map again.

'The cigarettes are left at Fonteneau et Delahaye,' she said phlegmatically. 'Then distributed across France. The Spanish consignments are taken across the border in the Garcia Saez olive oil lorries which are returning empty to San Sebastian, crossing at Hendaye where one of the senior customs officers is in their pocket. They've thought through every aspect. It all fits together.'

'Let's check the figures. Give us the times, Stig. Stig?'

Enqvist looked up. 'Uh?'

'You okay?' Sullivan said.

'Yeah. What is it?'

'Give me the time the *Maria Vasquez* left Rotterdam and the time she arrived in the Bay of Naples.'

Enqvist consulted the logbook.

'February seventh, leaves Rotterdam at nine am. February fifteenth, two am, stopped and boarded by the *Guardia di Finanza*.'

'That's, what, seven and a bit days. I make that a hundred and eighty-five hours,' Sullivan said, picking up the Lloyd's Register of Shipping and Reed's Marine Distance Tables from the one corner of the desk not covered by the map. He handed the register to Claire.

'Give me her speed.'

He opened the marine tables and calculated the distance between Rotterdam and Naples.

'Two thousand three hundred and fifty nautical miles.'

'Normal service speed thirteen knots,' Claire said.

She tapped the figures into her electronic calculator.

'A hundred and eighty hours,' Sullivan said.

Claire pulled a face.

'I wish you'd stop doing that.'

'Five hours less than she actually took,' Sullivan said. 'Even allowing for bad weather and reduced sailing speed that's more than enough time to stop in the Bay of Biscay and unload a few thousand cases.'

'She did the same run last November as well,' Enqvist said, leafing back through the logbook.

He frowned. 'There's something funny about this log.'

'How do you mean?' Sullivan said.

'I don't know. I can't put my finger on it.'

Enqvist flicked back through the pages. He wasn't in the mood for work. The pain in his head had eased but his eyes felt tired and sore. He wanted to rest his head on the desk and go back to sleep.

The telephone beside him rang. He picked up the receiver and listened lethargically, then suddenly came awake.

'*Merde!*' he said under his breath, continuing in French. 'Yes, I'll come straight away.'

He hung up and tossed the logbook across the desk.

'You two take care of it. See what you can find.'

'Why, what are you doing?' Sullivan asked suspiciously.

Enqvist went to the door and lifted down his overcoat from the peg, glad of an excuse to get out of the office.

'Stig,' Sullivan said. 'Who was on the phone?'

'Only Janvier.'

Richard Janvier was one of the 'delinquents', a senior official in the OCRDEFO.

'What did he want?'

'One of us. Don't worry, I'll take care of it.'

'Take care of what?'

Enqvist slipped on his coat and fastened up the buttons.

'Julius Wolf was found dead in an Antwerp hotel room this morning. Perhaps there is a God after all.'

Janvier met him in the foyer of the Hotel Rubens and escorted him upstairs in the lift. The Rubens was an old, long-established hotel, built in the nineteenth century for the wealthy merchants who came to Antwerp to trade in diamonds. It had been renovated and refurbished several times since, but still retained an old-fashioned ambience despite the air conditioning, double glazing and electronic work stations in the conference centre behind reception.

Julius Wolf's room was a large suite on the fourth floor facing west towards the River Schelde. It had been carefully furnished by an interior designer with a fondness for thick embossed wallpaper and polished mahogany, but it still looked like an ordinary hotel room: expensive, yet somehow dreary and unwelcoming. Its functional atmosphere wasn't helped that afternoon by the fingerprint dust sprinkled liberally over every surface and the quiet men in overalls and white gloves who were slowly and methodically inspecting every square centimetre of the place.

Enqvist took a look around from the doorway before following Janvier inside.

'He was in his bath,' Janvier said in French. 'The housemaid found him.'

Enqvist glanced automatically through the open door into the bathroom though there was nothing to see: the body had been taken away hours ago.

'Cause of death?' he asked.

'It looked like drowning. We won't know for certain, of

236

course, until after the autopsy. There was an almost empty bottle of cognac beside the bed, brought up by room service yesterday evening.'

'He drank it all?'

Janvier shrugged. 'We're waiting for the blood analysis results. On first impressions, yes. There was only one glass.'

Enqvist nodded, watching the scene-of-crime team going about their painstaking work.

'I assume from all this that you don't think it was an accident, or natural causes?'

'Come downstairs,' Janvier said. 'I've something to show you.'

They went down to the ground floor and through to one of the rooms in the conference centre which the police were using as their incident station. A coffee machine, the first priority after a few desks and telephones, had been installed in one corner. Janvier filled a couple of polystyrene cups and they sat down at an empty desk. The room was deserted except for a pretty uniformed policewoman who'd been dumped with the tedious task of manning the phone lines and taking messages.

'He checked in yesterday about four pm,' Janvier said. 'Went out for a couple of hours then came back, went up to his room and ordered the bottle of brandy and a sandwich. About nine o'clock he called reception to access the video channel on his television. They're centrally controlled. Choose your film from a list and the charge is added to your bill.'

'What did he watch?'

'California Cocksuckers.'

'Ah, a Disney fan,' Enqvist said.

'It's a Danish film, despite the title.'

'I didn't know Wolf spoke Danish.'

'I don't think he was watching it for the dialogue.'

Janvier drank some of his coffee. He was a short man in his forties with grey wiry hair and a slow, almost lugubrious way of talking that had fooled a lot of people over the years into thinking he wasn't very bright. Enqvist liked him. He had a relaxed, informal approach to his job which made him easy to deal with. He wasn't a believer in 'official channels', which did nothing except create delays and bureaucracy. If he wanted something from UCLAF or any other agency, he called them direct, circumventing both his superiors and the Ministry of Justice who, theoretically, were supposed to be notified of any transnational enquiries.

'What time did he die?' Enqvist asked.

'The doctor couldn't be specific. Not on medical grounds. But other evidence points to around eleven, eleven thirty.'

'What other evidence?'

'A woman in the room across the corridor. Says she heard someone knocking on Wolf's door about then. She couldn't be absolutely sure, she had her television on, but it looks as if Wolf had a visitor.'

'Any indication who?'

'No. The fingerprints are a mess, as you'd expect in a hotel room with people coming and going all the time. Reception didn't notice anyone coming in downstairs – certainly no one asked for Wolf's room number – but anyone could have walked in without attracting attention.'

'And the visitor killed him?'

'It's a theory,' Janvier said.

'You have any others?'

'No.'

'What makes you think it wasn't natural causes? A heart attack in the bath. He was an old man, after all.'

'The doctor examined the body before it was taken to the morgue. There were marks on Wolf's left shoulder. The kind of bruises you'd expect if he'd been held under the water. And a chunk of his hair had been half pulled out of his scalp.'

Enqvist looked across at the policewoman. She was speaking in Flemish into the telephone and scribbling notes on a pad of paper.

'Why?' he said.

Janvier swallowed some coffee and grimaced. He put the cup down on the desk and pushed it away.

'That's the worst thing about these incident rooms,' he said. 'The coffee. And these crappy polystyrene cups. Why?' he repeated Enqvist's question. 'You know why. A man like Julius Wolf. He had so many enemies they were probably queuing up to kill him.'

'Why *now*?' Enqvist qualified the enquiry.

Janvier gave a shrug. 'Maybe time just ran out for him. He was lucky, doing what he did for so many years without anybody catching up with him.'

'What was he doing here? Buying?'

Antwerp was the largest cigarette *entrepôt* in Europe. A huge proportion of the imports from the UK and America were held in bonded warehouses in the city. Both Enqvist and Janvier knew that Wolf had been a regular, if undesirable, visitor to the port.

Janvier unlocked the bottom drawer of the desk and pulled out an expensive-looking black attaché case which he placed on the top of the desk. The combination locks on the case had been forced open.

'Did you do that?' Enqvist asked.

Janvier nodded. 'It was in the hotel safe. It was the first thing I asked about when I got here. The local plods weren't too happy about my having it, but, you know, we're all on the same side, aren't we?'

There was a subtle undertone of irony in his voice. Janvier was a Walloon and, worse, a Walloon from the central authorities in Brussels. Antwerp was the capital of Flanders

239

and the city's police officers would have welcomed his arrival with about as much enthusiasm as they would a dose of the clap.

Janvier opened the lid of the case and lifted out some papers.

'Wolf left it at reception,' he said. 'They make interesting reading.'

'Can I take them away?' Enqvist asked.

Janvier shook his head. 'Evidence in a murder investigation. Sorry. But you can have a look at them.'

Enqvist read through some of the documents. There were letters, invoices, order forms, lists of phone numbers and addresses. There were names of companies, some of which Enqvist recognised, some of which he didn't. And there was a business diary full of times and appointments. It was all too complicated to remember or to make notes of.

'I need more time to study these, Richard,' Enqvist said.

Janvier glanced at the Flemish policewoman but she was showing no interest in their conversation.

'I'm going to find a toilet,' he said. 'There's a photocopier behind reception, but I didn't tell you it was there.'

Enqvist grinned at him. 'Make it a long piss,' he said.

Even in summer the apartment in Tervuren was gloomy and cheerless. But in winter, arriving there on a dank February day, it had a cold, forbidding oppressiveness about it that Kate found intensely depressing. She'd never liked it. The rooms were too big and bare, there was a smell of damp that persisted throughout the year no matter how warm the weather, and whatever she did it never seemed remotely like a permanent home.

It was only mid-afternoon when they drove down the narrow street and pulled in outside the ancient apartment building, but already it was dark enough to feel like dusk.

There were horse chestnut trees on the pavements on either side of the road which, though they were leafless, formed a canopy of interlocking twigs, blocking out the light even more than the grey clouds smeared across the sun. Climbing out, Kate felt the raindrops dripping down from the branches, pitter-pattering on the bonnet of the car and splashing her hair with icy pearls that trickled in rivulets down the back of her neck.

The boys loved those trees, particularly in autumn when the ground beneath them was scattered with shiny brown horse chestnuts that were left there to rot or to be carried away by the neighbourhood squirrels. The strange English custom of conkers was unknown in Belgium, the idea that small boys might devote hours of their time to throwing sticks into trees, collecting the fallen fruit to soak in vinegar and thread on to strings for fights in the playground some-how beyond the grasp of continental children who had more serious pastimes with which to amuse themselves. But that ignorance was Patrick and James's gain for the two of them went back to England after each autumn half term with so many conkers in their suitcases there was barely room for their clothes.

There were few other advantages to living in Tervuren as far as Kate was concerned. It was a pretty enough Flemish town, nestling in the Forêt de Soignes some thirteen kilometres east of Brussels. It had a sizeable expat British community, partly because the British School of Brussels was there, but that wasn't much of a plus: Kate had always found the British abroad worse than the British at home. It seemed to her an alien place, far away from the culture and language with which she was familiar, yet not sufficiently different or exotic to arouse her curiosity. It was wet and drab and boring and made her wonder why she'd driven three hundred miles when she could have stayed in Colchester, which was equally wet and

241

drab and boring but at least had the boys' schoolfriends nearby.

Keeping Patrick and James happy and entertained for the holiday was her most daunting challenge. They had the attention spans of hyperactive infants but much more energy, coupled with a surly awkwardness that drove her to distraction. They moaned constantly, bickered as if their lives depended on it and seemed incapable of enjoying any activity which wasn't dirty, dangerous or illegal. The journey had been bad enough, listening to them squabbling, but now they'd arrived and were unpacking the car, complaining about the weather and the apartment and God knows what, Kate was ready to scream.

'If I hear one more word, I'm leaving you here and going straight back to England. Do you hear?' she shouted at them in exasperation. 'Now get your bags inside.'

They went upstairs to the first floor and unlocked the apartment. It smelt musty inside, as if it hadn't been occupied for months, and Kate could see the dust on the polished wooden floor. She didn't believe Rob ever cleaned the place in between their visits; it certainly never looked as if he did. Her first day there was always spent vacuuming and dusting, hating herself for saving her husband the effort, but she just couldn't live in the squalor he seemed not to notice.

The boys went through into their bedroom with instructions to unpack their clothes and put them away in the chest of drawers and wardrobe. Kate, relieved to get them out of sight and hearing for a few minutes, sought refuge in the kitchen and made herself a pot of tea. There was milk in the fridge but that was about all. She swore under her breath. Did Rob not eat anything in the apartment when he was here alone? It annoyed her that, once again, she'd driven all the way from England to find that he hadn't bothered to stock up with any provisions for them.

'Mum, can we watch television?'

Patrick and James were standing in the doorway.

'Have you unpacked?'

'Sort of.'

'What do you mean, sort of?'

'We can do it later.'

'You can do it now,' Kate said, wishing that motherhood didn't have to turn you into a bad-tempered shrew.

'Aw, Mum.'

'Go on. No television until you've unpacked everything. I know you, you'll spend the whole week living out of suitcases.'

The boys groaned in the exaggerated theatrical fashion perfected by adolescents of all generations, but they went back into their room. Kate finished her tea and walked through into the master bedroom. The double bed was a crumpled mess. She pulled up the duvet and plumped up the pillows, then went to the window to close the curtains. The bedroom was at the front of the apartment, overlooking the street. Kate glanced out of the window. It was almost dark outside. The streetlights were on, the pavements glistening wet. She reached out for the curtains.

It was then that she noticed the car parked in the street below.

A dark Peugeot saloon with two men sitting inside.

Enqvist was excited. It had been obvious the moment he walked back into the office and dropped the sheaf of photocopied papers on to his desk.

'We've struck gold,' he announced with a flourish. 'Pure fucking gold. Take a look at that lot. Wolf's personal papers, even his diary showing who he met and when.'

Sullivan felt the contagious enthusiasm in his colleague's voice and manner but resisted it, suspicious of anything that hadn't been checked and crosschecked a dozen times.

'Oh yes?' he said cautiously.

'Don't be so fucking English,' Enqvist said. 'Look at them. You too, Claire.'

Sullivan left the papers on the desk. Claire made no move to pick them up either.

'Where did you get them?' Sullivan said.

'Janvier gave them to me. Wolf left them in the hotel safe. They're bloody complicated, but if we pick our way through them I reckon there must be a goldmine of information in them. Think about it. Julius Wolf, one of Europe's biggest cigarette dealers, a guy we've had our eye on for years without once catching him doing anything illegal. We've got letters, order sheets, times, dates, everything we need to piece together the secrets of his business. Whom he dealt with, when, where, how much he bought, whom he sold to.'

Enqvist threw off his coat and sat down, flicking eagerly through the papers. Sullivan and Claire watched him.

'How did he die?' Claire asked.

Enqvist repeated what Janvier had told him.

'He'll let us know the results of the autopsy when he gets them, but they're working on the assumption it was murder. The old bastard led a charmed life but it couldn't last forever.'

Enqvist collected together a pile of pages and passed them across to Sullivan.

'You take the diary, see what you can make of it.'

'And me?' Claire said.

'How far have you got with the log of the *Maria Vasquez*?'

She made a face. 'I get all the interesting jobs, I see,' she said dryly, flashing him a half smile to show there was no real resentment.

'Teamwork,' said Enqvist, 'is everyone else doing what I say.'

'Who do I have to sleep with to get a transfer back to olive oil?' Claire retorted, studiously avoiding Sullivan's gaze.

The sharp ring of the telephone interrupted them. Sullivan answered it in a businesslike voice, then shifted his tone to something softer, more affectionate. Claire knew he was talking to his wife.

'How was the journey?' he said.

Claire sat down at Nicoletti's desk, trying not to listen to Sullivan as he chatted, a little self-consciously, on the phone.

'Yeah, I shouldn't be late. How are the boys? I'm sorry, I meant to. I'll stop at the supermarket on my way home. Yeah, okay.'

There was a silence, then he said: 'What is it?' with a note of such concern that both Claire and Enqvist glanced up at him.

'It's probably nothing,' Kate said. 'You'll think I'm being silly.'

'No I won't. What's the matter?'

'You know I don't like this place on my own. It's creepy in the dark.'

'Kate, just tell me.'

'There's a car out at the front. There are two men inside it.'

Sullivan felt his stomach knot. It was pure instinct, there was no rational explanation for it. But Kate was obviously worried and her anxiety was rubbing off on him.

'So what?' he said, trying to sound reassuring. 'They're probably waiting for someone.'

'Yes, I suppose so. It just struck me as funny. You know how quiet it is here. When have you ever seen two young men sitting in a car outside the building?'

'Are they still there?' Sullivan said.

'I'll check.'

Kate put down the phone and went through into the

bedroom. She pulled back the edge of the curtain and peeped out. The Peugeot saloon was in the same place. She could see the shadowy faces of the two men through the windscreen. She went back to the phone.

'Yes.'

'I wouldn't worry,' Sullivan said. 'I'm sure it's nothing.' As an afterthought, he added: 'What do they look like?'

'Late twenties,' Kate said. 'Casual clothes, short-cropped hair. It's hard to see the details in the dark. One of them seems to have a bandage around his head.'

Sullivan became aware of a pain in his ear and realised he was pressing the receiver hard into the side of his head.

'A bandage?' he said calmly.

'Yes.'

'Look, I think I'll come home now.'

'Why?' Kate said quickly. 'Who are they?'

'Relax, I don't like you worried. Just to be on the safe side I'll come home and check. Are the boys inside?'

'Watching television.'

'Lock and bolt the doors.'

'Rob, what's going on?'

'I'm on my way, okay?'

Sullivan walked quickly down the corridor and out through the security door to the lift. He pressed the button and waited impatiently for the lift to arrive. He wondered if he was overreacting, but he remembered what had happened to Claire. This was his wife and kids; it wasn't possible to overreact where their safety was concerned.

He stayed calm as the lift took him down into the basement car park. But when the doors opened, he burst out through the gap and sprinted for his car.

Kate went to the front door and locked it with the keys before pushing the bolts into place at the top and bottom and attaching the safety chain. Her hands were trembling a little and she felt queasy, a reaction not just to the men waiting outside at the front but to Rob's response when she'd told him. She knew he was keeping something from her and that only added to her anxiety.

Going back into the bedroom, she peeked out of the window again. The men were still there. One of them looked up and saw her. He said something to his companion who lifted his eyes and fixed them on Kate. She suppressed a shiver. In the harsh light of the streetlamps their heads resembled faceless skulls: bony, hollow-eyed, devoid of skin or hair.

The two men opened the car doors and climbed out. One reached back inside and lifted out a sports bag.

Then they walked across the pavement and into the entrance to the apartment building.

Heading east away from Brussels on the Tervursesteenweg, Sullivan drove one-handed whilst punching in his home number on his mobile phone. He let it ring a dozen times.

There was no answer.

He pressed redial and let it ring again.

Still no answer.

He called the office. Enqvist answered.

'Stig, do something for me,' Sullivan said abruptly. 'Look up the number of the Tervuren police. Something's wrong. Tell them to get over to my apartment immediately.'

'What's going on?'

'Just do it, Stig. Now.'

Kate had frozen. This was way outside her experience. She didn't know what to do. The telephone rang but she ignored it. Maybe she was wrong. Maybe she was being stupid. She stood in the hall, staring at the locks on the door, the solid wooden panels, wondering if they would hold. She heard footsteps on the stairs outside. They jolted her into action. She picked up the boys' coats and went through into the living room. She switched off the television, slipping on her own coat. She turned to the boys, trying to keep her voice calm. She didn't want them to panic.

'Put your coats on. Do exactly as I say.'

Enqvist riffled through the Brussels area telephone directory, tearing at the pages in his haste. He found the number and dialled it.

It was engaged.

'What is it?' Claire said. 'Has something happened?'

Enqvist tried again.

Still engaged.

'Shit!'

He paused to think. Then he punched in a number he knew by heart.

'Get me Richard Janvier,' he said in French. 'Then *interrupt* him. This is Stig Enqvist, UCLAF. Tell him it's urgent.'

The first shuddering bang came as Kate and the boys stepped out on to the narrow balcony outside the living room French windows. Patrick and James turned their heads, startled by the noise.

'Mum.'

Kate didn't give them time to think, much less to speak.

'Over the rail. Quickly,' she said.

There was another blow from the front door. Kate urged the boys over the metal railing around the balcony. She knew they could do it: one of their favourite ways of riling her was to drop off the balcony into the garden instead of going downstairs to use the door. The question was whether *she* could do it.

Patrick went first, lowering himself from the top rail down to the concrete edge of the balcony floor, then letting himself go until he landed on the soft lawn below. James went after him with all the supple agility of a young boy.

'Get out through the gate,' Kate shouted to them.

They didn't move.

'Go!'

'Not without you, Mum.'

Kate scrambled over the railings, copying what her sons had done. Why didn't they run, the stupid children? she screamed inside her head. Don't worry about me. Just get out!

'We'll catch you, Mum. Come on.'

They held out their arms, standing underneath her on the grass. Kate heard another juddering bang followed by the crash of the door. They were inside the apartment. She looked down and let go. She felt the boys' arms support her as she hit the ground and stumbled.

'You okay?' Patrick said.

Kate nodded. 'The gate.'

They ran across the wet soggy lawn. There was a wooden gate in the brick wall that surrounded the garden.

It was locked.

Kate looked back. The key was on a hook just inside the rear door of the building, but there was no time to go and get it.

'Over the wall,' she said.

She gave Patrick a leg-up. He pulled himself on to the top and straddled it. Kate lifted James around the waist. Patrick grabbed his brother's hand and heaved him up beside him.

There was a shout from the apartment. A figure appeared in silhouette on the balcony. He started to climb over the railings. Kate bent her knees and leapt upwards, getting a hand on the top of the wall. Patrick and James caught her other arm and pulled her up. Her legs scraped against the rough brickwork but she managed to hook one foot over the top and lever herself into a sitting position. One of the men – with the bandaged head – was already running towards them across the lawn. The second was clambering down from the balcony.

Patrick and James didn't need to be told what to do. They swung their legs over and jumped down on the other side of the wall. Kate delayed a second too long, wanting to see them safe before she followed. The first man came up below her and grasped her left leg. Kate clung on to the top of the wall as he attempted to drag her off it. She felt her grip loosening, her fingers rubbing raw on the uneven bricks. She took a deep breath and, with a viciousness she didn't know she had in her, kicked down hard with her foot. The heel of her shoe slammed into the man's nose. He let go of her leg and clutched at his bloody face. Kate twisted round and almost threw herself over the wall. The boys were waiting below on the muddy path that ran through the woods to a lake. People jogged or walked their dogs here in daylight, but it was deserted now darkness had fallen.

'This way, Mum.'

Patrick and James took her hands, dragging her along the path. No questions, no wasted words, they knew the urgency of the situation. Kate had been along here a few times, but the boys knew every inch of the network of tracks that criss-crossed the woods. They'd spent hours exploring them.

They came to a fork in the path and went right, running as fast as they could in the thick darkness. The trees were like pillars lining the path, the undergrowth a dense wall which spread out before them, threatening to trip them up. Kate stumbled several times on the muddy, pot-holed ground but the boys held her up. They were children still but Kate felt them grow into men, protecting her as much as she was protecting them.

She glanced back. The two men couldn't be far behind.

They would be faster than them, stronger. She thought she saw a shadow flitting along the path but couldn't be sure. She listened. The rasping sound of her own breath drowned out any other sound. She knew running wasn't the answer. The men would catch up with them before they'd gone any distance. They had to hide, seek sanctuary in the blackness of the forest.

Patrick and James seemed to sense it too. They veered off the path, pushing through the shrubs, taking her along with them. The ground started to dip down into a hollow. There was a fallen tree at the bottom, its roots torn out of the ground to leave behind a shallow hole. Patrick and James slid down into the hole. Kate followed. They lay on the ground, catching their breath, trying to deaden the noise as they gasped for air. Around them, the trees were dark sentinels, the undergrowth a bastion. They waited, praying silently that the night would shield them from their pursuers.

Sullivan pulled in outside the apartment building and leapt out of his car. Kate's black Fiesta was parked just in front of him, a Peugeot saloon a few yards further up the street. Sullivan ran into the entrance to the building and saw that the lock on the main door was broken. He pushed it open and sprinted up the stairs. On the first-floor landing he stopped.

The door to the apartment was wide open. One edge of it was chipped and splintered with the marks of some heavy implement. The locks and bolts had been torn off, the safety chain dangled loose from its slot.

Sullivan walked in, knowing he was too late.

'Kate!'

He ran from room to room, calling his wife's name. Then he saw the French windows swinging open in the breeze. He walked on to the balcony and stared out into the night, looking beyond the wall at the black, impenetrable woodland.

'Kate!' he yelled.

He listened for a response, for any slight sound. Nothing. He turned to go.

Wait a minute.

He swung back. Crossing the lawn, bruising the surface of the long wet grass, was a series of tracks. Tracks which stopped at the wall at the bottom of the garden.

Sullivan spun round and ran out of the apartment. Downstairs on the ground floor, he snatched the key off the hook on the wall and threw open the door to the garden. He reached the perimeter wall and fumbled for the keyhole in the wooden gate. He turned the lock, whipped open the gate and ran out into the woods.

Kate could feel the two boys next to her, pressing in close. She had an arm around each of them, holding them tight. She knew they must be as scared as she was, but they were hiding it well.

'Who are they, Mum?' James whispered tremulously. 'What do they want?'

'I don't know,' Kate said, squeezing his shoulders.

'Where's Dad?'

'He's on his way. We'll be okay.'

'Sssh,' Patrick hissed.

Kate peered out over the lip of the hole. A tall figure was moving along the path about fifty metres away. He stopped. It was too dark to see his face, or where he was looking. Kate pressed her head to the ground, pulling the boys in against her, trying to reassure them. She could feel their slight, wiry bodies trembling.

The man glided away, running through the trees towards the lake. Kate twisted round but lost sight of him. Where was the second man? Kate didn't dare move until she knew. She wanted to get out of the woods and back to the houses, to streetlights, cars and people. They were vulnerable staying put, even under cover of darkness, but more at risk trying to move until they were sure they wouldn't be observed.

'Are they going to kill us?' James breathed in her ear.

Kate hugged him. 'We'll be fine, you see,' she said, submerging her own fears beneath the need to be strong for the boys' sake.

The undergrowth rustled suddenly behind them. Kate glanced over her shoulder, then sat up quickly. The man with the bandaged head was standing on the rim of the hole, looking down at them. The blood was smeared across his nose and cheeks. He shouted something, calling to his companion. Then he smiled wolfishly and slid down the muddy incline.

Sullivan heard the shout and stopped dead, trying to pinpoint exactly where it had come from. Somewhere to his right, and not too far away. He turned off the path and took the shortest course, running in a straight line through the trees.

Kate scrambled to her feet, pulling the boys up after her and backing away slowly. The sides of the hole rose steeply behind them. Their feet slipped on the damp earth. Kate kept her eyes fixed on the man while she pushed Patrick and James away.

'Run,' she said quietly.

The boys stayed where they were.

'Go on,' she urged them.

The man took a step towards them. Then lunged suddenly for Kate. She attempted to dodge his outstretched arms and lost her footing, toppling to the ground. The man loomed over her. Kate's fingers dug into the soft

253

earth. She hurled a fistful of soil up into his face and, while he was temporarily blinded, scuttled sideways and clambered to her feet. She looked around for a weapon: a rock, a branch. There was nothing to hand. She grabbed more earth, flinging it at the man's head. He lashed out with an arm and sent her flying.

Kate rolled over on the ground and saw Patrick and James going for the man, trying to push him, to hit him with their tiny fists. He knocked them both over like skittles. A fury, a maternal protectiveness overwhelmed Kate and she threw herself on to the man's back, clawing at his face with her nails, kicking his legs as hard as she could. His body was solid and muscled. He wrenched her hands off and tossed her to the ground. Then swung down with a clenched fist that never connected for, at that moment, another figure burst out through the undergrowth, a heavy branch raised in his hands which he brought down in a savage arc, smashing so hard into the man's back the timber broke in two.

It was Rob. Kate picked herself up and backed away, her immediate relief rapidly giving way to fear for her husband's safety. But he seemed to know what he was doing. The other man was younger, probably in better shape, but Rob had more to lose. Kate had never seen him so aggressive, so furiously violent. His foot sank into the man's belly, doubling him up, then he pummelled him with his fists, punching him to the ground where he rained more heavy blows down on him. Kate pulled the boys up the slope out of the way, averting their eyes from the bare brutality of male anger.

Then the odds changed. The second man appeared in the clearing. He took in the scene and raced to the assistance of his companion.

'Rob!' Kate screamed a warning.

Rob turned, but too late. The man dived on top of him,

knocking him over. They struggled and writhed, punching and kneeing each other in a rabid frenzy. Kate couldn't stand by and watch. She picked up a length of fallen branch and hurled herself back down into the hole, clubbing the man about the head and shoulders. He lifted his hands to protect himself and Rob rolled out from under him.

The two assailants staggered to their feet, bruised and bloody. In the distance, the sudden strident noise of police sirens ripped through the night. The men glanced at each other, then turned and sprinted away through the woods.

Rob let them go, too dazed and hurting to prolong the confrontation. He bent over, hands on knees, struggling to breathe.

'Rob, are you okay?'

He straightened up, nodding wearily. He held out his arms. Kate and the boys came to him and they held each other in a fierce, tearful embrace.

SIXTEEN

There were people everywhere. The apartment was crawling with them: uniformed police officers, plainclothes detectives, forensic specialists from the scene-of-crime team, a photographer and his assistant. A joiner and a locksmith were lounging in a couple of chairs, waiting for the fingerprint officers to finish with the front door and, in the bedroom, a police doctor was examining Kate and the boys.

Sullivan was in the kitchen with Stig and Claire and Richard Janvier who had taken charge of the operation.

'You'll get an armed police guard twenty-four hours a day,' Janvier said. 'Three shifts. I'll need some official paperwork from the Commission but I can make the arrangements without it.'

'I'll call Carlsen,' Enqvist said. 'He'll take care of it.'

Janvier gave a nod and looked at Sullivan. 'We'll need statements from your wife and children when they're up to answering questions. From you too.'

'I'll do it now.'

'Has the doctor seen you yet?'

'No. Kate and the boys are in a worse state than I am.'

Janvier grunted sceptically, studying Sullivan's face which had a livid bruise on one cheek, a cut and swollen mouth and dried blood matted into his hair from a gash above his ear.

'You look awful.'

'You should see the other two guys.' Sullivan tried a smile but abandoned it midway, it hurt his mouth too much.

'I hope so,' Janvier said. 'We've closed down the whole of Tervuren. If they're still here we'll find them.'

'What about their car?'

'Stolen earlier this afternoon from a car park near Zaventem.'

'You think they flew in today?' Sullivan said.

'We're checking the airline passenger lists. We'll have a photofit from your description we can show to cabin crews, see if anyone recognises them.'

'It's a long shot.'

Janvier shrugged. 'We don't have much else to go on.'

The police doctor walked in from the hall, his black bag dangling from his hand.

'How are they?' Sullivan asked anxiously.

'Physically, relatively unscathed,' the doctor replied. 'Some cuts, grazes, nothing serious. But mentally . . . well, you can imagine. They seem to be coping well. The boys seem resilient but don't let that fool you. Once they have time to reflect they may suffer considerable stress: nightmares, palpitations, that kind of thing.'

'And my wife?'

'She's worried about the boys. In some ways that makes it easier for her. She's suppressing her own emotions and concentrating on them. But it adds to the strain she's under. She's going to have a tough few days. I've given her some tranquillisers. Don't be afraid to use them.'

The doctor placed his bag on the kitchen table and snapped it open.

'Now you,' he said, pulling out a chair for Sullivan to sit down.

Claire went out into the hall. The joiner was patching

up the front door, replacing the sections of timber which had been damaged. She pushed open the door to the main bedroom and went in. Kate was sitting on the bed, her arms wrapped around Patrick and James. All three were pale and drawn. They looked up at her with tired eyes.

'Is there anything I can get you?' Claire said. 'Something to drink perhaps.'

Kate shook her head listlessly. 'Where's my husband?'

'In the kitchen. The doctor's seeing to his cuts and bruises.'

'The men . . .' Kate's voice trailed away. She seemed too drained to talk.

'They haven't been found yet. The police are still searching the woods and the streets.'

'And all the people? Out there?'

'They'll soon be finished. Are you sure I can't get you anything?'

'Yes, I'm sure.'

Claire found herself assessing Kate, trying to work out what kind of a woman she was. She was a few years older than Claire, her figure heavier through age and the inevitable side effects of having children. But she was still attractive, even now after the trauma she'd just been through. She looked intelligent, able, determined. Not all that different from me, Claire thought.

Kate was looking at her curiously, frowning a little. 'Are you with the police?'

'I'm a colleague of your husband's.'

'Are you?'

'Claire Colmar.' Claire smiled. 'Not the best time to be introduced, I know. I came with Stig. I'll see what's happening for you.'

She went out of the room and closed the door to shut out the noise and the constant comings and goings. She had an idea what Kate was going through. It must have been similar to what she herself had felt after her ordeal at the cottage on the coast. Similar, but probably worse. Kate had children to fear for, and she was a spouse on the periphery of everything, which must have left her feeling impotent and bewildered. Claire, at least, was an active participant. She'd faced risks before and was better equipped to deal with them. But an investigator's wife and children, they were supposed to be sacrosanct.

She returned to the kitchen. The doctor was still attending to Sullivan's face. Claire walked to the far end of the room with Enqvist.

'Why?' she said in a low voice she knew Sullivan couldn't hear. 'Why go after a woman and two young boys? What did they intend to do, kidnap them, kill them?'

'Neither makes much sense,' Enqvist said. 'A hit team wouldn't sit outside in a car in full view for all that time. They'd come straight in, probably the back way, do the job and leave.'

'So what were they doing?'

'Scaring them. Warning us off. That would be my guess. They must be worried, whoever they are, to do something so extreme.'

'Worried?' Claire said.

'We're getting close to something big, I can feel it here.' Enqvist touched his belly, then glanced at his watch. 'You busy tonight?'

'No.'

'Good. We've got a lot of work to do.'

They waited until everyone was gone and the boys were in bed before they sat down together to talk. After the chaos of the previous few hours it was a relief to be alone. Rob put his arms around his wife and they held each other for a long time. He felt her tremble and start to shake, then the tears came in cathartic sobs. He let her cry, not saying anything. It was the best thing she could do.

'I'm sorry,' she said eventually, wiping her eyes. 'This isn't going to help.'

'It is. Let it all out.'

'I was so scared. The boys were incredible. They wouldn't leave me. I told them to but they wouldn't. They stayed with me even though they must have been terrified. I don't know what would have happened if you hadn't come just then.'

She blew her nose and sniffed away more tears. 'Do you think they'll be all right?'

'They'll come through it,' Rob said.

'How can you be sure? What if they're permanently damaged?'

'We can help them. With our support they'll be okay.' He brushed away a stray tear from her cheek. 'It's all my fault. The moment you phoned, I should have called the police.'

'You weren't to know what would happen.'

'I shouldn't have taken the chance.'

'It won't happen again, will it?'

'No,' Rob said, wanting to reassure her.

But he was worried. The two men hadn't been caught, though the police had been scouring the neighbourhood for several hours. It was a difficult task in the dark. The men might have holed up somewhere, but it was more than possible they'd got out of Tervuren before the orchestrated search began.

'I want to go home,' Kate said.

'You're safer here. With me.'

'We'll be safe at home.'

'Things are simpler here,' Rob said gently. 'Brussels is a Commission town. The Commission wields a lot of power. The police understand that. They're used to dealing with diplomats, with international residents. I'm a Commission employee in Brussels and the Commission will make sure you're properly protected. If you go back to England, what do the British police care? To them you're a suburban schoolteacher and I'm a customs officer who just happens to be working abroad. The European Commission means nothing to them. It has absolutely no clout in Colchester.

'Besides,' he added. 'I want you here with me. You're going to need me. And I need you.'

He pulled her close to him, trying not to dwell on what had happened, feeling guilty because it was his job that had put them in danger.

'I think you'd better tell me everything,' Kate said. 'What's changed? Why did those men come after us?'

'That I don't know,' Sullivan said. 'But from the moment we seized the *Maria Vasquez* things have been different. It's not been like other investigations. Too many people have died.'

'I'm frightened for you, Rob. It's never been like this before.'

'I'm quite safe,' he said soothingly. 'So are you and the boys now.'

'You don't know that.'

'They won't get near you again. You're too well-protected.'

'And your investigation?'

'Carries on as before. They're not going to stop us. Whoever sent those two men, I'm going to nail the bastards.'

Kate rested her head on his shoulder. Then she said: 'Who's Claire Colmar?'

'Claire?' He was taken by surprise. 'She's standing in for Maurizio.'

'She's attractive.'

Rob didn't acknowledge the remark.

'You haven't mentioned her before.'

'She's only just transferred.'

'She seems nice.'

'She is.' He changed the subject. 'Why don't we go to bed? You must be shattered.'

He stood up and offered Kate his hand, pulling her to her feet. They looked in on the boys before they went into their own bedroom. Both Patrick and James were sleeping soundly, physically and emotionally exhausted. Rob put his arm around Kate as they watched the unconscious figures in the beds, listening to their soft breathing. He felt a surge of protectiveness, of love for them all; a moment of bonding and gratitude to his wife, the mother of his children, which overpowered him with its intensity. He drew Kate into his arms and held her close in a pledge of commitment and fidelity.

Stig Enqvist rubbed his eyes and got up from his desk, stretching his arms above his head to ease the stiffness in his back. It was approaching eleven o'clock. He and Claire had been sifting through Wolf's papers for nearly five hours and the strain was beginning to show. Claire was on the telephone, talking in English and making notes on a pad. Enqvist walked around the office and waited for her to finish.

'The number in the diary is a cargo warehouse at East Midlands Airport,' she said. 'A company called Freightstorage Services Limited.'

'Clean?'

'As far as UK Customs are aware, yes.'

'Why would Wolf have their number?'

'Maybe he's used them for legitimate cargoes.'

'Hmm.' Enqvist went back to his desk and sat down. 'Let's see if we've got anything on them.'

He logged on to his computer and accessed the UCLAF database. There was no listing for Freightstorage Services.

He checked Companies House Direct. The company's registered office was an address in Nottingham. There were
only two directors: Clyde Barrow and Kyril Shafranov.
Enqvist read the names out to Claire.

'Shafranov. What nationality do you reckon that is?'

'Sounds Russian,' Claire said. She paused. 'Or maybe
Ukrainian.'

Sullivan woke early next morning and slipped quietly out
of bed, leaving Kate sleeping peacefully under the duvet.
He pulled aside the curtain and looked briefly out of the
window. The unmarked police car was down below in
the street, two plainclothes officers sitting in the front.
Reassured, Sullivan went out to the kitchen and made
some coffee.

The night had been easier than he'd expected. The boys
hadn't woken at all and Kate only once that he was aware
of – a short natural interruption after which she'd quickly
gone back to sleep. He was relieved, but suspected future
nights might not be so tranquil. The after-effects of an
ordeal like the one they'd endured were not easy to
predict.

Breakfast was a subdued affair. Patrick and James were
never at their best first thing in the morning, but today they
seemed to be even less communicative than usual. Sullivan
left them alone for a while, then probed them gently.

'Don't bottle anything up,' he said. 'If you want to talk
about it, we're here to listen.'

The boys nodded silently.

'Everything's going to be okay. You're bound to be
affected by what happened. Just say if you need to talk.'

'We don't need to talk,' Patrick said stoically. 'We're
all right.'

'Well, you know we're here,' Sullivan said, not wanting
to push them.

He wondered if they blamed him the way he blamed himself. Children, even your own, were hard to read.

During the morning Carlsen telephoned, as he had the previous evening, to ask how they were and reaffirm that Sullivan didn't need to come into work. Then Janvier called, checking that the protection officers were in place and confessing apologetically that, despite the overnight police search, the two men had not been caught.

'They've gone, haven't they?' Rob said.

'I fear so,' Janvier replied. 'They've slipped the net.'

Sullivan took a shower and went into the bedroom with the phone. The sombre, but understandable, atmosphere in the apartment, such a contrast to the previous times when the family had stayed, was getting to him. It was dispiriting and he felt powerless to help.

He rang Stig Enqvist and they talked for a while about how they were coping.

'What's happening?' Rob asked finally.

'You don't want to worry about that,' Enqvist replied.

'I do. I want to know. I *need* to know.'

Enqvist said nothing.

'Stig,' Rob said, sensing something even at the other end of a phone line. 'What's happening?'

Enqvist sighed. 'You really want to know? Claire and I worked late last night. Checking through the papers we found in Wolf's attaché case, making a few phone calls. When he arrived in Antwerp, he went out and had a meeting at Laterveer Voorden.'

'Oh yes.' Laterveer Voorden was a bonded warehouse company down by the docks.

'He ordered two thousand cases of cigarettes, Marlboros, and arranged for them to be transported to Kiev. They were flown out yesterday morning from Antwerp airport.'

'Even though Wolf was dead by then?'

265

'The freight company didn't know that. Anyway, it wouldn't have made any difference. Wolf placed the order on behalf of Steinhammer Weiss with payment from his bank in Zürich. We checked with Customs at Antwerp and . . .'

Rob could tell by the way Enqvist paused that something important was coming next.

'And?' he prompted.

'And discovered that the plane used to transport the cigarettes was an Ilyushin-76.'

'Shit!' Rob said. 'Registration mark?'

'You can guess.'

'You sure it's the same?'

'No doubt. A different charter company but it's the same plane all right.'

'There's more, isn't there?' Rob said.

'Claire found it. There were other papers in the attaché case. I won't bore you with the details, but we found a telephone number scribbled on one of them, a number that was repeated on a page of Wolf's diary.'

'Which page?'

'The day before he died. It was a UK number. We checked it out. It's a cargo warehouse at East Midlands Airport owned by a company called Freightstorage Services. One of the directors is a Kyril Shafranov who turns out to be of Ukrainian origin.'

'Go on.'

'And Shafranov's son-in-law is Ivan Kravchenko, manager of the clothing warehouse in Nottingham raided by UK Customs last summer.'

'And brother of Vasili, Frans Maartens' drug-dealing friend in Hull. This gets better and better,' Sullivan said. 'You reckon they're flying cigarettes in, storing them at the airport and using a network of Ukrainians to distribute them?'

'I can think of worse guesses. Claire called Customs at East Midlands and what do you know, they're expecting a cargo flight from Kiev via Athens this evening. A shipment of Ukrainian pottery.'

'*Pottery?*' Sullivan said.

'Yeah, interesting, isn't it? I know you're not exactly well-informed on these matters, but would you say Ukrainian pottery was all the rage in England right now?'

Sullivan was silent for a moment, thinking through everything he'd been told.

'The Ilyushin again?'

'Uncle Romeo 79705. It's them, no question about it.'

'You're going over?'

'This afternoon.'

Sullivan hesitated. 'I ought to come too.'

'That's not necessary, you know that.'

'I should be there.'

'Claire and I can handle it,' Enqvist said. 'Take some time off, your family needs you.'

'When's your flight?'

'Rob, how many times? You don't need to come.'

'Yes, okay. Let me know how it goes.'

Sullivan hung up. The apartment was very quiet. He went out of the bedroom and found Kate in the kitchen, scrubbing the draining board beside the sink as if housework were some kind of therapy.

'Don't you ever clean this?' she said, throwing the remark at him over her shoulder.

Sullivan didn't respond immediately, sensing the opening line of an argument they'd had many times before.

'You don't need to do that,' he said, sitting down at the table.

'Well, as you never do,' Kate said. 'This place is absolutely filthy.'

She scrubbed vigorously at the stainless steel with a

scouring pad. She was angry, but Rob knew the state of the apartment had nothing to do with it.

'Come and sit down,' he said gently.

'I'm fine here.'

'Kate.'

He stood up and took the scouring pad from her hand, then led her to a chair. She offered no resistance.

'I have to do something,' she said. 'Cooped up here all day.'

'I know it's not going to be easy for you,' he said. 'But it will get better. Things will get back to normal.'

'Oh yeah? When?'

'It's been less than twenty-four hours. Try and forget about it.'

'You know I can't forget it. Nor can the boys.'

'I'll make us some coffee.'

Sullivan filled the kettle and switched it on.

'They haven't caught them, have they?' Kate said.

'No.'

'Great. So they're out there somewhere just waiting to do it again.'

'They're not out there. I doubt they're even in the country by now. And you have two armed policemen sitting outside. They have instructions to check you're all right every hour, and there's a panic button in the hall you can press if you need them in between. You couldn't be safer.'

Sullivan spooned coffee grounds into the cafetière and filled it with boiling water.

'Who was that on the phone?' Kate said.

'Only Stig.'

He took two mugs out of a cupboard and put them down on the table. Kate was watching him.

'You want to go back to work, don't you?' she said.

'No,' he said quickly.

'Jesus, Rob, do you think I can't tell? You hate this, playing nursemaid to your family.'

'I don't. I'm concerned about you.'

'I know you're concerned, of course you are. But you're prowling about the place like a caged animal. What did Stig say?'

'A consignment's on the move. The Ilyushin we caught at Vitoria but had to hand back to the Ukrainians is taking a cargo from Kiev to East Midlands tonight.'

Kate kept her eyes on his face. 'And you want to be there to meet it.'

'It's our operation.'

'Why can't UK Customs handle it?'

'We're supplying the information. It's our responsibility.'

'Stig's going, I suppose?'

'Yes.'

'And Claire?'

'She's going too.'

Kate sighed. She depressed the plunger on the cafetière and filled the mugs with coffee.

'You can't bear to be left out, can you?'

'It's not that.'

'Isn't it? Come on, Rob, you always like to be in on the kill. It's what you enjoy.'

'Okay,' he admitted. 'But there are other reasons in this case.'

'Oh yes?' She waited.

'The men who attacked you may have been Ukrainians. One of them looked very similar to a thug who nearly killed Claire at a beach house near De Haan. She fought him off with a tyre iron, wounded him badly in the head, but he got away.'

'A tyre iron? That pretty, petite girl?'

'She's not a girl.'

'Christ, I hope you never borrow her pencils without asking.'

Sullivan ignored the remark. 'The crew of the Ilyushin are going to be Ukrainian, I'm sure of that. I want to be there when they're caught red-handed with a planeload of contraband cigarettes. If we can crack them, we may find out who attacked Claire and who attacked you. That's what I want above all.'

'You never told me before she'd been attacked. Why not?'

'I didn't want to worry you. Besides, you didn't know who she was until yesterday.'

Kate drank her coffee, wondering why Rob's colleagues had never interested her greatly until now. She resisted the temptation to probe further.

'Have you told Stig you're going?'

'No. I'm not, if you don't want me to.'

'You're asking me to make the decision?'

'I'm saying, if you want me here, then I'll stay.'

'Don't *you* want to be here?' Kate said.

'Yes, of course. You always come first.'

'But?'

'No buts.'

Kate shook her head. 'I don't believe this. One minute you're telling me we can't go home to England because we'll be safer here with you to look after us, the next you're pissing off to England on business leaving us here on our own.'

'You won't be on your own. There are . . .'

'Yes, I know. The US fucking cavalry are waiting outside the front door.'

'It's my *job*, Kate.'

'And we're your family.'

'Look, let's not argue about it. I understand how you feel. I'm not going.'

He got up from the table. Kate reached out and took his hand.

'You're right, it's not worth an argument.'

She thought of the old joke about give and take in a marriage, wondering why it was always the wife who had to do the giving. Perhaps that was the only way the institution survived.

'Go,' she said. 'We'll be all right.'

'No, I'm staying.'

'Go on, before I change my mind.'

There was a crackle of interference on the radio, then a faint, garbled voice relaying some information that Enqvist, Claire and Sullivan, standing ten yards away, didn't quite catch. Tony Fitzpatrick, from UK Customs, acknowledged the message and nodded across at them.

'This is the one,' he said.

They stepped out of the shelter of the hangar doors, exposing themselves to the piercing wind gusting across the airfield, and looked up at the clear night sky. A couple of lights glowed brightly on the horizon to the east, one of them flashing intermittently as the plane made its final approach. The lights came gradually lower, descending in a shallow curve over the hidden carriageways of the M1, and across the perimeter fence of the airport. The harsh roar of the engines became audible, throbbing over the flat terrain. The wheels touched down and the bulky snub-nosed silhouette raced along the runway in front of them.

Enqvist watched the Ilyushin slow and turn off, taxiing across the apron towards the cargo hangar. It was months since he'd had such a feeling of excitement, such a sense of purpose and anticipation. There were three dark blue transit vans parked on the concrete just outside the hangar doors. As the plane came to a standstill and cut its engines, two of the vans sped out and slewed to a halt beside it. Officers from the Nottinghamshire Constabulary Armed Response Team jumped out and took up positions around the Ilyushin. Steps were manoeuvred into position and the door on the side of the plane swung outwards. Two officers wearing helmets and Kevlar jackets sprinted up the steps into the cockpit, their sub-machine-guns gripped in their hands. More officers followed.

Moments later, the rear door of the third transit van, the ART communications unit, opened and a uniformed inspector climbed out.

'The target has been secured,' he announced laconically, pulling on his leather gloves and strolling across the apron.

The crew of the Ilyushin were being herded down the steps and into a cluster by one of the vans. They were protesting angrily in accented English.

Enqvist, Claire and Sullivan walked out with Fitzpatrick and waited for the rear loading ramp of the Ilyushin to be lowered, revealing the vast cargo hold inside the bowels of the plane. Thousands of cardboard boxes, stacked inside wheeled mesh cages, were lined up down the length of the fuselage. A cargo service truck was brought in to tow the first of the cages down the ramp on to the apron. Fitzpatrick glanced at the UCLAF contingent.

'Your honour, I think,' he said, holding out a pocket knife.

Enqvist took the knife, aware that everyone beside the plane – crew, police and customs officers – was watching him. He lifted down one of the boxes and slit open the top, Sullivan and Claire standing next to him. He cut open a second box, then a third, working his way through the whole stack.

He rummaged through the contents of each box and straightened up, unable to meet the eyes of his colleagues.

He took a deep gulp of the chill night air and looked away, across the airfield to the string of runway lights which sparkled in the darkness like fallen stars.

SEVENTEEN

'CRACKPOTS!'

The headline was splashed across the front page of the newspaper in huge screaming type. Every other British tabloid had something similar. Even the broadsheets had given it prominence, though in less hysterical fashion.

Carlsen tossed the pile across his desk for them to see, giving them time to absorb the embarrassing details, to squirm uncomfortably in their seats.

'So what happened?' he said.

He was a man of great self-control, who took care to suppress his emotions, both good and bad, but this morning there was no doubting he was angry. Livid. And Ole Carlsen was not angry very often.

The others didn't say anything. Sullivan was staring down at the carpet and Claire had her eyes fixed on the wall next to the window. Enqvist was slumped in his chair, subdued, completely chastened by their experience. They'd got it wrong, but none of them had expected their mistake to be blazoned across every newspaper in Britain and quite a few of the continental ones too.

Carlsen picked up a couple of tabloids from the pile and selected a few choice quotes at random from the text, rubbing salt in their wounds with uncharacteristic callousness.

'"Europe's so-called elite team of fraudbusters staged an

armed ambush on British soil last night and netted – fifteen hundred boxes of crockery."

'"What is UCLAF, this cowboy outfit of gung-ho foreigners who think they can come over here and throw their weight around? We say *they* are the Eurofrauds, wasting taxpayers' money on foolish antics like this."

'"Britain's Boys in Blue were put on full alert, at vast cost, to help these Brussels Buffoons intercept a cargo of cups and saucers."'

Carlsen paused. 'You want me to go on?'

Sullivan looked up. 'We made a mistake. No excuses, but these things happen. You know they do.'

'Is that all you can say? Is that what you want me to tell the Director when I see him in half an hour? Is that what you want the Commission to put in the press statement, these things happen? The British papers will have even more of a field day.'

'They're blowing it up out of all proportion,' Enqvist said feebly.

'Are they?' Carlsen retorted. 'Let's look at the facts. You organise the search of a cargo plane belonging to a foreign government. You call in UK Customs and the local police armed response unit. You surround the plane with gun-toting cops, arrest the crew and find nothing on board except Ukrainian pottery, exactly as stated in the cargo manifest. That's pretty blown up already, don't you think?'

He looked at each of them in turn and his anger seemed to wane, its place taken by disappointment.

'The papers are right,' he continued sombrely. 'It makes us look like buffoons. We were humiliated last night, made to look like a bunch of amateurish clowns. And it wasn't just UCLAF that looked foolish, it was the entire Commission. You've given every Europhobe in Britain an excuse to mock us, to lambast us as incompetent idiots.

And they will grab that excuse with both hands. Do you think it will end here? There will be questions in the British parliament, I can guarantee that. In Strasbourg too. The British press will keep hammering away at the incident because it fits in perfectly with their Eurosceptic agenda. This isn't going to go away.'

Enqvist held up his hands. 'It was all my fault,' he said resolutely.

'No way,' Sullivan demurred.

'We were all responsible,' Claire added. 'But we acted in good faith.'

'I was reckless,' Enqvist insisted. 'I should have checked everything more carefully.'

'Stig,' Sullivan said. 'You didn't have time. We had to move quickly.' He glanced at Carlsen. 'Besides, we all know that if you check every last detail, word gets back to the traffickers and they abort the run. Christ, this isn't all *that* unusual. Customs officers all over Europe, all over the world, stop and search regularly without finding anything of consequence.'

'Unfortunately for us, they don't all have such a high profile as this case,' Carlsen said. 'The scale and nature of the operation makes our failure all the more visible. And all the more embarrassing. Did you really need armed police? Especially in the UK where they're so sensitive about things like that.'

'You know who we were dealing with. You know what happened at Vitoria, how we had to block the runway with fire tenders to stop them escaping,' Sullivan said. 'We had every reason to think they'd try to get away again this time.'

'Only if they'd been smuggling in cigarettes.'

'Hindsight, Ole,' Sullivan said. 'We thought they were. How do you think we'd have looked last night if they *had* been smuggling cigarettes and the Ilyushin had taken off leaving us standing on the airport waving goodbye? We took all the right precautions. We just got the wrong cargo.'

'And that's all anyone is going to remember,' Carlsen fired back. 'I know it's unfair, but no one out there either knows or cares about our successes. It's our failures they will use against us.'

He sighed, running his fingers through his coarse grey hair. 'I'm not blaming any of you. I understand the difficulties under which you are forced to operate, but I'm warning you that we will have questions to answer about everything we did. There will have to be an inquiry. There may be calls for resignations. I will do my utmost to make sure those calls are not heeded, but they may become too strong for the Director to resist. Now take me through every single detail of the operation, from start to finish.'

'We were set up,' Enqvist said bitterly. 'We were fucking set up.'

He kicked the metal wastepaper bin by the side of his desk and watched it skitter across the carpet and bang against the base of the office wall.

'The papers, the diary, they were all planted for us to find. How could we have been so stupid?'

'Because Wolf was dead,' Sullivan said calmly.

Enqvist turned to look at him, then nodded, acknowledging the truth of the remark. That was the crux of the matter. If they'd come across the papers in any other circumstances, they would have gone through them in minute detail, checking the authenticity of every reference: noting the times and dates of Wolf's movements, of the cargoes he'd ordered and where they'd gone. They'd have crosschecked every single bloody item to build up a complete picture of how he operated.

But the Swiss had been dead. It was that which had lulled them into abandoning their usual caution. Wolf himself had placed the documents in the hotel safe, their provenance was impeccable and his subsequent murder seemed only to give the papers more credence. There was no reason to suspect they were fakes. Even now, the debacle at East Midlands Airport fresh in their minds, it was hard to accept the implications of what had happened.

Claire put into words the key concern that was troubling all three of them.

'Are we saying Wolf was killed just to discredit us? I find that difficult to believe. What if there was no connection between his murder and the forging of the papers?'

'They have to be connected,' Sullivan said. 'Someone went to a lot of trouble to mislead us with the documents. Wolf's death was no coincidence or accident.'

'You'd have to be pretty ruthless to think of a plan like that,' Claire said.

Sullivan nodded. 'They *are* ruthless.'

'But Wolf must have been in on it.'

'He was.'

'And they sacrificed him to make us look stupid?'

'Not just for that. They must have wanted him out of the picture for other reasons too.'

'Such as?'

Sullivan shrugged. 'Wolf was a frail old man, but he was still working. Maybe someone wanted to take over his territory.'

'Montague?' Enqvist said.

Sullivan walked to the window of the office. It was raining again outside – he could see the droplets above him on the glass roof – but none of it penetrated through to the atrium whose plants and shrubs had to be artificially fed and watered. The Beaulieu complex was a strange sealed environment, protected from the vagaries of the weather by glass and concrete walls. It seemed to Sullivan like a metaphor for the entire European Commission, a bureaucracy of self-absorbed careerists and time-servers who lived in isolation from the real world. Most of them led lives of dull, sheltered tranquillity. They had no idea, and no interest, in the corrupt, disturbing currents that shaped and distorted the existence of those outside.

But UCLAF was different. It was the only part of the whole organisation whose *raison d'être* was crime, whose staff were steeped – albeit at one sanitised remove – in the murky sediment of human greed and savagery. Sullivan knew how much money was at stake. To an ambitious criminal the murder of an old man was a small price to pay for a larger share of the booty.

'Everything points to him,' he said. 'Wolf was at his house for the few days before his death. That has to be when the papers were prepared.'

'It was a big job,' Claire said sceptically. 'They must have been forging them for weeks.'

'I don't think so,' Sullivan said. 'I think most of those documents are genuine. That's what's clever about it. Even if we *had* checked them more thoroughly we'd have found they added up. All Montague did was slip in a couple of telephone numbers, an order form from Laterveer Voorden and let us do the rest for him.'

'And we walked straight into it,' Enqvist said through gritted teeth. 'If the Director wants a head for this cock-up, it has to be mine, okay? I'm nearly at the end of my time anyway.'

'If you go, Stig, we all go,' Sullivan said. He glanced at Claire and she nodded in agreement. 'We ride out the storm,' he continued. 'And we make sure that next time – and there will be a next time – we get him.'

No one asked the obvious question, how? But Claire was already thinking through the possibilities.

'If most of the papers are genuine,' she said, 'we still have a briefcase full of dynamite. Don't we?'

'They're genuine,' Sullivan replied. 'But useless. Montague will have made sure of that. They'll either be stuff we already know, or false trails leading us into some unsolvable maze of companies. We might manage to implicate Wolf in something, but why waste our time? Wolf is dead.'

'So where do we go from here?' Enqvist said. 'We have no hard evidence against Montague at all.'

'Then we have to find some. My guess is he's going to make his next move soon, while we're still in disarray. He thinks he's got us on the ropes, that we'll be too frightened of getting it wrong again to take any risks. That makes it the perfect time to hit back.'

'Carlsen won't like it,' Enqvist said. 'He's going to want us to lie low for a while until this blows over.'

'We don't tell Carlsen. Not until we've got something positive for him. Something we're absolutely sure of.'

Enqvist stared at him pensively, chewing his lower lip. Sullivan met Claire's eyes, keeping all emotion, all memories of shared intimacy out of his expression. They had to make this decision independently of each other. All three of them. But Sullivan had no compunction about influencing their choice.

'There's a Ukrainian connection,' he said. 'The Ilyushin last night proves that. This is bigger than just Montague. A Ukrainian attacked Claire and Ukrainians threatened my family, I'm sure of that. We can't afford to sit back and do nothing while Carlsen organises an inquiry to placate a few shit-stirrers in the British press.'

Sullivan turned away to let them think about it. He wondered what Kate and the boys were doing, wondered whether his common sense was being submerged by some

281

inflamed, irrational desire for revenge for what had happened to them. He didn't think so. This was business, pure and simple.

'You have something in mind?' Claire said, and Sullivan knew she'd made her decision.

He walked back to his desk and sat down.

'Stig?'

Enqvist sighed and gave a reluctant nod. 'Okay.'

'There are several strands here which we have to link together somehow,' Sullivan said, counting them off on his fingers. 'Montague, Van Vliet, Gilles Lafon, the *Maria Vasquez*, the Camorra, the Ukrainians. Claire, can you call Hellendoorn and ask him if he can put the Golden Valley Inn under surveillance? So far, that brothel's the only link we have between the key players in this. I'll ask UK Customs if they can keep an eye on Montague.'

'What else?' Enqvist said.

'As I said when we went for lunch in Jezus-Eik,' Sullivan replied. 'You don't smuggle cigarettes with a suitcase and a couple of couriers. You don't do it even with an Ilyushin-76 which can carry only a couple of thousand cases at one time and has to land at official airstrips. You do it by sea. You take advantage of miles of unguarded coastline to make your drops. The *Maria Vasquez* is out of the picture, but Montague will have another ship somewhere. We have to identify it.'

Enqvist pulled a face. 'That could take us weeks.'

'We haven't got weeks,' Sullivan said. 'If I'm right, we have just a few days at the most to identify it, and find it.'

The paper was piling up on the desks. Sullivan looked at the growing mound with a sinking heart. Enqvist was right, this could take weeks. And there was no guarantee of success even then.

They'd done their best to narrow down the search, concentrating on shipments from Rotterdam and Antwerp, the two largest cigarette ports in Europe. There were bonded warehouses elsewhere on the continent, but they were too small to supply the quantities a large-scale, serious trafficker would have required. And Sullivan was sure of one thing: Hal Montague, though he'd evaded identification until now, was a big-time smuggler.

They had faxes from Customs in both ports detailing all consignments of cigarettes due to sail in the next seven days. It was a daunting list, comprising some fifty-four ships of varying nationalities.

'It's too many,' Enqvist said.

'Then cut it down,' Sullivan said. 'Let's take out the flags of convenience and concentrate on those.'

They consulted the Lloyd's Register of Shipping and went through the list, ticking off the ships which were registered in the classic flags-of-convenience countries: Liberia, Costa Rica, Panama, Honduras, the Bahamas and Vanuatu.

'How many have we got?' Claire said.

Enqvist counted them. 'Thirty-six.'

'Let's start with the ones taking consignments from Van Vliet's warehouse,' Sullivan said. 'Mark the stated destination of the cargoes, then check with Customs in those countries to see if the ships have been there before and when.'

Enqvist picked up the log of the *Maria Vasquez* and looked at the map of the world they'd taped to the wall. There were sheets of coloured stickers on the desk.

'Red triangles are the *Maria Vasquez*,' he said, peeling off the stickers.

He studied the log and put a red triangle beside each port the ship had visited over the previous two months: Rotterdam, Hull, Algeciras, Istanbul, Odessa, Massawa, Limassol, Bilbao.

Then Sullivan handed him a list of ships to check. He gave Claire another and kept the last few for himself. He reached out for the phone but it rang before he got there. He picked it up.

'UCLAF, Sullivan.'

'This is Janvier,' a voice said in French.

'Richard,' Sullivan said. 'What's new? Any sign of the two men?'

'I'm afraid not,' Janvier replied. 'But we have an ID on one of them. We showed the photofit to airline personnel at Zaventem and got a positive. He came in on an Aeroflot flight from Moscow on Tuesday morning.'

'Moscow?'

'His name's Drozhkin. Mikhail Drozhkin. You were right, he's a Ukrainian.'

'Any form?'

'No, but here's something interesting. His father is Yevgeny Drozhkin. We have a file on him.'

'Should I know the name?' Sullivan said.

'Before the collapse of the Soviet Union, Yevgeny Drozhkin was the GRU Resident in Brussels.'

'Jesus!'

'When the Ukraine became an independent state he went back to Kiev and set up a private security business hiring out bodyguards, providing protection, confidential vetting, you know what I mean. Half the senior officers of the GRU went into the same lucrative line of work. By the looks of it, his son did too. If I get anything more I'll let you know.'

Sullivan hung up. Enqvist and Claire were looking at him expectantly. Sullivan repeated what Janvier had told him.

'The GRU?' Claire said in disbelief. 'Soviet Military Intelligence?'

Sullivan nodded.

'Great,' said Enqvist. 'That's all we fucking need.'

*　　*　　*

It was late afternoon, the winter darkness closing in around the office, when Sullivan finally remembered to ring Kate. She didn't sound happy.

'You said you'd call this morning,' she said tersely.

'It slipped my mind, I'm sorry.'

'The least you could do was ring. How long does a phone call take?'

'I'm sorry, okay?' Sullivan said, trying not to get irritated by her combative tone.

'We're stuck here in this bloody flat going spare with boredom and you can't even be bothered to see how we are.'

'You're not stuck,' Sullivan said, knowing he was inviting a prolonged argument. 'You can go out.'

'Oh sure, wonderful,' Kate retorted. 'Go out where?'

'Anywhere you like.'

'What, with a couple of plainclothes cops following us?'

'They're there for your protection.'

'We're virtually prisoners here. That's not why we came. The idea was that you would be able to spend more time with your family, take a few days off work. Remember?'

Sullivan controlled his rising feeling of resentment. She had a point, but he didn't want to be reminded of it.

'We've a lot on here,' he said. 'Things we have to clear up.'

'Can't Stig and Claire handle it?'

'It's not that simple.'

'What things?'

'It's too complicated to explain. You wouldn't under-stand.'

'Oh, pardon me for being so dense.'

'Kate, this isn't helping me.'

'You think going back to work is helping *us*? Have you considered that?'

'We ballsed things up in a big way last night. The British

285

papers are crucifying us. It's important we recover some of our credibility. That's why I'm here, not with you.'

'Credibility? How much credibility do you think you have with the boys now?'

'Don't bring them into it.'

'They're in it already, or hadn't you noticed?'

Sullivan snorted with annoyance, frustrated at the way the conversation was degenerating into an all-out row.

'Look,' he said firmly, 'I wouldn't be here without a damn good reason. If we don't sort this out now, I might be out of a job by the weekend.'

'You know, that might not be such a bad thing for all of us,' Kate said and hung up.

The map of the world was gradually filling up with small coloured stickers: squares, diamonds, circles, stars, some with numbers written on them, each denoting a different ship. Sullivan added another beside the port of Mombasa and turned as Enqvist walked back in carrying a couple of faxes. Sullivan gave him an enquiring glance. Enqvist shook his head.

'*Santa Maria IV* and the *Donna Elvira* both look clean,' he said. 'The *Santa Maria* was in Lagos last month with a mixed cargo including twelve thousand master cases of cigarettes. The *Elvira* took fifteen thousand cases to Haifa five weeks ago. Nothing unloaded en route.'

Sullivan consulted the key beside the map and placed the appropriate stickers next to the ports. Claire came off the phone and scribbled a note on her pad.

'The *Sheerness* looks clean too,' she said. 'Ten thousand master cases to Dakar a month ago. Every case arrived and was checked through Senegalese Customs.'

Enqvist swore in Swedish and sat down at his desk.

'We're wasting our time. All these ships are in the clear.'

'That doesn't mean they're not involved in trafficking,' Claire said. 'If you're a smart smuggler, you'll mix legitimate cigarette shipments in with the contraband shipments to muddy the waters.'

Enqvist sighed. 'I know. But we've got to narrow the field down somehow.'

'None of them are in the clear until we know every single shipment they've made and checked it with the ports concerned.'

'We don't have access to that information,' Enqvist said. 'Not without their logbooks or the owners' records, and we can't get hold of either of those.'

Sullivan was studying the map on the wall. 'We're doing this the wrong way round,' he said.

'What?'

'We should be starting with the ports, not the ships. We have the log of the *Maria Vasquez*. That's the one ship whose movements we know exactly. What we should do is contact each port the *Maria Vasquez* visited with a list of the thirty-six ships we're checking and see if any of them went there too. See if there's a pattern common to more than one of them.' He tapped the map. 'Particularly ones that also called at Odessa.'

'Odessa?' Enqvist said. 'Shit, yes, I should have spotted that immediately.'

They photocopied the list and Enqvist went down the corridor to fax it to every port mentioned in the *Maria Vasquez*'s log. Claire looked across at Sullivan, but before he could say anything his telephone rang. He picked up the receiver.

'UCLAF, Sullivan.'

'You were lucky last time,' a voice said softly. A man's voice, educated, definitely English.

'Pardon?' Sullivan said.

'We gave you a sporting chance. Let your wife see us first. You won't be so lucky next time.'

287

Sullivan jolted forwards in his seat. A sudden spasm of nausea shuddered through his stomach.

'Who is this?' he demanded.

'Think about it,' the voice said. 'A woman, two young boys. Think how vulnerable they are, how easy it is to get to them.'

'Who the hell are you?' Sullivan was almost shouting into the phone.

'Does it matter?'

'What do you want?'

'You know what we want. Back off, Sullivan. Find someone else to pick on. We don't like it.'

'Tough shit.'

'I'm serious. Think about your wife and kids. Why take the risk?'

The line went dead. Sullivan replaced the receiver and swallowed hard, taking deep breaths to ease the sickness in his belly. Claire was watching him.

'Them?' she asked.

Sullivan nodded. He stood up and grabbed his coat.

'I'm going home.'

'They'll be safe, Rob. The police are there.'

'I know. I should be too.'

Claire came round from her desk and pushed the door shut.

'Claire, look . . .'

She stopped him with a shake of her head. 'Let's not talk. It won't help.'

She reached up and kissed him on the mouth. He returned the pressure of her lips, feeling her arms around his neck, her body soft against him. With an effort he broke away.

'I'd better go.'

He pulled open the door and walked out.

Kate was watching television in the living room. She

glanced up at him as he came in and turned her head back to the screen. Sullivan sat down in an armchair. His wife exuded a perceptible air of hostility.

'The boys in bed?' he said.

'It's nine o'clock.'

'How are they?'

Without looking at him, she said coldly: 'If you'd come home, you could have asked them yourself.'

The tone was set. Sullivan decided to get it over with now. It would be much worse if he left it until they were in bed together.

'I'm sorry,' he said contritely. 'We had a lot on.'

'Oh yes?' Kate tilted back her head and sniffed a few times.

'I can smell perfume.'

'It's probably Claire's.'

'Ah.' There was a whole wealth of meaning in that short exclamation.

'She wears it,' Sullivan said.

'Did she give you a dab to try too?'

Sullivan gestured in exasperation. 'Come on, Kate, this is silly.'

'It's very strong.'

'It's like cigarette smoke. The smell gets everywhere.'

She was looking at him pensively. For a moment Sullivan thought she was going to come out and ask him directly. But to his relief she changed the subject.

'We're going back to England tomorrow.'

'You're . . . ?' He stared at her. 'That's not a good idea.'

'It's bad enough here at the best of times. I can't take any more of it.'

'You have to stay. For your own safety.'

'The boys want to go home too.'

Sullivan leaned forwards, alarmed. 'You can't. I told you, you'll be better protected here.'

289

'How long is this going to go on? The boys have to be back at school on Monday. So do I.'

'That's not important right now. You can take a few days off until this all settles down.'

'Like you did, you mean?' she said acidly.

'For Christ's sake,' Sullivan exploded. 'This is their safety we're talking about. Have you thought of that?'

'I've thought about nothing else for the past two days. Which is more than you have.'

'That's not fair.'

'It's true. We've seen what your priorities are. Well my priorities are to get home and back to a normal life for the boys as soon as possible.'

'Give it more time,' Sullivan said.

'For what? You said yourself those men are probably out of the country by now. What real danger are we in?'

Sullivan hesitated. He'd hoped he wouldn't have to tell her about the phone call. He didn't want to worry her any more than necessary. But he had no choice now.

'They called me at the office before I left,' he said. 'Not the men themselves, but someone speaking for them. Maybe the man who sent them. He made threats.'

'Against us?'

'Yes. You have to stay, Kate.'

'What did he say?'

'Not much.'

'What did he say?' Kate repeated.

'Just how you were vulnerable.'

'Was he serious?'

'Yes.'

'And are we vulnerable?'

'You might be.'

'Are you saying that because you believe it, or because you want us to stay here?'

'I'll feel happier with you here.'

290

'Oh, *you'll* feel happier. Sitting in your office carrying on as normal while we're stuck out here.'

'Kate, let's discuss this rationally. You might still be in danger.'

'Are you going to be with us?'

Sullivan was silent. Then he said lamely: 'That's not the point.'

'No, it's not, is it? Not to you. If you're so concerned, then you'd better arrange for someone to keep an eye on us in Colchester, because that's where we'll be.'

Kate stood up and switched off the television.

'I think we should give this more thought,' Sullivan said.

'I've done all the thinking I need.' She headed for the bedroom.

'Don't you care what my views are?'

Kate stopped. 'Right now, Rob, I don't give a toss what your views are.'

She went into the bedroom and closed the door firmly behind her.

EIGHTEEN

Montague stood by the window, looking out through a narrow gap in the blinds, while Doyle went through his customary routine of checking the room for bugs. The Singel canal outside was a murky brown colour, its surface smeared with the rainbow traces of oil from the passing boats. To his right the floating flower market was an inferno of colour. The wooden platforms were smothered with carnations and chrysanthemums, lilies, roses, irises and a hundred other species. Montague watched the bustle of the market, listening to the cries of the stallholders, the lap of the water against the sides of the pontoons. There was a subdued normality about it all he found soothing.

Behind him, Doyle was packing away his electronic equipment. Montague turned and waited for him to finish.

'It's clean,' Doyle said.

Montague gave a nod. The trolley of coffee and biscuits had already been wheeled in. He poured himself a cup and wandered to the head of the table to sit down. Lafon and Luciani were always late. They had a Mediterranean indifference to punctuality which Montague had learnt to accept though it irritated him immensely. They were the buyers and, as in any other trade, they were always right.

Ten minutes elapsed before the Frenchman and the Neapolitan arrived. Montague always thought of Luciani as Neapolitan, not Italian. There was something coarse, primitive about him. He had a crude vitality and a streak of ruthless cruelty which Montague associated with the *Mezzogiorno*, the southern half of the Italian peninsula where feudal tradition still held away and where men like Armando Luciani ruled over their cowed subjects like medieval warlords.

The two men sat down and waited in silence for coffee to be brought to them in their seats. Montague made no attempt at small-talk. They were none of them friends. Outside their shared business interests they had absolutely nothing to converse about.

Luciani waved away his bodyguards and fixed his dark, hooded eyes on Montague.

'When do I get my shipment?' he said, getting straight to the point of the meeting.

'The ship leaves Antwerp on Monday morning,' Montague replied. 'She'll be in the Bay of Biscay three days later, the usual location . . .' He looked at Lafon and the Frenchman nodded. '. . . then off the coast of southern Italy in the middle of the following week.'

Luciani scowled. 'No earlier?'

'It's as soon as I can manage. We're having to be very careful this time.'

'How many cases?'

'Twenty-five thousand each. Payment on the usual terms. The master of the ship will contact you when he's nearing the rendezvous positions. I trust that's acceptable to you both.'

Lafon gestured his assent. Luciani grunted, then gave a grudging nod. Even he couldn't complain about twenty-five thousand cases – that was two hundred and fifty million cigarettes with a street value in Naples of approaching twenty million US dollars, more than enough to keep his *camorristi* busy for a few weeks.

'The ship,' Luciani said. 'How safe is she?'

'As safe as I can make her. She's never been stopped or searched. Everything about her is above board and there is no way – absolutely no way – she can ever be traced back to us.'

'What's her name?'

'The *Reunion Star*,' Montague said.

It was a relief to Montague when the meeting was over and Ilse Ameling came in with the girls. Luciani and Lafon seemed to relax immediately and Montague escaped from their surly company to find solace with the house madam. He'd known Ilse for more than fifteen years, since the time she'd been a call girl for one of the high-class, discreet escort agencies in Amsterdam – less obvious than the sordid prostitution available in the city's red-light district and more suitable for Montague's business partners, who would never have dreamt of trawling the streets for their pleasure. She'd set up the Golden Valley Inn at his instigation, tapping into the rich market of peripatetic businessmen who lived their lives away from home and were prepared to pay a premium for the comforts of a five-star hotel with a few extras thrown in which the Hiltons, Sheratons and Dorchesters didn't provide. Montague used her for a lot of his clients. Money oiled the wheels of business but he found that sex was just as good a lubricant, sometimes better.

They drank champagne and chatted casually for a while, then Montague noticed Christine talking to Doyle on the other side of the room. He caught her eye and beckoned her over. He offered her a glass of champagne and lit up a cigar the size of a *baguette*.

'How are you today, my dear?' he asked formally.

Christine smiled archly. 'Don't you want to find out?'

Montague chuckled. 'All in good time.' He puffed contentedly on his cigar then removed it from his mouth and tapped the ash off into a small silver tray. 'How is your assignment going?' he asked.

'I don't want to rush it,' Christine replied. 'But I'm making good progress.'

Montague nodded. 'I trust I'm going to see a return on my investment soon.'

'Oh, you will,' Christine said with conviction. 'Believe me, you will.'

The nondescript white Ford transit van was parked on the other side of the Singel canal, its curtained rear window facing the entrance to the Golden Valley Inn. Inside, sitting on collapsible camping chairs, were two bored-looking men in crumpled suits. One of the men was peering out cautiously through a slit in the curtain.

'Here we go again,' he said, pulling the slit wider.

His partner lifted his camera to the glass and focused the 400mm lens, clicking off a number of shots in quick succession while the first man spoke quietly into his radio. Five minutes later and, again, a further ten minutes after that, they repeated the exercise. Then they removed the film from the camera, clambered into the front seats of the van and drove away.

Claire was holding the fax sheets in her hand, reading through them one by one, trying to make sense of the information they contained.

'It's hard to know where to start,' she said.

Neither Enqvist nor Sullivan replied. Enqvist was drinking yet another cup of coffee and rubbing his bloodshot eyes. Sullivan was gazing distractedly out of the window, his mind elsewhere. Claire guessed he was thinking about his family.

'Hey, guys,' she said. 'Are we going to do this or not?'

Enqvist nodded unenthusiactically. Claire wondered if it

was her imagination or if she could really smell alcohol in the office. Maybe it seeped out of the pores of the skin like sweat.

'Rob?'

Sullivan turned. 'Uh?'

'Come on, we've got all this to sort out. I'm not doing it on my own.'

'Sorry.'

Sullivan drifted back to his desk and got his brain in gear for the job in hand.

'Okay, what do the faxes say?'

Claire read out the names of the ships and the ports. Sullivan scribbled numbers on coloured stickers and handed them to Enqvist who placed them on the map on the wall. There were so many it looked as if a multi-coloured rash had swept across the world.

'What now?' Enqvist said.

Claire looked at Sullivan. 'We match the movements with the route of the *Maria Vasquez*, I suppose. See if any ship followed exactly the same course.'

Sullivan nodded and picked up the log of the *Maria Vasquez*. 'Let's start with Rotterdam.'

He read out each port in order while Enqvist and Claire checked the map and fax sheets. No other ship had called at all the ports. Twenty-six had been to Rotterdam at some point, not surprising given its importance in the world shipping business. Eight had been to Hull, fifteen to Algeciras, ten to Istanbul, eight to Odessa, one to Massawa, seven to Limassol and thirteen to Bilbao.

'Let's take Odessa,' Sullivan said. 'Give me the names of the eight ships which have been there, and the dates.'

Claire read out the names and Sullivan wrote them down on a pad of paper.

'*Sierra Blanca, Allport Castle, Reunion Star, Simonetta, Catriona, Charlotte Anne, Navarino Princess, Nancy Dawson.*'

297

'The *Charlotte Anne* is in the clear already,' Enqvist said. 'I checked her out yesterday with the Van Vliet shipments.'

'That leaves seven,' Sullivan said. 'Stig, you take the first three on the list, Claire the second two. The remaining two I'll handle.'

They picked up the telephones and the directory of customs posts around the world and started to dial.

By mid-afternoon the information was beginning to trickle back from the ports. Sullivan called out the names of the seven ships in turn.

'*Sierra Blanca*?'

'Clear,' Enqvist said. 'She took fifteen thousand cases to Istanbul on her last trip. All accounted for according to Turkish Customs.'

'*Allport Castle*?'

'Clear.'

'*Reunion Star*?'

'Ditto.'

'*Simonetta*?'

'I'm still waiting for a reply,' Claire said. 'The same with the *Catriona*. Freetown Customs are calling me back when they've located the documentation.'

'The *Navarino Princess* looks to be in the clear,' Sullivan said. 'No word on the *Nancy Dawson* yet.'

He reviewed the list.

'*Simonetta*, *Catriona* or *Nancy Dawson*. It's one of those three.'

It was growing dark outside. Sullivan could see the distant flicker of car headlights on the roads, the dull glow of the streetlamps. He thought about Kate and the boys yet again. They would be almost home in Colchester by now. He considered ringing but decided not to, unsure of the reception he'd receive. He and Kate had parted under a cloud of frosty politeness, still smarting from the previous night's row. He'd made another attempt to persuade her to stay on in Brussels but she'd refused. They were both stubborn, unwilling to give ground. There'd been other moments like this in their marriage, but they'd always come through them. Maybe they would this time too. Sullivan wasn't sure.

Enqvist came in with two more faxes. He shook his head.

'*Simonetta* and *Nancy Dawson* look to be clear,' he said.

That left the *Catriona*. Claire was on the phone to Customs in Freetown. Sullivan and Enqvist waited for her to finish.

'The *Catriona* took seventeen thousand cases to Sierra Leone in January. Every one arrived,' she said. 'She seems to be in the clear too.'

'Fuck!' said Enqvist.

'Maybe it's not a flag-of-convenience ship,' Claire speculated.

'It has to be,' Sullivan said. 'Doing offshore drops, they need a compliant Third World crew. Guys who don't care what the ship does provided they get a pay packet at the end of the trip.'

'So maybe we're making a mistake concentrating on Odessa.'

'Maybe.' Sullivan wasn't convinced. He was sure the Ukrainian connection was important.

'We've ruled out Van Vliet and Odessa,' Enqvist said. 'Where do we go from here?'

'We check the remaining ships,' Claire said.

Enqvist grimaced. 'We'll be here all night.'

'Probably longer.'

They were getting nowhere slowly. Twenty-four of the thirty-six ships had been eliminated from the list, but that still left a further twelve to consider. Phone calls had been made, faxes sent. No replies had yet been received. They were starting to get tired, hungry.

'We need a break,' Enqvist said wearily. He was listless, jaded by their lack of progress.

Sullivan was studying the map on the wall, his eyes roving across the names of the ports, the clusters of coloured stickers.

'Somewhere we're missing something,' he said.

Enqvist walked over and stood next to him, looking at the map too.

'I don't know what it is,' Sullivan continued, 'but I know we've overlooked it.'

Behind them the telephone rang. Claire answered and spoke in Dutch for a time.

'Hellendoorn,' she said, coming off the line. 'The surveillance operation on the Golden Valley Inn. There was a meeting there this morning. Three visitors identified as Hal Montague, Gilles Lafon and Armando Luciani. He's faxing through the photos for us now.'

'The vultures are gathering,' Enqvist said. 'Let's go and eat.'

Sullivan stayed behind for a few minutes to call Kate.

'When did you get back?' he said.

'A couple of hours ago.' Her voice was flat, tired.

'You should have called me.'

'Why? You didn't call us.'

'Are you still cross with me?'

'Does it show?'

He tried again.

'Have the police been in touch?'

He'd asked Janvier to arrange for a watch to be kept on them by the Essex police.

'A patrol car came round. They checked the doors and

windows, gave me a bleeper to use if anything happened.'

'You should be here.'

'Are we starting all that again?'

Sullivan sighed. 'What about the boys?'

'They're in bed.'

'I'll ring tomorrow. Speak to them then.'

Silence.

'Anything else?' Kate enquired sourly.

He couldn't swallow his anger. 'What do you mean, anything else? I'm your husband, not some bloody nuisance caller.'

'Don't swear at me.'

'How long are you going to keep this up?'

'I'm tired. I'm going to bed now. Good night.'

He couldn't believe she'd hung up on him. He dialled the number again. It rang but there was no reply. He knew it was the line ringing, not the phone. She'd unplugged it from the socket.

He slammed down the receiver and sat motionless for a time, trying to contain his fury. He realised his hands were clenched into tight balls and forced himself to relax before he stood up and went out after Claire and Stig.

The surveillance photographs from Amsterdam, grainy long-distance snaps showing various individuals coming and going from the Golden Valley Inn, were in the fax tray in the secretaries' office down the corridor. Sullivan paused to flick through the pile, wanting to take a good look at the opposition. Montague he recognised from their encounter at Horningtoft. The others, Lafon, Luciani and a third man identified as Simon Doyle, were all new to him. He studied their features, committing them to memory, then tossed the photos back into the tray and went down in the lift.

Sullivan studied the map of the world again when they came back from dinner. It was getting late but none of them wanted to call it a night just yet. Then he opened the log of the *Maria Vasquez* and read through the pages carefully. He noted the dates and times and did some arithmetic in his head. He returned to the map and peered at it intently.

'What're you doing?' Enqvist asked.

'Pass me the Reed's tables.'

Sullivan checked some of the distances, then did a few more mental calculations.

'I knew something didn't add up. The *Maria Vasquez* was in Massawa, Eritrea, on December fifteenth last year. The next port of call, according to her log, was Limassol, Cyprus, on December twenty-second. It's thirteen hundred nautical miles from Massawa to Limassol. At the *Maria Vasquez*'s normal service speed of thirteen knots it should have taken her four days, say five to allow for delays in the Suez Canal. Yet it took her seven.'

'So she took her time.' Enqvist said.

'Not these ships. They cram in as many cargoes, as much mileage as they can. It's the only way they pay.'

'You think she went somewhere else on the way?' Claire said.

Sullivan nodded. 'And didn't record it in the log.'

Enqvist stared at the map. 'Like where?'

Sullivan turned to Claire.

'Can you ring Dutch Directory Enquiries and get a number for Gerda Faassen?'

'Frans Maartens' sister?' Claire said in surprise.

'It's a long shot, but worth a try.'

Claire replaced the receiver and eyed Sullivan narrowly.

'What on earth made you think of her?'

'I remembered she said she collected them.'

'Her brother sent her a postcard from Port Said, in Egypt, dated December twentieth.'

*   *   *

302

They checked with Customs in Port Said, then called Massawa and Bilbao, the *Maria Vasquez's* next port of call after Limassol. Sullivan assimilated the notes he'd made and smiled ruefully.

'These guys are good,' he said. 'Very good. You have to admire them. The *Maria Vasquez* loaded ten thousand litres of palm oil in Massawa, Eritrea. At Port Said she took on thirty thousand litres of hazelnut oil. The documentation was changed in transit so that by the time she reached Bilbao she was offloading forty thousand litres of palm oil from Eritrea. No mention of the stop in Port Said or the hazelnut oil.'

'Which went to Garcia Saez in San Sebastian and from there to Bayonne,' Claire said, working it out for herself. 'No security paid and Fonteneau et Delahaye got their regular supply to adulterate their olive oil.'

'But this is the bit I like,' Sullivan said. 'Eritrea is a Lomé Convention country entitled to preferential import tariffs. Egypt isn't. So they pass the hazelnut oil off as Eritrean palm oil and pay no customs duty on it either. It's brilliant. These guys are ripping off the EU in every direction.'

He turned to Stig. 'There was one other ship on our list which called at Massawa. Which one was it?'

Enqvist rummaged through the messy pile of papers on the desk and extracted a single sheet. He ran his finger down the names.

'The *Reunion Star*,' he said.

'That's our baby.'

They double-checked with Bilbao to make absolutely sure. The *Reunion Star* had been there two weeks earlier and unloaded a cargo of palm oil from Eritrea.

'The same run, the same scam,' Sullivan said. '*And* she went to Odessa en route to Massawa. There's no question, she's the target.'

Claire consulted the information they'd received from Customs in Rotterdam and Antwerp.

'She's taking fifty thousand master cases from Laterveer Voorden in Antwerp to Accra.'

'When does she sail?'

'First thing Monday.'

Sullivan glanced at his watch. It was two fifteen in the morning.

'Who wants the pleasure of waking up Carlsen?' he said.

NINETEEN

The aeroplane started to bank as it made its approach into Capodichino and Doyle caught a glimpse through the window of the barren summit of Vesuvius and then the waters of the bay shimmering in the morning sunshine. He pinched his nostrils and blew out through his nose to ease the pressure on his eardrums. He felt them pop and leaned his head back, closing his eyes. He enjoyed flying, but the descents played hell with his ears. For up to an hour after they'd landed he knew he'd be partially deaf. The thought didn't disturb him unduly. This was Naples, after all: partial deafness was probably a blessing.

Outside the airport terminal he took a taxi into the centre of the city, asking the driver to drop him in front of the central station. A scruffy kid who looked as if he should be in school was on the forecourt selling black-market cigarettes from the bonnet of a parked car. There were children like him on practically every street corner in the city. Doyle watched him for a moment, wondering which Camorra gang he was working for, then went through into the station concourse.

He paused briefly for an espresso at one of the bars before slipping out of a side entrance and hailing another cab to take him to the Castel Nuovo. At the castle, he walked across the piazza, down the street past the Teatro San Carlo and into the Galleria Umberto I. When he emerged from the Galleria, he flagged down a third taxi and gave the driver directions to a bar in a side street near the Piazza Dante. They were elaborate precautions, and probably unnecessary, but Doyle was a careful operator. These were dangerous men he was dealing with.

He was met in the bar, as he always was, by a stocky bull of a man in a sharp grey suit who spoke English like an extra in *The Godfather* but looked like a navvy on his way to church. A dented lump of rusty scrap metal masquerading as a Fiat Punto was parked in a yard behind the bar. Doyle had come to realise in the time he'd been visiting Naples that though the Camorra *capi* had a fondness for vulgar ostentation, their foot soldiers were expected not to draw attention to themselves.

A twenty-minute drive through the belching Naples traffic took them up into the hills behind the city and in through the gates of a magnificent castellated villa which was protected like a fortress. The windows in the house were glazed with bulletproof glass, the sleek gardens patrolled by discreetly armed guards and the reinforced front door looked strong enough to stop a tank. Very little made Simon Doyle nervous, but coming here did.

He was searched once at the main gates, then again when he entered the villa. Yevgeny Drozhkin and Dino Falzone – tanned, svelte, Armani-clad – were waiting for him in the large sitting room at the back of the house. They shook hands and Falzone offered him coffee and *strúffoli*, small balls of dough dipped in honey and fried, which Doyle declined. They exchanged a few courtesies in English, a language Falzone spoke fluently though with a strong American accent, then the Camorra boss smiled, showing his gold fillings, and shot Doyle a glance of icy penetration.

'Shall we get down to business?' he said.

*   *   *

306

Ole Carlsen lived in Overijse, one of the Flemish-speaking communes which, like Tervuren, was out beyond the Forêt de Soignes on the south-eastern side of Brussels. His house – two-storey, detached with gardens all around – overlooked the local golf club where he was a keen eight-handicap member and had a regular Saturday morning four-ball which, much to his annoyance, he was having to forego.

Claire arrived first, then Sullivan, who sat down at the opposite end of the living room. Neither said much. Sullivan seemed preoccupied, far away. Claire tried to read his body language, the tone of his voice, but it was impossible to tell what he was really thinking.

Finally, Enqvist turned up half an hour late. Carlsen brought in coffee on a tray and distributed the cups, making sure there were coasters under each one to prevent them marking the polished surfaces of the occasional tables placed around the living room. In his private life Carlsen exhibited the same fastidious neatness he applied to his work. The room was spotlessly clean and so tidily arranged it seemed unnatural. Every ornament had its own allotted position – Carlsen even paused to adjust one which had strayed a couple of millimetres out of line as he circled the room with the coffees – and there was an air of perfection which Sullivan, for one, found intimidating.

Carlsen remained standing by the window. He was dressed in his casual weekend attire of pressed grey trousers and V-necked pullover, under which he wore a plain white shirt and navy-blue tie. Sullivan had never seen him without a tie. Sometimes he wondered if he slept in one. The section chief was clear-eyed and alert. He showed no sign that his rest had been disturbed by a phone call at 2.30 am.

'Let's recap what you told me last night – early this morning,' he corrected himself, looking at Sullivan. 'Just to ensure we have all the facts right.'

Sullivan outlined again how they'd pinpointed the *Reunion Star*. Carlsen listened carefully, taking small sips of coffee from his cup.

'We're guessing she'll make a drop off the coast of France,' Sullivan said. 'Somewhere in the Bay of Biscay beyond the territorial limit. The Gascony coast is perfect for a clandestine landing. Then another drop off the Italian coast. We don't know where. The Bay of Naples is getting too hot for them so I'd guess they'll try somewhere further south.'

'Where?' Carlsen said. 'Calabria?'

'Not Calabria,' Enqvist replied. 'The 'Ndrangheta control too much territory down there. Maybe Puglia or Basilicata. There are plenty of isolated bays they can use.'

'You have some intelligence to back up this guesswork?'

'We know the *Maria Vasquez* made a drop in the Bay of Biscay,' Sullivan said.

'Know?' Carlsen said.

'Well, we're pretty certain. Cigarettes from the ship ended up in a warehouse in Bayonne. The Bay of Biscay seems the most logical place they were offloaded. And we know Hal Montague is supplying both the French and Italian black markets.'

'Do you?'

Sullivan told him about the customs surveillance of the Golden Valley Inn. Carlsen stroked his moustache with the side of his forefinger, something he did when he was thinking, and when he was nervous.

'You *have* been busy,' he said. 'It might have been better if you'd informed me about this earlier.' He gave them a glance of mild reproof.

'We had to move fast,' Sullivan said.

'Hmm.' Carlsen didn't press the point.

'Montague, Luciani, Lafon, a triumvirate who between them control a sizeable part of the European contraband business,' Sullivan continued. 'And the *Reunion Star* is their ship.'

'More guesswork?'

'To some extent,' Sullivan admitted. 'We don't know much about her. Five-thousand-tonne general cargo ship, registered in Vanuatu so the true ownership will be hard to verify. The Vanuatu registry of shipping in New York is closed over the weekend so we won't be able to find out any more about her till Monday, late afternoon Brussels time.'

'And she sails?'

'Nine am, from Antwerp.'

Carlsen turned away to look out of the window. Across the road outside, on the other side of a low wooden fence, was the Overijse golf course. Two men in caps and showerproof jackets were about to tee off on one of the holes. Carlsen watched the first man drive, following the ball as it soared away through the air and landed on the mowed stripes of the fairway.

'What are you proposing?' he asked without looking round.

'Twenty-four-hour surveillance from the moment the *Reunion Star* leaves Antwerp.'

Carlsen turned back. He finished his coffee and placed the empty cup carefully on the tray before he spoke.

'On the high seas?'

'And along the French coast,' Sullivan said.

'That will mean satellite surveillance. That's not easy, and it's very expensive. And the coast, what are you suggesting? That the whole west coast of France is watched? Have you spoken to the *Douane*?'

'Not yet,' Claire said. 'I was going to call Allard after this meeting. Assuming you gave us the go-ahead, of course,' she added tactfully.

Carlsen acknowledged the remark with a terse snort. He fixed Claire with a look that was almost a glare.

'And what do you think Allard will say?'

Claire shifted uncomfortably in her seat. 'I don't know.'

'I'll tell you what he'll say. He'll say he doesn't have the manpower to mount an effective surveillance of that length of coastline.'

'It won't be the whole coast,' Claire retorted. 'We can narrow it down. Once the *Reunion Star* heaves to and starts to offload, we'll know roughly where the boats intend to come ashore. If we move fast, we can be there waiting for them.'

Carlsen pursed his lips doubtfully and wandered back to the window. Enqvist pressed their case.

'We know these are big-time smugglers, Ole. Now's our chance to get them.'

'Like you did on Wednesday night?' Carlsen said. Then he sighed. 'I'm sorry, that was unfair. But you see my point? You were certain then and look what happened. We're working on supposition, not hard evidence.'

'It's not supposition,' Enqvist said. 'We know the *Reunion Star* has been involved in smuggling.'

'Hazelnut oil, not cigarettes. There's a difference,' Carlsen said.

'The *Maria Vasquez* also smuggled hazelnut oil. The pattern is the same.'

'But we know almost nothing about this ship,' Carlsen said. 'You want me to authorise a massive surveillance operation on little more than guesswork. Even if the *Reunion Star has* shipped contraband cigarettes in the past, it doesn't necessarily mean she will this trip. What if we mobilise French Customs and the *Reunion Star* sails straight past France and on to West Africa? How will we look then? We can't afford another fiasco like East Midlands.'

'There's always an element of risk. Nothing is foolproof,' Sullivan interjected.

'I know what you're saying. But the Director is taking a

310

lot of political criticism after what happened on Wednesday night. It's a bad time to attempt something with this degree of risk attached to it.'

'That's exactly what the smugglers want,' Sullivan responded heatedly. 'They want to tie our hands. That was what East Midlands was all about. If we do nothing they've beaten us. For God's sake, Ole, we're an operational unit. We're not a bunch of pen-pushing bureaucrats waiting for our pensions like everyone else in the Commission. We're here to take action, to *do* something about trafficking. So sometimes we make mistakes. The only people who never make mistakes are people who do nothing all day. If we play this the way the smugglers want it, we might as well give up and go home now.'

Carlsen gazed out of the window again. From his silence, Sullivan knew that his argument was having some effect. But Carlsen wasn't going to be steamrollered.

'I still don't like it,' he said. 'It's too hurried. Something like this has to be carefully planned and executed.'

'We don't have time,' Sullivan said. 'They're making their move. We have to counter it. They only met yesterday, but I'm certain their next shipment leaves on Monday. We know Montague is connected to Julius Wolf. He may well have been trafficking for years using Wolf as a cover. Gilles Lafon is linked to Montague and implicated in the payment of bribes to at least one senior French customs officer. Armando Luciani is one of the two most powerful Camorra bosses in Naples. And the *Reunion Star* has smuggling written all over her. How much more evidence do you need?'

Out on the golf course a thin stick of a man in a garish yellow sweater was teeing off, hooking his ball far into a patch of long rough. He snatched up his tee angrily and stomped off down the fairway with his partner. Carlsen watched him, then turned and walked to the tray. He poured himself some more coffee, buying a little extra time to think.

Finally he looked up and sighed. 'You'd better be right about this.'

'You're giving us the okay?' Sullivan said.

'Yes, I'm giving you the okay.'

'*Ciao*, Antonio. How's the *Maria Vasquez* investigation going?' Sullivan said.

'Don't ask,' Casagrande replied curtly. 'It's a sore point.'

'Did you find the blue Fiat van?'

'Yes, abandoned in Bari docks.'

'Bari? They went across to Yugoslavia?'

'We don't know where they went. The trail's gone cold. What are you doing anyway, ringing on a Saturday? Haven't you got anything better to do?'

'Things have been happening.' Sullivan explained what they'd agreed with Carlsen.

'I'll see if I can increase the surveillance on Luciani,' Casagrande said.

'It'll only be for a short time. Something's going to happen in the next couple of days, I'm sure of that.'

'I'll put some men on to it. I was intending to ring you in any case.'

'Oh yes?'

'Those names you gave me last week: Montague and Doyle. I had someone keep a lookout on the incoming airline passenger lists. Simon Doyle flew in on Alitalia this morning. A team covered his arrival. He knows his stuff. We lost him for a couple of hours around lunchtime but we were right behind him the rest of the time.'

'What was he doing? Visiting Luciani?'

'Strangely no. He went to see Dino Falzone.'

Sullivan frowned. 'The other Camorra boss. Why?'

'Ah, if only we could eavesdrop on Falzone's meetings.

We don't know. Doyle was with him for half an hour. Perhaps they've fallen out with Luciani and are changing sides.'

'Or perhaps they're selling cigarettes to both of them.'

'Now that,' Casagrande said, 'would be a very dangerous game to play.'

They were alone in the office. Enqvist had just left for some unspecified evening appointment. Claire walked over and perched herself on the corner of Sullivan's desk.

'You want to go for dinner?' she said.

Sullivan looked at her. She was very beautiful. He felt the same physical attraction, the same stirrings of desire, but something inside him had changed since Tuesday night. Since Kate and the boys had been attacked. Things were no longer so simple, and it wasn't merely guilt overriding his libido. The attack had jolted him. It had made him reconsider his priorities, reassess his loyalties and what really mattered to him. He wondered what he was going to do.

'Maybe not tonight,' he said.

'What's the matter?'

'I don't know. I'm sorry. I've things on my mind. Worries.'

'Your family?'

Sullivan nodded. 'It's a bad time. I'm sure you understand.'

Claire pursed her lips, giving him a long searching glance.

'Yes, I understand,' she said.

Lying back on the shiny leather sofa in the study of his town house, Montague stared at Doyle with a mixture of puzzlement and surprise.

'He wants to do *what*?' he said.

313

'Make the payment in person.'

Montague sat up and swung his legs on to the floor.

'What the fuck's he playing at?'

Doyle gave a shrug. 'He wants to see the merchandise for himself before he pays. He says he doesn't see why he should take all the risk.'

'He doesn't trust us?'

'Not after last time. His view is that he paid in advance and ended up with nothing. He thinks we should share the loss if the cigarettes are seized.'

'Does he now?' Montague clenched a fist in anger. 'And where does he think he's going to get his supplies from if we call off the deal? The market's sewn up tighter than a camel's arse in a sandstorm. Does he think the multi-nationals will deal directly with a known racketeer like him?'

'I don't know what he thinks,' Doyle said mildly. 'I'm just telling you what he said. He'll pay for the cigarettes when he sees them for himself.'

'Cash? Does he know what fifteen million dollars looks like? What's he bringing, a removal van?'

'He'll pay in bearer bonds.'

Montague scowled at the wall for a time. Then he said: 'What's he doing? This doesn't make sense.'

'I'll handle it,' Doyle said. 'Leave it to me.'

Montague turned his head to look at him. His lip twisted into a cynical smile.

'Leave you with fifteen million in bearer bonds?'

'I'll look after them.'

'Not without me you won't.'

There was a knock on the door. Serena walked in.

'Hal . . .'

'Yes, yes, I'm coming,' Montague said tetchily. 'We're just finishing.'

'If you don't change now, we'll be late for the show.'

'I'm coming.'

'What are you going to see?' Doyle said.

'Some shitty musical,' Montague said. 'What is it, *Camelot*?'

'It's *Carmen*, the opera,' Serena explained patiently.

'They're all the same to me.'

Montague heaved his large frame up from the sofa and went out of the study. Serena listened for his footsteps on the stairs before gently closing the door.

'Well?'

Doyle nodded. 'It's all fixed.'

'Falzone too?'

'Exactly as we discussed.'

Serena smiled archly. 'What a good boy you are, Simon. And good boys deserve a reward.'

'Give it a rest, Serena.'

'Spoilsport,' she said, stepping nearer and kissing him playfully.

She unzipped his fly. Doyle pushed her hand away.

'Are you mad?'

'Don't you like it? The possibility of getting caught *in flagrante*. Doesn't it turn you on?'

'Not now. Soon we'll have all the time in the world.'

'But I don't want to wait,' Serena said petulantly.

She slipped her hand inside his trousers.

'Christ, Serena, at least lock the bloody door.'

It had been a long time since Enqvist had felt this way about a woman. Since he'd experienced the nervous sickness, the sleepless nights and obsessive thoughts that were the hallmark of sexual infatuation. He thought he'd long passed the stage when a woman could arouse such powerful emotions in him. He was troubled. Unreasoned passion in adolescence was understandable, a necessary stage in the process of growing up. But in a middle-aged man it seemed grotesque, somehow indecent.

He'd dated a few women in the three years since he'd split up with his wife, slept with some of them. But none of them had afflicted him with the fierce irrational desire he felt for Juliana Rietveld. She was in his thoughts most of his waking hours, a distant, tantalising dream that distracted and unsettled him. He wanted her, but he knew there was something rash about his ardour. He was being a fool, yet the sensation was so intense and pleasurable he didn't want to lose it by letting his head overrule his lust.

Even now, sitting together in a *trattoria* enjoying pepperoni pizza and a cheap Chianti, he could feel the raw sexual power of her presence. Juliana was across the table from him, her lovely features touched by the flickering candle-light. Stig watched her surreptitiously as she ate. He had no idea how she felt about him, she'd never opened out in that way, but she seemed to want to be with him and that was more than enough for the time being.

'When do you have to go back to Amsterdam?' he said.

'Tomorrow evening. I have a fitting first thing on Monday morning. But I'm free tomorrow afternoon. The photo shoot should be finished by two at the latest. You could show me some of Brussels.'

'I'd like that,' Stig said. 'But I have to work tomorrow.'

'On Sunday?'

Stig made a face and nodded.

'I thought you Eurocrats only worked Monday to Friday.'

'Something urgent's come up. I can't cancel it, I'm afraid.'

'What time will you finish?' Juliana said. 'Maybe we could have dinner before I catch my train.'

'I may not be in Brussels.'

'Oh. Never mind.'

The disappointment was transparent in her face. Stig took her hand and squeezed it.

'I don't know what I'm doing yet, it hasn't been decided. I might have to leave town at short notice.'

'Somewhere exotic, I hope.'

Stig laughed. 'I'd hardly call Antwerp or Bordeaux exotic.'

'Bring me back a present.'

'I will.'

They went to his apartment after they'd eaten. It was a cramped one-bedroom flat on the second floor of an old converted house. Enqvist hadn't chosen it for its ambience, nor its location, on the seedier fringes of Schaerbeek. He gave so much of his salary to his ex-wife and daughter – by guilt-ridden choice, not compulsion – that it was all he could sensibly afford. But he'd cleaned and aired it and tidied away the clutter – a rare occurrence – in the hope that Juliana would accompany him home. He had a bottle of champagne in the fridge and Godiva chocolates to go with it. And for once he had a clear head, having made sure he'd drunk only a couple of glasses of wine.

He went into the kitchen and poured the champagne. When he returned to the living room, Juliana was standing by his desk, leafing through an old pile of European Commission periodicals he'd never got round to throwing away.

'This lot looks boring,' she said.

'I wouldn't know. I never read them,' Stig replied. 'Like everyone else in the Commission.'

He handed her a glass and held out the box of chocolates. Juliana shook her head.

'I shouldn't.'

'Go on. Just one.'

Juliana took a sip of her champagne.

'Why don't we take them to bed with us?' she said.

Stig was lying on his back, snoring gently, when Juliana pulled aside the duvet and slipped out of bed. She waited a few seconds. Stig didn't stir. She crept softly to the door and went out. The living room was in darkness, but she knew exactly where she'd left her handbag. She rummaged inside it and took out a cellular phone. She listened again, then went into the bathroom, shutting the door carefully behind her. She sat on the lid of the toilet, the phone in her hand, and tapped in a number.

It was two o'clock in the morning when the sudden, jarring noise of the phone woke him. Montague reached out from the warmth of his bed and fumbled for the receiver.

'Yes?'

It was Ilse Ameling.

Montague sat up and switched on the bedside lamp. He listened for a few minutes, interjecting questions as Ilse spoke. Then he hung up and punched in a number.

'Simon, it's me. Get over here now. I don't care what fucking time it is. Now. There's been a change of plan.'

TWENTY

Sullivan rose early, woken by the dawn chorus of birds in the horse chestnut trees outside the bedroom window. He took a shower and was dressed and finishing breakfast by eight o'clock. He thought about ringing Kate – the bitter rancour of their last exchange still weighed heavily on his conscience – but it was only seven am in England, an ungodly hour to attempt a reconciliation, so he telephoned Stig instead. A prearranged alarm call. They had a lot to get through during the day and Enqvist could never drag himself out of bed on weekdays let alone a Sunday.

There was no reply. Maybe he wasn't home, maybe he'd left for the office already, maybe he was sleeping off a Saturday night on the town. Sullivan knew which option was most likely. He gave him half an hour then called again. Still there was no answer. Sullivan threw on his coat and went out to his car.

The Tervurenlaan through the Forêt de Soignes felt almost deserted the traffic was so thin compared to the weekday rush hour. Sullivan drove at a steady pace and was in Schaerbeek in twenty minutes. He parked up the street and walked the last hundred metres to Stig's apartment building. The front door was swinging open as if someone had just come in or gone out and forgotten to close it properly behind them. Sullivan went upstairs. Approaching the second floor he heard a door click shut and the sound of a woman's high heels on the wooden floorboards. A tall blonde in a black overcoat with a velvet collar was coming away from Enqvist's door. She glanced at Sullivan as she passed him and he turned his head to watch her go down the stairs. There was something familiar about her face. He stood there on the landing for a time, trying unsuccessfully to remember where he'd seen her before. He shrugged and headed for Stig's door. He was about to ring the bell when it came to him.

Dear God, no. It couldn't be.

Perhaps he was mistaken. He'd caught only a brief glimpse of her. Maybe it was simply a likeness he'd detected, some faint similarity that was leading his memory astray. But he had to make sure. He went back out to his car and drove to Beaulieu.

The surveillance photographs from Amsterdam were in the secretaries' office where he'd left them on Friday night. He went through them quickly and found the one he was looking for. He'd hoped he was wrong, but there was no mistake. With dread in his heart, he slid the print into his pocket, returned to his car and drove back to Stig's apartment.

He rang the bell and knocked on the door for almost half a minute before Stig finally answered. He was unshaven, bleary-eyed and barefoot. The navy-blue dressing gown he was wearing was open at the top. Curls of fine blond hair poked out through the gap.

'Did I wake you?' Sullivan said.

'What time is it?'

Sullivan walked into the living room. He pulled open the curtains. Enqvist winced and held up a hand to shield his eyes as the sunlight flooded in. The apartment was tidier than Sullivan had ever seen it. The clothes, the junk, the takeaway food containers and empty beer cans which normally featured prominently were nowhere to be seen. Sullivan could smell traces of a woman's perfume in the air.

'You never told me you had a new girlfriend,' he said.

'Uh?'

Enqvist blinked at him, still half asleep.

'I saw her leave,' Sullivan said.

'That was ages ago. Have you been outside all this time?'

'I went to the office to get something. Have you known her long?'

'A couple of weeks. Why?'

'Nice-looking. Very tasty. Where did you meet her?'

'What is this?' Enqvist said.

'What's her name?'

'What business is it of yours?'

'Her name, Stig. Tell me her name.'

'Juliana Rietveld.'

'Dutch?'

Enqvist stared at him. He was fully awake now.

'What's your problem? Why are you being so aggressive?'

'Where did you meet her?' Sullivan repeated.

'In Rotterdam. She's a model. What the hell is this, an interrogation?'

Sullivan pulled out the photograph and gave it to him.

'That's her, isn't it?'

Enqvist studied the print. 'It looks like her. Where did you get this?'

'It's one of the surveillance pictures from the Golden Valley Inn.'

Enqvist's mouth fell open. He swallowed.

'So?' he said hoarsely.

'You can do better than that. She was photographed coming out of a brothel. What do you think she is, a stunning beauty like her, the cleaning lady?'

'I'm sure there's another explanation,' Enqvist said defensively.

'She's a whore, Stig. Hellendoorn identified her as one. And her name's not Juliana Rietveld, it's Christine Stokkel.'

Enqvist slumped down into an armchair, still holding the photograph. He passed a hand over his face, rubbing his bloodshot eyes and the stubble on his jaw.

'How did you meet her?' Sullivan said.

Enqvist didn't reply. He seemed too numb to speak. His eyes were fixed on the photograph. On the grainy close-up of a woman emerging from a door, the wind catching at her blonde hair, throwing a few strands across her cheeks.

'Stig?'

'Outside the hotel,' Enqvist replied in a whisper. 'We went for dinner.'

'How many times have you seen her?'

'Just three.'

'Didn't you suspect?'

'Why should I have suspected?'

Enqvist lifted his head and gazed bleakly at Sullivan. Sullivan turned away, unable to look at him. There was no easy, no kind way of doing this.

'Look at her. Then look at yourself.'

It was cruel. But he had to do it.

'I'm not that bad-looking,' Enqvist said plaintively. 'Women fall for uglier men than me.'

'Rich men, famous men, charismatic men. Why would she go for someone like you?'

'Thanks.'

Sullivan sighed. 'Jesus, Stig, wake up. They set you up with a prostitute. What did you tell her?'

'Nothing.'

'You'd better come clean on this. What did you tell her about your work?'

'Nothing. I'm always careful about things like that.'

Sullivan studied him clinically, trying to forget for a moment that Enqvist was his friend.

'You knew, didn't you?'

'No,' Enqvist replied vehemently.

'Or guessed.'

That was closer to the mark. Enqvist heaved himself out of his chair and went to the drinks table against the wall. He poured himself a shot of brandy and gulped down a mouthful. Sullivan didn't try to stop him. One more wouldn't make any difference.

Enqvist returned to the armchair and sat down heavily, the glass clutched between his hands.

'It's all right for you,' he said. 'You have a wife, kids, some kind of life outside the office. What do I have? Nothing. She's a beautiful woman. I fell in love with her.'

'She's a prostitute,' Sullivan said harshly. 'And you got the hots for her.'

Enqvist gave no sign that he'd heard for he went on: 'She's the best thing that has happened to me in years. It's the male business traveller's fantasy, isn't it? Get picked up by a gorgeous woman and screw away the boredom of the Karlsruhe Holiday Inn, or wherever. But it never happened to me. Until Rotterdam.'

He drank some more brandy and stared down at the floor.

'Why should I have guessed? Am I really that unattractive? I was lonely. I thought she genuinely liked me. What was wrong with that?'

His voice cracked. Sullivan hoped he wasn't going to break down on him. He didn't think he could cope with that.

'Did you take money from her?'

'No, never,' Enqvist said fiercely. 'I swear. We just had dinner a few times.'

'Just dinner? You were set up, Stig. Someone paid her to lay you.'

Enqvist was silent. He looked at the photograph again.

'I know,' he said quietly. 'But she was one illusion I could have lived with for longer.'

Sullivan sat down opposite him on the sofa.

'What did you tell her about your work?' he asked again.

'Not much. Nothing of any importance.'

'Think, Stig. Have you mentioned anything about Montague, or Lafon or Luciani?'

'No.'

'Or the *Reunion Star*?'

'No. I told her I had to work tomorrow, but that's hardly classified.'

'Is that all? I need to know, Stig.'

Enqvist drained his glass. He glanced up, then away across the room. Sullivan saw the momentary flicker of guilt in his eyes.

'What else?' he said.

Stig went to refill his glass. Sullivan stood up and snatched the bottle from him.

'What else?'

The reply was a long time coming.

'I mentioned I might have to go to Antwerp or Bordeaux,' Enqvist said eventually, adding hurriedly: 'But that wouldn't mean anything to her.'

'It would mean something to Montague.' Sullivan was angry now. 'You arsehole, Stig. You think they can't interpret a piece of information like that and work out exactly what we're doing?'

'They'd need more than that.'

'You think they'll take the chance? They know we're on to the *Reunion Star* as sure as if you'd told them so in writing. Christ, Stig, what the fuck were you doing?'

Sullivan walked across the room to the telephone.

'What are you going to do?' Enqvist said.

'What choice do I have?' Sullivan replied. 'You've blown the whole bloody operation.'

'Rob, give me a chance.'

Sullivan paused, his hand hovering over the telephone. Enqvist was gazing at him like a remorseful child, his eyes frightened, despairing.

'You make that call and I'm finished,' he said despondently. 'Not just my career but my life. If this comes out I'll never work again. The *Tullverk* won't take me back and who else would employ me? I know it's what I deserve and I can understand why you're angry.'

'I'm not angry,' Sullivan said. 'Disappointed, sad, but not angry. It was so stupid, so unnecessary.'

'Help me, Rob. I swear that's all I told her. I never took any bribes. I'm not corrupt, just foolish. Give me a chance to redeem myself.'

Sullivan studied him compassionately, remembering the two years they'd worked together and feeling acutely the bonds and responsibilities of friendship. He moved away from the phone and sat down again.

'Redeem yourself how?'

'I don't know. We can work something out. We can sort out the mess without anyone else knowing. I know we can.' He saw the doubts in Sullivan's face and continued: 'I won't jeopardise your future, I promise. If anything happens, I'll say you never knew.'

Sullivan let out a long, weary sigh. 'We'll have to tell Claire.'

'Will we?'

'She's part of the team. She has to be on board. That's the only way it will work.'

'Okay.'

'Get dressed. We'll discuss it on the way to the office.'

*   *   *

325

Claire sat by her desk in stunned silence, listening to the
two men talking, sharing out the explanation between
them. Then she turned to Sullivan and said: 'I need to
talk to you in private.'

They went down the corridor to the secretaries' office.
No one else was in. The building was eerily quiet, all the
other doors shut and locked. Claire pushed the door to and
looked at Sullivan, her face tight with anger.

'You expect me to go along with this?' she demanded.

'No, I don't expect it. You have to make the decision
yourself.'

'And if I say I'm calling Carlsen now?'

'That's your choice.'

'Jesus, Rob, what are you doing?'

'He's my friend. He's made a mistake, but he deserves
a chance.'

'A mistake? Is that what you call it?'

'He's not corrupt. He's taken no pay-offs, sold no information.'

'He's blown a major operation. He's slept with a prostitute hired by organised criminals. Don't you think that's
serious?'

'Claire, calm down.'

'Don't tell me to calm down.'

Claire took a deep breath. Her eyes were on fire. Sullivan
moved towards her and tried to put his hand on her arm.
She backed away.

'Don't try that, Rob. This isn't the time. This is business,
a question of professional ethics.'

'He made one slip, that's all. As far as Stig was concerned
it was an innocent relationship. Have you never told a
boyfriend a few details of your job?'

'I've never compromised an important trafficking investigation.'

'Don't be so hard on him.' Sullivan paused. She was

hostile, unreceptive, but he was sure he could persuade her. 'Look, you said it's a question of professional ethics. Do you think it's ethical to ruin him because he fell in love with a woman? Is that such a crime?'

'You stick together don't you, you men? It's something you can all see yourselves doing, making fools of your-selves over a whore.'

She turned away, shaking her head. 'You're asking me to cover it up.'

'I'm not. If what we're suggesting works, it won't matter any more.'

Claire looked back at him. 'You think so?'

'Montague knows we're on to the *Reunion Star*, so he'll find another way of getting cigarettes through to his cus-tomers. By road or rail. He'll try to do it quickly. He has a distribution network to feed. This is a regular business, he does it all the time. My guess is he'll want to do it today before we find out the *Reunion Star* isn't going to offload. Because while we're concentrating on the ship we won't be watching other routes.'

'You don't know that.'

'I know. It's a risk. But I think it's worth taking.'

Claire didn't respond. She didn't like it. Her head told her to wash her hands of the affair and look out for herself. But there was something selfish, even disloyal about doing that. She was part of a team, and a team could only function on the basis of absolute solidarity between its members. You stuck together or you were nothing.

'Just one day,' Sullivan said. 'Stig deserves that, at least.'

'And if you're wrong?'

'If I'm wrong, we're all in the shit.'

The waiting was beginning to get to them. Sitting in the

office, drinking coffee and staring at the walls. Waiting for something to happen.

With each hour that passed Claire began to wonder again whether they were doing the right thing. No one talked much. Once or twice she caught Sullivan's eye and he looked away, distancing himself from her. She could sense he was cooling towards her. It made her angry. She didn't like being used.

Enqvist walked over to the filter machine and refilled his cup, glancing enquiringly at the other two. They shook their heads. Sullivan felt sick. He was tired but his system was so saturated with caffeine he couldn't relax.

The phone rang, breaking the silence like an alarm. Claire snatched up the receiver.

'Yes?' She listened. 'When?'

She scribbled down a few notes. Then her face fell.

'Yes, thanks anyway.'

She hung up.

'Antwerp,' she said. 'Laterveer Voorden have asked Customs for clearance to release fifteen thousand cases for shipment by rail to Munich.'

'Munich?' Enqvist looked away, disappointed.

They could rule out consignments within the EU, when duty would have to be paid before the cigarettes left the bonded warehouse. They were looking for a destination outside the Fifteen, for cigarettes in transit duty free.

'It's not going to be today,' Claire said pessimistically.

It wasn't what the others wanted to hear.

'Give it a few more hours,' Enqvist said.

Mid-afternoon there were two phone calls in quick succession.

The first, from UK Customs. Montague and Doyle had taken a British Airways flight from Heathrow to Charles de Gaulle, Paris.

The second, from Casagrande. Armando Luciani had flown Alitalia from Naples to Turin.

Enqvist permitted himself a small smile.

'What did I say? More coffee anyone?'

Half an hour later, the phone rang again. Claire answered.

'It's your wife,' she said to Sullivan.

He took the receiver, turning away and saying quietly: 'Hi. Are you at home? I'll call you back immediately.'

He hung up, sensing Claire watching him, and went out. Down the corridor in the secretaries' office, he clicked the door shut behind him and rang Colchester.

'Sorry, I didn't want Stig and Claire listening in,' he explained. 'How are things?'

'Okay. Very quiet,' Kate said.

'The boys?'

'They're fine. They're out in the garden playing football.'

'And you?'

'I'm fine too.'

Sullivan listened, gauging her mood from the tone of her voice, from the silences between the words. There was no hostility, but he could sense a tension in her; something she wanted to say.

'Rob,' she said and paused. 'I'm sorry about the other day. I was angry. I shouldn't have upped and left like that.'

'I don't blame you,' Sullivan said. 'I was in the wrong. I should have been with you. You needed me.'

'Well, anyway, I behaved badly. I'm sorry.'

'I'm sorry too. It was my fault.'

'Okay, it was your fault,' Kate said.

Sullivan laughed. They'd been together for a long time. They understood each other. There were bonds between them which no row could threaten. Which no casual infidelity could sever. Sullivan felt the permanence of those ties with a profound sense of relief and certainty.

'I wish you were here,' he said. He wanted to hold her, to give her some physical confirmation of his loyalty.

'Me too,' Kate replied. 'We're not meant to be apart. It's not right, we're a family.'

'I'll take some time off when this is out of the way. Come home for more than a weekend.'

'I'd like that. We need it, Rob. Nothing's changed, has it?' Her voice was soft, a little tentative.

'No, I'm still the same. We can make this work. Two more years and I'll be home permanently.'

'I want it to work, don't you?' Kate said.

He didn't hesitate. 'Yes, I want it to work.'

Queyras and Pigout were waiting for Montague and Doyle outside the arrivals terminal at Charles de Gaulle. They followed the Englishmen's taxi into Paris, crossing the *périphérique* at the Porte de la Chapelle and continuing on towards the city centre. Approaching the Gare du Nord, the taxi turned off west towards Montmartre, finally coming to a halt outside a restaurant near the Place Pigalle. Montague and Doyle paid off the driver and, carrying their small overnight bags, went into the restaurant. Queyras and Pigout watched from their parking space fifty metres up the street.

'Something's not right,' Queyras said, looking out of his window at the seedy shopfronts, the litter-strewn pavements. 'A couple of guys like that, an area like this.'

'Relax,' Pigout said. 'They're crooks. They're at home here.'

'We needed more than one car to do this properly.'

'On Sunday afternoon overtime? Think of the budget,' Pigout said with heavy sarcasm.

Queyras fidgeted restlessly in his seat, tapping his fingers on his outstretched legs. Finally he pushed open his door and got out.

'I'm going to take a look round the back.'

The package was inside the cistern in the men's toilet at the rear of the restaurant, tightly wrapped in oilskin and plastic. Doyle lifted it out and tore off the protective layers. Inside, clean and dry, was a loaded SIG-Sauer automatic pistol and spare clip. Doyle slipped them into his pocket and went back out into the dining area.

The place was almost empty. A few stragglers left over from lunchtime were drinking coffee at their tables but the evening rush was a few hours away yet. Montague was at the bar, sipping an Armagnac while the barman kept out of his way washing glasses at the sink. At the other end of the counter a pug-nosed man in a tan leather jacket was nursing a bottle of beer and a Gauloise. He glanced round as Doyle walked up to the counter and nodded at him, then stubbed out his cigarette and stood up. Doyle and Montague followed him out through the kitchens to the waiting BMW.

Coming round the corner into the backstreet, Queyras was just in time to see the three men climbing into the car and driving off.

Hellendoorn rang from Amsterdam at five thirty in the afternoon. Claire took the call, speaking in Dutch, then relayed the message in English to Sullivan and Enqvist.

'He's just had a fax from Customs in Rotterdam. They've cleared a consignment of twenty thousand master cases for shipment by rail to Belgrade. A last-minute order.'

'Which warehouse?' Sullivan said.

'Van Vliet.'

'And the route?'

'Paris, Lyon, Turin, Trieste, Zagreb.'

Sullivan glanced at Enqvist, feeling a pulse of excitement which he refrained from showing. The ingredients looked right but he'd learnt not to jump to conclusions without a lot more information.

'When does it leave?'

'He's finding out and will call back.'

'Do we know the name of the shipper or the consignee?'

'The shipper is an agent in Rotterdam,' Claire said. 'The consignee, a company in Yugoslavia, Zoric Repajic.'

'Spell that,' Enqvist said, switching on his computer terminal and logging on.

He ran the name through both the UCLAF database and Dun and Bradstreet. The company wasn't listed in either.

'Dead end.'

'I have an idea,' Claire said.

She made a short phone call, speaking in Dutch. Sullivan looked over her shoulder and saw her writing down a number which she then dialled. She had a longer conversation, again in Dutch, taking notes, and hung up.

'That was the agent's office,' she said. 'I said I was ringing from Van Vliet's warehouse, checking the method of payment for the consignment. They gave me a number to call in Liechtenstein. Someone called Baumann.'

'Try it,' Sullivan said.

Claire dialled the number and waited. She let it ring for a long time. There was no reply.

'Another dead end,' Enqvist said.

Sullivan was looking down at Claire's notes.

'Two three seven Konstanzerstrasse, Vaduz? Is that an address for Baumann?'

'Yes. Why?'

Sullivan had his desk drawer open and was sifting though a file. He pulled out a piece of paper.

'Two three seven Konstanzerstrasse is also the address of Herr Walter Busch, the man who paid for the cigarettes on the *Maria Vasquez*. Now is that a coincidence?'

*   *   *

Twenty minutes later Claire took the call from Hellendoorn. She listened, then said something in Dutch which could only have been an expletive.

'The application for customs clearance was made at three o'clock this morning,' she repeated to Sullivan and Enqvist. 'The night shift handled it. The freight arrangements were made shortly afterwards with *Nederlandse Spoorwegen* and the SNCF.'

'And the train? When does it leave Rotterdam?' Sullivan said.

'There was a mix-up at Customs. The information got left in an out-tray and was only noticed at shift change at four o'clock this afternoon. The train left Rotterdam three hours ago.'

They drove flat out to Lille, covering the hundred kilometres in a little under an hour. Philippe Allard had hastily arranged for a helicopter to be waiting there to fly them to Paris. He met them at the heliport at Orly and they transferred to a Customs plane for the flight to Lyon.

Allard had a map of Europe which he spread out over the table inside the plane.

'The train has by-passed Paris and should be somewhere around here by now.' He pointed to a spot about fifty kilometres south of the capital. 'It's scheduled to reach Lyon at half past ten this evening. That's the first stop it makes according to the SNCF freight timetable. It waits there for an hour and a half to unload some wagons and take on more freight, then leaves at midnight for Italy. If they're going to offload the cigarettes within France, Lyon is where they'll do it.'

'There's no possibility of an unscheduled stop before then?' Sullivan said.

Allard shook his head. 'You don't just stop a freight train in the middle of nowhere and unload a few containers. It's not possible, even if you bribed the driver. The SNCF know exactly where all their trains are at a given moment. Lyon is the only place they can do it.'

'And Montague?'

Allard winced. 'We lost him in Paris. He could be anywhere.'

'Shit!'

'Worse. Luciani has disappeared too.'

The freight-marshalling yard was spread out beneath them like a huge steel-ribbed fan, hundreds of wagons lining the silvery tracks.

Allard was by the window of the darkened office, looking out through a pair of night glasses.

'Over there in the middle,' he said. 'Next to the oil tankers. The light grey containers with the black vertical stripes. You see them? That's her.'

Sullivan followed Allard's outstretched arm. There was a line of containers immediately behind the SNCF locomotive. He counted them. Twenty. A thousand master cases to each container, five hundred packets to each case. That was a total of two hundred million cigarettes.

The yard was illuminated by high floodlights placed at intervals across the sidings but much of it, particularly in between the rows of wagons, was in shadow. There was a lot of activity, despite the late hour. Freight cars were being unloaded, their cargoes transferred to waiting lorries, the huge overhead gantry crane was removing containers from flat-backed wagons and a couple of stubby diesel locomotives were shunting rolling stock up and down the tracks. It would have been a relatively simple, inconspicuous operation to unload twenty containers of cigarettes, but there was no sign it was going to happen. In fact, as they watched, more freight cars were being coupled to the rear of the train, making it impossible to detach the cigarette wagons.

They waited ten minutes, then fifteen. Sullivan glanced at his watch. It was nearing eleven o'clock. The fist around his stomach was tightening its grip. No one spoke, the tension in the office had stifled all desire for conversation. They stood by the windows in silence, watching for someone to make a move.

Another ten minutes passed. Then Allard lifted his night glasses and trained them on the wagons.

'Here we are,' he said softly. He picked up his radio and spoke into it.

The others peered out through the glass. The wagons were two hundred metres away but they could just make out the shadowy figure of a man walking down the length of the train and stopping by the cigarette containers.

Allard's radio crackled and a faint voice said something garbled in French. Allard responded with a curt '*Non*'.

He watched the figure through the glasses. The man lit a cigarette, the sudden flare of the match highlighting his face and peaked cap, then he walked on past the wagons.

'SNCF security,' Allard explained. 'Or looks like it.'

'Can we get him out of there?' Sullivan said.

Allard called to one of his colleagues. 'Alain, find out who he is.' Then to Sullivan: 'He might be one of theirs. You can be sure they'll be watching, looking for signs of surveillance. We don't want to show ourselves too soon.'

The man strolled on, seemingly in no hurry to finish his inspection of the train.

'What's he doing?' Enqvist said. 'They're not going to unload with him standing there.'

Allard turned to his colleague who was on the telephone. Alain held up a finger, listening, and came off.

'He's legitimate.'

Allard barked an order into his radio. In the distance, two customs officers jumped down from a wagon parked on the adjacent siding and ran up to the security guard. Words were

335

exchanged and the guard was unceremoniously bundled away.

'Hold him until we've finished,' Allard said into the radio.

Sullivan consulted his watch again. He noticed Allard and then Claire doing the same. Something wasn't right.

'They're not coming,' he said. 'There's no time to unload now.'

'Give it a while longer,' Allard said.

Sullivan shook his head. 'The train leaves in thirty-five minutes. Unless they uncouple the wagons and leave them behind, they're not going to be able to do it.'

'Maybe they're offloading them all in Turin,' Allard said. 'That's the next stop and that's where Luciani disappeared.'

'Maybe,' Sullivan said doubtfully.

They gave it another twenty-five minutes. A final group of wagons was coupled to the back of the cigarette train. Allard checked the cargo manifest they'd obtained from the SNCF.

'That's the lot,' he said. 'It's ready to go now.'

He looked at Sullivan, Claire and Enqvist. 'Perhaps we got the wrong train.'

'No way,' Enqvist said vehemently. 'This is the one. They're going to offload in transit, I'm sure of it.'

Allard shrugged. 'But obviously not here.'

'I want to look inside it,' Sullivan said suddenly.

'What?'

'Just a gut feeling I have. I want to look inside the containers.'

Allard shook his head. 'That's not a good idea. They're sealed.'

'Then we'll unseal them.'

Sullivan headed for the door.

'Rob, don't be hasty,' Enqvist cautioned. 'It might be Turin. We don't want to tamper with the containers if it is.'

'And if it isn't? That train leaves in ten minutes. We need to know now.'

Sullivan broke the customs seal on the first container and swung open the heavy side doors. Crammed tightly inside were brown cardboard boxes marked with serial numbers and the words 'Philip Morris Products Inc, Richmond, VA, USA.' He reached up and dragged one of them out, putting it down on the hard core beside the track and ripping open the top. He shone his torch down. There were red and white cartons of Marlboro cigarettes inside. Sullivan checked a couple, then tipped the box upside down. The cartons tumbled out on to the ground.

'What're you doing?' Allard said, starting to get angry.

Sullivan pulled out another box. Allard grabbed his arm to stop him tearing the top off.

'You can see what's inside. Why open more? You could jeopardise the whole operation.'

Sullivan looked at the faces encircling him: Allard, Claire, Enqvist, a couple of French customs officers. He could see the doubt in their expressions and wondered for an instant whether he was wrong.

'One more,' he said, shaking off Allard's hand.

He ripped open the box and stared down at the cartons inside.

'You see,' Allard said furiously. 'What did you expect to find?'

Embarrassed, Sullivan lifted up the box to replace it in the container. He hesitated. The box didn't feel right. It was too light. He put it back down on the ground.

'What're you doing now?' Allard demanded.

Sullivan lifted out the top layer of cartons. Underneath them was nothing but packing: newspapers and straw and ballast to fill the empty space.

'*Merde!*' Allard said.

337

Sullivan walked to the second container and broke open the seals. He swung back the doors. The container was completely empty.

He went down the line, checking the other containers. They were all empty, but in the final one was a single cardboard box. Sullivan carried it back up the track and opened it in front of his colleagues. There was only packing inside. He dug down with his fingers and encountered something hard – a china cup glazed with a dull blue and red pattern. He shone his torch beam on the bottom of the cup and held it up so the others could read the words 'Made in Ukraine'.

'I think they're rubbing it in,' he said.

'How did they *know*?' Stig Enqvist said in disbelief.

'They didn't,' Sullivan replied. 'But Montague's a careful man. That's one of the reasons it's taken us this long to identify him. He couldn't know, but it was worth taking the precaution, running a decoy shipment to keep us busy. What did he have to lose?'

'So where does that leave his trafficking? Where does that leave us?' Enqvist said.

They were back in the office block overlooking the marshalling yard, only this time in a conference room with the lights switched on and the blinds pulled shut. Allard and his team were on one side of the long table, the UCLAF contingent on the other.

'We're missing something,' Claire said. 'Montague's over here, maybe Luciani too. Why, if there's no shipment? What are they doing in France?'

'There is a shipment,' Sullivan said.

'We've checked all the customs clearances,' Enqvist said. 'That train was the only possible target crossing France today.'

'We're overlooking the obvious,' Sullivan said.

Claire sat up abruptly and swore. 'Jesus, of course.'

Enqvist rubbed his eyes. His body was drooping with fatigue.

'Go on,' he said. 'Make me feel stupid.'

'Rotterdam Customs cleared twenty thousand cases for shipment to Yugoslavia by rail,' Claire said. 'If they weren't on the train, and we know now only a few full cases were loaded for show, then where are all the others?' She answered the question herself. 'They're going by road.'

Enqvist blinked. 'How are we going to find twenty-plus lorries in a country the size of France?'

Claire came off the phone to Rotterdam, her face stony.

'The lorries left the warehouse at two o'clock this afternoon, heading for the *Nederlandse Spoorwegen* freight depot in the Europoort,' she said grimly. 'But they never got there, of course. Or at least not those particular lorries. Montague sent substitutes while the real cargo was heading south for France.'

'Two o'clock,' Sullivan said. 'That's ten hours ago. An average speed of, what? Eighty kilometres an hour? Let's say ninety to be safe. They'll have covered nearly a thousand kilometres by now.

They leaned over the map of Europe on the conference table. Allard measured off a length of string according to the mileage table and, putting one end on Rotterdam, drew a pencil arc across France with the other. It formed a curved line starting at the Bay of Biscay just north of Bordeaux, continuing across through the Dordogne, Tarn and mid-Provence and ending at the Italian frontier near Briançon.

'They could have offloaded every single case already,' Claire said. 'And we'll never know where.'

'I think some are going to Italy,' Sullivan replied. 'That's why Luciani's involved.'

339

Allard glanced at the pencil arc and cursed. 'They could be over the frontier by now,' he said.

He snatched up the telephone, punched in a number and had a short urgent conversation. In mid-flow he broke off and said to Claire: 'Do we know what the lorries look like? Any names, markings?'

Claire shook her head. 'We know nothing about them.'

Allard went back to the phone and resumed his conversation, speaking rapidly, giving instructions.

'We're in luck somewhere at least,' he said, hanging up. 'There's been heavy snow in the Alps. All the northern passes and the Mont Blanc and Frejus tunnels have been closed to traffic since ten o'clock. They'll have to come south, right to the Riviera, to get across into Italy, and every frontier post will be watching for them. They won't get out of France.'

'I wonder if they may be going elsewhere too,' Claire said thoughtfully, looking down at the map.

'What?'

'Some will be offloaded in France, some will be going to Italy, but some may be heading for Spain.' She turned to Allard. 'Can you find out if Bignon is on the night shift at Hendaye?'

Allard gave a nod and picked up the phone. Claire watched him as he spoke, following every word. She knew the answer before he put down the receiver.

'How did you guess?' he said.

'Can you get a team there?'

'You bet I can. The plane is on standby at Lyon airport. I'll make the arrangements now.'

Claire stood up and walked over to the window. She opened a gap in the blinds with her fingers and peered out into the night.

'Something else on your mind?' Sullivan asked. He was standing by her shoulder.

'Montague will expect the frontier customs to be extra vigilant,' she said. 'Land borders are risky. Lorries are too easy to stop and search. What if they're not crossing by road into Italy?'

'How else will they get there?'

'By sea. Lafon runs his business from Toulon. What better way than to transfer the contraband to fast boats and take them along the coast?'

'It's possible,' Sullivan said. 'Perhaps more than possible.'

'What do you say?'

Sullivan reflected for a moment, then nodded. 'Let's go for it.'

Claire looked round at Allard on the phone.

'You'd better make that *two* planes,' she said.

TWENTY-ONE

The atmosphere inside the house was strained. Gilles Lafon, for all his wealth, was an awkward host. He seemed ill at ease in the plush surroundings of his own home, and his obvious discomfort was unsettling for his guests. He'd ordered in drinks and watched them being served by his maid, but his idea of hospitality seemed to go no further. He made no attempt at conversation and constantly drifted in and out of the living room as if he didn't know what to do with himself. Luciani too was on edge, a brooding silent presence who sat in a corner with his two bodyguards, sipping Scotch and glaring at the furniture. Only Montague seemed relaxed. He made a few abortive attempts to break the ice, then gave up when his urbane charm made no inroads into the hostile atmosphere. Losing patience, he escaped on to the terrace at the back of the house with Simon Doyle.

'It's like a fucking funeral in there,' Montague complained irascibly. 'What's the matter with them?'

'They're nervous,' Doyle replied. 'They've never been at the sharp end before. They usually leave all the messy stuff to their subordinates.'

'Nobody made Luciani come, it was his choice,' Montague said. 'Besides, nothing's going to go wrong. I don't know what they're worried about.'

He pulled a cigar from his pocket and lit it, blowing

smoke out over the stone parapet. Below them the garden of Lafon's house fell away in a series of steep terraces, each one carefully landscaped with rockeries and shrubs and winding gravel paths. A low brick wall marked the boundary of the property and beyond that was nothing – literally nothing, for the ground ended abruptly in a precipitous cliff which plummeted a hundred feet or more to the rocky shore of the Mediterranean.

Doyle shivered and buttoned up his jacket. The weather was closing in. When they'd first arrived, half an hour earlier, it had been possible to see the glow of lights in the sky above Toulon. Now the skeins of mist had obliterated everything outside a radius of two hundred metres. And the visibility was getting worse. The mist was becoming thicker, the ghost trails merging into a dense sheet of fog which twisted and swirled in the gusting breeze, wrapping ever tighter around the exposed peninsula.

Doyle felt the damp air soak into his flesh, chilling him to the bone. His ears were still aching from the private jet flight that had brought them from Paris to the south coast. The cool wind made them hurt more and he wanted only to go back inside to the warmth of the living room. But Montague was in the mood for talking.

'I don't expect my business dealings to be a party,' he said, 'but those two, Christ, they're like a couple of corpses. Lafon's a miserable sod, isn't he? All that money and, you know, I think he'd be happier if he were still driving a truck. And Luciani, well, he's just an uncouth thug. Has he got the bearer bonds?'

'In his briefcase, I reckon. He hasn't let it out of his sight.'

Montague sucked on his cigar and exhaled. The smoke drifted out across the garden and was lost in the eddies of mist.

344

'I don't trust the little shit. What's this all about, bringing me down here to do the deal? Is he plotting something with Lafon?'

Doyle shrugged. 'What would they have to gain? They need you more than you need them.'

'You think so.'

'With Wolf out of the way you control a considerable chunk of the European cigarette market. They can't afford to cross you.'

'Hmm.'

Montague didn't sound convinced. He watched the fog settling over the garden, coiling around the trees and shrubs, insinuating itself into every hidden corner. Beneath the groan of the wind was the distant roar of the waves breaking over the rocks at the base of the cliff.

'Where's your gun?' Montague said quietly.

'Under my jacket.'

Montague nodded. 'Keep it handy.'

The door swung open and four men walked into the customs post. The sudden draught caught at the papers on the desk, blowing them on to the floor.

'Who the devil are you?' Bignon snarled, bending down to retrieve the documents.

Stig Enqvist pulled out his identity card and held it in front of Bignon's nose.

'We're taking over this post for the night.'

'You're *what*? On whose authority?'

'How many men are on this shift?'

'I don't see what . . .'

'How *many*?'

'Three, including me. What's going on?'

'You'll soon find out.'

Montague looked up at the sky, aware suddenly of a milky

luminosity which hadn't been there before. Turning his head, he saw the lance of headlights piercing the mist, the hazy outlines of the lorries behind as they came up the drive from the road.

'About bloody time,' he said, tossing his cigar away.

The haulage depot was on the western fringes of Toulon, an ugly collection of metal-roofed warehouses clustered around a yard filled with trailers and trucks bearing the legend 'G Lafon – haulier'. Allard was searching the inside of the main warehouse with his team of customs officers and a squad from the tactical support unit of the local *gendarmerie*. Sullivan and Claire were checking the yard, examining the containers stacked three high in rows next to the chainlink perimeter fence. The depot had been closed up tight for the night when they'd arrived, a nightwatchman and a security guard the only people on the premises. There was no sign that any lorries had either recently unloaded or were expected.

Claire came out from behind a container and shrugged at Sullivan.

'I can't see anything suspicious. Can you?'

'Is this his only depot?'

'As far as we know.'

'What about the docks? Maybe the lorries are unloading down there.'

Claire shook her head. 'Customs have been on the alert since we left Lyon. There's no way any cigarettes could have been offloaded on to boats without their noticing.'

She stared around the yard. The low mist, tainted a garish yellow by the streetlights, looked like some noxious gas seeping from the earth.

'I'm still sure we're right,' she said. 'Where the hell are they?'

She took a step forward, about to walk out across the

yard. Suddenly, Sullivan grabbed her arm and hauled her roughly back into the shelter of the container.

'What the . . .'

'Sssh.'

He gestured at her to be silent then jabbed a finger towards the main warehouse. They peered out carefully, hidden by the bulk of the container. A door down the side of the building had opened and a figure was waiting in the shadows. It was the security guard. He turned his head, scanning the yard and the road at the front of the depot. Then he sprinted for a gate in the perimeter fence and was momentarily lost from sight. Claire and Sullivan ducked out. The guard was climbing into a Citroën saloon parked in the side street next to the depot. The engine turned over and the headlights blazed out through the darkness. Sullivan and Claire ran to the front of the warehouse. Claire tore open the door of the car they'd arrived in.

'Allard?' Sullivan said.

'No time.'

She was already in the driver's seat, turning the key in the ignition. Sullivan jumped in beside her, pulling his door shut as the car slewed round across the yard and out on to the road. Claire turned down the side street, accelerating hard then jamming on the brakes as they reached a T-junction.

'You see it?' she said.

'No.'

'Shit!'

'Yes, there. Left.'

Claire spun the wheel. The Citroën was a hundred metres in front, turning left on to the main road out of Toulon. Claire sped after it and settled in behind, letting two other cars come in between them. They took the road around the west side of the bay, passing through La Seyne-sur-Mer before climbing the hill towards Cap Sicié. There was less traffic on the road now. Claire let the Citroën pull away a little, following the dull red glow of its rear fog lamps as they twisted their way around the headland. Sullivan suddenly remembered Allard. He pulled out his mobile phone and punched in his number.

'Philippe? Philippe, can you hear me?'

The interference was a harsh, intermittent crackle in his ear. He tried again.

'Philippe, it's Sullivan. We're on Cap Sicié, heading south-west after the security guard. Did you hear me? Fuck!'

The signal broke up altogether, disintegrating into a continuous roar.

'Did he get the message?' Claire said.

'I don't know.'

Enqvist stepped out into the road, swinging his flashlight in an arc. The lorry slowed a little, the brakes hissing, the engine growling as the driver changed gear. Enqvist saw the driver's face in the glare of the frontier floodlights and something about it, the eyes, the expression, made him sure this was the one. He lifted a hand, signalling it to stop.

Then the engine noise changed. Enqvist took a moment to register the difference, to realise the lorry was not slowing now, but accelerating. He flung himself sideways, feeling the current of air tugging at his coat as the lorry raced past. Rolling over on the damp asphalt, he twisted his head round and was just in time to see the chain of steel spikes springing up across the road.

The lorry's front tyres punctured immediately. The cab veered across the carriageway, the tyres shredding, the trailer swinging dangerously out of control behind. The driver braked, fighting to keep the vehicle on the road. The front wheels locked and the cab slewed round. But the articulated trailer kept going, jack-knifing into an unstoppable skid. It swayed violently, its nearside wheels lifting off the road. For a moment it seemed as if it might stay upright, but then, almost in slow motion, it began to keel over. The side of the container hit the ground and with a scream of tortured metal, sparks flying, the trailer slid fifty metres along the road and came to a stop blocking both carriageways.

Enqvist picked himself up, the noise of the crash still ringing in his ears. Two of the customs officers he'd brought with him from Lyon were already at the lorry, clambering on to the side of the cab to get the driver out. The other officers were flagging down traffic, stopping another four identical trucks which were following the first.

Enqvist walked to the overturned lorry. Using a crowbar, he broke open the rear doors of the container. A stack of cardboard boxes tumbled out on to the road. Enqvist ripped one open. A violent spasm of relief and elation surged through him as he looked down at the red and white cartons of cigarettes.

Ten lorries were parked in the wide open courtyard to the side of Lafon's house and on the grass beside the drive. Floodlights on the walls of the buildings around the courtyard illuminated the open doors of one of the containers. Luciani's two bodyguards were hauling out cases of cigarettes and cutting open their tops to check their contents while the Camorra boss watched impassively from the steps leading up to the house.

'It's all in order,' Montague said, unable to conceal his irritation. 'Why would I try to cheat you when I know you're going to open every single case at the other end?'

Luciani said nothing. He waited for his bodyguards to open five or six more boxes and inspect the cartons of cigarettes inside.

'We're wasting time,' Lafon snapped. 'Let's get them out.'

He signalled to a group of thick-set unshaven men standing in front of the servants' quarters. They came across the courtyard, pushing Luciani's bodyguards out of the way, and formed a line from the lorry to the rear of the house where a long flight of steps disappeared over the edge of the cliff. Above the steps, slung between metal pylons, was a thick steel cable which descended in a parabola to the rocky cove below. A metal cage was suspended from a pulley on the cable. The first cases of cigarettes, passed along the line of men, were loaded into the cage and dispatched over the cliff. It was a slick operation, one which the men had obviously carried out many times before.

Montague watched for a moment then went back into the house with Doyle. They waited for Luciani and his bodyguards to join them in the living room.

'Satisfied?' Montague said.

Luciani sat down and slipped his leather briefcase along the side of the armchair.

'Are you going to give me the money now?' Montague demanded.

The Italian's eyes rolled up slowly from below their heavy lids.

'We have things to talk about first.'

The fog started to thicken as the car sped up the winding coast road, the headlights dancing over the hillside, tracing patterns in the shifting curtain of mist. Sullivan risked a look out of his window as Claire threw the vehicle into another bend and wished he hadn't. The drop to the sea was almost vertical, a sheer wall of rock disappearing into a dark, swirling abyss.

Up ahead, the security guard's Citroën was swinging back and forth across the road, going way too fast for the treacherous conditions. Claire kept pace with him, her mouth clenched tight in concentration. Sullivan hung on to his seat and closed his eyes in silent prayer.

At the brow of the hill, the road straightened out, still running close to the clifftop, then turned inland up a gentler incline. There was forest on one side, rough meadowland on the other – coarse grass and the occasional tree clinging precariously to the slope before it plunged over the edge. In the distance, on a slight promontory, a house was just visible through the ebb and flow of the mist. Its forecourt was a harsh puddle of light, a bright hole cut out of the surrounding blackness. Figures could be seen moving around in the centre, and on the periphery, little more than hazy shadows, was a cluster of lorries.

The security guard turned off the road into a long drive-way leading to the house. Claire braked and pulled over on to the verge, extinguishing the headlights. Sullivan punched in Allard's number on his mobile again. The interference was still there, so loud he had to hold the phone away from his ear. He switched it off and tossed it angrily on to the dashboard.

'We're on our own,' he said.

'What are you talking about?'

Montague maintained his air of pained bemusement, but beneath the frown his mind was racing, calculating the odds, assessing his chances of emerging unscathed from this confrontation.

'You know what I'm talking about,' Luciani said.

'I assure you I don't.'

'Don't fuck with me. I *know* you've been supplying Falzone.'

'Armando, I don't know who told you that, but . . .'

'I *know*,' Luciani broke in fiercely. 'You and the fucking Ukrainians.'

Montague gave an involuntary start. He was alarmed now, his legendary self-assurance starting to slip. Luciani almost smiled.

'I know it all, you *cazzo*. You deal behind my back with my greatest enemy and think I won't find out.'

'I have never dealt with Falzone,' Montague said emphatically.

'No? But you trade with the Ukrainians knowing they're shipping the stuff over from Montenegro into my back yard. Competing directly with me in my own territory. You expect me to sit and take that?'

'You're wrong.'

'Don't tell me I'm wrong.'

Luciani thrust himself up out of his chair to within spitting distance of Montague. Doyle stepped between them, fending Luciani off.

'Calm down,' Doyle said, his hands raised, palms outwards in a gesture of peace.

Luciani glared at Montague and turned away towards his bodyguards who were hovering uncertainly on the edges of the dispute.

Montague recovered his composure but his legs were trembling. He wasn't a physical man; violence scared him.

'I don't know which Ukrainians you mean,' he said. 'I'm sure there's been a misunderstanding.'

Luciani snorted. 'I'll tell you which Ukrainians I mean. I mean the Ukrainians who came to Naples and blew up the *Maria Vasquez*. *Those* Ukrainians.'

'What?'

Montague gaped at him, genuinely stunned.

Luciani grinned. 'You didn't know that, did you? You made a big mistake dealing with *them*. They have no honour, no sense of loyalty. They trade with you then betray you behind your back.'

'They sank her,' Montague whispered. 'Why?'

'Because you're a fool. Work it out. Because the *Maria Vasquez* was supplying me, and they were supplying Falzone. They cut me out of the market there's all the more for them.'

Luciani wiped the spittle off his lips with the back of his hand.

'But we've talked enough.'

He signalled to his bodyguards. They stepped forward, hands reaching inside their jackets. Montague felt his legs give way. His bowels turned to water.

Then suddenly the door banged open and Lafon burst in, his face twisted with panic.

'The *Douane*, they know,' he shouted almost incoherently. 'We have to get out.'

Lying flat in the long wet grass just inside the gates, Claire looked across towards the house. It was half a kilometre away, but the courtyard was so brightly lit it was possible, even in the mist, to see the vertical wall of the cliffs plunging away behind the outbuildings.

'They must have a harbour, a jetty at the very least, down at the bottom,' she said.

Sullivan nodded. 'We have to block their escape routes. Contain them until we can get some back-up.'

'You check the cliff, I'll deal with the drive,' Claire said.

She pulled herself to her feet and took off in a low crouch towards the line of parked lorries.

Lafon was in a state of extreme agitation, babbling uncontrollably, saying the same things over and over.

'They'll come here next, I'm sure of it. After they've finished at the warehouse they'll come here. They know. They *know*, you understand me?'

353

'Shut up,' Doyle said curtly, stepping in to take charge. He could see from the faces around him that he was the only one calm enough to think clearly.

'They're searching my depot, did you hear me?' Lafon yelled. 'We have to get out.'

'I said shut up. How much time have we got?'

'How should I know? Ten minutes, half an hour.'

'How many lorries have still to be unloaded?'

'What?'

'Get them up to the house now. The cigarettes are what count. We get as many on to the boats as possible and burn the rest.'

'Burn?' Lafon frowned at him.

'Without the cigarettes they have nothing on us. Move yourself, Gilles. Now!'

Lafon stared at him for a second, then spun round and ran out of the living room. Doyle walked over to the window and pulled back the curtain. He could see the lorries lined up down the drive and the curve of the road beyond, but nothing else. No vehicles approaching, no lights, no people. He turned back to the others. The Italians were flustered, thrown by Lafon's interruption. But Luciani was regaining his composure, remembering what he'd been saying. Doyle slipped the SIG-Sauer from the waistband of his trousers. Very coolly, he stepped up behind the two bodyguards and shot them in the back of the head. Luciani whipped round, his mouth hanging open in stunned horror. Doyle shot him between the eyes.

'Jesus!'

Montague, licking dry lips, was gaping at his aide. Then his eyes dropped to the three crumpled bodies on the floor, the blood seeping from their heads and soaking into the carpet.

Doyle tucked the pistol away under his jacket and picked up Luciani's briefcase. He snapped it open and looked inside, going very still. He turned the case round to show Montague. It was completely empty.

Claire was climbing up into the cab of the nearest articulated lorry when she heard shouting from the house and saw men running out from the courtyard and down the drive. She clicked the door shut behind her and cast an eye over the controls. No keys in the ignition. Crouching down, she risked a look out over the dashboard. The men were splitting up, taking a lorry each. A short man in a quilted jacket was heading straight for hers, the last in the line. Claire ducked down and rummaged under the seats. Her fingers encountered a lumpy plastic satchel – a toolkit. She felt inside and pulled out a heavy spanner. Holding her breath, she listened to the footsteps of the driver as he ran up beside the truck.

He threw open the door and clambered up the steps. As his head came into view, Claire lunged forward, the spanner thudding down on to the top of his skull. The man emitted a low moan and fell backwards off the cab. Claire jumped out. The man was unconscious on the drive, the keys to the lorry next to his outstretched arm. Claire snatched them up, climbed back into the cab and started the engine. She had no licence but she'd been in enough freight depots and stopped enough HGVs to know how to drive one. She engaged reverse gear, removed the handbrake and backed the lorry down the slope, turning the wheel so the trailer swung across in front of the gates, blocking the exit. She leaped down from the cab and hurled the keys away into the night.

Sullivan peered cautiously over the edge of the cliff. Down below was a small semi-circular cove hemmed in by steep rock walls. The sea, confined by jagged outcrops on either side of the cove, raced in through the open mouth in turbulent waves, crashing furiously on to the small shingle beach.

At the far side of the bay, at the bottom of the steps from the house, was a tiny harbour – horseshoe-shaped with a quayside and two concrete jetties protruding into the sea. Three boats were moored inside the shelter of the harbour: two cabin cruisers, the sort of expensive leisure boats that would arouse no suspicion along the Côte d'Azur, and a larger, sleeker craft that most certainly would – a former East German torpedo boat, the cigarette trafficker's favourite vessel, capable of carrying two thousand cases and, with a top speed in excess of fifty knots, of outrunning every coastguard ship in the Mediterranean.

There were four or five men on the quayside, hurriedly unloading cardboard boxes from the metal cage at the foot of the cable run and carrying them to the torpedo boat. One of them pressed a button on a control panel next to the bottom pylon, activating an electric motor. Swaying violently in the wind, the empty cage started to ascend back up the cliff.

Sullivan scanned the wall below him. It was nothing like as sheer as it first appeared, and it wasn't all rock. In places there were ledges of coarse grass and bare earth cutting across the face. He looked up towards the house. To reach the steps to the cove entailed getting across the brightly lit courtyard in full view of half a dozen people. He had no choice. He lowered his legs over the edge and began to climb down.

'Something's wrong.'

Doyle was standing in the courtyard, staring across the grounds at the HGV blocking the gates.

'Why hasn't that lorry been moved? Where's the driver? What the hell is . . .'

He broke off abruptly. He'd seen something else, an outline on the drive too far away to identify clearly.

'Stay here,' he ordered Montague.

He sprinted across the lawn and down the winding drive. Within fifty metres he knew what the shape on the ground was. He pulled the SIG-Sauer from his jacket and dropped instinctively into a simian crouch as he approached the body. He felt the driver's pulse, saw the sticky coagulated blood on the top of his head. Squatting down, he peered around intently, his spine tingling. He could see nothing suspicious.

He straightened up and ran to the lorry, climbing up into the cab and checking the dashboard. There were no keys in the ignition. He dropped down to the ground again and raced back up the drive.

'Can you move it?' Montague asked anxiously.

'No.'

'*What?* That's the only exit. How do we get the car out? How do we . . .'

'Shut up!' Doyle snarled, his eyes roaming over the grounds, the courtyard, the clifftop. 'Stay close to me and do exactly as I say.'

The fog was getting worse, drifting down into the cove in pea-soup waves. It gusted along the cliffs in patches, one moment revealing the drop to the rocks, the next concealing it. Sullivan was ten metres down, traversing across towards the centre of the bay where the edge had given way to form a spur that dropped in a steep, but not vertical, line to the shore.

He felt his way across, choosing his foot- and handholds carefully. The vegetation was wet and slippery. He dug into the thin layer of underlying soil with his fingers and inched cautiously down, his body pressed hard against the edge.

He reached an outcrop of solid rock, its surface pitted

357

with holes and cracks. This was the first really dangerous moment. There was nothing below the outcrop but a
thirty-metre drop to the beach. And no alternative but to
cross it.

Sullivan studied the rock face, looking for the darker
shadows, the changes in texture which indicated possible
ledges or crevasses. Then he stretched out and ran his
fingers over the greasy surface, searching for a handhold.
His fingers slipped into a narrow gap. He tested it. It was
strong enough to hold him. He found a cleft for his toes
and pulled himself out on to the outcrop. Very slowly,
he manoeuvred his way along it, testing every handhold
before he risked his weight on it. The blood was throbbing
in his head and he was aware of the sweat beading his
forehead. He reached a narrow ledge and paused. He was
halfway across the outcrop. Ten more feet and he'd be at
the spur.

He went on. He found another crevice for his feet and
handholds higher up, spread-eagling himself over the rock.
He pulled himself along, feeling with his toes, hanging on
tight with his fingers. The spur was almost within reach
when he put his left foot on to a tiny ledge and searched
for a hold with his left hand. He jammed it into a fissure
above his head and swung his right foot across.

Suddenly, the ledge gave way. The rock snapped off
with a splintering crack. Sullivan's left foot jolted down
and his body dangled loose in space, the weight tearing
at his shoulders and arms. He hung on, ignoring the pain
in his tendons, feeling desperately for purchase with his
feet. His right hand started to slip. He clung on with
his fingers till he could feel the jagged rock breaking his
skin. His shoes scuffed the cliff below him, searching for
something, for anything that would hold. His right foot
located a cleft. Sullivan forced his toe in and tested the
rock. It held. He eased the pressure on his arms and

straightened up, taking his weight on his right leg. Then he slid his left foot into another crack and rested his face on the damp rock, breathing heavily, sick with terror.

He pressed on quickly before he lost his nerve. He concentrated solely on the few feet of rock immediately in front of him, taking each bit as it came. The rest of the outcrop, the drop to the shore didn't exist.

The side of the spur came into view. Sullivan heaved himself up on to it and drew breath.

The ground sloped away beneath him, its surface a mixture of soil and boulders and loose scree. Below, on the quayside, he caught fleeting glimpses of the men loading cases of cigarettes on to the torpedo boat. The fog was so dense now he knew he couldn't be seen on the spur, even if the men looked his way. He scrambled down as quietly as he could, climbing some of it, sliding the rest until he dropped the last few feet to the shore. The concrete harbour wall was to his right, a couple of metres above the level of the beach. He clambered on to a group of large fallen rocks and peered over the top of the wall.

Just in front of him was a brick boathouse. Sullivan heaved himself over the wall and scuttled into the lee of the building, crouching down to poke his head round the corner. The men were further along the quayside, still carrying cases to the torpedo boat. Sullivan ruled out any hope of disabling the vessel. But the two cabin cruisers, moored on either side of the harbour, were a different matter. They had yet to be loaded and neither appeared to have anyone on board. Sullivan waited for his moment. The men all had their backs to him, faint figures moving around in the black fog. He shot out along the concrete jetty towards the nearer of the cabin cruisers, dropping swiftly over the edge on to the aft deck of the boat.

Claire pressed close to the wall of the house and waited.

359

She'd circled round to approach from the far side, away from all the activity in the courtyard. She listened, trying to ignore the thud of her own heartbeat. It seemed safe. Softly, she crept through the gateway into the back garden. There was no one about. She passed the French windows fronting the terrace and glanced inside, stopping abruptly when she saw the three bodies on the floor. There was no doubt they were dead, she could see the blood spattered across the carpet. The sight unnerved her momentarily. She fought back the rising nausea and hurried past the windows, leaning back on the brickwork to ease the feeling of sickness. Where was Sullivan? She'd been to the clifftop but had seen no sign of him. She wondered if somehow he had got inside the house, if something had happened to him.

The sound of footsteps startled her. She stayed exactly where she was and turned her head a little. Two men had come round the corner of the house from the courtyard and were pausing at the top of the steps to the cove. Claire saw enough of their faces to recognise them from the surveillance photographs. Montague and Doyle. They exchanged a few words in muffled voices, then headed down the steps.

Claire darted across the terrace and dropped to the ground by the low garden wall. The two men were following the steps across the face of the cliff, the flights descending to the shore in a long winding zig-zag. In the other direction, at the rear of the courtyard, Lafon's men were finishing loading the cage with more cases of cigarettes. The electric motor whirred and the cage swung out over the edge. Claire watched it drop. It was gliding only a matter of feet above the shallow incline at the top of the cliff.

She acted almost without thinking. Vaulted over the wall and across the steps. Slithered down the slope a few feet then dived forwards. Her fingers hooked around the mesh on the underside of the cage. It lurched violently and sagged under her weight but continued its descent. Claire hung on tight. Her feet lifted off the ground. Below her she could see the cliff falling suddenly away into a sheer drop. The cage slid out into space. There was nothing underneath now but fog and thin air. Claire gritted her teeth. The mesh cut into her fingers like cheese wire, her shoulders felt as if they were being prised from their sockets. But she barely noticed the agony. She was too concerned with just hanging on.

She counted the seconds. One, two . . . A pylon loomed up out of the mist. Was that halfway or were there more to come? Six, seven . . . Christ, how much longer? She looked to her right. She could see the steps but not Montague and Doyle. Were they behind or in front of her? Eleven, twelve . . . I'm going to let go. I can't take this, it's too much. Fourteen, fifteen . . . Just a while longer. You can do it. You can *do* it.

She saw the ground below sweeping up towards her. There were figures on the quayside. Figures standing still, then suddenly running. Through the throbbing haze of pain she became aware of a noise outside and beyond her body. Sirens. The loud, unmistakable shriek of police sirens.

The cage started to slow. The smooth concrete surface of the quay emerged through the fog. Claire let go, dropping heavily to the ground and rolling over to break her fall. The sirens were louder now, getting nearer. Claire looked around for the men. They'd abandoned the remaining cases of cigarettes and were clambering on board the torpedo boat. The boat surged away from the harbour and out of the cove, heading straight out to sea where it was quickly lost from sight in the mist.

Claire sensed a movement along the cliff. Montague and Doyle ran down the last few steps and stopped on the quayside. Claire ducked swifly behind the boathouse before they saw her.

'What kept you?' a whispered voice asked in her ear.

Claire spun round, stifling a cry of shock. Sullivan was leaning on the wall in the shadows.

'Jesus,' Claire breathed. 'What the hell are you doing?'

The sound of automatic gunfire from the top of the cliff stopped him replying. The noise seemed to paralyse them both for a few seconds. Only when it ceased did Claire nod urgently towards the steps and say: 'Montague and Doyle.'

She peered out along the quayside. The two men were still at the base of the steps, apparently listening as there was more sporadic gunfire from above. Then they ran for the first of the two cabin cruisers.

'Fuck,' Sullivan murmured. 'That's the one I haven't disabled yet.'

Montague and Doyle were out on the jetty. They disappeared behind the superstructure of the boat.

'Now!' Claire said.

She sprinted across the quay and in one seamless movement dropped over the edge into the water. Sullivan followed without hesitation. It was only about twenty metres to the cabin cruiser. The mist was drifting low over the harbour but through the cloudy veil they could see Montague on the deck by the controls. Doyle was still on the jetty untying the ropes. Claire and Sullivan filled their lungs and plunged under, swimming hard through the inky water.

They surfaced under the hull and, unseen, worked their way round to the bow. Sullivan reached up and grabbed the forerail. He pulled himself up out of the water and checked the aft deck. Doyle was jumping on board, saying something to Montague. Neither man was looking towards the bow. Sullivan swung his legs up and slithered under the rail. He unclipped the hatch cover on the foredeck and pulled it open as Claire came up behind him. They snaked down through the opening and pulled the hatch shut on top of them.

Montague depressed the starter button. The engine turned over and kicked into life. Doyle leaned over the gunnel and pushed the boat away from the jetty, then threw himself abruptly to the deck as a shower of bullets peppered the water beside them. The gendarmes were halfway down the cliff steps. They fired another warning burst but Montague was already opening up the throttle, sending the cabin cruiser foaming out across the cove. He accelerated. The hull slapped against the waves, dipping and rolling in the swell. Once out on the open sea, Montague turned the wheel to starboard, heading west around the headland.

'There must be a chart somewhere,' he said. 'Look around for it.'

'We don't need a chart,' Doyle replied, hanging on to the taffrail as the boat suddenly pitched forwards. 'The first suitable bay we find, we go ashore. We're not staying out here any longer than absolutely necessary.'

'How long have we got?'

Doyle shrugged. 'The weather's on our side. They can't get a chopper up, but there's half the fucking French Navy in Toulon. If they put out a couple of boats, with radar they'll spot us in minutes.'

Montague throttled back a little in the turbulent sea. He stayed as close to the shore as he dared, keeping clear of the submerged rocks but not losing sight of the land. The fog was so thick now that, at times, the headland was almost invisible.

'What the hell was all that about Falzone and the Ukrainians?' he said. 'What's going on?'

Doyle didn't reply. Montague turned his head to look

at him. Doyle had the SIG-Sauer out, swinging loose by his side.

'You knew, didn't you?' Montague said shrewdly.

'Of course. I arranged it,' Doyle said. 'And tipped off Luciani. I needed him here. That was part of the deal with Falzone.'

Montague stared at him.

'What are you talking about?'

'Dead men's shoes, Hal.'

'What?'

Doyle raised the pistol, his finger tightening on the trigger. Montague pulled down hard on the wheel, sending the boat lurching to port. Doyle fell over sideways. The bullet shot up through the awning above the deck. Montague hurled himself down the steps into the main cabin and lumbered clumsily towards the bow.

Crouching dripping wet in the forecabin, Sullivan and Claire were thrown against the bunk as the boat veered violently to the left. The report of the gunshot reverberated through the walls.

'Was that . . .' Claire said, the question tailing off into nothing.

Sullivan nodded. He lifted the lid of a wooden locker next to the bunk and rummaged urgently through it. There were ropes and life jackets and floats inside and at the bottom, underneath all the sailing paraphernalia, two curious metal objects which looked like oversized handguns with swollen barrels. Sullivan examined one of them.

'Flareguns,' he said. 'Loaded. It's the best we can do.'

He handed one to Claire.

'I'll take the deck,' she said.

She stood on the bunk and reached up, unfastening the hatch and pulling herself out through the narrow opening. Sullivan swung back the cabin door and looked out. Montague was scrambling towards him down the central passageway, his face twisted into a paroxysm of fear. Their eyes met and Montague stopped for an instant, stunned surprise then a flicker of hope transforming his fleshy features.

'He's going to kill me. Do something,' he gasped. 'Please.'

He pushed past Sullivan into the cabin and looked around desperately.

'He's going to kill me,' he repeated. 'You have to stop him.'

He noticed the open hatch in the cabin roof and stretched up, trying to haul his heavy frame through the gap. Sullivan saw Doyle come down the steps at the far end of the passageway, a pistol in his hand. He slammed the door shut and locked it automatically though he knew it afforded little protection. Montague was halfway out through the hatch. Sullivan grabbed his legs and pushed him the rest of the way. The door handle rattled. Sullivan grasped the edge of the hatch opening and heaved himself up. The door cracked, then splintered as something heavy smashed into it. It burst open and Doyle stepped into the cabin, his pistol searching for a target. Sullivan propelled himself up through the hatch, whipping his legs out and rolling away across the deck as a bullet sizzled out from below.

Sullivan knelt up, trying to keep his balance with the cabin cruiser corkscrewing out to sea. Montague was crouching on the foredeck, watching him hawkishly. Sullivan's eyes swept around the boat. There was nowhere to hide. Where was Claire? Where was Doyle for that matter? Sullivan pointed the flaregun at the hatch, his hands shaking. He waited, but Doyle didn't appear.

Montague edged round behind him. Sullivan sensed the movement. He glanced over his shoulder, but a moment too late. Montague's fist caught him full on the temple. Sullivan keeled over, his head spinning. Montague made a grab for the flaregun, attempting to wrench it from Sullivan's hands. Sullivan, half dazed, lashed out with his arm. His elbow sank hard into Montague's belly. Montague grunted and fell backwards, still clutching at Sullivan's hand. The flaregun skittered away across the deck, coming to rest against one of the bow cleats only inches from the side. Montague crawled towards it. Sullivan dived on top of him and they rolled over, punching, kneeing, jabbing at each other. Sullivan's fist hammered into Montague's face. Montague lifted his hands instinctively to shield himself and Sullivan broke away.

The boat dipped forwards suddenly. The flaregun started to slide towards the edge. Sullivan hurled himself across the deck, one arm outstretched, and caught it as it went over the side. Hooking his arm around the bowrail, he pulled himself to his knees. Montague was still lying on the deck, his face smeared with blood.

'You keep back, you understand?' Sullivan gasped.

'He's going to kill me.'

'You think I give a shit?'

Sullivan dropped to his stomach and slithered away along the starboard gangway. He paused, listening, watching for Doyle. Then he snaked towards the stern, the flaregun in his right hand, his left gripping the bottom of the deck rail to stop himself rolling overboard in the violent churning of the hull. He could see the waves curling and foaming below him.

The boat plunged abruptly to starboard and the sea smashed over Sullivan's head. His body thudded against the rail and for an instant his legs swung out over the side. He clung to the stanchion, the water pouring off the deck, almost dragging him with it, then the boat dipped to port and he was hurled the other way against the raised side of the main cabin. He coughed, spitting out the foul salty water, and lifted his head to peer around. Montague was

right behind him, close enough to touch. He was hanging
awkwardly on to the rail, endeavouring to pull himself
upright. The cabin cruiser listed heavily to starboard again.
Montague was thrown over the rail, but somehow managed
to hold on to the top bar. He screamed.

'Help me!'

Sullivan turned to look.

'For God's sake, help me!'

Sullivan reached back and grasped Montague's wrist
with his left hand, wrapping his right arm around the
metal upright to hold himself fast to the deck. Another
wave surged over them. Sullivan shuddered under the
impact but kept his grip on Montague, trying in vain to
pull him back on board.

Montague's face, streaming with water, was screwed up
in agony as he struggled to hold on. His legs were trailing
in the water, the forward motion of the boat dragging him
backwards. He turned his head. Something in his eyes
made Sullivan twist round. Doyle was on the starboard
side of the aft deck, only a few metres away. He brought
up his pistol and fired twice. Montague jolted back, flailing
out over the water into the fierce, enveloping waves.

Doyle swung the pistol round. Sullivan fumbled with
his flaregun, his fingers slipping on the wet surface. Then
a figure moved on the port side. Claire came forward out
of the shadows. Her flaregun blazed. The missile exploded
across the aft deck, shooting out over the ocean mere
inches from Doyle's head. Doyle wheeled round and fired
once, the pistol bucking in his fist. The bullet hit Claire
in the shoulder and she staggered backwards, a rose of
blood sprouting from her jacket. Sullivan squeezed the
trigger of his flaregun. The flare smashed into Doyle's
torso, the explosion lifting him into the air and back on
to the deck.

Sullivan turned in time to see Claire toppling over the

port rail into the sea. He didn't hesitate. He ran to the side and dived over after her.

The water was ice-cold, frothing in the wind. Sullivan swallowed a mouthful and coughed it out, treading water and straining to see in the darkness. There was no sign of Claire. He swam back the way they'd come, fighting against the rolling waves. He tried to guess exactly where she'd gone over, calculating how far the cabin cruiser had travelled before he dived in. It had to be somewhere about here. He stared around desperately. The waves were so high he could see only a few metres. Maybe it was further. He swam on, keeping his head high, snatching quick breaths before the next wave crashed over him.

The visibility was deteriorating. There was no moon, not even a glimmer of light in the sky, and the fog was trailing low, almost kissing the tops of the waves. He took a few more strokes and paused again. He'd caught a glimpse of something pale up ahead: a hand, a face, he might have imagined it. He splashed towards it and saw a tiny sliver of whitish flesh, a cloudy opalescence sinking slowly beneath the surface. He ducked under and swam down, kicking so hard that he almost collided with the body. Her eyes were closed, her hair floating loose. He grasped her under the arms and dragged her back up to the surface.

She was unconscious but he could feel a pulse. He held her against him, protecting her face from the buffeting of the waves. *Hold on, Claire. Just hold on.* He turned on to his back, gripping her under her arms, and struck out for the shore.

He had no idea how far it was. He felt drained of energy. His clothes, sodden with water, weighed him down, making every stroke an effort. But from somewhere he found the strength to stay afloat.

Twisting round, he could see nothing but a wall of water

behind him. A surge of spume hit him full in the face. He choked and trod water, trying furiously to clear his lungs. Claire's body began to sink. He held her up, whooping for air. Then another wave hit him. He lost his grip on Claire, felt himself start to founder. His body was leaden, growing heavier. The water was lapping around his chin. He threw back his head and gulped in more air. He pulled Claire to him and held her in his arms, pressing her face to his own, feeling her skin cold and clammy. He was too exhausted to go on.

Then suddenly a beam of light pierced the fog, glancing off a nearby wave. Sullivan turned his head and saw a coastguard patrol boat looming up through the darkness. He lifted an arm and waved frantically as the spotlight swung round and settled on his face.

Sullivan had lost track of how long he'd been waiting. There was no clock in the tiny refreshment area next to the surgical wing of the hospital, and his own watch had stopped working after its immersion in the sea. But he knew it was several hours because of the way the sky outside the window had grown gradually lighter and from the mounting stack of empty plastic cups on the floor by his chair. One of the night nurses had brought coffee out to him at regular intervals, to warm him up after his ordeal, and to give him something to do. It was the only sign of activity he'd seen since they'd brought Claire in.

The naval hospital was eerily quiet, the long echoing corridors devoid of people. Occasionally he heard footsteps in the distance, the faint sound of voices, but they didn't come nearer. He was alone. Sitting on a cheap plastic chair in the ill-fitting clothes lent to him by one of the coastguard officers. Alone, unable to think of anything except Claire in the operating theatre a hundred metres down the corridor.

He stood up and walked around a little, too tense to stay in the same position for long. Through the glass panes in the door he saw Philippe Allard coming towards him from the main reception.

'We recovered the boat,' Allard said, pushing open the doors. 'One body on board.'

Sullivan nodded blankly. He knew he'd killed Doyle. At that range an explosive flare was as lethal as a bullet.

'Lafon's dead too,' Allard continued. 'Killed in the shootout at his house. We're still looking for Montague's body.'

Sullivan didn't say anything. He wasn't interested. He sat down and stared at the wall. The silence was too much for Allard.

'We got most of the cigarettes. The *Guardia di Finanza* are on the lookout for the torpedo boat. They should pick it up very soon.' He paused. 'Are they looking after you? Do you need anything?'

Sullivan shook his head. Allard watched him awkwardly, then turned away.

It might have been half an hour later, an hour maybe, that they heard the surgeon coming down the corridor from the theatre. He was still in his operating gown, his rubber boots padding over the linoleum floor tiles.

'Your colleague was seriously injured,' he said phlegmatically. 'She'd lost a lot of blood. We've done all we can, but she remains in a critical condition.'

'Will she live?' Sullivan said.

'It's too early to say. I'm sorry.'

Sullivan turned away and walked through the swing doors. Down the long corridors, through door after door, not knowing, or caring, where he was going. He emerged through an exit and found himself on the quayside, looking out over Toulon harbour. The ships of the French Mediterranean fleet were moored in front of him. He walked along the quay past them. The mist was lifting, the first glimmers of a new dawn breaking through from the east.

Sullivan walked on, oblivious to everything around him. There was an emptiness inside his head, like a bleak wasteland, riven by the scream of seagulls and the howl of the wind.

EPILOGUE

Six weeks later

Sullivan got to his feet and walked to the window. It was wet and grey outside, a steady drizzle spattering on the glass roof of the atrium. It was spring in Brussels, but how did anyone tell?

He gazed into the distance, reflecting how things changed yet everything remained the same. Behind him, Maurizio Nicoletti was back at his desk, talking on the telephone in Italian to Casagrande. Enqvist's replacement, a grim, humourless German named Erwin Halsch, on secondment from the *Zollkriminalamt* in Cologne, was leafing through the files, acquainting himself with past cases. Sullivan's own in-tray was brimming over with papers, information that would have to be digested, collated, disseminated to the appropriate parts of the EU. It was all so relentless, so ultimately futile, but someone had to do it.

'You want to go to Naples with me at the weekend?' Nicoletti said, coming off the phone.

Sullivan turned. 'Me?'

'Casagrande's had word of a shipment coming over from Montenegro.'

The thought of two days in the sun was appealing, but Sullivan didn't succumb. He shook his head.

'Take Erwin, throw him in at the deep end.'

Halsch looked up, frowning earnestly. 'I would like that.

373

It will be good for me,' he said. 'I've never been to Naples before.'

'It's an experience,' Sullivan said.

'You don't fancy a trip?' Nicoletti asked Sullivan.

'I'm going home for the weekend. See Kate and the boys.'

'You went home last weekend.'

'I know. And every one from now on. It's the only . . .'

He broke off, staring across the office. Claire was standing in the doorway. Her left arm was in a sling, her jacket draped casually across her shoulders.

'Hello,' she said.

'Claire,' Sullivan said. 'Hi.'

He paused, thinking what to say. 'It's good to see you back. How are you?'

'I'm fine.'

She looked at him. His manner was cool, professional, nothing more. He made no move to come to her. Even to shake hands.

'We didn't expect you back so soon,' he said.

'I was getting bored at home. My shoulder's almost healed now.'

'Good.'

'Who's this?' Claire asked, glancing at Halsch.

Sullivan introduced them. Halsch stood up and offered his hand formally.

'I hope you enjoy your time here,' Claire said.

'Thank you.'

There didn't seem to be much else to say. Claire felt awkward, exposed, standing there in the doorway.

'Ah well, back to counting olive oil bottles,' she said, unable to keep the bitterness from her voice. 'I'll see you around.'

'Yes,' Sullivan said. 'See you around.'

She forced a smile that went nowhere near her eyes and walked away down the corridor.

Sullivan drifted back towards his desk, feeling hollow, suddenly low. The telephone rang and Halsch picked it up.

'It's for you,' he said to Sullivan.

'Who is it?'

'He didn't say.'

Sullivan took the receiver. 'Yes?'

A familiar voice said: 'Okay, ten famous Hungarians.'

Serena vaulted the last hedge and urged her horse into a gallop, leaning forwards over the stallion's neck, enjoying the raw power of the animal, the feel of the breeze in her face. They raced across the field adjoining the house and round the front into the stable block where she dismounted and handed the reins to the stable hand. She was flushed, sweating from the exercise. Removing her riding hat, she shook loose her dark hair and walked across the yard into the house.

She showered and changed into a short black skirt and jacket, then went to the window of her bedroom. A dark grey Mercedes was pulling in on the gravel forecourt below. Serena waited a few minutes before going downstairs. The housemaid had shown the visitors into the dining room. Serena checked her appearance in the hall mirror, smoothing back a stray hair, and made her entrance.

Yevgeny Drozhkin and Dino Falzone were standing by the long rosewood table. Serena smiled and shook hands with them, conscious of their cold eyes on her face, her figure, her clothes – assessing her not just as a woman, but as a partner.

'Please sit down,' she said. 'I've ordered coffee.'

The two men pulled out chairs and waited politely for Serena to take her place at the table before they joined her.

'I was very sorry to hear about your husband,' Falzone said. 'It was a tragic business.'

'Yes, it was. But we must put all that behind us. It's what Hal would have wanted.'

She looked at each man in turn, appraising them now. They would be unsure of her, perhaps wary. She had to reassure them that she was someone they could deal with safely, professionally.

'As you know,' she said smoothly, 'my husband left me everything in his will. His property, his land, his stocks and shares, including a controlling interest in all his companies. I intend to honour all outstanding supply arrangements with you.'

Drozhkin sniffed and glanced at Falzone. 'But can you deliver?'

'Of course. The cigarette manufacturers traded with my husband's companies, not with him personally. Those contracts are still in place and will be fulfilled.'

'On the same terms, in the same way?'

Serena smiled, knowing she could handle them.

'Gentlemen, as far as I'm concerned, it's business as usual.'